Jenn McKinlay
Summer Reading

PENGUIN BOOKS

PENGUIN BOOKS

UK | USA | Canada | Ireland | Australia
India | New Zealand | South Africa

Penguin Books is part of the Penguin Random House group of companies
whose addresses can be found at global.penguinrandomhouse.com

Penguin
Random House
UK

First published in the US by Berkley, an imprint of Penguin Random
House LLC, New York, in 2023
First published in the UK in Penguin Books 2023
001

Printed and bound in Great Britain by Clays Ltd, Elcograf S.p.A.

The authorised representative in the EEA
is Penguin Random House Ireland,
Morrison Chambers, 32 Nassau Street, Dublin D02 YH68

A CIP catalogue record for this book is available from the British Library

ISBN: 978-1-804-94503-2

www.greenpenguin.co.uk

MIX
Paper from
responsible sources
FSC® C018179

Penguin Random House is committed to a
sustainable future for our business, our readers
and our planet. This book is made from Forest
Stewardship Council® certified paper.

For Natalia Fontes. The greatest gift my brother ever gave me was you for my sister-in-law. You inspire me every day with your kind heart and generous spirit, and your commitment to always try to be the best possible version of yourself. I am ever grateful that I get to call you my sis. Love you forever.

Dear Reader,

Having been an avid reader my entire life, I can't imagine not having books and stories to escape into when life gets difficult. But I'd watched up close as several of my family members did not find reading as enjoyable as I did and had to navigate a world that was incredibly unfriendly to those with dyslexia. Books weren't the safe place for them that they were for me, and it made me much more aware of how many people find decoding the written word a challenge.

When the idea for **Summer Reading** came to me, I knew I wanted to flip the script. I hadn't read many stories where the female lead is the unbookish person, and I wanted to change it up and have a book-loving hero and a nonreader heroine. It immediately put a chasm between them that I knew would be interesting to watch them navigate. Because dyslexia is a very individual condition, manifesting differently in each person, I knew that having a heroine with a neurodivergent brain was going to be interesting and an incredible learning opportunity for me. I went all in.

I learned from interviewing the neurodivergent people in my life that some find letters a challenge, for others it's numbers, and many have attention deficit disorders in addition to their dyslexia. Using my librarian skills, I was able to dig even deeper, reading books and articles about dyslexia, watching TEDx talks, and reading memoirs of successful people who have dyslexia who talk about how it shaped their lives. Two of my beta readers are women with dyslexia who helped me craft the character of Sam with their own personal stories and have been invaluable in the creation of her journey.

The one thing I discovered that is common to most neurodivergent people is the tremendous number of coping skills they developed to navigate the challenges they face in day-to-day life—such as ordering from a menu, reading directions, or filling out paperwork—things that many of us take for granted. There is true genius at work in these individuals, and I am so incredibly impressed by their perseverance and fortitude.

Statistically, one in five to one in ten people (I've seen both stats with no definitive number) have a variation of dyslexia. With this new awareness, when it came time to turn in my manuscript, I made my pitch to have **Summer Reading** published in a dyslexic-friendly font. To my delight, our book designers were eager to use their skills to adjust not just the font but the overall design of the book to improve the accessibility of the novel with a dyslexic-friendly design. To that end, when reading this book, you will find certain things are different. The text is in a sans serif font called Verdana, the words that would usually be in italics are bold instead, no words are cut in half with a hyphen at the end of a sentence, and even the size of the margins were adjusted. It is our hope that this makes reading the book an easier and more pleasant experience for our neurodivergent readers.

We are fortunate to live in an age when stories come to us in a variety of formats—books, audiobooks, and movies, to name just a few. My hope in writing this book is to appreciate the value of stories in all their formats and the connections they help us make with others.

Happy reading or listening or watching,
Jenn

Summer
Reading

Chapter One

The ferry from Woods Hole to Martha's Vineyard was standing room only. Shoulder to shoulder, hip to hip, the passengers were packed as tight as two coats of paint. I had a rowdy group of college kids at my back, which was fine, as I'd carved out a spot at the rail near the bow of the ship and was taking in big gulps of salty sea air while counting down the seconds of the forty-five-minute ride.

It was the first time I'd returned to the Gale family cottage in Oak Bluffs for an extended stay—I'd only managed quick weekends here and there around my busy work schedule—in ten years, and I was feeling mostly anxious with a flicker of anticipation. Preoccupied with the idea of spending the entire summer on island, I did not hear the commotion at my back until it was almost too late.

"Bruh!" a deep voice yelled.

I turned around to see a gaggle of man-boys in matching T-shirts—it took my neurodivergent brain a moment to decipher the Greek letters on their shirts, identifying them as frat boys—roughhousing.

Is **gaggle** the right word? I'm sure they'd have preferred something cool like **crew**, but honestly, with their baggy shorts, sideways ball caps, and sparsely whiskered chins, they looked more like a cackle of hyenas or a parliament of parrots. Either way, one of them was noticeably turning a sickly shade of green, and his cheeks started to swell. When he began to convulse as if a demon was punching its way up from his stomach, his friends scrambled to get away from him.

I realized with horror that he was going to vomit and the only thing between him and the open sea was me, trapped against the railing. In a panic, I looked for a viable exit. Unfortunately, I was penned in by a stalwart woman with headphones on and a hot guy reading a book. I had a split second to decide who would be easier to move. I went with reader guy, simply because I figured he could at least hear me when I yelled, "Move!"

I was wrong. He didn't hear me and he didn't move. In fact, he was so nonresponsive, it was like he was on another planet. As the dude doing the herky-jerky lunged toward me, I gave the man a nudge. He still didn't respond. Desperate, I slapped my hand over the words in his book. He snapped his head in my direction with a peeved expression. Then he looked past me and his eyes went wide. In one motion, he grabbed me and pulled me down and to the side, out of the line of fire.

The puker almost made it to the rail. Almost. I

heard the hot splat of vomit on the deck behind me and hoped it didn't land on the backs of my shoes.

Mercifully, reader man's quick thinking shielded me from the worst of it. Frat boy was hanging over the railing, and as the vomiting started in earnest, the crowd finally pressed back, way back, and we scuttled out of the blast zone.

My rescuer let go of me and asked, "Are you all right?"

I opened my mouth to answer, when the smell hit me. That distinctive stomach-curling, nose-wrinkling, gag-inducing smell that accompanies undigested food and bile. My mouth pooled with saliva, and I felt my throat convulse. This was an emergency of epic proportions, as I am a sympathy puker. You puke, I puke, we all puke. Truly, if someone hurls near me, it becomes a gastro-geyser of Old Faithful proportions. I spun away from the man in a flurry of arms that slapped his book out of his hands and sent it careening toward the ocean.

He let out a yell and made a grab for it. He missed and leaned over the railing, looking as if he was actually contemplating making a dive for it.

I felt terrible and would have apologized, but I was too busy holding my fist to my mouth while trying not to lose my breakfast. The egg-and-bacon sandwich I'd enjoyed suddenly seemed like the worst decision ever, and it took all of my powers of concentration not to hurl. I tried to breathe through my mouth but the retching sounds frat boy was making were not helping.

"Come on." Reader guy took my arm and helped me move farther away. I turned my head away in case I was sick. I could feel my stomach heaving and then—

"**Ouch!** You pinched me!" I cried.

My hero, although that seemed like an overstatement given that he had just inflicted pain upon my person, had nipped the skin on the inside of my elbow with enough force to startle me and make me rub my arm.

"Still feel like throwing up?" he asked.

I paused to assess. The episode had passed. I blinked at him. He was taller than me. Lean with broad shoulders, wavy dark brown hair that reached his collar. He had nice features, arching eyebrows, sculpted cheekbones, and a defined jaw covered in a thin layer of scruff. His eyes were a blue-gray much like the ocean surrounding us. Dressed in a navy sweatshirt, khaki shorts, and black lace-up work boots, he looked like a local.

He stared at me expectantly, and I realized he'd asked a question and was waiting for an answer. Feeling like an idiot for blatantly checking him out, I attempted to play it off as if I was still wrestling with the urge to upchuck. I raised my hand in a "wait" gesture and then slowly nodded.

"No, I think I'm okay," I said. "Thank you."

"You're welcome," he said. Then he smiled at me—it was a dazzler—making me forget the horror of the last few minutes. "You tossed my book into the ocean."

"I'm so sorry," I said. Nervousness and relief that I hadn't lost my breakfast caused me to attempt to make light of the situation. This was a bad play. "At least it was just a book and not an essential item, but I'll absolutely buy you a replacement."

"Not necessary." He frowned at me and then looked at the sea, where the paperback was now polluting the ocean—one more thing for me to feel bad about—and then back at me and said, "I take it you're not a reader."

And there it was, the judgmental tone I'd heard my whole life when it became known that I was not a natural-born reader. Why were book people always so perplexed by nonbook people? I mean, it's not like I wanted to have dyslexia. Naturally, when feeling defensive about my neurodivergence, I said the most offensive thing I could think of.

"Books are boring," I responded. Yes, I, Samantha Gale, went there. I knew full well this was likely heresy for this guy, and I was right. His reaction did not disappoint.

His mouth dropped open. His eyes went wide. He blinked. "Don't hold back. Say what you feel."

"Why would I read a book when I can just stream the movie version, which allows me to use both hands to cram popcorn into my face at the same time?" I asked.

"Because the book is **always** better than the movie."

I shook my head. "I disagree. There's no way the book version of **Jaws** was better than the movie."

"Ah!" he yelped. If he'd been wearing pearls, I was sure he'd be clutching them.

When he was about to argue, I cut him off with the **duuun-dun duuun-dun duuun-dun dun-dun dun-dun** sound from the iconic **Jaws** theme music.

Reader guy laughed and raised his hands in defeat. He glanced back out at the water. "Did you pick that movie because we're on our way to the location where it was filmed?"

I shrugged. "Maybe. Also, it was the first movie that popped into my head."

"I wonder if sharks are big readers?" he asked. He glanced back down at the water. His book had soaked up enough of the sea that it was slowly dropping beneath the surface, sinking down to Davy Jones's locker forevermore. I glanced back at his face. He looked as if he was in actual physical pain.

"You all right?" I asked.

"Not really," he said. He rubbed his knuckles over his chest as if his heart hurt. "I was just getting to the good part."

I had to force myself not to roll my eyes. It was

just a book. I thought about abandoning reader guy to his grief, but it seemed impolite since he **had** saved me from a fountain of barf, he **was** cute in a "buy local" sort of way, and I **had** accidentally smacked his book into the drink.

"I really am sorry," I said. "Was it a rare book or super valuable?" I hoped not. Being in between chef jobs was not leaving my bank account flush.

"No, it was just the latest Joe Pickett mystery from C. J. Box." He shrugged. "I'm just stuck at a cliff-hanger without it."

"Oh, that is a bummer." Personally, I hated cliff-hangers on my shows—**Just give her the rose, already!**—so I imagined the feeling wasn't any better with a book. I glanced at the choppy water below as if I could manifest the book and make it rise out of the ocean and float back to the boat in perfect condition. See? Just because I don't read doesn't mean I don't have an imagination.

"It's fine, really," he said.

One thing I'd learned in my twenty-eight circles around the sun was that when a person said it was fine, it never ever was. I glanced up and noticed we were approaching the pier.

"Listen, I'm happy to replace it, really," I said. I reached to open my shoulder bag, wondering how much cash I had in my wallet. My nausea threatened to punch back at the thought of how broke I was.

He reached out and put his hand over mine, stopping me. His skin was warm despite the cool breeze blowing in from the water. He gave my fingers a quick squeeze before he let go and said, "It really is okay. Accidents happen."

We'd leveled up to okay. Well, all right then. Okay usually did mean exactly that. I smiled at him, relieved. His gaze met mine, and for a second I forgot about everything—my anxiety about returning to Oak Bluffs after so long, the nature of my responsibilities while on the island this summer, the low balance in my checking account, the future of my culinary career—and suddenly it was very important to me that this guy not think badly of me. Why? I have no idea, it just was.

"You know, it's not so much that I'm not a reader as my occupation keeps me too busy to find time," I said. "There's not a lot of downtime to curl up with a novel in my world."

The wind whipped my long black hair across my face as if to chastise me for being a fibber. Whatever. I hooked my finger around the hank of hair and pulled it away from my mouth.

Reader guy leaned an elbow on the railing. Now I had his attention. "When you do have time, what do you like to read?"

Uh-oh. I hadn't really thought the natural conversational trajectory through. Shit. I scanned my brain for the title of a book—**any** book.

"Stephen King," I said. One does not grow up in New England and not know the King. "Big fan. Huge." Not a lie because I'd watched all of the movies repeatedly.

"So, you like the scary stuff?" he asked. "Like Stephen Graham Jones, Riley Sager, and Simone St. James?"

The heat of the sun beat down on my head. Why was it suddenly so hot out here? Who was I kidding? This guy was book smart and I was a book moron. Why was I even trying to converse with him?

"Yup, all those guys. Horror's my jam," I agreed. Before he could ask me any more questions, I spun it around. "How about you? Who are your go-to authors?"

He looked thoughtful and said, "Oh, you know, Kafka, Joyce, Proust . . ."

Even I, the nonreader, knew these were literary heavy hitters. My voice came out a little higher than normal when I asked, "For fun?"

His gray-blue eyes met mine, and I saw a spark of mischief in them. Relieved, I burst out laughing and swatted his forearm. "Funny, really funny."

His return grin was like getting hit by a blast of sunshine at the end of a long winter. "What gave it away?"

"Joyce is not really known for his cliff-hangers," I said. I hadn't read any of that stuff since my D minus attempt at English 101, but even I remembered there were no creepy cornfields to be found in James Joyce. Pity.

He snapped his fingers. "Should have gone with Shakespeare."

A gentle bump indicated that we'd landed, and as the boat rocked beneath our feet, he reached out a hand to steady me. A current of awareness rippled through me, and I was about to ask his name, when a shout brought my attention back to the direction of the puker.

"Hey, miss!" I turned and saw one of the frat bruhs had my duffel bag by the handle. "Is this yours?"

It was! I had completely forgotten it. I took a few steps toward the guy when I remembered my new friend. I turned back but the crowd was already filling the space between us.

I called back to reader guy, "Sorry, I have to—"

A large family shuffled into the gap, cutting off my words as everyone scrambled for the exit, while avoiding the vomit-contaminated area. I was jostled right into the young man with my bag, and when I glanced back, all I could see of my new friend was the top of his head. He raised his hand and waved over the crowd. I returned it, feeling very unsatisfied by our parting. I hadn't gotten his name or anything, which did not stop me from hoping I ran into him again.

Martha's Vineyard was less than one hundred square miles. Surely, I'd see him at some point. Right?

Chapter Two

"Sam, you're here!" Tony Gale, my dad, stood on the pier and waved at me. At least, I thought it was my dad. The man in question had face hair, specifically a goatee—hello, 1990s!—and was wearing skinny jeans. Skinny jeans! I tried not to stare. I failed.

I returned his wave and skirted around the disembarking crowd to reach him. Before I could say hi, Dad kissed both my cheeks, a custom from his Portuguese upbringing that was as ingrained in him as his love of linguica, and hugged me tight as if proving to himself that I was real. The faint scent of Old Spice aftershave engulfed me—thankfully that hadn't changed—and I instantly felt as if I were a kid again.

"Come on, let's get out of here," he said. He grabbed my suitcase, which I'd retrieved from the luggage area on the ferry, while I shouldered my duffel bag and followed him to the car. "How was the ferry ride?"

I gave this low-rent hipster version of my dad side-eye

and thought about the hot reader guy I'd met. I scanned the area, looking for him. No luck.

"Quick," I said, thinking how I'd have liked more time to talk to my book buddy.

"Good, that's good," he said, but he seemed distracted. He stopped beside a tiny two-door convertible that had more rust than paint on it.

"What's this?" I asked.

"My project car," he said. "Like it?"

He popped the trunk and stuffed my suitcase inside.

"Project car?" I asked, surveying the wreckage in front of me.

"Yeah, to fix up on weekends," he said. "I had one like it in my teens, way before you were born. It's a classic."

"Is that a euphemism for rust bucket?" I asked.

"No." He looked mildly offended, which I felt bad about, but seriously, this thing looked like it was held together with duct tape and dental floss. "Wait until you see how she drives, then you'll understand. Hop in."

I climbed into the passenger seat, relieved that it was just me and him for the moment, mostly because no one else would fit but also because this was what I'd been hoping for this summer, some Dad-and-me time. After all, neither one of us was getting any younger.

Plus, given my current impoverished circumstances, I was going to have to make an unexpected withdrawal from the bank of Gale, which, at the age of twenty-eight, made me feel like such a loser.

"Steph and Tyler would have come to meet you but . . ." His voice trailed off.

"Where would they sit?" I asked.

Dad smiled.

"It's okay," I said. "After your trip, we'll have the rest of the summer to hang out."

"I'm glad you see it like that." He nodded. "We'll be gone a little over a month, and I really hope you'll take the time while we're away to get to know your little brother a bit better."

Tyler Gale, my half brother, was fourteen years younger than me, so about half my age. He'd arrived in my world when I was fourteen, right on the heels of my parents divorcing, so as you can imagine, his arrival was fraught with a lot of drama. Although I saw Tyler a couple of times a year, mostly on holidays, we were not what I'd call close. In fact, we were more like distant cousins who had nothing in common but tolerated each other for the sake of the family.

My dad was looking at me encouragingly, so I forced a smile and a nod. "Absolutely."

"Great, that's great," he said.

So, he'd gone from a distracted good, that's good to great, that's great. Hmm. Something was up with the old man if the skinny jeans, sports car, and goatee were any indication. Selfishly, I hoped it would not negatively impact my summer at the beach.

Silly me. if I'd known how my summer was going to play out over the next few weeks, I probably would have jumped out of the car and run back to the ferry and the safety of the mainland.

Traffic was thick as we merged with the cars getting off the ferry. We wound our way onto Beach Road out of Vineyard Haven toward Oak Bluffs. Thankfully, the landmarks I'd always used to navigate the island remained unchanged. Oak Bluffs, the quaintest village on the island, with its colorful gingerbread cottages and large town green, had always been my favorite.

The Gale house, which had been in the family for generations, which was the only way we could afford it, was on the outskirts of Oak Bluffs on a small side street. A classic wooden shingle house with two bedrooms and one bathroom, it was going to be a tight squeeze. I assumed I'd be relegated to the living room couch when Dad and Stephanie returned from their trip, which was fine as I didn't plan to be there as much as the beach.

As we drove along the familiar streets, I noticed the island and the town looked exactly the same. It felt strange, as if the shortest distance between two points wasn't a straight line but rather like someone had folded the line and brought the two points together, making the distance in between them disappear. That was how familiar it felt, as if no time had passed and nothing had changed between my last visit and today. Weird.

It was also not terribly reassuring, as my last full summer here had been rife with drama. Dad had insisted I go away to college, but I had just wanted to move to Boston and start working in a restaurant kitchen, learning my trade the hands-on way. The argument that followed had shaken the house with what my mother called "Gale-force winds."

I shook off the memory. I was not a kid. We had come to an understanding back then, and I'd done one year in college before transferring to a culinary school. We'd had no such drama for the past ten years, so there was no reason to think this was going to be a repeat of the disaster that was my last summer on Martha's Vineyard even though I was currently unemployed with no work in sight. Really.

Dad parked in the tiny driveway beside the cottage. While the island hadn't changed that much, the cottage had definitely gotten a face-lift in my absence. Fresh white paint had been applied to the formerly dark green trim, and the furniture on the front porch looked to be a recent purchase, with big squishy navy cushions on bright white wicker furniture. In my recollection, nothing in our house had ever matched before. If this was a warning shot, I was curious to see how the interior had changed as well.

Dad climbed out of the car and circled around to the back. I went to help him.

"Place looks pretty good, right?"

"It looks great," I agreed.

"You're going to have a wonderful summer, Sam," he said. And then as if I'd argued, he added, "You'll see."

We rolled my suitcase up the cement walkway and hefted it up the steps to the porch. The white front door, also new, opened wide, and there was my dad's second wife, my stepmother, Stephanie. How did I feel about her? Honestly, I liked her. I liked her a lot.

Stephanie Gale was smart, pretty, even-tempered, and she put up with my dad, who could be a handful, so there wasn't much to dislike about her. She was always warm and welcoming and respected my boundaries, so she was most definitely not a Disney stepmother.

But—there's always a but—she and my dad had started dating during my parents' separation, and teenager me had had a hard time not making her the focus of my ire at the time. I had said some horrible things to her. Then, of course, once I realized I liked her, I'd had to work through all the guilt I felt about being disloyal to my mom, which was ridiculous but, again, teenager. I still felt awful about our rough-and-tumble beginning so, as usual, I overcompensated in my greeting.

"Stephanie! Hi!" I dropped my shoulder bag and hugged her tight, practically squeezing the breath out of her. I let go and stepped back. "How are you? You look fantastic. I swear you simply do not age."

She shook her blond bob and looked at me with the same affectionately tolerant expression in her blue gaze that I'd seen her bestow upon my dad a million times. When she smiled, her eyes sparkled, which was another thing I'd always adored about her. She was abundant with her affection, even with me, her problem stepdaughter.

I lowered my voice and leaned in close and whispered, "What's with the goatee and the skinny jeans?"

"You noticed." She laughed.

"Kind of hard to miss," I said. "Is he okay?"

She grinned. "He's fine but possibly feeling a bit nostalgic for his youth."

"Which explains the jalopy."

She winced. "We don't talk about that."

Sore subject. I nodded. "Got it."

"I'm so glad you're here, Sam," she said. She gave me one more quick squeeze. "It's been too long since you've visited the Vineyard."

"Yes, it has," I agreed. "Summers for chefs are just so hectic."

"Well, it's good that you're taking some time off, and this summer should be restful, since all you have to do is—" The window above the porch slammed shut. She frowned. "Excuse me for a second."

She disappeared inside while Dad and I exchanged a look.

"You guys did tell Tyler that I was coming, right?" I asked.

"Of course," he said. "He was thrilled."

I stared at him with my eyebrows raised in disbelief. As I mentioned, my half brother and I were not close. It's not that we didn't get along. We'd never spent enough time together for that to be tested.

"Thrilled?" I asked. "Really?"

"Well, as thrilled as any fourteen-year-old boy is about anything," he said.

I took that to mean Tyler was not very jazzed that I was here and would be acting as his babysitter while Dad and Stephanie were away.

Dad picked up my suitcase and gestured for me to enter while he brought up the rear. I crossed the threshold and stumbled to a stop. Gone was the old wooden paneling. Yes, I said paneling. I know, pause to shudder.

With its removal, creamy white walls had been revealed. Pale gray furniture, all matching, filled the living room, and the old redbrick fireplace had been refurbished in mottled shades of gray from a soft dove's wing to deep charcoal. Gone were the kitschy family tchotchkes of generations, and now a tasteful glass vase here and a short stack of books there adorned the minimalist shelves. It looked amazing and yet not at all like the summer home I'd once known.

The half wall that used to separate the kitchen from the living room had been removed, making the space an open floor plan that flowed right into the brightly lit kitchen with new cabinets, also white, quartz countertops, and steel appliances.

"Wow!" I said. It was the only word that came to mind. "No more avocado appliances and country blue cupboards."

"We've been working on it, room by room, for over a year," Dad said. He put my suitcase and shoulder bag at the foot of the stairs.

I could hear voices above. They didn't sound heated. Stephanie wasn't a yeller. In fact, in all the years I'd known her, I'd never heard her raise her voice. Still, there was a tension pouring down from upstairs that led me to believe not everyone was happy about this summer's arrangement.

"I think I'm going to need a more detailed accounting of how Tyler reacted to being told I'm going to be his babysitter?" I asked.

Dad crossed his arms over his chest, then he uncrossed them and shoved his hands into his pockets. No small feat given the skinny jeans he was wearing.

"We didn't use the word 'babysitter,'" he said. "We thought the term 'chaperone' was more appropriate given his age and all."

"Uh-huh," I said.

Dad gestured for me to take a seat, and I sank into one of the new armchairs. I wasn't sure what to say. When Dad had asked if I could take some time off from the restaurant to come out to the island to watch Tyler, he'd had no idea that he was throwing me a lifeline I desperately needed.

The truth was I had lost my job as a chef. I had been in between gigs and poised to sell most of my worldly possessions online if I didn't come up with a job immediately, when my dad called and asked me to babysit . . . er . . . chaperone while he and Stephanie took the trip of a lifetime to Europe. Of course, I said yes. The timing had been epic.

I hadn't told either of my parents about my unemployed situation, not because they wouldn't be supportive but because I was ashamed. It's hard to look up when you're in a downward spiral, and twenty-eight and jobless felt like I was circling the bowl compared to where I'd planned to be at this age.

"Don't you think, Sam?"

I shook my head, realizing Dad had been talking to me. "Um, sorry, what was that?"

"I was saying that your brother never really got to know your vovó as well as you did, and this might be a good time for you to share stories about her with him," he said.

Vovó was my dad's mom, Maria Gale, my

grandmother, and easily the most influential person in my life. She was the one who taught me to cook, encouraged me to be my authentic self, and just loved me for me, no expectations or conditions. Just pure Portuguese grandma love. A pang of grief hit me hard in the chest. Even though she'd been gone for seven years, it still knocked the wind out of me sometimes.

"I know," Dad said. He patted my knee, and I glanced up to see the same grief I felt reflected in his gaze. "I miss her, too."

We sat silently for a while in the house that had been Vovó's. Widowed young, she'd raised all three of her children here, my dad and his two younger sisters Tia Luisa and Tia Elina. Both had married and left the island. They still came to visit when they could, but their lives were busy with their own families and careers, and I knew Dad regretted that he didn't see his sisters more often.

Still, the three of them were very close, and they called each other all the time. I knew every single prank and misdeed my cousins had pulled just like they knew mine. This was another reason I didn't want to share the news about my job situation. The entire Gale family would know in minutes, and I just wasn't up for that.

I wondered if that sibling bond my dad shared with his sisters was why he wanted me to get closer to Tyler. Maybe he felt we needed to be as close as he had been to his sisters growing up. I resisted the urge to remind him that I was twenty-eight and any opportunity to bond that Tyler and I might have had was likely past us.

"Tony, I'm not sure this trip is a good idea," Stephanie said as she came back down the stairs and joined us, sitting beside Dad on the love seat. "I don't think I can leave when Ty needs me."

Dad's eyes were in a half roll, when he thought better of it—smart man—and instead he closed his eyes and said, "He doesn't need you."

"But—" She looked offended, and he started explaining himself immediately.

"Ty is fourteen. He enrolled in this robotics competition so that he could win the scholarship to the Severin Science Academy. That's his dream and he's working hard for it. It's on him to win it, not you."

"I know, but I want to be here to give him support," Stephanie said. "I'm a teacher. I could help."

"You're a history teacher. This is robotics camp. You're a fabulous mom for wanting to pitch in," Dad said. "But this is our time. We've been looking forward to this trip for years. You've never been to Europe, and you've always wanted to go. From a pure financial perspective, if we don't do it now, by the time we're finished paying for his college—which if he gets into this elite high school, he'll likely go on to a top-tier university and it'll be expensive—we'll be old and poor."

"We won't be that old," she protested.

"Well, we won't be as young as we are now," he said.

Feeling awkward about being in the middle of their discussion but not knowing how to excuse myself, I hunkered down in my armchair and tried to blend in with the upholstery.

Stephanie glanced around the living room, as if she was trying to imagine leaving it. When she spoke, her voice was soft. "What if something terrible happens? We'll be hours and hours away. It'll be like the movie **Home Alone**, except instead of Christmas in the suburbs, it will be Tyler scared and alone on the island while we're off gallivanting around ancient Greek ruins."

"Steph, Sam will be here," Dad said. "She can handle anything that could happen."

I didn't move. I was half hoping they'd forgotten I was in the room, because when my dad had asked me to watch Tyler, it seemed like a no-brainer, but now I was seeing Stephanie's very real panic that something bad could happen, and I would be responsible for it. Suddenly, I wasn't so sure I was ready for this, but what choice did I have?

"But is it fair of us to ask this of her?" Stephanie said.

They turned to look at me. This was it. This was my moment. The one thing about not being bookish was that I'd had to develop other skills, such as talking my way into opportunities that might otherwise have been off-limits to me because of my learning issues.

"You're not asking me, I'm telling you," I said. "I'm twenty-eight and I've lived on my own for ten years. There is nothing that can happen—clogged toilet, power outage, or flat tire—that I can't handle. Trust me, I can totally watch over him for you."

Dad and Stephanie exchanged a look. They looked unconvinced, which made me wonder if they questioned my babysitting abilities. Not gonna lie, I was a little offended. So, even though watching over some angsty teenage brainiac for the summer was nowhere near my list of favorite things to do, I now felt compelled to prove myself.

"We just don't want to take advantage of your kindness, Sam—" Stephanie began, but I interrupted. So rude, I know.

"It's not kind of me, I assure you," I said. "I offer my services as a guardian to the teen, simply because this is a two-bedroom house. If you don't leave on this trip, I'm stuck sleeping on the couch all summer, so shoo. Go. Git. Adios. Have a great time and bring me back something cool."

The parentals just stared at each other, clearly speechless. I studied them as they pondered my magnanimity.

My dad was a handsome guy. A few fractions of an inch shy of six feet, he was on the tall side of medium in height, his thick head of jet-black hair was just beginning to sprout random silver threads. He had dark brown eyes that crinkled in the corners when he laughed, which he did often. He was deeply tan from hours spent on the tennis court with Stephanie, and his build was strong and lean from his many hours jogging along the beach.

He carried himself with a sense of purpose, as if he had places to go and things to do. But he was also aware enough of others to always try to put them at ease with a smile or a joke. I felt like I had inherited that from him, just like his black hair and brown eyes, and it had served me well in my life.

Stephanie was his perfect counterpart. She was tall, lithe, and fair, athletic enough to keep up with him but also content to spend hours in front of a fire reading. She was happy to let him have all the limelight while she stood offstage, enjoying his zest for life, supporting but not always participating. They had always seemed a perfect match to me, and there was no question that they deserved this trip of a lifetime together.

"Teenagers can be tricky," Dad said. He sounded cautious, as if he, too, was rethinking the situation. Unbelievable.

I looked at him with one eyebrow raised. "Seriously? Do you think I've forgotten what hell on wheels on an icy road I was?"

Stephanie flinched. So I knew she remembered.

"I've got this," I said. "There is literally nothing that kid can throw at me that I haven't already done."

"Not the most reassuring pep talk," Dad replied.

"You said on the drive over that you wanted me to take the opportunity this summer to get to know Tyler better," I said. "Well, we're never going to have a better chance than this."

"You said that?" Stephanie asked him. She sounded surprised.

"I thought it would be nice," Dad said.

Stephanie gave him a soft smile that made my dad sit up straighter, as if her approval filled his happiness bucket. I wondered how long it had been since these two had been alone together for an extended period of time. Probably before Tyler was born. They were overdue. Besides, fam is fam, and you do what you must. And not for nothing, but if I had to borrow some money from my dad, I felt that a charitable deed beforehand would definitely put me in his good graces.

"Listen, I know teenagers are awful. They're loud, rude, and self-involved. Basically, they're me but with less manners," I joked. No one laughed. Tough crowd. I rolled my eyes. I put my right hand on my heart and held up my left. "I promise I will take excellent care of your baby boy. I will not let him get into trouble, I will make sure he's fed three squares every day and that he gets his eight hours of shut-eye every night. I'll even tuck him in and read him a bedtime story if he wants. Tyler will be safe and sound with me, I promise."

"For the record, I think it's pretty clear that they want **me** to keep an eye on **you**."

At the sound of a man's voice, I spun around and glanced at the stairs in the corner. There stood a very tall, very skinny man-child with his hands thrust in his pockets and a scowl puckering his lips. I blinked. **Tyler?** What had happened to the gap-toothed, stained-T-shirt-wearing, goofy boy I remembered? I realized that in my mind he was stuck somewhere at age eight even though I'd last seen him at Christmas. I took in his markedly more grown-up appearance and wondered how much he'd heard of my opinion on teens.

"Just so you know, I'm not a baby and I'm definitely old enough to take care of myself. I don't need **you**." He shrugged with the disdain only a teen could convey with a shift of the shoulders.

Well, that answered that. He'd heard all of it, even the not-nice parts. So this summer was off to a fabulous start.

Chapter Three

"We're going to be late, Sam!" Tyler said. He paced around the island in the kitchen while I removed the pots and lids to arrange them in a more efficient way to utilize the limited cupboard space. Dad and Stephanie had left on the red-eye out of Boston the night before, and I wasted no time in making the kitchen mine.

I had no idea why I felt the need to do this now. To put my stamp on the room that held so many memories for me of cooking at Vovó's side? Maybe.

I knew we had to leave. I knew I didn't have time to finish this project, so why had I started it? It was just the way I was wired. I'd always struggled with multitasking because my dyslexia disorganization would hit and I'd get sidetracked, and before I finished one project I was off on another and then another, forgetting the original task. This, of course, sent my anxiety into hyperdrive. Honestly, some days it was exhausting being in my own head.

"I'm almost done," I said. Feeling the need to

defend myself, I added, "Besides, it's just camp. It's not like school, where they take attendance."

"Are you kidding me?" he cried. He dug a hand into his thick black hair as if he wanted to pull it out by the roots. "This robotics camp is sponsored by Severin Robotics. If I want to get into their science academy this fall, then I have to make a good impression. I have to be the best every single day, and it has to start with arriving first!"

"Relax, we won't be late," I said. The bro was wrapped pretty tight, and I noted this as a person who played **Mortal Kombat** with her own anxiety on a daily basis. "And finish your French toast."

"I did," he said. The words were pushed out through gritted teeth as if that was the only way he could keep himself from shouting at me. I glanced at the sink. Sure enough, his empty plate was sitting at the bottom. Huh.

The pile of pots and pans was calling to me. I really wanted to finish sorting them before we left, but Tyler was not having it.

"Sam, now . . . please." He struck a pleading stance with sad eyes and his hands clutched in front of his chest, softening the demand.

"You sound an awful lot like Dad when you get all bossy," I said. I grabbed the keys to Stephanie's SUV and my shoulder bag and strode out the door.

"Sorry. It's just this is really important to me," he said.

We climbed in and I backed out of the driveway, turning onto the road. I gestured at the sign posted on the side. "I can only go so fast. The speed limit is seven miles per hour."

"Ugh!" Tyler groaned and clapped his palm to his forehead.

"Is this really how you want to spend your entire summer?" I asked. A bicyclist cut in front of me, and I had to slow down even more. I saw Tyler wiggle in the seat beside me. I half expected him to open the door and run to the library. "There's so much to do on the island. You could be out sailing, biking, playing tennis, or just loafing on the beach. Why do you want to spend it indoors all day?"

"You wouldn't understand," he said. The way he said it, so dismissively, as if I wasn't intelligent enough to appreciate his genius, really smarted, and being the mature twenty-eight-year-old that I am, I naturally clapped back.

"You're right," I said. "I don't understand. At your age, I was too busy having fun."

It was a shit thing to say. Ty's mouth tightened, and he turned his head away. I felt like a complete asshole.

"Listen, I'm sorry," I said. "I didn't mean—"

"Yeah, you did," he interrupted. "Just forget it."

I blew out a breath. Right. The subtext to his words sounded more like "forget you," and I couldn't really blame him. I was supposed to be the mature older sister. It was time I started acting like it.

"I'm not going to forget it," I said. I turned onto the road for the library. It was a long one, passing several older homes. I turned left at the top of the short hill, drove past a building under construction, and parked in front of the two-story gray building with the bright white trim. Tyler was out of the car before I had fully parked, and I had to jog to catch up to him.

A large dogwood tree was in full bloom to the right of the entrance. A book truck was parked to the left of the front door, offering activity grab bags for local kids. Genius! The sliding doors were just closing behind Tyler when I hurried in behind him. He took the stairs two at a time, using his long legs to his advantage. I hustled after him.

On the upper level, I passed the service desk and was gaining on Tyler when he stopped short. He had his backpack slung over one shoulder, and it cushioned my impact as I slammed into him.

He stumbled forward, catching himself on a bookcase. His brown eyes were wide when he turned to glare at me. He hissed, "What are you doing?"

"Walking you to camp," I teased.

Before I could explain that I'd actually come in to see my best friend, there was a giggle from the other side of the bookshelf. I hunkered down and peered through the books, where I saw two teen girls staring at us. Tyler went redder than the peppers I grind for my pimenta moída, Portuguese pepper sauce. I smiled and waved at the girls, and they giggled again before dashing toward a room on the far side of the building.

"You're a menace," Tyler said. "Stay here. Do not walk me to the door." The look of fury he sent me almost seared my eyebrows off. He spun around and stormed off after the girls.

"Pick you up at five," I shouted after him.

He waved a hand at me without looking back. Well, that put me in my place, now, didn't it?

I did a quick tour of the library, but I didn't see my friend Emily, who worked there. I should have texted her and checked her hours, but the kitchen project had distracted me. I left the library, feeling discouraged. I'd hoped Tyler and I would grow closer this summer, especially with Dad and Stephanie being away, but this was not an auspicious start.

After I stopped at the local Stop & Shop grocery store to stock up the pantry, I returned home and before I dove into my project set three different alarms just to make sure I didn't get distracted from picking Tyler up. It took me the rest of the day to arrange the kitchen to my specifications.

Chefs and their work spaces. It's a thing. In my case, I needed the spice rack set up near the main workstation, alphabetized and expiration dates verified. The disorganized jumble of pots and pans below the counter sorted by size and shape and paired with their proper lid. Knives in the knife block sharpened—they had needed it quite desperately—and ready for use. I also found some old cast-iron cookware of my grandmother's shoved into the far back of the cabinet, and I took the pieces out and seasoned them. I remembered using them with Vovó, and for a moment it felt almost as if she was here with me.

Right on time, my phone, the oven timer, and the alarm clock in my bedroom all chimed a half hour before camp ended. I decided to leave right then just to make sure I was waiting when Tyler finished. Surely after a long day he'd be happy to see me, right?

The library was busy when I entered. Parents with kids streamed past me, so I assumed another program had just gotten out, as this was the toddler set and definitely not members of the robotics camp.

On the second floor, I noted that the double doors to the robotics room were still closed. I checked my phone. I had about fifteen minutes to kill. I glanced at the short shelves stuffed with books and ran my fingers along the spines. Despite our complicated relationship, I actually loved books. I liked the weighty feel of them in my hands and the way they smelled of paper and ink, and I especially loved it if there were pictures—I tended to think in pictures, especially pictures of food.

My calling to become a chef had come early in life. My vovó watched me mornings and later after school while my parents worked. We'd lived in New Bedford back then. The cottage on the Vineyard became a summer home after I was born. I didn't know it then, but I had been a surprise. Because my parents were just starting out, Mom as a real estate agent and Dad in insurance, same as now, it was decided that Vovó would leave the island and come live with us to watch me so my parents didn't have to quit their fledgling careers or pay for day care.

I spent my childhood learning all of the family recipes by her side. Vovó spoke in her own mix of Portuguese and English but never wrote any of her recipes down, so I'd learned by watching her and doing what she did. I discovered even at a young age that learning came easiest to me if I was allowed to use my hands and do the work myself—kinesthetic learning, it's called.

From my first successful queijo de figo, I knew exactly what I wanted to do with my life—cook. For the food lovers, **queijo de figo** is loosely translated as "fig cheese," but it's not cheese, it's cake—delicious cake with figs and anise—but it resembles a cheese wheel, thus the name.

I checked my watch. I had ten more minutes until camp was done, so I wandered over to the next bookshelf and saw that it displayed the latest magazines. I scanned the covers until I found one with food and recipes. I laid it on top of the short shelving unit and began to flip through the pages. The photographs were excellent. The fonts were a nightmare. There is no cure for dyslexia. There's no pill to take or brain surgery to be done that can keep the words and letters from flip-flopping or hopping around the page.

There are, however, fonts that are friendlier to the dyslexic brain than others. Sans serif or bottom-heavy typefaces that differentiate the **p**'s and **b**'s and **d**'s are super helpful. This magazine had none of that. Given that one in ten people have some form of dyslexia, you'd think mass-market publications would catch on with their fonts, but no.

Someday, when I published my own cookbook . . . yes, this was a secret dream of mine. I never told anyone, ever, for fear that they would laugh at the girl with dyslexia wanting to publish a book. Anyway, if, no, **when**, I published my cookbook, the fonts were going to be dyslexic friendly.

I happily flipped through the pages until I saw the most beautiful pan-seared Atlantic salmon on a bed of jasmine rice that I had ever seen. My eyes strayed to the recipe. Did they use a rub? A marinade? How had they seared it so evenly with an extra char on the edges? I studied the words with a sigh.

In addition to being a kinesthetic learner, I was a visual learner, too, and spent most of my time watching online cooking videos to learn how to do things. The

Internet had literally saved me in culinary school. Still, I wanted to know about this salmon. I forced myself to focus on the words that were as slippery as a freshly caught fish. It was a struggle.

"Sam? Is that you?"

I ripped my gaze from the page. I blinked, trying to get my bearings. I glanced at the woman standing in front of me. Medium in height, like me, but thinner, with a head of bright red hair, she wore overly large glasses, had a button nose and full lips. She grinned and asked, "It hasn't been that long since we've seen each other, has it? Do you really not recognize me?"

"Emily! Emster! Em!" I cried. "Of course I recognize you. You're just out of context. I mean, usually we're drunk in a bar in Boston when I see you."

I hurried around the short shelf and grabbed her in an exuberant bear hug. Clearly not prepared for my enthusiastic greeting, Em was caught off guard, and we stumbled before she grabbed the bookshelf for balance.

"Sorry! I'm just so glad to see you," I said. "I meant to call you as soon as I landed, but there was minor family drama happening and I'm still trying to get my bearings with being here and all."

"That's all right," Em said. She waved a hand at me. "I know how busy you are."

"Eh." I shrugged. Not that busy since I'd lost my job, but I didn't need to share that just yet.

Even though I considered Em one of my closest

friends, I hadn't told her about my situation. Being passed over for the promotion to executive chef at the Comstock, when I'd been there for seven years, had crushed me, and I'd quit. Now I was flat broke and unemployed and full of my old familiar friend—shame. I hadn't told anyone about my aborted career. Instead, I let everyone think I was just taking the summer off. Ha! As if that ever happened when you were a chef.

I knew the restaurant owner's decision to hire someone else was not reflective of my culinary skills. Straight up, he told me he felt a man would be a better fit in the hierarchy of the kitchen. Misogynistic jerk! Still, there was a part of me that felt that the food I'd busted my tail to create should have guaranteed me the job of executive chef, and it was hard to let it go, especially when I suspected deep down that it was my dyslexia that caused him to pass over me.

An executive chef had so many organizational duties, like the menu, inventory, schedules, and budget. The owner knew I had dyslexia, and I suspected he didn't want to take a risk with me. Whatever. I decided that sharing the current events of my life could wait at least until we had drinks in front of us.

Em stared at me expectantly. I'm the extrovert, the talker, while she'd always been the introvert. It had been my job to do the heavy lifting conversationally, and usually it was no problem, but at the moment it just felt too difficult to open up.

I scouted the room, looking for something to say. I noticed that the library was still hopping for a Monday evening and the doors to the robotics room were still closed. "I looked for you this morning when I dropped Tyler off for robotics camp."

"I'm working the evening shift today," she said.

"Yeah? It must be nice to have the morning off," I said. Why was this conversation feeling so difficult? Where was our usual camaraderie?

"It is," she said. She didn't elaborate.

We stood awkwardly watching the patrons bustle around the building. I tried to remember the last time we'd hung out. It had to have been during the holidays when she came to Boston to do some shopping. We'd had a blast stuffing our faces at the food stalls in Quincy Market and then having a nightcap at Durty Nelly's pub. Why were things so weird now?

Had something happened since we'd seen each other? Was she mad at me? I did a mental check that I'd been good about keeping in touch. I mean, we were both busy, but we managed to video chat at least once a month. Had we chatted last month? I couldn't remember. I'd been involved in a lot of work drama.

Self-involved much? Yes, but that wasn't new, and I still didn't understand why this conversation was the verbal equivalent of putting on jeans that were two sizes too small.

I glanced at my friend, but Em wasn't looking at

me. Instead, she was staring past me, and her eyes were wide. I turned to see why her expression was one of high alert.

My jaw hit the ground, which, for the record, is never a good look. Leaning on the bookcase behind me, with a twinkle in his blue-gray eyes, was hot reader guy from the ferry. And here I was with no makeup on, my hair in a ball on top of my head, wearing my dingiest jean shorts and a baggy T-shirt with a faded unicorn on it. Clearly, the universe really did hate me, probably because of the book now polluting the ocean or some other offense of which I was unaware. Couldn't really blame it.

Now, a normal person might have been embarrassed to see the man whose property they had destroyed, but not me. Being shoved into the special needs class in high school when I could no longer fool everyone about my reading issues and the residual teasing that came with it had hardened me to humiliation. Seriously, I had a hide like a rhinoceros.

"Don't tell me, let me guess," I said. "You're here to replace the copy of the book that I accidentally sent to sleep with the fishes."

I heard Em gasp behind me but I didn't explain. Too complicated.

Reader guy laughed and held up a paperback book. "I got the last one on the shelf."

"But I ruined your personal copy. I still feel awful

about that. Are you sure I can't buy you a replacement?" I asked. My dad had thankfully left me a chunk of money to pay for our essentials this summer, and I figured replacing a damaged book would definitely be considered an essential.

"No need," he said. "But I appreciate the offer." He was wearing a pale blue dress shirt and a dark blue tie over beige slacks, all of which looked excellent on his muscular frame, so I assumed he must have come to the library from work. I tried to guess what he might do for a living. Banker? No. Salesman? No. Lawyer? No, none of those felt right. Hmm.

"So, you're just here to check out a book?" I asked. Yes, I was fishing, with all the subtlety of shooting trout in a barrel, but fishing nonetheless.

"Among other things," he said. He exchanged a knowing smile with Emily, and I had a panicked thought that he might be her boyfriend. Oh, sweet chili peppers on a biscuit! Had I been checking out my friend's boyfriend? The horror!

"Actually, Ben is my new boss," Em said. She stepped forward and glanced between us. "Samantha Gale, this is Bennett Reynolds, interim library director."

"Library director?" I almost choked on my own spit.

"No need to be so formal. Call me Ben," he teased. He held out his hand.

I gave a half-hearted chuckle. So hot reader guy was actually hot librarian guy. I had knocked a

librarian's book into the ocean. The universe certainly loved irony, didn't it?

I shook his hand. His grip was firm but not aggressively so. Meanwhile the shock I was sustaining made my hand sweaty and limp. Argh! I firmed up my grip and he winced.

"Sorry," I said. I let go. I wondered if he'd noted the calluses, scars, and burns that marred my chef's hands. If he did, he didn't mention it.

"No problem." He smiled as if he understood that I was a freak. Of course he did. After our puke-infused book drowning of a first meeting, what else could he think of me?

"How do you two know each other?" Ben asked.

Relieved to have the subject changed so that I could process the fact that hot reader guy was even cuter the second time around, I turned to Em and said, "I'll let you explain."

Em looked momentarily taken aback. Yes, I had ambushed her by inviting her do the talking. She rallied to the assignment, however. She smiled at me and said, "Sam and I go way back."

"To diapers," I confirmed. Em gave me a look, and I asked, "Inappropriate?"

"He's my boss," she said.

"Oh, right." I glanced at Ben. "Scratch that. We really met in jail."

Em burst out laughing and Ben looked alarmed.

"Not literal jail," Em said. "We were toddlers, and some boys playing cops and robbers on the playground locked us up in their pretend jail. We staged a breakout, and Jimmy Basinski had a complete meltdown tantrum."

"Truly, the stuff of playground legends," I said. "We weren't allowed to play with the boys anymore after that."

"It sounds like you two have long histories on the island," Ben said.

"Sam more than me," Em said. "I moved here as a full-time resident when I was a baby, but your family has lived here for generations."

I nodded. "But only part-time since I was born. My great-grandfather helped establish the Holy Ghost Association."

Ben tipped his head to the side in silent inquiry.

"That's the name of the Portuguese American club over on Vineyard Avenue," I said. "My dad still belongs."

"Your island roots run deep," he said.

"They do. Our house was my grandmother's and her grandmother's before her. My cousin Dominick says that back in the day, you couldn't throw a rock in Oak Bluffs without hitting a Gale," I said. "There are fewer of us now since so many have moved off island to the Cape."

"You might be just the person I need, Samantha," he said. The intensity in his gaze made my heart stutter stop. To be on the receiving end of that blue-gray gaze was heady stuff.

"Do tell," I said. And, yes, I am a horrible person

because I completely forgot that Em was standing next to me. In fact, I'd have been hard-pressed to remember my own name at the moment.

"I took the interim director job, since I have the summer off from my academic research library position at MIT, primarily to do some family research over the summer," he said. "I'm trying to track down a person who was here in the eighties."

"That's a bit before my time," I said. I glanced at Em, and she nodded.

"Same," she said. "We arrived in the nineties."

"Who are you looking for?" I asked.

"Just some relatives," he said. "My mother lived in Oak Bluffs in '89 but then moved to Maine. She's come back to the island recently, and I followed her, hoping we could reconnect but also to do a deep dive into the family history. Unfortunately, she's not as interested as I am."

I nodded, thinking about my brother, and said, "I'm doing something like that myself this summer. Maybe I can help."

Ben's brows lifted as if he was surprised by the offer. "I'd really appreciate that."

"Not at all," I said. "It's the least I can do since the 'incident.'" I made air quotes as I said the word.

He grinned at me, and I felt myself return his smile. Em glanced between us, pausing on me with a "you're going to explain all this later" look.

"Excellent. Can I get your number so we can discuss

it some more?" he asked. He pulled his phone out of his pocket, and I was about to tell him my number, when I was interrupted.

"You have got to be kidding me," a voice said from behind me.

I whipped around and there stood Tyler. He glanced from me to Ben and back. He looked furious.

"Seriously?" he asked. "You're actually standing here hitting on the director of the library?"

"What? I'm not—" I protested. I should have saved my breath.

Tyler didn't wait to listen to a word I said. He turned on his sneaker, threw his backpack over his shoulder, and stormed to the door.

"Well, hell," I said. I glanced back at Em, whose expression was surprised yet sympathetic, and Ben, who looked mostly shocked. I threw up my hands, feeling my face get hot with embarrassment. "So, this got crazy awkward. Sorry. I'd better go catch him." I glanced at Em. "Call you later."

"You'd better," she said.

I ran for the stairs, wishing the industrial carpet would swallow me whole. No such luck.

Chapter Four

"Tyler, wait!" I cried and was soundly ignored.

He was already across the parking lot and headed for the street. One part of me was so ready to let him walk home, but then I thought about my dad and Stephanie and imagined trying to explain to them that Tyler got run over by a car on his first day of robotics camp because he was miffed with me. Yeah, no.

I dashed to the SUV and hopped in. I drove across the lot and pulled up alongside Tyler. I rolled down the passenger-side window so I could talk to him. He had earbuds in and was aggressively ignoring me. Fine.

I honked the horn. He jumped a foot in the air. I almost laughed but managed not to as I was quite certain that wouldn't go over with the prickly teen. He shot me a dark look. I honked again.

He glanced around as if to be sure no one was witnessing his embarrassment of a half sister honking her horn at him. I honked again.

"Stop that!" he cried.

"Then get in," I said. "Otherwise, I'm following you and honking the whole way home."

"You're so immature," he said. He heaved a very put-upon sigh and opened the passenger door. It took everything I had not to prank him and step on the gas. He tossed his backpack into the foot well and then his body into the seat. He buckled himself in with a click.

"About what you overheard at the library—"

"I'm not talking about this."

"Excuse me?"

He pointed to his earbuds, and I watched as he raised the volume on his phone so that he couldn't hear a word I was saying. I turned back to the road and drove us home, fuming.

I'd always thought the care of babies was an excellent method of birth control. I mean changing diapers and constant squalling, no thank you, but in that moment, I realized that teenagers were a much better deterrent. Honestly, how did parents not leave them by the side of the road with a **Free to a Good Home** sign taped to their backs?

I pulled into the driveway, and Tyler was out of the car before I'd completely stopped. I watched as he darted up the porch stairs, unlocked the door, and slammed it behind him.

I glanced at the clock on the dashboard. It read 5:20 p.m. or, as I liked to think of it, beverage o'clock.

I locked the car and entered the house. There was no sign of Tyler, so I assumed he'd escaped to his room. Perfect. I could use a little alone time.

I surveyed the contents of the liquor cabinet in the kitchen. It was lightly stocked but that was okay. I decided I needed a little sunshine in my day and made a spiked sort of lemonade and then headed back out to the front porch. I sat on the love seat and put my feet up on the coffee table. Our little cul-de-sac was off the beaten path, but a few tourists wandered by, checking out our quaint houses and the abundance of blue hydrangeas that decorated just about every front yard.

I let the cool breeze wash over me while I mentally planned dinner in my head. Tyler was obviously growing, and I was betting that hunger would get him out of his room more effectively than any request by me, so the trick would be to cook something that beckoned him like a siren to a sailor.

He had stubbornly refused to let me pack his lunch today, taking a sad-looking peanut butter and jelly sandwich and an apple instead. If I didn't know for a fact we were related, I'd have questioned his parentage.

I sipped my drink, lemony with just a hint of vanilla, and waved at Mr. Dutton across the street as he mowed his very petite patch of grass with the precision of a pilot coming in for a landing.

There wasn't a lot of yard to tend around the houses of Oak Bluffs, which was why so many of the regular summer residents were in each other's business. Mr. Dutton waved back and switched off the engine.

I hadn't seen him, or any of the neighbors, very often over the last ten years, and while his hair was grayer, he still wore his baggy shorts and festive Hawaiian shirts. It made me feel as if I might be able to slip back into Vineyard life without too much fuss. He looked like he was about to cross the narrow street and come chat, when a motorcycle stopped in front of my house.

Interesting. I didn't know anyone on the Vineyard who rode a motorcycle. I watched as the rider switched off the engine and set the kickstand. He was wearing a white T-shirt, which framed his broad shoulders, and well-worn jeans that clung to his slim hips like he was a walking advertisement for a lickable man pop. The black lace-up boots looked familiar, but I couldn't place them.

I watched as the rider unfastened his helmet and lifted it off. He shook out his dark wavy hair and set the helmet on the seat. With a flash of recognition, I knew who it was before he turned around, and I thought I might keel over in my seat. Hot librarian guy, Ben, rode a motorcycle! OMG!

I resisted the urge to fan my face with my hand, but the fluttering feeling inside me refused to be still. Instead, I tried to look casual and took a bracing sip of my spiked lemonade as Ben started up the walkway.

Mr. Dutton across the street saw that I had a visitor, and turned back to his mower, which was fine. We had all summer to catch up.

"Hi, Ben." I waved him up onto the porch. Was my voice coming out too high? I cleared my throat, trying not to stare at his shoulders, his hips, his wavy hair. Gah! I didn't know where to look. Was there an unattractive part of him anywhere? Maybe a nostril or an earlobe?

"Hi, Samantha," he said. His steps were heavy on the stairs. "I hope I'm not interrupting anything."

"Not at all. You're just in time. Happy hour started about ten minutes ago," I babbled. "I'm working on my mixology skills. The jury is still out on this concoction, care to have one and offer an opinion?"

He looked at the cocktail in my hand appreciatively. "Are you a professional mixologist?"

"No, I'm a chef by trade, but I like to dabble with beverage recipes and raise my skill set," I said.

He grinned and my brain went a little fuzzy. "Well, if it's for the sake of research, I'll try one."

"Sit." I gestured to a chair. "I'll be right back."

I hurried into the house and quickly fashioned him a cocktail just like mine. I might have been a bit more careful with his, not that I was trying to impress him or anything. Okay, yes, I totally was, which was ridiculous because for all I knew he was married or had a girlfriend. Never mind that he was obviously a book person and I wasn't. I pushed all of that aside and went back to the porch.

"Here you go." I handed him the drink.

I watched as he lifted the glass to his lips, which were puckered ever so slightly. I glanced away. Staring is rude, you know, and I imagined that ogling a librarian was even worse than that. Sort of like checking out a nun. I picked up my own glass and took another sip. The hint of vanilla was subtle, but it mellowed the tartness of the lemon perfectly. I really thought I had a winner here.

"This is good," Ben said. He glanced at me and nodded. "Really good."

"Not too girlie?" I asked. "I don't want to be reinventing the appletini."

He laughed. "It's not as macho as a scotch neat, but the lemon provides a nice punch. So I'd say it's no more girlie than a mojito. It's the name that'll clinch it. You need a very gender-neutral name."

"I was thinking of calling it Liquid Sunshine," I said. I frowned. "That will never fly with the XY chromosomal set."

"Probably not," he agreed. 'You need something more manly, like Scorched Earth."

"Sounds delicious," I said. "I'm imagining subtle notes of ash."

"And dirt," he added with a laugh. It was a good laugh.

We sipped our drinks and watched the world go by for a moment. Mr. Dutton had finished his lawn and put his mower away. The silence should have been awkward since I really didn't know hot librarian guy at all, but surprisingly, it felt comfortable having him sit here. I glanced at him, and he seemed perfectly at ease, relaxed in his chair, his glass held loosely in one hand. It belatedly occurred to me that despite his easygoing manner, this obviously wasn't a social visit, and he probably had a reason for dropping by.

"I'm guessing you aren't here just to be my cocktail taste tester," I said.

He grimaced. "Sadly, no. I'm here to see how Tyler is doing."

"Doing?" I repeated. I had a sudden feeling of foreboding. Had I messed up this teen-watching thing already? We were only a day in. "As far as I know, he's okay. I mean I'm watching him for the next six weeks since our parents, well, our dad and his mom, I have a different mom, are away in Europe. We're actually half siblings."

Ben blinked. I knew I was talking too fast and info dumping all over him—he probably heard the beep of a truck backing up over my words—but I couldn't seem to stop the insipid chatter.

"Honestly, I don't know anything about teenage boys," I confessed. "I think Tyler's okay, but he's not talking to me at the moment and has merely grunted at me since he left the library, you know, after the . . . er . . . misunderstanding."

"Yeah, I think I might know what fueled that," he said.

I sat up straighter. "I'm listening."

"Apparently, while I was talking to you, there was an altercation in the robotics room."

"Altercation?"

"Ryan Fielding, who is the head instructor of the robotics camp, told me there was a disagreement and another student pushed Tyler down," Ben said.

"What?" I jumped to my feet. "Are you telling me some bully put his hands on my brother? Who was it? Because I will march over to his house and demand to speak to his parents—"

"Her parents," he said.

"Her pa—wait . . . what?"

"The student Tyler got into an altercation with was a girl named Amber Davis," he said.

I stared at Ben. My brother got trounced by a girl. This was bad, and on so many levels. I wondered how far my dad and Stephanie were into their trip, because this situation was well above my pay grade and they could just turn their tail feathers around and come deal with it.

"A girl?" I asked just to make sure I was getting it right before I had a complete freak-out. "Tyler had an altercation with a girl?"

"Yes."

I took a huge swallow of my beverage.

"Just to be clear," Ben said. "Tyler handled it perfectly."

"Okay."

"He pointed out to Amber the potential difficulties in the design she was presenting, and she responded by knocking him down in front of the entire team."

I felt my fingers tighten on my glass.

"But he didn't push back or engage with her in any way other than to tell her to stop," Ben said. "Which, quite frankly, is commendable."

"Yeah," I agreed. I sank back into my seat. Poor Tyler. I felt my heart pinch. He was in a lose-lose situation. Hit the girl back and you're an asshole, do nothing and you're a weakling getting beaten up by a girl. Ugh, no wonder he'd ripped my head off when he saw me talking to Ben. He'd needed to lash out at someone and there I was. "So what happens now?"

"That's why I'm here," he said. He looked pained. "As the library director, who is ultimately in charge of the robotics camp, I have to determine the consequence for what happened today, and I wanted to get Tyler's input on the situation."

I nodded. I could feel his discomfort. Most places operated on a zero tolerance policy for bullying, so he was likely feeling that he needed to boot this thug Amber out of the program, but as I understood it, there was scholarship money attached and it was something that couldn't be done lightly.

"I'll call him—"

That was as far as I got when the front door banged open and Tyler came striding out. He was already pleading his case, so Ben and I finished our drinks while he spoke.

"Mr. Reynolds, I know why you're here, but whatever you heard, it's not true," Tyler said. He began to pace the length of the short porch. "I tripped, that's all. There's no reason anyone should be punished for my clumsiness. I mean, look at the size of these feet. I'm a size twelve and a half. It's like trying to walk around in a pair of canoes."

Ben pressed his lips together as if trying not to laugh, and I had to look away for the same reason. Little brother was on a roll. I wasn't going to stop him.

"I mean, Sam will testify, I'm so clumsy I can barely cross the room without tripping," he said. He lifted up one foot and pointed to his shoe. "I should have rubber bumpers built onto these bad boys to keep myself from harm when I bump into everything, which I do all the time. In fact, I might look into wearing a helmet for when I fall down like I did today."

"So, what you're saying is that you tripped and fell without any assistance from anyone else?" Ben asked.

"That's what I'm saying," Tyler said. He couldn't hold Ben's gaze and instead looked down at his shoes. Ben and I exchanged a bemused glance. I wasn't happy that

Ty was covering for Amber Davis, but I was impressed that he wasn't ratting her out, even though she deserved it.

"How do you think the situation should be handled?" Ben asked.

Tyler glanced up. "I wouldn't kick anyone off the team. I would treat it as the misunderstanding it was and just put it behind us." His eyes took on an intensity that was riveting. "If we're going to win the Severin Robotics competition at the end of the summer, we need every person on this team. Each member brings something unique, and we need to tap all of that potential if we're going to win, and I really want to win."

Ben nodded. "You've certainly got the spirit."

Tyler gave him a tentative smile, as if he was hoping that he'd won Ben over.

"The robotics camp is meant to be an inclusive, constructive, sharing space with zero tolerance for bullying," Ben said. His tone was firm, brooking no argument.

"Yes, sir."

"If I take your word for what happened today and let this episode go, I will expect you, if you experience any bullying or observe it happening to others, to come and talk to me."

"Absolutely, one hundred percent," Tyler agreed. He glanced at me, and I gave him a double thumbs-up and smiled.

Tyler rolled his eyes as if I was the most annoying person who ever drew breath, which, for the record, I am not. I'd also had no idea how irritating an eye roll could be. It was big-time irritating, like supersonic aggravating. Before I could share this opinion, Tyler looked back at Ben.

"Thank you, I won't let you down," he said. He turned and slammed back into the house, leaving the screen door vibrating on its hinges in his wake.

I glanced at Ben and said, "He does have very large feet."

"Canoes," he agreed.

We both laughed and then immediately tried to stifle it in case the teenager was listening.

"Between you and me, I'm on my way to go have a chat with Amber Davis just to make certain we're all on the same page," Ben said.

"Oh, good, if you could sweat her a little, that would be great," I said.

Ben laughed and said, "Consequences will be discussed."

"Can I ask a question?"

"Sure."

"How does this robotics camp work?" I asked. "My parents mentioned that it was an opportunity for a scholarship to the Severin Science Academy, but . . ." I shrugged.

He nodded. "I get it. When I took the job as interim

library director, I had questions, too. Ryan Fielding, who works in outreach for Severin Robotics, is the main instructor for this group on the Vineyard. There are ten different camps all over the country, and they have ten students each. They are all competing for the top prize, which is scholarship money and automatic entry into the academy for their entire team."

"Which is why Tyler didn't want Amber kicked off?"

"I suspect so," he said. He rose from his seat. "I'd better go speak with her before it gets late. Thanks for the cocktail."

"Anytime." Oh no, did that sound too desperate or too friendly? I'd been working nights at the Comstock for so long I had no idea how normal people interacted.

Ben turned and headed toward the stairs. I put down my drink and followed him, as it felt weird to stay on the porch and wave goodbye from a distance.

We walked down the short path to the street. He paused beside his motorcycle. It was a big old beast of machine.

"So is this the house that used to be your grandmother's?" he asked.

I glanced back at the cedar shake shingled cottage that had been my happy place every summer. "It is."

"How did your family come to live on the Vineyard?"

"They were Portuguese fishermen," I said. "Recruited from the Azores to work whaling ships, they eventually settled on the Vineyard. My family has owned this house and a couple of others since the before times, when the area was called Cottage City."

Ben's eyes took in the modest house, which was well over one hundred years old. He nodded slowly as if he could see the ghosts of my ancestors walking the grounds. Sometimes I could, too.

"That's an amazing thing to have so much family history," he said. His voice was wistful, and I watched him swing his leg over the seat and pick up his helmet. I had a feeling Bennett Reynolds was looking for more than just some relatives, and my curiosity demanded to know what.

"I'll see you tomorrow when I drop Tyler off," I said. There I was sounding desperate again. I downshifted to casual. "You know, if you're around."

"Oh, I'll be around." His gaze met mine, and there it was. That spark of awareness that made my pulse pound and my hearing get fuzzy. How the heck had I managed to get a scorching case of "yes, please" for the hot librarian guy? No idea.

Ben Reynolds was way more than I'd bargained for this summer. Good thing I was flexible. I watched him put on his helmet and fire up his bike. With a wave, he shot down the street, and I discovered I was actually looking forward to going to the library the next day. Who'd have thought?

Chapter Five

I went back into the house to find Tyler foraging through the pantry like a bear in a dumpster. He was pulling random things out, smelling them, and then shoving them back as if he feared they carried a contagious strain of disease.

I folded my arms and leaned against the counter. "Can I help you find something?"

"Food," he grumbled. "I don't even know what most of this stuff is."

"What mystifies you?" I asked. "The almond butter? The loaf of bread that's not presliced? Or is it the plethora of fruits and vegetables?"

He turned to me with a glower. "I can't eat this stuff."

"Can't or won't?"

"I only eat pasta with butter, plain rice, or peanut butter and jelly, and occasionally chicken nuggets, but they have to be fresh from McDonald's."

"What are you, five?" I asked. I was appalled. What

fourteen-year-old ate the diet of a constipated old man? "Come on, we're going out."

"I don't want to eat out," he said. "They never serve anything I like."

"I am positive we can find something plain enough to suit even you," I said. "Besides, I'm in charge of meals, and if you want food, you're coming with me."

He slammed the door to the pantry, and his scowl deepened. "Why do you even want to go out to eat with me since you hate teenagers so much?"

I sucked in a breath. So he had heard me talking to Dad that first night. Great. I stood next to him, thinking of what I could say that might make him stop using what I had said about teens as a club to bludgeon me with every time I opened my mouth, otherwise it was going to be an excruciatingly long summer.

It occurred to me as I was considering and discarding snappy comebacks that I was looking up at him. Up. At my little brother. **When the hell did that happen?**

"This spring," he said.

"Did I say that out loud?"

"Yes," he said. "Since Christmas, I grew four inches and three shoe sizes."

I glanced down at his feet. "I thought we'd established those aren't shoes, they're canoes."

"Thanks for reminding me," he said. He looked annoyed.

How had I forgotten how miserable the teen years were? The uncomfortably awkward feeling that your skin and bones and hair don't fit right anymore. The absolute certainty that everyone is watching you all the time, judging your coolness and just waiting for you to slip up so they can laugh at you and cause you to die of embarrassment. The brutal stage of having perverted thoughts about, well, just about everyone, combined with sprouting hair in places that had no business having hair, and sudden problematic body odor. Yeah, it was a wonder anyone survived it.

I knew better than to look at my brother with sympathy or he'd just lob it back with some cutting barb that would either annoy me or hurt my feelings.

"Just because you're taller than me," I said, planting my hands on my hips just like Stephanie did when she lectured us. "Don't think you're the boss of me."

He looked down at me, and a smile started in one corner of his mouth and slowly slid across to the other side. Then he patted me on the head.

"Whatever you say, short stack."

"Short stack?" I sputtered in mock outrage. "Short stack?!" Then I ruined it by laughing. He ducked his head, but not before I saw his grin.

"Where are we going to eat?" he asked. He moved around me and headed for the door. "I'm starving."

"Oh, now you want to go eat," I said.

He gestured to his body. "I'm a growing boy. I have

to eat every fifteen minutes or I'll die, literally starve to death."

"Fine." I stepped out onto the porch with him, locking the door behind me.

We stared at each other for a moment, and I noticed for the first time that we had the same black hair, brown eyes, and heart-shaped face. I don't know why I'd never noticed before, but it hit me that we both took after my father and his Gale DNA and seeing my own features mirrored back at me made me feel a connection to Tyler that I'd never felt before.

"What?" he asked. He glanced down at his shirt. "Did I spill something?"

"No, you're fine," I said. I was in no way prepared to deal with all of these feelings. I'd been a solo unit for a really long time. I had no idea what a sibling bond even meant. "Let's go."

We walked through the neighborhood to the more touristy part of town. We had to duck and weave through the crowds, but we finally arrived at the Flying Horses Carousel.

"Seriously?" Tyler asked. "Don't you think I'm a little old for this?"

"You're never too old for a carousel," I said. "But that's not why we're here."

We walked past the vintage carousel—which boasted being the oldest in the country, as it had been brought to the Vineyard from Coney Island, New York, in 1884—

and crossed the street, where a small mom-and-pop shop crafted the best pizza outside of New Haven, Connecticut.

"You do eat pizza, I assume?" I asked.

"Cheese only," he said.

"Of course."

I led the way into the shop, and we ordered a couple of slices each and sodas. I figured after the day Tyler had, Dad and Stephanie couldn't be too disapproving of pizza for dinner. I'd finagle a way to get him to start broadening his palate another day. I was a chef, after all. I couldn't be in charge of a sibling who only ate bland and bland on nothing. The horror!

We found an empty bench on Lake Avenue that looked out over the marina. We people watched while we ate, and I decided it was as good a time as any to do an informational deep dive.

"So, what's up with Dad and the chin hair?" I asked.

I caught Tyler on a sip of soda, and he hacked and laughed at the same time.

"Sorry," I said. "Need me to thump you on the back?"

I may have sounded too eager, as he shook his head and said, "Nah, I'm good."

My pizza slice had a nice thin crispy crust, a light coating of sauce, and a heavy hand with the cheese. In other words, perfection. I nibbled while I waited for Tyler to answer. Surely he had noticed the goatee.

"I have no idea what's going on there," he said. Before I could ask a follow-up question, he said, "And I don't understand the skinny jeans or the fixer-upper sports car either."

"How fragile are you?" I asked.

He looked at me in confusion. "What does that mean?"

"It means I want to ask about Dad and Steph's marriage, but if it makes you feel vulnerable, I won't go there," I said.

He looked surprised.

I shrugged. "I know we aren't that close and we haven't spent that much time together over the years, but I like Dad and Steph together, and I just feel like . . ."

"He's having a monster midlife crisis," Tyler said.

"He is?" I asked. It's what I'd been thinking, but it was weird to have it confirmed.

"That's what Mom yelled at him when he showed up with the clown car," Tyler said.

I snorted, and soda went up my nose. This made Tyler laugh, naturally.

"Need me to thump your back?" he offered. I laughed harder and his grin deepened.

We smiled at each other for a beat, and it hit me that I liked having a younger brother. Thankfully, I did not say this out loud and freak him out.

I was just gnawing the last of my crust when a man popped up from his boat docked across the walkway. He looked familiar, and I must have looked the same to him because he did a double take.

"Samantha Gale, is that you?" he asked.

I swallowed. The crust went down hard, and I had to take a quick sip of soda to get it all the way gone. I forced a smile and said, "That's me."

"I'm sorry, you just look so much like your father, but of course I see your mother, Lisa, in you, too," he said. He extended his hand, which I shook out of reflex more than friendliness.

"You probably don't remember me, but your parents used to go sailing with my wife and me all the time. You came with us but you were only about this big." He held his hands a foot apart as if I'd been a fish they'd caught.

"Oh, well, it's good to see you again, Mr. . . ."

"Stuart Mayhew. Call me Stuart," he said.

"I vaguely remember you," I said. It was a lie. I had no idea who this guy was, but he seemed to want me to recognize him, and I hated to disappoint.

"Are you being kind?" he asked.

I shrugged. "Maybe."

He laughed. "You're as diplomatic as your father."

I grinned. "I'm not the only one. This is my younger brother, Tyler, the brains of the family."

Tyler looked surprised that I'd introduced him, but he shook Stuart's extended hand and said, "Nice to meet you, sir."

Stuart glanced between us. "Yup, you two are definitely Gale siblings."

I have no idea why this made me feel good, but it did. I glanced at Tyler to find him looking at me as if he wondered what I thought about this. I winked at him to let him know I thought it was cool, and his lips turned up in the corner just a teeny bit.

"So where are your parents? I'd love to catch up," Stuart said.

"Dad and Stephanie are on a trip to Europe at the moment," I said.

"Stephanie?" Stuart looked confused. It hit me then that he was a friend from way back when my parents were still married.

"Stephanie is Dad's second wife and Tyler's mom," I said. "She's also my stepmother, and I adore her." Why did I feel compelled to add that? As if this could get anymore awkward.

"Is Lisa, I mean is your mother, I'm sorry, is she . . . ?" Stuart looked aggrieved, and it took me a moment to realize he was asking if my mom was dead.

"My mom is fine," I assured him. "Living large in Boston, happy as can be."

"So your parents got divorced?" he asked. He sounded shocked.

"Yes." I couldn't even look at Tyler. I decided to steer the conversation in another direction, any direction. "I take it you've been away from the Vineyard for a while."

He nodded. "I left the Vineyard after my wife, Jeanie, passed away." His voice was wistful and he glanced back at his boat. "I couldn't bear to be here without her, so I moved down to Florida, and I've been there for the past twenty-three years."

"I'm so sorry for your loss," I said.

"Me, too," Tyler added.

I felt a flash of pride that he could put our own familial weirdness aside to acknowledge Stuart's pain. My brother had layers.

"Thank you both," Stuart said.

He pushed the baseball cap back on his head, revealing a fringe of gray hair around an otherwise bald head. He was tall and lean, with deep brown skin and arms that were roped with muscle. He wore a T-shirt, cargo shorts, and old-school boat shoes with no socks. He looked like a man who was most at home either on or adjacent to the water.

"What brought you back here?" I asked.

"Business," he said. "And I missed it. There's no place like the Vineyard. Besides, I thought being here would bring Jeanie back to me a little, so I bought the Tangled Vine Inn."

"Oh, I love that place," I said. "My grandmother used to take me to afternoon tea there every Saturday.

Some of my best memories were spent on that patio. I didn't realize it was still open."

"It wasn't for a long time. I'm trying to scrape off the neglect and rehabilitate it. Say, you don't happen to know a caterer who specializes in appetizers, do you?" he asked. "I'm trying to infuse some life into the Friday nights with a happy hour, but my dining room chef can't manage both that and dinner."

"Seriously?" I asked. I felt my heart rate increase. If I could score a job, I could make some scratch and possibly avoid hitting up my dad for a loan, which would go a long way to making me feel like less of a loser. "I'm actually a chef."

He blinked at me as if he thought I was joking. I realized I was going to have to do a hard sell.

"I'm summering here to keep an eye on this guy while the parents are away, but I was recently one of the head chefs at the Comstock in Brookline."

"You're not there anymore?" he asked.

"No," I said. I didn't elaborate. No need for him to know that I was passed over for a promotion. I felt Tyler's laser-like gaze on the side of my face. I ignored him. "Family duty first and all."

Stuart nodded. I had a feeling he wasn't completely sold on hiring a perfect stranger with no credentials. Go figure.

"Not to be all braggy or anything, but I was written

up in several Boston magazines as one of the thirty under thirty to watch."

He studied me, considering. I was going to have to go all in.

"Tell you what," I said. "I'll cater your happy hour pro bono, and if you hate it, you don't have to pay me."

His eyebrows lifted and he started to protest.

"No, I mean it," I said. There was a tiny voice inside of me screaming, **Shut up, shut up, shut up!** I wasn't listening. "If you're happy with the happy hour, you can reimburse me for the food and my time, and if you're not, we part ways with no hard feelings."

Stuart was silent. My heart was pounding in my chest. I almost called it off. What was I thinking? The only way I could afford to pay for the food was if I raided the money Dad had given me to feed Tyler and myself. If I blew this, we'd be eating butter noodles and popcorn until the parents got back. I must be insane.

But if I pulled it off, I stood a chance of having a job. And, oh, I wanted to be working so badly.

"I don't see how I can refuse," Stuart said. He looked thrilled. "This is great. Give me your phone number and we can hammer out the details. Can you start this Friday?"

"Absolutely," I said. We exchanged numbers and shook hands again.

"I'm looking forward to working with you, Sam. Nice

to meet you, Tyler," Stuart said. He held out his hand and Tyler shook it. "I hope we meet again soon."

"Oh, you will," I said. I had no idea where that statement came from, but I doubled down. "Tyler's my sous-chef."

"Fantastic," Stuart said. "The Gale siblings in the house!" He raised his hands in the air like he was raising the roof, and I laughed. I liked Stuart.

He departed with a wave, and I slumped back in my seat. My mind was racing with possible menus. I refused to consider the ramifications of failure at this point, when Tyler pushed up to his feet, glared at me, and snarled, "I am not your sous-chef and I will not be cooking with you."

He threw his paper plate and cup into the nearby trash can with more force than was necessary and began to stalk away back toward home. Now what had I done?

I sighed, then followed.

"Tyler, wait!" I called.

He walked faster.

I thought about letting him take the lead and just follow him like a stray dog all the way home, but that sort of passivity was not in my nature.

When he was forced to wait at a crosswalk amid the throngs of tourists, I crept up behind him and said, "Why don't you want to be my sous-chef? I'd pay you."

"It's not about money."

The light turned, and the crowd moved as one big gelatinous mass across the street. I drafted in behind him.

"Then what's it about?" I asked. "I thought we were bonding there."

"Well, we weren't."

"That disappoints."

"Welcome to my life."

He couldn't see me, so I squinched up my face and stuck my tongue out behind his back. A trio of girls coming toward us burst out laughing, and Tyler whipped his head around to look at me. Thankfully, I managed to iron out my expression to one of contrite concern before his gaze landed on me. His eyes narrowed in suspicion, so I widened mine with every bit of innocence I could muster. I'm not sure he bought it.

"Aw, come on, Tyler," I cajoled. "Help a sister out."

He glowered.

We turned off Lake Avenue onto a quieter side street that would lead us through the Oak Bluffs neighborhood to home. As we passed the famed gingerbread cottages, I looped my arm through his.

"Why are you so mad?" I asked.

"You had no right to volunteer me to be your sous-chef without asking me first," he said. He shrugged me off. "Maybe I have plans."

"You don't have plans."

"I might have plans. You don't know."

I considered what he said. He was right. Oh, not that he had plans. I seriously doubted that, but I should have asked him first.

"You're right," I said. "I should have asked you first. I apologize. I was just so excited to be offered a cooking gig, I got carried away."

"Yeah, a cooking gig because the place you used to work booted you," he said. He gave me side-eye. "Dad said you took the summer off to spend time with us, but that isn't it, is it? You lied."

He was speculating, throwing a guess at the wall and seeing if it stuck. Still, I felt busted. Shame swamped me. For a second I thought about telling him the truth about being passed over for a promotion that I had earned and quitting because of it. Tyler would be the first person I'd told. Nope, nope, nope. There was no way I was dumping my tale of woe on a teenager. Too humiliating. It was bad enough that I thought of myself as a loser, I didn't want to see my little brother look at me that way, too. Not now, not when we were just getting to know each other.

"You know how you love robotics?" I asked. He nodded. "Well, that's how I feel about cooking. Even if I'm on a hiatus from my career, for whatever reason, I still love it. The kitchen is my happy place. Like, even if you weren't trying for a scholarship to the Severin Science Academy, you'd still be doing something with robotics this summer, right?"

"Probably." His tone was grudging.

I stared up at him, which was still so weird, and said, "You're fourteen. You can't get a job yet, but this job could make you some serious cash. Don't you want your own income stream?"

He considered me. "How much?"

"Five bucks an hour?" I asked.

"What do you take me for, child labor?"

"All right, ten," I said.

"Fifteen, plus a cut of the tips," he said.

I leaned back and gave him my most offended look. Then I patted down my pockets.

"What? Did you lose the house key?" he asked.

"No, but I'm pretty sure I was just robbed."

He laughed. Then he stuck out his hand and said, "Deal?"

I heaved a put-upon sigh. "Fine." I shook his hand. "But you'd better be in shape, because I'm going to work you into the ground."

"For fifteen bucks an hour, I'll let you." He wagged his eyebrows at me. I tried not to laugh. I failed.

Chapter Six

I got up early the next morning. I did not want to be late again and risk the fragile connection Tyler and I had established by getting distracted before we needed to leave for camp. When we'd gotten home last night, I was sure Tyler would shoot up to his room to play video games, but instead he hung out downstairs with me and we ended up watching a **Great British Bake Off** marathon.

The kid had no idea what he was in for. I tried to warn him that you get attached to the bakers. He didn't listen. When his favorite baker didn't make the cut, we called it a night so he could recover from the emotional trauma. I resisted the urge to say, "I told you so," and was quite proud of myself for that.

I was just forking the Belgian waffles out of the iron when Tyler appeared in the doorway. He looked shocked to see me. "You're up?"

"And ready to walk out the door as soon as you eat," I said. "I promise."

I dumped the dishes in the sink, unplugged the

waffle maker, and sat at the dining table with my hands curled around my coffee cup.

Tyler tucked into the waffles that had nothing on them but powdered sugar. I know how to serve plain with panache. "These are amazing. Thank you."

"You're welcome." I sipped my coffee, feeling pleased with myself. Maybe watching a teenager wasn't so hard after all.

"Are you just going to sit there, staring at me?" he asked.

"No." I glanced away, but then the dishes grabbed my attention. I should really wash those. Surely I had time. I was half out of my seat, but then I sat back down. Nope, I was not going to get distracted. I was going to stay on task.

"I might have to stare at you," I said.

Tyler frowned. "For real?"

"I don't want to lose my focus, which is getting you fed and delivered to camp early so you can be first."

"Oh." He swallowed a huge bite of waffle. "Do you lose focus a lot?"

"I do, because I have a scorching case of ADHD. It's part of the whole dyslexia gift basket," I said. "Not for everyone with dyslexia but for a lot of us."

"How do you run a kitchen then?" he asked. "I mean, aren't there a ton of moving parts, how do you keep track of it all?"

I shrugged. "Coping mechanisms. I developed them

as a kid to try and keep up, and a lot of them translated into my professional life."

"Such as?" he asked.

I'd have given him the short answer that I usually used when people asked about my neurodivergent brain, but Tyler seemed genuinely interested. We were supposed to be getting to know each other this summer. I took a deep breath and decided to go all in. I was nervous. I really didn't want my supersmart brother to think less of me. I almost changed the subject at the last second—almost. Instead, I tapped into a reserve of courage I didn't know I had, and shared.

I stared into my coffee cup, thinking about my life in the restaurant. "For starters, I do things like group my tasks, so if I have to chop onions for one dish and peppers for another, I do them all at once. I plan out the timing of each dish so there aren't any surprises, and even then, I make sure to give myself extra time just in case. Shutting out external noise is helpful, although difficult in a busy kitchen, and I prep as much as I can ahead of time so I don't get freaked out by the utter chaos that is the dinner rush hour."

Tyler stared at me as if trying to process what I was saying. "So, what you're saying is you have to come up with ways to compensate for the executive function in your brain being asleep on the job."

I narrowed my eyes at him. "How do you know that? You just described exactly what ADHD means."

"I might have done some reading up on dyslexia and ADHD," he said. His gaze went down to his plate.

"You did?" I was oddly touched by this.

"Yeah, you're not mad?"

"No," I said. Which was true. "I appreciate that you want to understand."

That might have been the wrong thing to say. It felt too emotional or too vulnerable. I wasn't sure which, but it felt weird, and the awkwardness that mushroomed between us confirmed it wasn't just me.

"Maybe you could build me a robot to help me out," I said. I was going for a laugh to lighten the moment, but instead Tyler looked thoughtful.

"You know, that's not a bad idea."

"Yeah, yeah." I looked at the clock. "Let's get going so you can maintain attendance dominance."

"You make me sound like a maniac," he said.

"Takes one to know one."

"Right," he agreed. But he didn't sound offended.

We pulled into the library parking lot with time to spare. Tyler glanced at me when I climbed out of the car with him.

"You're coming in with me?" He looked appalled.

"Relax," I said. "I was teasing yesterday, and I'm sorry about that. I should have taken your feelings more seriously. I'm just going inside to see my friend Em."

"Okay, but you won't go anywhere near the robotics room," he clarified. He stared at me as if he had the power to freeze me in place. "And you're not going to talk to any of the kids in the program."

I rolled my eyes. "No."

"Promise me," he demanded. He didn't blink, not once.

"I promise, you weirdo," I said. "Sheesh."

I waved him off, pretending I needed to get my bag out of the back of the car so he could get a head start and walk into the building alone. He didn't want to be seen with me. I got it. It wasn't as if I'd wanted to be seen with him when I was his age and he was a baby. Turnabout was fair play, I supposed.

I waited until he entered the building, and then I locked the car and followed. I wanted to catch up with Emily and see how she was doing, and maybe I'd get a glimpse of Ben, formerly known as hot reader guy. This thought thrilled me way more than it should have.

I wondered if it was ridiculous for me to want to see him again. I mean, what did we really have in common? He was a reader and I was . . . not. But it wasn't just that he enjoyed reading, he was **a librarian**. The man had chosen a profession where putting books into the hands of readers was literally his reason for being. Hot reader guy was all about books, meaning his idea of the perfect woman was undoubtedly someone with whom he could share that passion. That wasn't me.

For the record, the English language is not kind to people with dyslexia with its **there**, **their**, and **they're** and its words that look nothing like how they're pronounced, like **subtle** and **yacht**. Who came up with that shit anyway?

And I'd rather Ben see me with spinach in my teeth than witness what passed for my version of spelling. So no love notes then. I decided not to overthink it. I was attracted to Ben and I wanted to see him again. It didn't need to be more complicated than that. For all I knew, he had a girlfriend, and friends was the most we could ever be. I felt a flicker of disappointment and then stomped on it. Friends was fine. I had a fourteen-year-old to keep an eye on. I didn't need any other complications. Really.

I saw Emily seated at the service desk on the second floor. The robotics group was meeting in the teen area at the far end of the room, so I didn't think Tyler could get too miffy about me talking to Emily. If he'd taken out a restraining order on me, I was far enough away not to violate it.

Em smiled when she saw me approaching, but there was a concerned look in her eye, as if she wasn't sure how I was doing today. I'd left on a rather awkward note last night, racing after my brother, so I understood the worry.

"Hey," I said.

"Hey back," she returned. In a dry tone, she continued, "Nice to see that Tyler didn't actually expire from teenage indignation."

"It would have been tough to explain to the parents," I said.

"Right," she said. "Much easier to blame it on quicksand or spontaneous human combustion."

I laughed. Good old Em, she always knew how to make me feel better.

"Ryan told me what happened at robotics yesterday. Is Tyler okay?"

"Yes, or mostly," I said. Very dramatically, I wiped my brow with the back of my hand. "Thank goodness. I didn't want to have to call Dad and Stephanie and say I'd failed on day one and Tyler got beat up and was already booted out of camp. Can you imagine?"

"You'd have to flee the island," she joked.

"Possibly the country," I agreed.

"Which would be totally unfair since taking on a teenager is no small task," she said. "Stephanie mentioned to the bunco ladies, she and my mom play together, that you were watching Tyler for half of the summer. Even Stephanie said she hoped Tyler didn't wear you out."

And just like that my self-doubt reared its ugly head, and for a second I wondered if there had been a notice in the **Vineyard Gazette**, asking everyone to keep an eye on Tyler since I was in charge and had no idea what I was doing. Paranoid much? Um . . . yes.

Desperate to change the subject, I asked, "What are you working on?"

There was a stack of books at her elbow. I glanced at the titles, and even with my reading issues, I noted one word common to each book spine. Cancer. I glanced back up at her, and she quickly moved the stack of books to the cart behind her.

"Research for a patron," she said.

I noticed the rainbow of sticky notes poking out of each book.

"You're an awesome librarian," I said. "Marking pages and everything. I wish I'd had someone to do that for me when I was in school."

She was wearing a cute sleeveless sage green dress with a lightweight white cardigan over it. Her wavy red hair was tied at the nape of her neck, and she looked very much the professional librarian. Her glasses were perched on the end of her nose as she peered at me over the computer monitor in front of her. She fiddled with the button on her cardigan. "It's the job."

She didn't sound thrilled, but at least she had a career. I glanced down. I was wearing a faded Dead & Company T-shirt, baggy shorts, and checkered Vans. Of the two of us, I was clearly the one who was unemployed and going nowhere. I tried to shake off the critical voice in my head, but its grip was fierce.

"You said a few weeks ago that you were going for the executive chef position at the Comstock," she said. "Did you get it?"

If it was anyone else, I'd have hedged and not done a full disclosure, but Em was my best friend. She was one of the few people I'd told about the job. I knew I could trust her not to make me feel worse about the outcome, which, frankly, would be hard to do.

"What happened was that I was passed over for the promotion and I quit," I said.

"Passed over?" she cried. "What? Why? That's utter bull—" She caught herself, clearly remembering where she was. She lowered her voice and said, "You've given the Comstock **years** of your life. How could they not give you the job?"

And that was why Em had been one of my very best friends since we were babies. She was definitely the sort that when you called her in the middle of the night and asked her to come over, she came, no questions asked, whether the task was burying a body or night harvesting Chardonnay grapes.

"The owner said he didn't think I was ready," I said. "Also, he admitted he preferred to have a man run the kitchen."

"Oh, that's so sexist," she fumed. "You should sue him."

"That costs money," I said. "He blathered something about the amazing reputation of the chef he hired, but I've had more press than that guy, and I've been a chef longer, too."

"'Guy' is definitely the operative word," she said.

I nodded. I didn't add that I hoped that was the case. It was much easier for me to accept being overlooked because I had boobs than because I had dyslexia of which the owner was aware, because when I first started at the Comstock, there had been a steeper learning curve for me than other chefs. The fact that I was still there when most of the others had moved on had lulled me into thinking the owner was confident in me and my abilities, but apparently not. Yup, it still stung.

"It makes no sense. You were written up in the **Boston Globe** as an up-and-coming chef to watch," Em ranted. "You're a rising star in the culinary world. I hope the Comstock gets a million one-star reviews."

See? Loyalty. I may not have gotten it from my old boss, but I was getting it from my friend.

"It is what it is." I shrugged.

"It's crap is what it is," Em said. She studied me for a moment. "It must be weird for you to be here for the summer. Your life was so glamorous in Boston, like a rock star but with food." Her voice held a note of longing I'd never heard before. I felt the need to offer a reality check.

"Which part was glamorous?" I asked. "The crummy hours, lousy pay, frequent third-degree burns, lazy sous-chefs, uptight managers, or the misogynistic owner?"

"Well, when you put it like that . . ."

"Don't get me wrong," I said. "I love cooking. It's just the restaurant biz is brutal. It will chew you up, swallow you down, and then spit you back out."

"Ew." She cringed.

"Exactly."

"Well, so much for living vicariously through you."

Em's tone was light and teasing, but there was an underlying heaviness to it, as if the truth weighted her words like dry beans held down a piecrust. She shook her head as if I'd just dispelled any fanciful notions she had about me or my life. If I wasn't mistaken, she looked disappointed that I wasn't quite the immense success she'd thought I was. Huh.

I'd always thought that Em and I had a friendship that went beyond the surface trappings. In my mind, we were the human embodiment of a pinkie swear with a sisterhood forged in the hellfire of raging hormones, both of us, and no impulse control, mostly me. It had never occurred to me that she might see my life in Boston as something to aspire to, and I wondered if Em was happy.

She'd lived on the Vineyard most of her life, leaving for college but then coming back to live at home and work as a librarian. Growing up, she'd always said she wanted to see the world, but when she didn't pack a bag and head for parts unknown, I'd assumed that she changed her mind. But now I wondered if that was accurate. Had she abandoned her dreams? And, if so, why? I didn't know how to ask, so I went for a diversion instead.

"We'll have to get up to some shenanigans while I'm here for old times' sake," I said.

She grinned. "I'd like that."

When our gazes met and held, it felt as if we were still teenagers riding our bikes on Beach Road, sneaking beers, and breaking curfew, much to our parents' deep disappointment.

It goes without saying that I was the bad influence. I had a lot of anger pulsing through me during my teen years, and Em was my wingman. Thankfully, she reined in some of my dumber ideas while I made sure she actually got out and lived a little bit. We'd been good for each other that way.

"You know you're going to be fine, better than fine, right?" she asked.

I glanced at her. She was looking at me with a surety I hadn't felt since packing up my knives and leaving the Comstock.

"Maybe."

"Maybe?" she cried. "You're one of the best chefs in Boston, no, Massachusetts, no, the United States."

My eyes went wide. "That's high praise."

"I mean it," she said. "Remember I visited you at the restaurant when I came to Boston. I sat on a stool in the corner and watched you work. You're going to find your footing again. I know you will."

"Thanks, Em," I said. I was feeling a bit choked up. Whenever Em came to Boston, which was a couple of times a year, she always stayed with me and frequently hung out at the restaurant while I worked. This was a pep talk that only a best friend who had seen me in my element could deliver. "I really appreciate that."

She considered me for a second. "What do you think

about doing a cooking demonstration for our teen summer reading program?"

"Cooking program? As in teaching teens to cook?" I asked.

"Yes," she said. "I'm in charge of the teen programming, and I haven't been able to think of anything that's engaging, but a cooking program . . ."

"Will likely bore them to death unless I'm teaching them how to make their favorite fast food at home," I said.

Her eyebrows shot up. "That's it. That's brilliant. Could you do that?"

"You're serious?"

"Yes," she said. She bounced on her chair and clapped as if she'd just won a cakewalk. "That would be so much fun. Say you'll do it."

"Okay, I'll do it," I said.

"Excellent." Her face fell. "But I probably can't pay you."

I shrugged. "Pay for the food and we'll call it even."

"Really?" she asked.

"It's not like I have anything else to do," I said. "Other than one random catering job, my calendar is wide open."

Did I sound bitter? I was afraid I might. I forced a smile, but it made my face hurt.

"We can work out the details when I get the idea approved," she said.

There was a noise at the end of the room where the

robotics group was gathering. We both looked in that direction and I half expected to see Tyler frowning at me for being in his designated area. Thankfully, he wasn't. In fact, all looked calm.

I reached into my bag and pulled out a big fat Chunky candy bar. "Look what I found at the store yesterday."

She glanced at the silver-wrapped square of chocolate, and a slow smile spread across her face. "Do you remember—?"

"Of course I do," I said. "That's why I bought it. It brought me right back to one of the most humiliating moments of our adolescence. How could I not buy it?"

Em laughed out loud at that. "I truly thought I might die of embarrassment that day."

I grinned. "I know. Who knew that shoving candy bars in our back pockets on a hot summer day would make them melt?"

"Yeah, and that when we went to take them out to share with Timmy Montowese, the cutest boy on the island, it would look like we pooped ourselves because the wrappers had opened and melted chocolate was all over our fingers and our butts," she concluded.

We grinned at each other, and then a giggle escaped Emily, met by a belly laugh from me.

"It took me **years** to live that down," she said. "You're lucky you wintered off island."

"No doubt," I agreed.

I opened the package and snapped the candy bar in two, handing half to Em. She promptly broke it in half again and popped a piece in her mouth. "Still one of my favorites."

"Same." I shoved a quarter piece in my mouth as well.

"Is this a Vineyard thing?" a voice asked from behind me.

I felt a prickle of awareness on the nape of my neck, and I knew without turning around that it was Ben.

"No—" Em began, but I interrupted.

"Yes, it is," I said. "At the top of every hour, we islanders have to have a bite of the chocolate of our choice. It's totally a Vineyard thing."

As if to back me up, Em nodded while I handed Ben the remaining square of my chocolate.

To my surprise and delight, he took it and ate it. His thick dark hair had just a bit of wave in it, curling away from his collar. He chewed thoughtfully, giving me the opportunity to study his lips. They were a warm shade of pink and full with a dip in his upper lip that was positively bitable. I glanced away and tried to focus my eyesight on something, anything, else.

Get it together, Gale. I made my expression blank and glanced back at him.

"Not bad," he said. "I'm more of a Milky Way guy, but this'll do."

"It's got raisins and peanuts," I said. "It's practically trail mix."

Emily snorted, and we both turned to look at her, causing her to turn a faint shade of pink. She glanced at Ben and said, "Sam has volunteered to teach a cooking class to our teens. Isn't that great?"

I glanced at her in amazement. Her definition of volunteer and mine were clearly two very different things.

"That's right. You're a chef," Ben said.

"Currently between gigs," I confirmed.

He studied me as if trying to figure out what the subtext was to that. As in, had I been fired? Was I a lousy cook? I wanted to defend myself and explain, but I didn't.

"She's not just a chef," Em said. "She's one of Boston's finest. She's been written up in papers and magazines all over New England."

I felt my face get warm. I loved Em's enthusiasm, I did, but it was also a teeny bit embarrassing and a bit over the top. I wasn't that great. Okay, potentially I was pretty great, but still, I didn't want to set the expectation bar too high.

"I think that would make a terrific teen program,"

Ben said. "But, of course, I feel like I should sample your cooking before I okay it."

I studied his face, noted the twinkle in his blue-gray eyes and the small smile on his lips. He was playing me, and dang if it wasn't working.

"You're doing quality control for a free program, really?" I asked. "Or are you just angling for dinner?"

He shrugged. "Can't blame a guy for trying."

"No," I agreed. "But I have a better idea. I'm catering a happy hour at the Tangled Vine Inn. Why don't you help out and you can see me in action?"

"So you're planning to have me work for my supper?" he asked.

"Can't blame a gal for trying."

That surprised a laugh out of him. Then he nodded, he held out his hand, and we shook.

"All right. Give me the date and time and I'll be there."

"This Friday, at five o'clock," I said. "You can follow us to our house after camp, since Tyler's my other crew member and there's limited parking at the inn."

Ben turned to Emily. "Why do I feel like I was just set up?"

She smiled. "Once you taste Sam's cooking, you'll only regret that she didn't feed you sooner."

"Now I'm definitely going to be there," Ben said. "See you Friday."

He left with a wave, heading toward the room where

the robotics kids had gathered. I glanced at Emily who, like me, watched him walk away. What was she thinking? Was she crushing on him? Sure, she'd said he was just her boss, but he was a hot librarian guy. Those had to be rare in the female-dominated library world, mythical even, like unicorns. How could she not be into him at least a little? I decided to see if I could figure out how my friend felt about Ben, in a subtle way, of course.

"That guy is smoking hot," I said. See? Subtle.

"Ben?" she asked. She frowned at me as if I'd made a lewd suggestion about Santa Claus.

"You can't be serious," I said. "Look at him. He's all thick wavy hair, broad shoulders, sexy lips, and he rides a motorcycle. He's the very definition of F-I-N-E."

Em clapped her hands over her ears. "La la la la. I'm not hearing this. I can't be thinking about my boss that way. Ugh, it's like walking in on your grandparents when they're . . . you know . . . getting busy."

"Really? A hot boss makes you think of **that**?"

"Stop calling him that," she said. "The man signs my paychecks. It'd be tawdry to even think of him that way." She sounded horrified, but her eyes were twinkling with laughter. So, no crush on the boss man then. Cool. I smiled at her, and it occurred to me that I had really missed my bestie.

"Hey, Em," I said. "I don't want to impose, but I have no idea how this happy hour is going to go. Is there any chance you could help out, too?"

"Sure," she said without hesitation. "It definitely beats another Friday night, sitting at home alone reading . . . wait . . . or does it?"

"It does!" I laughed. "It definitely does."

She nodded. "All right. I'll do it, but I'll meet you at the inn, as I have to feed Mr. Bingley."

"Your mom's cat is still alive?" I asked. "He must be almost thirty."

"Eighteen," she said. "He's officially a grumpy old man, and he has the sour disposition to prove it."

"He had that disposition when he was a kitten," I said.

"You're not wrong," she agreed. "Either way, I have to feed him first."

"All right, meet us at the inn," I said. A library user was coming toward the desk, so I started to back away so she could get back to work. "Black pants, white shirt. Tell Ben."

"Fancy," Em said. She put her hand to her throat, posing like a model from the forties. "You got it."

Glancing at the clock, I realized I had better get home and start planning what I was serving. I was going to need every minute before Friday to make sure this went smoothly. I now had two major cooking commitments on my calendar. I felt a thrum in my chest. I wasn't sure if it was fear or excitement. I decided I would call it excitement until it became excitement. I just hoped that worked.

Chapter Seven

One thing I knew, from a lifetime of working around my unique way of seeing things, was that preparation was key, so I spent all week working on my menu. Stuart had said he wanted me to focus on small plates and bar bites, but what did I want those items to be?

I decided this happy hour needed to be different. Not the standard fare of potato skins and sliders. Rather, I wanted it to be so distinctive and delicious that people would talk about it all week. I wanted the foodies on the island to hear the buzz and realize they had missed out and demand my return next week. Pretty high aspirations for a single happy hour, I know. But the beauty of my neurodivergent brain is that sometimes I can picture the forest better than the individual trees, and this vision guides me toward my goals.

I didn't know where to start with my menu, so I hit the West Tisbury Farmer's Market to look for some inspiration. Held in the Martha's Vineyard Agricultural Hall, rain or shine, spring through fall, this farmer's market had been founded in 1934 in response to the Depression. My vovó hadn't even been born yet, but she often told me stories about my relatives, farmers and fishermen, trying to survive those lean years.

The farmer's market was revived in the seventies, and twenty years later, when I was a kid, Vovó brought me every Saturday. Some of my best memories were of wandering through the stalls and booths with her, watching her haggle over a few pounds of fish or a big old melon.

My throat got tight and I paused beside a booth full of honey and wildflowers. I missed my vovó with an intensity that almost took me out. She had been such a constant in my life as a kid. I knew she would have thought I was crazy to quit a paying job when I didn't have another one lined up, but I also knew she was my biggest champion and she would have told me I could do anything I set my mind to. Whenever I had struggled to master a recipe she was teaching me, she always told me to trust myself and keep trying. I could really use her confidence in me right now.

It was then that inspiration struck. I'd been looking to cook exotic fare for the Tangled Vine's happy hour, thinking it had to be some crazy food trend so that I could get noticed, but it didn't have to be that. It just had to be something different that was also delicious. A memory of Vovó popped into my head. She was standing by the stove in our summer house and she was making kale soup. She tested it, made a face, and said, "Mais sal." I remember laughing at the time because she never measured anything, she always cooked to taste—her taste.

And that's what I was going to do. I decided right then and there in the middle of the market that I was going full Portuguese. I dragged the memories of all the dishes Vovó had taught over the years out of my brain. My menu would consist of peixinhos da horta, or batter-drenched fried green beans—yes, it's a classic and, little-known fact, the Portuguese are believed to have invented tempura. I'd also make bolinhos de bacalhau, which are small round cod and mashed potato fritters, and torresmos, a recipe for marinated pork that had been known to make grown men weep it was so good.

I grabbed pork ribs from the Grey Barn stand and potatoes and green beans from the Milkweed Farm booth, then I zipped over to the Menemsha Fish Market to pick up some fresh cod. I spent the next two days doing practice runs at the house, which caused Tyler to complain about the fish smell. Whatever. It felt so frigging good to be a chef again. I was giddy.

The Tangled Vine Inn was nestled on the outskirts of town. It sat prominently on East Chop Drive surrounded by garden beds of thick hydrangea that burst into colors from white to powder blue to vibrant magenta. They looked artlessly arranged as if they'd naturally sprung up around the stone walls, but of course the lush lawn that swept out from the side of the inn made it clear that the grounds were scrupulously maintained.

Happy hour was to be held on the enormous stone terrace at the back of the inn. There were small high-top tables, a DJ playing yacht rock in the corner by a small dance floor, and paper lanterns strung around the perimeter that would light up as soon as the sun went down. I was surprised to find I was nervous. I'd cooked for hundreds of events in my time as a chef, but this one felt more personal since my younger brother was here. I could admit it, at least to myself, that I wanted him to be impressed with me. Also, I'd spent all of our grocery money on the food, so it really was do-or-die time.

Stuart and I had discussed my ideas for catering the happy hour, and we went with three dedicated food stations that Tyler, Ben, and Em would host. Meanwhile, I would run back and forth to the kitchen, which I shared with the regular chef, Mark Chambers, who was not at all territorial, thank goodness, and quite happy to have me fill in for happy hour so he didn't have to do it.

As I set up the stations, I could smell the brine on the incoming tide, and it triggered a lifetime of summers spent on the island. For the first time since I'd arrived, I felt like I was home. It hit me then that I'd missed summers on the Vineyard. I'd missed them a lot, and it felt good to be back. I just wished my dad was here to see me crushing it, because I absolutely was. I suffered a lot of insecurity about myself but never about my cooking.

Stuart popped in to say hello while I worked in the inn's kitchen all afternoon, prepping for the evening. He acted suitably dazzled by the appetizers I was preparing. I didn't know if his enthusiasm was just because he'd been friends with my parents back in the day or not, so I insisted he try a little bit of everything. He cleaned his plate sopping up the leavings with a bolo lêvedo, similar to an English muffin but better, dozens of which I'd baked that morning and planned to set, freshly warmed, in big baskets at every food station. He sighed—actually sighed—when he was finished, and then he gave me a chef's kiss.

"Sam, you are a culinary genius," he said. "And I'm not just saying that because my mother was Portuguese."

I bowed my head. "Thank you." And in that moment, I could feel the devastation from being passed over at the Comstock easing just a smidge. Maybe I was going to be all right.

I ducked out and picked up Tyler at the library. Ben followed us back to the house, where he parked his motorcycle. I drove the three of us to the inn, and Em met us there. All three of my helpers were wearing black pants and white shirts per my request. Despite my prep work, we ran around like crazed contestants on **Chopped** just before happy hour was about to start, getting each food station fully stocked.

Given how swiftly the patio filled up, I was relieved to have Em and Ben there, too. If it had been just Tyler and me, we would have been overrun.

"How are you holding up, Chef?" Ben asked from behind his station.

"Fine. Why? Do I look nervous?"

"Not at all."

"Liar," I said. "I'm petrified. It shows, doesn't it?"

He studied me for a second, and I felt as if he was looking past the pleated hat and white coat into the woman who had found her identity in the culinary arts, when it seemed like she wasn't good at anything at all.

"Not a bit," he said. His gaze held mine, and it was warm and full of admiration. "You look as if you were born to do this."

I grinned. It was a perfect answer. "I was," I said. "Everything important I learned about cooking, I learned from my vovó. I'm half-Portuguese, after all, and we know how to cook."

Ben lifted the lid off the warming tray in front of him. He inhaled deeply of the torresmos. "It smells amazing."

"I'll make a plate for you in the kitchen on your break," I said. "I can't let my help starve to death, plus it will help you decide if I have the chops to do a program for the teens."

He gave me a mock severe frown. "I'm reserving judgment until I taste the goods." His gaze dropped to my mouth, and I felt my pulse pound. Was I "the goods"? Oh my.

Two young women in mini-sundresses and wedge-heeled sandals, smelling faintly of coconut-scented sunscreen, with their long hair parted in the middle and hanging halfway down their backs, arrived at his station. They gave Ben a synchronized hair toss and looked at him as if he were on the menu. All of a sudden I felt as dowdy as a laundry sack in my chef coat, and I backed away, letting him serve them.

I turned on my heel and started to walk away, when Ben called after me, his voice low, "Don't forget me, Samantha."

"As if that's even a possibility," I said. It came out wrong. I saw the women glance speculatively between us, but they fuzzed out of my vision when Ben grinned.

"Good to hear," he said.

"I . . . uh . . . meant about your food, getting your food," I said. I pulled my chef coat away from my chest. Why was it so hot out here? I was flustered and sweaty and decided it was time to beat a hasty retreat. But I couldn't resist just one more look.

I glanced over my shoulder at Ben, and he winked at me. Okay, I'd been on the receiving end of some pretty good winks before, but this one made my breath short and my heart speed up, and I wished, quite desperately, that I had the wherewithal to wink back. I didn't. Instead, I blinked stupidly and gave him a dorky thumbs-up.

In a panic, I went to check on Emily. I needed an infusion of normal. Stat. She had a line of people, as the cod fritters were a huge hit. I stepped behind the station and helped her for several minutes before it was clear I was going to need to make more. Thankfully, I had left plenty of everything prepped in the kitchen. All I had to do was fry them up and get them out here.

I had almost reached the kitchen when Tyler waved me down. I pivoted and headed in his direction.

"How's it going?" I asked.

"Running low on the green beans," he said. I glanced at his face and noticed a bit of food in the corner of his mouth.

"Could that be because you're eating them?" I asked. I clapped a hand over my heart. "Don't tell me you ate peixinhos da horta voluntarily."

"I just had a tiny nibble so that I could insightfully answer questions," he said. "I swear."

"Why do I feel like your idea of a tiny nibble and mine are measurably different?"

He blinked at me, the picture of innocence.

"I have more," I said. "I'll be right back." I took two

steps but then spun around and said, "No more sampling."

"But they're really good," he protested.

"Are you sure?" I asked. "I don't think batter-fried green beans aligns with your usual 'plain with a side of boring' menu."

He shrugged. "It's fried. Anything is good if you batter fry it. You should fry up some Twinkies. If you wanted to make people really happy, you'd make those."

"Twinkies?" I was horrified. "I'd rather cut out my own liver and serve it with onions."

His shoulders started to shake, and it was then that I noticed the glint in his eyes.

"Are you messing with me?" I asked.

He held up two fingers about an inch apart. "Tiny bit."

"There is one thing Gales do not joke about," I said. "And that is food."

His grin broadened and he saluted me. "Yes, ma'am."

"And just for that, you have to sample everything I cooked tonight and not just the fried green beans," I said.

He looked appalled. "Even those fish thingies?"

"Especially those," I said.

"Well, you'd better have an ambulance on speed dial," he said. "I haven't eaten anything fishy in years, if ever."

"Your body will thank you tomorrow," I said. "All those omega-3s and such."

"Maybe, but my taste buds won't," he retorted.

I rolled my eyes and headed for the kitchen. The rest of the night passed in a blur. The run on the food was relentless, which was fabulous. I gave my crew breaks with heaping plates of food. Not for nothing, but even Tyler ate every single bite, yes, even the fritters.

By the time the happy hour was over and the patio was beginning to clear, we were almost out of food. This was perfect because my vovó had raised me to believe that if the food was good, it would be devoured, but if there weren't any leftovers, then someone went hungry. Eek! So you always wanted a little food left, just not very much.

We did not run out, and I watched my crew box up the last of it. There was just enough for Em to take to work for lunch the next day. As I watched my team, I told myself I was just assessing how the night went, but I was really indulging myself in studying Ben. I'd noticed that no matter how many people were in line at his station, he never got rattled. Just like on the ferry, when catastrophe struck and I knocked his book into the water, he didn't get riled or upset. He just rolled with it.

He had an easy way about him that I found reassuring. Being on the slightly manic side, I didn't have a lot of calm in my life. He felt like the human equivalent of a cool cloth on the forehead, or a weighted blanket. I liked him.

He chatted with everyone who stopped by his station, but I noticed that he paused frequently to watch men of a certain age. He studied them, and I wondered if maybe that was his type. Not gonna lie, I was a teeny bit disappointed.

The DJ played his last song, and the crowd left the patio. I wasn't sure if I wanted to collapse into a heap or jump up and down for joy. There was no question tonight had been a major success.

"Sam," Stuart Mayhew called from where he stood beside the patio bar.

I braced myself for the moment of truth. It didn't matter if I thought tonight was a success, it only mattered what Stuart thought. A tiny part of me wanted to run. Ben came up beside me and gave me a gentle nudge.

"You crushed it. Don't worry. It'll be all right," he said.

What did he know? This could be horrible. Stuart could be disappointed. He might even refuse to pay me. It had happened before with a woman who asked me to cater her daughter's baby shower. She'd decided that I had overcharged her for the cake, never mind that the price had been listed on the invoice she signed, and she tried to sue me. My cooking scars ran deep, and not just from burning myself on the stove.

"Tonight was fantastic! You exceeded my expectations and then some," Stuart said. As if he'd popped my worry balloon with a pin, all the anxiety whooshed out of me.

"Thanks," I said. "I felt like it went well."

"Better than well," Stuart said. "People were raving about your food. So, what are you doing every Friday evening for the rest of the summer?"

My eyes went wide. I almost dropped to my knees in relief. I hadn't spent all of Dad's money for nothing. We were going to be okay, more than okay. Still, I held my breath and asked, "Really?"

He nodded.

"I think I'm cooking happy hours for you," I said. I glanced at Tyler, Ben, and Em, who were hydrating from the long night with ice waters. "I don't know if I can bring my own help every time, though."

"Don't worry," Stuart said. "We'll get some of our regular waitstaff to man the food stations. They saw the tips your people earned, and they want in."

I grinned. "It was pretty great."

"Stop by my office tomorrow and we'll discuss your salary and food budget, and be sure to invoice me for the money you already spent. From now on all you have to do is let Mark know what you need and we'll get it for you," he said. "Good job, Sam. This is for you and your staff for tonight." He handed me a fat wad of cash, and it was all I could do not to dance right there.

I didn't move until he walked back inside the inn, because I was trying to contain my fist pumping, jumping up and down, and clapping until he was out of sight. You know, trying to be cool.

"Don't leave us in suspense, Sam, what did he say?" Em called from across the patio.

I couldn't find the words. I was so relieved and happy. Hearing the music coming from the portable speaker one of the waitstaff had brought out onto the patio to listen to while they cleaned up, I busted out one of my favorite shuffle dance moves, the running man.

"Oh no," Tyler said. He looked mortified.

"I take it this is a victory dance?" Ben asked Em.

She smiled. "Oh yeah."

The server collecting the plates stopped what she was doing and watched me for a second. To my surprise, she then jumped in and matched my steps.

We were grinning at each other, and then she rotated into a Charleston step, which I copied. She looked impressed. I decided to kick it up a notch and rolled into the T-step. She followed me. We traded more moves back and forth until the song ended. There was a smattering of applause, and I saw that my squad was watching and we'd drawn a bit of a crowd from the inn as well.

"I'm Sonu," my dance partner said. She was a bit winded, like me. Her thick black hair was styled in one fat braid that reached halfway down her back. She wore the standard waitstaff uniform of a white shirt and dark pants. There was a sparkle in her deep brown eyes that I understood completely. Shuffle dancing had helped me work out a lot of anxiety in my life.

"Sam." I held out my hand and we shook. "You've got some nice moves."

"You, too," she said. "Do you know this one?"

She executed a sideways moonwalk that was so smooth it was like she was gliding on ice.

"Let me see," I said. I studied her feet and then fell into rhythm beside her. It took a few tries but I got it and we began to move in sync.

"Nice," Sonu said when we both slid to a stop. We exchanged a high five and paused to catch our breath.

"Is that your sister?" I heard someone ask.

I glanced over at Tyler and saw a girl about his age standing next to him. He looked pained when he said, "Yes."

"She is so cool," the girl gushed. She was almost as tall as Tyler, willowy, with shoulder-length hair that had a faint pink tinge to it. "I wish I could dance like that."

Tyler looked at her as if she must be joking, but the girl looked at me as if I was the raddest person ever. In that moment, with the success I was having both in the kitchen and on the dance floor, I felt like she wasn't wrong.

"Sonu, let's go!" a waiter called from the door of the kitchen.

"Gotta bounce," she said. "We'll have to meet up again."

"I'll be here every Friday," I said.

"Excellent. See you around," Sonu said before she disappeared into the kitchen.

As I rejoined my group, the girl who'd been talking to Tyler left with her family. He turned on me and demanded, "**What** was that?"

"**Who** was that?" I countered.

"You first," he said.

"Shuffle dancing."

"She's no one special," he said.

I blinked at him. He was a terrible liar. He was sweating and his face was so red he looked like he had a rash.

"No one special?" Ben asked. "Sophie's one of your fellow robotics campers."

Tyler shrugged.

"Sophie?" I asked Ben, knowing I would get nothing from Tyler.

"Sophie Porter," he said.

I glanced at Em. "Know the family?"

"What?" Tyler asked. "No, you are not asking questions about my robotics friends."

"Why not?" I asked. "Maybe we know the family."

"We don't," he said.

I glanced at Em for confirmation.

She shook her head. "They're not island regulars. In fact, I think this is their first summer. They're staying over in Chilmark."

"Do you two know most of the residents on the island?" Ben asked. He glanced from me to Em.

"I used to," I said. "But I've been out of the loop for a few years."

"I know most of the year-rounders," Em said. "Especially if they're library users."

Ben nodded. I figured he was trying to get the Vineyard vibe. There was no other place quite like it, maybe Nantucket, but each island had its own peculiarities. The Vineyard had six towns to Nantucket's one, so the Vineyard was much bigger, and with so many tourists coming and going, it was a bit looser, less buttoned up than Nantucket.

"I hate to leave you with kitchen cleanup," Em said. "But I have to go since I'm opening the library tomorrow." She held out a wad of money. "Here are the tips from my station."

"Keep them. Those are yours." I said. I pulled the wad of bills Stuart had given me out of my pocket. "In fact, I owe you more."

Em waved me off. "No, don't even think it. You worked all week for that. I'm happy to have earned tips."

I turned to Ben with the cash in hand. He shook his

head. "Same. I'm good with my tips and you can buy me a beer."

"I'm not," Tyler said. He held out his hand and wiggled his fingers.

"All right, but you have to finish earning it," I said. I held a couple of big bills in the air. "If you pack up the car, these are yours."

Sure I wanted to help my brother earn extra money, but honestly the adrenaline of the night, heck, of the whole week, was draining away, and I was actually exhausted. The thought of packing up all my gear made me want to lie down on the dirty patio and nap.

"Deal!" Tyler said. He snatched the bills and started counting his wad.

"Smart move." Em laughed and waved at us as she left. She called over her shoulder, "Talk tomorrow?"

"Of course," I said.

I glanced at Ben, wondering if he really wanted a beer or if he was just being nice. He was watching Tyler count his money and smiling at Tyler's obvious glee.

"You might want to put that cash away before you lose it," I said. Ugh, I sounded like such a nagging older sister. Mercifully, Tyler didn't call me out for it.

"Right," he said. He shoved the money in his pocket. When he glanced at me, he had a little frown in between his eyebrows. "So where did you learn to shuffle dance? I mean I've never seen Dad do anything like that."

I laughed trying to picture our dad doing anything beyond a basic side-to-side sway. "Um, not from Dad, that's for sure."

I thought that would be it, but Tyler was staring at me expectantly. Clearly, he was looking for full disclosure. Ben was watching me, too, making me self-conscious.

"EDM was my thing in high school," I said.

"Electronic dance music?" Ben made a face like he smelled something bad.

"Hey, don't be judgy," I said. "There was a lot going on in my life at the time."

I did not look at Tyler, as I didn't want him to know that he'd been one of those things.

"Such as my arrival," Tyler said.

So much for protecting his feelings.

"Yeah." I nodded. "I was at a school dance, under duress, as I didn't want to go, and this guy started to bust some moves that just blew my mind. He told me it was called shuffle dance and that it began in Melbourne, Australia, in the early eighties but had since merged with hip-hop to become something new. I could not get enough."

"EDM, huh? Who were your faves?" Ben asked. The concerned frown in between his brows resembled Tyler's, and I didn't know if it was my taste in music or my love of dance that they both found so worrisome.

"To dance to? Avicii, Skrillex, or Alesso," I said. "I think 'Levels' was my anthem as a teen."

Ben looked dubious, while Tyler looked as if I'd started speaking in tongues. He had no idea what I was talking about. That's what a fourteen-year age gap between siblings created.

"Who did you listen to when you were a teen?" I asked Ben.

He looked thoughtful for a moment and then said, "Classic rock, because **Guitar Hero**, at which I might add I was a beast. But to listen to, it was Linkin Park, the Killers, OutKast, you know, the standards for the aughts."

"'Hey Ya!' is totally danceable," I said. Then I grinned at him. "I can prove it."

I opened the music app on my phone and raised the volume. As soon as the song started to play, I bobbed my head to the beat.

"I'm sure you can," Ben said. He raised his hands to wave me off, but I tipped my head in Tyler's direction. He was studying me with the intensity of a scientist. I gave Ben a pointed look, and he visibly drooped.

"Fine, teach me," he said.

Tyler turned to Ben with wide eyes. He looked shocked. "You're going to learn to do that?"

Ben nodded. "Sure. It looks like fun, doesn't it?"

"Yeah, I guess, if you're into that sort of thing,"

Tyler said. He was trying to appear casual, but he could not hide the spark of interest in his eyes. Sophie had clearly made an impact.

"All right!" I clapped my hands and spun around so Ben and Tyler were behind me. I could see them in the reflection of the kitchen window.

Tyler was staring at his feet as if uncertain about whether they would betray him or not. But Ben, with his scruff of a beard and piercing eyes, met my gaze and mouthed the words **You owe me**.

A little thrill shivered through me, and I quickly glanced away so he didn't see my reaction. **Focus, Gale, focus.**

Chapter Eight

Over my shoulder I said, "Okay, running man is the basic step for everything. Master this and you are good to go. Now watch."

I did the moves slowly so they could see. Then I picked up the tempo until my feet were a blur. I looked back at them, and they had matching looks of confusion on their faces. I laughed. I couldn't help it. I'd taught a few men to dance in my time, and it never failed to entertain.

"Think of it this way. Flamingo." I paused to hold my right foot up like the pink bird. "Pyramid." I put my right foot down in front, making a pyramid out of my legs. "Flamingo." I raised my left foot while sliding my right foot back at the same time. "Pyramid." I put my left foot down in front. "Got it?"

I turned around to watch them attempt it. They looked like they were trying to stamp out a fire. I pressed my lips together to keep from laughing. They were cute. They were earnest. They were terrible.

Tyler stumbled and then got his feet mixed up. He

was trying to hop from left to right without sliding back the foot that was in front while popping up the other leg at the same time. He was a hot mess. Ben was a little bit better but also looked like he was made out of tin and his joints had gone rusty.

"This is hard!" Tyler said. He stopped and doubled over, panting for breath.

"Yup, but once you get it, it's all muscle memory." I turned back around and began to dance slowly so they could see me. When it looked like they might be catching on, I moved into a T-step so they'd have a chance to catch their breath with the lower-impact move.

"I think she's trying to kill us," Ben muttered to Tyler, who laughed.

"Hey, you're the ones who asked," I protested. I caught Tyler's gaze reflected in the window, and he smiled at me. It was a grin of complete joy, and it made me stumble a step. In all of his fourteen years, my half brother had never looked at me like that, not even when he was a toddler and actually liked me.

My gaze slid over to Ben as he glanced between us. He met my stare and winked, and I knew he got it. He understood how huge this was for me. I smiled and he returned it. In that moment I felt purely connected to him, as if we understood each other on a level unique to us, which was crazy since I hardly knew him, but it felt amazing.

When the song ended and rolled into another one on my playlist, Ben yelled, "Freestyle!"

He and Tyler made up dance moves that looked like they were starting a lawn mower and then mowing a lawn. I laughed so hard I lost my rhythm.

"Come on, Sam, keep up!" Tyler heckled me.

"Miss, I'm sorry to interrupt your . . . um . . . but we're going to need this patio." I turned to find a hostess standing beside me. I let out a yelp and stopped dancing.

"Of course," I said. "Sorry!" I cut the music on my phone and shooed both Tyler and Ben into the kitchen.

Tyler was choking on his laughter. "She didn't even know what to call that."

"I think I'm offended," Ben said. He glanced at me and said, "I also think you still owe me a beer."

"Sounds fair."

I grabbed the plastic tubs for my cooking supplies and shoved them at Tyler.

"Start packing, kid." I gestured to my cookware that was stacked on a drying rack, as I'd washed up as we went along during happy hour. "We'll be right back."

"Yes, Boss," Tyler said. He sent me a saucy smile.

We headed into the inn and took two stools at the end of the old-fashioned bar near the wall.

"Good to see you again, Sam," the bartender said. He was tall and wide with reddish blond hair and pale blue eyes. He had a full beard that hung down the front of his shirt, and his matching mustache was waxed and curled on the ends. I had no clue who this guy was.

"I'm sorry," I said. "I don't—"

"Recognize me?" he asked. "I'm not surprised. I haven't seen you in over ten years. I went into the Coast Guard and have been gone almost as long as you, from what I hear."

My mouth dropped open. There was only one person I knew who'd joined the Coast Guard. "Finn Malone, is that you?"

"In the flesh," he said. He opened his arms, and I hopped up and leaned over the bar to give him a hug.

"The beard totally threw me off," I said. "When I knew you, you didn't have enough facial hair to cover a pimple."

He laughed. "Didn't stop me from getting into trouble. Remember the night we stole that car from that asshole?"

"Shh." I put my finger to my lips. I jerked my head in Ben's direction. "I have a reputation to protect. I'm trying to convince the director of the library here that I'm capable of teaching teenagers how to cook."

"Good luck with that," Finn said. "After all of the trouble you got into as a teen? I think your reputation is beyond saving."

"Well, it is if you keep oversharing," I said. I pointed to Ben. "Ben Reynolds, this is Finn Malone, and any bad things I did as a teen are one hundred percent his fault."

"What? That's what I always say about you," Finn protested. They shook hands.

"It's a shame we can't blame Em. No one would ever believe it," I said.

"True," Finn agreed. "What can I get you two?"

"Something locally brewed?" I asked Ben. He nodded.

"Two Bad Marthas coming up," Finn agreed. He wandered off toward the taps.

"I can explain about the stolen car thing," I said.

Ben rested his chin on his hand. It was a good chin, square and strong, maybe a little stubborn. "I'm listening."

"Finn, Em, and I were walking home from the arcade one night, and this guy was driving a Camaro and weaving all over the place," I said. "And then, he just parked it in the middle of the street, doors open and engine running, while he staggered over to some bushes to . . . how do I say this delicately?"

"Splash the boots, strain the noodle, shake the dew off the lily?" Ben guessed.

"The only delicate word in there was 'lily,'" I said with a laugh. "But, yes, all of those. Anyway, my dad had recently taught me to drive a stick shift, so I jumped in the car and Finn jumped in with me."

"But not Em?" he asked.

"Her rebellion streak did not run as wide as mine," I said.

"Are you at the good part yet?" Finn returned and pushed two pints in front of us.

"I'm at the part where we got in the car," I said.

Finn nodded at Ben and tugged on his beard. "Yeah, that's the good part. You should have seen this one"—he paused to point at me—"it was like driving with Mario Andretti."

"If he was a fifteen-year-old girl who could barely reach the pedals and was afraid to take it out of second gear," I said.

Finn howled. "But you did have to, didn't you?"

"The guy noticed that we'd gotten into his car," I explained.

"Uh-oh," Ben said. He was smiling at me as if he thought I was the coolest kid in the class. My head felt fuzzy, but I hadn't even taken a sip of beer. Who knew a man's smile could be so intoxicating?

"Yeah, he started to chase us while holding up his shorts in one hand and throwing up at the same time." Finn laughed.

"What did you do?"

"I drove the car to the police station," I said. "I turned the car and the keys over to a friend of my dad's and said someone had left their car running with the doors open. I just didn't mention where they had done it or that I had driven it to the station."

"You probably saved that drunk's life," Finn said. "Or someone else's."

I looked at Ben. "That was our line of defense with our parents."

"Did it work?" he asked.

Finn and I exchanged a look of remembered pain and punishment.

"No," I said. "Instead we spent the weekend trimming the lawn in my front yard."

"That's not so bad as punishments go," Ben offered.

"With scissors, children's scissors," Finn clarified. "It took us two full days, and I blistered my thumb."

Ben laughed a great big belly laugh. He didn't even try to hold it in.

"Em did bring us lemonade and cookies, though," I said.

"Homemade chocolate chip cookies to die for," Finn added.

"Totally worth it," I agreed.

"Then there was the time you, me, and Em put Bubble Wrap under all of the doormats on the street," Finn said. He chuckled and I did, too. "If only we'd shot video of the residents jumping as soon as they stepped out their front doors. We'd have gone viral before going viral was a thing."

I shrugged at Ben. "This is what happens when your parents don't let you play video games all day."

"Then there was the time—" Finn said, but I interrupted him.

"No, no more," I said. I pointed at the end of the bar, where a customer waited. "I'm on island all summer and working here every Friday. We have plenty of time to discuss the good old days."

"Excellent," Finn said. He nodded at Ben. "Nice to meet you. See you around, Sam."

"For sure."

We watched him move away. I took a long sip of my beer, also known as liquid courage, and said, "Now I have a question for you."

"Shoot." Ben wrapped his hand around his beer glass.

"I don't want to pry—no, that's not true—this is totally prying. Sorry. But I noticed you seemed to be checking out certain guests at the happy hour tonight."

Ben went still with his beer halfway to his mouth, and his eyes widened in surprise. "Was I?"

"Yes," I assured him. "I don't want to overstep, but you're new here, and if older guys are your thing, I'm happy to introduce you to some single men that I know."

Ben blinked at me, and then he burst out laughing. I felt a whoosh of relief that perhaps I'd read the situation wrong.

"Is this because I'm a librarian?" he asked. "Because a lot of people assume if you're a man who loves books you must be gay."

"No, not at all," I said. "My assumption is because I saw you staring at a few guys in their fifties, so I just thought you might be looking to meet a man on the more mature side."

He leaned back and studied me. "You don't miss much, do you?"

I didn't, but I couldn't exactly explain that it wasn't nosiness so much as yet another coping mechanism. I tried to have a handle on what was going on around me at all times so that there weren't any unforeseen surprises. Basically, it was like I went through life always anticipating a pop quiz and trying to be ready for it. Exhausting but effective, mostly.

It helped that I was a visual learner and I'd discovered in school that if I watched and listened to my teachers closely and memorized their lessons, I could usually bluff my way through assignments and tests and such.

"I'm a people watcher," I said. That seemed like a safe response.

"You're half-right in your observation about me," he said. He took a long sip from his beer. "The truth is I'm—"

"Hey, Sam, look who's here!" Finn called from behind the bar.

Damn it! I wanted to hear what Ben had been about to tell me. What did he mean I was half-right? Why was he looking at older men? I almost ignored Finn, but then I heard my name being called, and I spun on my barstool in the direction he indicated.

Standing there was Mrs. Braga, one of our neighbors and my grandmother's best friend when she'd lived on the Vineyard. She looked overjoyed to see me.

"Excuse me," I said to Ben.

He nodded, and I hopped off my stool and hurried over to give Mrs. Braga a hug. She had to be well into her eighties now, but she smelled exactly like she had when we were kids, faintly of rose water and baby powder, and just like that I was ten years old again.

How many summer afternoons had I spent in her kitchen with Vovó, listening to the two of them gossip in Portuguese while cooking together? I had learned almost as much from Mrs. Braga as I had from my grandmother. When Vovó had passed away when I was in culinary school, it was Mrs. Braga who convinced me to stay, to make Vovó proud. I owed her so much.

We agreed to meet up soon for afternoon tea, and she went back to her tablemates and I rejoined Ben. I was just about to ask him what he'd been about to say, when Tyler appeared in the doorway to the kitchen.

"Sam, the car is all packed," he said. "Let's go!"

Shoot, there went my opportunity. I forced a smile at Ben as if I wasn't feeling thoroughly thwarted, and we finished our beers. I paid the tab and left a healthy tip, waving to Finn as I went.

"Check me out," Tyler said. He broke into a much smoother running man than he'd been doing before, so I assumed he'd been practicing while packing. Ben joined him. His was still terrible.

"No dancing in my kitchen!" Mark yelled. Tall and wide and wielding a ladle like a cudgel, he looked like he meant it. Couldn't blame him, professional kitchens were hazardous enough without people breaking into dance.

"Pull it together, you two," I hissed at them.

We slipped out the side door to the gravel lot where the staff parked. A busser and a dishwasher were sharing a vape, and we passed them on our way to my car.

"Nice moves, Chef," the dishwasher called after us.

I glanced back to see if he was mocking me, but he looked as if he was sincere, so I flashed him a smile and kept going. We climbed into the SUV, with Tyler taking the back seat just like he had on the way to the inn.

"Nice work tonight," I said. I drove down the narrow dark road, keeping an eye out for pedestrians. "Thank you both for your help. I couldn't have done it without you."

"I'll say," Tyler said. "It was crazy busy." He fished his phone out of his pocket and began scrolling. "Are you going to help out next week, Mr. Reynolds?"

"If I'm needed. Since we're coworkers, you should call me Ben."

"Yeah?" Tyler asked.

"Yeah."

"All right." Tyler collapsed back against his seat, looking pleased.

I glanced at Ben. The car wasn't small, but he filled the passenger seat, with his head almost grazing the ceiling. "Thanks for **everything** tonight."

He nodded, understanding what I meant. "It was . . . unexpected."

I glanced in the rearview mirror at the back seat. Tyler was engrossed in his phone, watching a video with his earbuds in.

"Unexpected?" I asked. "Is that in a good way or a bad way?"

"Other than throwing my back out during the impromptu dance sesh, I'd say it was good."

I laughed. "Thank you for that. I could tell someone wanted to know how to do those moves but didn't want to ask and needed a buddy."

"Happy to help," he said. He turned in his seat and watched me while I drove. I tried not to be self-conscious. I failed.

"What?" I asked.

"You're an extrovert, aren't you?" he asked.

"You say that like it's a bad thing," I said. I was absolutely an extrovert. It was another coping mechanism. I found people were much more accepting of my neurodivergence if they knew me and liked me before they found out about it. I wondered if Ben would respond the same way. It was hard to say given that he was an über-reader.

"Not bad," he said. "Just . . . different."

"From you, you mean?" I asked. "You're an introvert?" There was doubt in my voice because he hadn't struck me as someone who shied away from crowds.

"I prefer to think of it as being highly selective

about whom I spend time with," he said. I glanced at him, and a small smile curved his lips. It felt delicious to be on the receiving end of that smile. I cut my eyes back to the road.

"I'm guessing your idea of a perfect evening is being home, reading whatever book you're into at the moment," I said. "Sounds thrilling."

"And yours is to find the noisiest nightclub around and go shuffle dancing," he said. "Not torture at all."

I laughed at his pained tone of voice. He wasn't wrong. On the very rare nights I'd had off in Boston, that's exactly what I'd done for fun. It appeared hot librarian guy and I had nothing in common, even less than he realized, given that he didn't know how much of a nonreader I was.

It was a shame, as the pull I felt for this man was undeniable. Did it really matter if he was an introvert and I was an extrovert if we were only going to be on the island for the summer? How deeply involved could we really get in just a few weeks? This was assuming of course that he was interested. I still needed to hear his explanation for why he was checking out older middle-aged men. Was he trying to track down a library offender? Some guy who had racked up overdue fines and refused to pay? My curiosity was dialed to high, but I didn't want to finish this conversation in the car. I'd wait until we got home.

Ben asked me about some of the island's summer

events, so I told him all about Grand Illumination, the annual summer event when the gingerbread cottages of Oak Bluffs were lit up with paper lanterns, which I had always thought was the most magical night of summer.

He listened without interrupting, which I realized was a rare talent not many people possessed, including myself. When I parked in front of our house, we all climbed out, and I opened the back so we could haul the tubs of cookware back into the kitchen.

Ben went to take one, but I felt as if I'd taken advantage of him enough. "Oh, you don't have to help with that. We've got it."

"I don't mind," he said. He grabbed the plastic container and followed Tyler into the house. I took the last one and followed.

We dumped the tubs onto the counter, and Tyler shouted, "Good night."

We didn't even get a chance to respond before he bolted up the stairs to his room.

"Well," I said. That was all I got out before the booming beat of some dance music came from above. I raised my voice and shouted, "I'll walk you out."

Ben nodded and led the way. The noise dulled, mostly, when we stepped onto the porch, making me thankful for the house's insulation, which was not something I could recall ever being grateful for before.

We stood on the porch for a moment, and I found I was reluctant to see him go. I liked Ben. Regardless of whether he was single, interested, or interested in someone else, I genuinely liked him. He had a very calming way about him that soothed my busy brain.

"I suppose I need to go tell him to turn it down before the neighbors start lighting torches and sharpening their pitchforks," I said.

"I expect you're going to regret teaching him those sick dance moves," he said.

I glanced up at the second floor and sighed. "I think you're right. Let's hope this phase passes, or my dad is going to kill me when he gets back."

I grinned at him to let him know I was kidding, but he didn't smile back.

"That would be tragic," he said. "Given that I've just found you."

Found me? I swallowed.

There was a shift in the air. I wasn't sure if it was the space between us vibrating with awareness or if it was just me, but suddenly the chirp of the crickets and the sound of Tyler's music faded beneath a steady hum that coursed through my whole body. The night air seemed to thicken, and I was having a hard time drawing a breath.

Did he mean that the way I thought? Was I overthinking things? Probably. His gaze met mine, and beneath its scorching heat, every coherent thought I had flew right out of my head. Instinct took over and I stepped closer to him.

His eyes darkened with an intensity that made my stomach drop in anticipation. He held out his hand as if in invitation. I had no idea to what, but I didn't hesitate. I put my hand in his, and he tugged me close. I didn't resist the pull and found my front pressed up against his chest just like I had been on the ferry boat when we first met.

"You fascinate me, Samantha Gale," he whispered.

I would have said the same about him, but I was too distracted by the crispness of his shirt, the feel of his hands catching my hips, the way the yellow porch light picked up the copper strands in his hair. I was on sensory overload, but for once it was intoxicating, like drinking too much champagne.

He ducked his head and placed his lips on mine. His kiss was firm but gentle, and I could feel the rough rub of his close-shaven beard against my chin. It was a tentative getting-to-know-you kiss, delivered in little sips and slides, gasps and sighs. It was lovely, and then it turned hot.

He pressed one hand on my lower back and pulled me in tight. His other hand slid up my back and dug into the hair at the nape of my neck, holding me still while his tongue traced the seam of my lips, encouraging my mouth to open to him. I welcomed all of it, and heat rushed through me much like the wave of hot air that's released when opening an oven door. My hands slid up his shirtfront and clung to his shoulders, while the kiss deepened and my insides melted into a puddle of fiery, aching need. Mercy.

When I would have instinctively pressed up against him and demanded more, he eased back the throttle, gentled the kiss, and released me, pressing his forehead to mine while we both attempted to get our bearings. I was lost. It was like getting just a taste of something that dazzled the senses only to have it taken away.

My body tipped toward his, inviting more, but he didn't pull me in. His hands lowered to my hips, keeping me at a safe distance, which was weird, because the moment his mouth met mine, I hadn't felt safe at all. Instead, I was quite certain that every wall I had built, every shield I'd employed, and every safety net I had strung could be demolished by this man. The realization shook me.

It must have shown on my face, because he dropped his hands from my hips and said, "Sorry. Too soon? I should have warned you I was making a move."

I shook my head. "No, your signals were very clear. I could have shut you down."

"You sure about that?" he asked. "I can be very single-minded."

That surprised a laugh out of me. "So can I."

We stared at each other in bemusement. Oh, I enjoyed this man, but it was complicated. First, Tyler was my responsibility this summer, and I could not get distracted from my purpose, which was to take care of him. Second, I had absolutely no idea how I was going to tell Ben, whose passion was books, that I was not a reader. When I dropped that bomb on him, hot librarian guy was definitely going to leave skid marks. It had happened before, and I had no doubt it would happen again. And I understood. I mean, it would be like him telling me, the professional chef, that he didn't eat. How could this ever work?

Perhaps I should have been more on my guard and stopped that kiss in its tracks, but it'd been so long since I'd dated anyone, and he was so ridiculously attractive. Even more so now with his rumpled hair and swollen mouth, I could feel my body leaning in just to be near him. I arched my back.

"Why did you kiss me?" I asked. It came out more bluntly than I'd intended, but he didn't seem to mind.

"You mean aside from the fact that I've been thinking about it since I met you on the ferry?" His smile was pure mischief and he said, "After our conversation at the bar, I felt the need to be clear about who I'm interested in."

My heart thumped hard in my chest, and it was all I could do not to clarify and ask, "Me?" Instead, I just nodded, trying to be cool when I was anything but.

"See you Monday, Samantha. We need to talk about your cooking program for the teens, among other things."

I sucked in a breath. How did the man make two

simple words, other things, sound so wicked? Wait. What did he say? I shook my head to clear it.

"You're approving the program?" I asked.

"Of course," he said. "You're clearly a brilliant chef."

"Yes!" I did a fist pump. I was back! Plus, I'd get to see him, which was even more exciting to me than cooking. Shocking, I know.

He turned and headed for the stairs.

"Ben, I—" I began—yes, I was stalling him, not quite ready to let him go—but the front door banged open, and there was Tyler. Probably a good thing before I confessed all about myself and scared the man off island.

"Sam, you have to show me that T step again," Tyler said. He was breathing hard and soaked in sweat.

I glanced from him to Ben and said, "Never mind, we can talk on Monday."

Ben nodded. "Looking forward to it. Good night."

I would have watched as he fired up his motorcycle and rode away, but Tyler started dancing, thumping the floorboards of our old porch hard enough that I thought he might fall through. Clearly, I'd created a monster.

Chapter Nine

Shorts and a T-shirt and my beat-up bucket hat. No. A sunflower-print sundress with Converse high-tops. No. Jeans and a button-down shirt tied at the waist over a hot pink tank top. No. No. No.

It was Monday morning, and I was having a fashion crisis of epic proportions. What was I supposed to wear to see Ben this morning? I had to set the right tone. It couldn't be too flirty but also not so casual that I looked like I'd climbed out of the hamper. Mascara and lip gloss and a messy bun were a for sure, but what clothes to wear? I looked at the mountain of discarded outfits on my bed. Nothing spoke to me.

"Sam, come on!" Tyler cried from downstairs. "We're going to be late."

"You mean we're going to be less early than everyone else," I said.

"Whatever," he said. "Can we go **now**, please."

I was standing in my underwear. At least that outfit was a definite no.

"All right, all right, I'm coming!" I grabbed the first

thing on the bed. A flirty swing dress with a muted tie-dye pattern in swirls of dusty pink and sage green. Cute but casual. It would have to do. I slipped on my beige Tory Burch sandals, grabbed my shoulder bag, and hurried downstairs.

Tyler was waiting by the door, looking impatient. "What happened to the shorts you were wearing at breakfast?"

"I changed," I said.

"Why?" he asked. Yes, he of the baggy shorts and **Minecraft** T-shirt was questioning my fashion choices.

"Because I'm hoping to see hot librarian guy and kiss him again" did not seem like a good answer, so I said, "Just felt like it."

"Oh." He shoved his earbuds in and ignored me for the rest of the ride.

I rode the brake through the neighborhood, avoiding a pack of kids on bikes, two moms with jogging strollers, and a tourist who was walking down the middle of the road, chatting on his phone. I thought about honking at him. In Boston, he'd already be a speed bump, but I took a deep breath, reminded myself I was not in the city, and tried to tap into my Vineyard Zen.

The road to the library was mercifully clear, and we made great time. I'd had two days to think about the kiss Ben had planted on me, and I was desperate to find Em and ask her advice. I'd hoped to catch up over the weekend, but she had family commitments and Tyler and I had chores like laundry, cleaning, and grocery shopping. Adulting blows, FYI. Tyler also badgered me to help him with his dance moves, and despite the hamstring I'd pulled while teaching him, I have to admit he was getting pretty decent.

It was good that I'd had two days of not seeing Ben. It clarified a few things for me. I knew I liked him—a lot. But whatever this attraction was between us, it was definitely not long-haul type of stuff. We were ships passing in the night, which I found ironic given how we'd met on a ferry.

He was the interim library director, so he was only here temporarily, and I was on island just until I figured out my life, which I hoped would not take longer than the summer season. I couldn't get all turned around because of a relationship and lose my career in the mix, but that didn't mean a no-strings-attached summer fling was off the table, or so I told myself every time I thought about that brain melter of a kiss we'd shared.

I parked in the lot, and Tyler shot out of the car. Amazingly enough, he'd let me pack his lunch today. It was a very unadventurous turkey and Swiss on white bread, but he'd let me go crazy and add some mustard. I'd also tucked in fruit salad and some homemade chocolate chip cookies. It was a start.

"See you later, Sam," he said. He jogged to the

building. I wasn't sure if it was his need to arrive first or his desire to leave me behind. Most likely a bit of both.

I found Em on the second floor. She was seated at the reference desk. Today she was wearing a navy blue dress with a fit-and-flare skirt and the same white cardigan. She was reading a book and didn't see me walking toward her. I saw her take a sticky note and mark the page. Her face looked pale and tight with tension. As I watched, she reached up and rubbed the side of her neck as if trying to check her glands. I wondered if she was feeling all right.

"Hey, Em," I said.

She glanced up and dropped her hand. She slammed the book shut and put it on the book truck behind her.

"How was your weekend with the fam?" I asked.

She pushed her glasses up on her nose. "Good. Great. Fine. How was yours?"

"Solid. I worked recipes for the next happy hour, taught Tyler some new dance moves, and we went paddleboarding at Inkwell, although I had to threaten to throw Tyler's computer into the ocean to get him to come with me."

"Sounds fun," she said. "Not the threats, the paddleboarding."

She seemed distracted, and I wondered if she'd heard about the kiss between Ben and me. We'd been on the front porch, where anyone could have seen us. Darn it, I wanted to be the one to tell her I'd bagged the hot librarian guy. I went for it anyway.

"Ben kissed me," I said.

"What?!" she cried. Her eyes went wide behind her glasses, and she beamed at me. "How was it?" She raised her hands in a "stop" gesture. "No, don't tell me. **Gah**. I won't be able to look at him in the staff meeting."

I laughed. "I would never kiss and tell."

"Really?" She looked at me with a pointed stare.

"Okay, maybe just the PG version," I said. "For the record, it was ah-mazing."

She grinned. "Are you like boyfriend and girlfriend now?"

"No." I shook my head. "We're both here temporarily, and he's a book person and I'm . . ."

"Not," she said. I appreciated her simple acceptance sans judgment.

"Exactly," I said. "If we have anything, it's strictly a summer fling sort of thing."

"Are you sure?" she said. "The way he was looking at you at the happy hour was not a 'swipe right for a fun night' look. It was definitely more."

"But I can't offer him more," I said. "I mean, I have no idea where I'll be in a few months."

"So, you don't think you'll stay past summer?" she asked. She sounded forlorn.

"I can't," I said. "I have to get back to work . . . somewhere."

"Oh." She glanced down at her hands.

I didn't know what to say, so I studied the book truck behind her. I recognized the stack of books from the colors of their spines. They were the same cancer books she'd been looking at the other day.

It hit me like a punch to the face that she had lied to me. She wasn't looking up cancer information for a patron. It was for herself. Oh no, Em!

I couldn't believe she hadn't told me. I was her friend. And I had a million questions. What type of cancer was it? Had she been to the doctor? What had they said? Was it bad? Was she going to die? I couldn't breathe.

Em looked up from her hands and followed the line of my gaze and then back at me. She turned a faint shade of pink. She was embarrassed. Embarrassed? About cancer?

Of course I stood there like an idiot, saying nothing. How could I? She hadn't told me. I knew it shouldn't have felt like a betrayal, after all health is a personal thing, but it did.

"Em, is everything—"

"Ben said that he approved the teen cooking program," Em interrupted me. I couldn't tell if she did it on purpose or not. "We should talk about that, you know, make a plan."

"Okay," I said. If she didn't want to talk, I couldn't force her, but I could be here. I could try and take her mind off things at least for a moment. But why hadn't she told me? It occurred to me that it was because I had been so self-absorbed with my own career drama of late, I hadn't given her a chance. Ugh.

Em grabbed a pad and pen and said, "Come on. We can work at the table over there, and I can still monitor the desk."

I followed and took a seat across from her at the wooden table. The chair was hard, and I shifted trying to find a comfortable position. There wasn't one. Guilt for being such a shitty friend was like a thumbtack on my seat making me restless and unable to sit still.

"We need a snappy name for the program," she said. "Like 'Tasty Teens.'"

"Sounds like a cannibal support group," I said.

She huffed a laugh. "Fair point. What do you have?"

"I have a question," I said.

She glanced down at her notebook, across the room, up at the ceiling, anywhere but at me.

"I think you know what I'm going to ask," I said.

"I do," she said. "And I don't have an answer for you."

"Okay, then let's start with questions you can answer. Have you been to the doctor?"

"Not yet," she said.

"Em, if you have concerns, if you think you have cancer, you have to go."

She glanced around the room to make certain we couldn't be overheard.

"But what if they find something?" she asked.

"All the more reason to go sooner rather than later," I said.

"But it's just a little bump," she said. She put her hand on her neck. "It's probably nothing."

"Probably," I agreed. "But wouldn't it be great to find out and not have to worry anymore."

"I suppose," she said.

"Make an appointment and I'll go with you," I said.

"I already have one," she said. "It's for tomorrow at ten."

"All right," I said. "I'll meet you there."

"You don't have to—" she said, but I interrupted.

"You haven't told your mom, have you?" I asked.

"No, I don't want to worry her," she said.

"Then I'll be there," I said. "Every patient needs an advocate. I'll be your advocate."

Her shoulders slumped, and she looked like she was about to cry. "Thank you, Sam."

"Hey, that's what friends are for," I said.

We spent the next half hour plotting the teen program for cooking, which we called Teen Chef, sort of like Top Chef but with Teen. Clever, I know. We decided to have it in the middle of the summer reading program as a push to keep the teens engaged through the end. The menu was still under consideration. I knew I could teach the kids some fast-food techniques, but I also wanted them to learn something that raised their game as a chef.

In spite of myself, I kept one eye on the movement of the library around us, looking for Ben. When he'd said that we'd talk, I didn't know if it was this morning or in the afternoon, if I was supposed to find him or he would find me or what. This was poor planning, which went against my entire way of being. I was feeling antsy and decided it was best that I go. I could always talk to Ben later, if he wanted. Maybe he didn't want to. Maybe the kiss had meant nothing to him. Maybe he'd already forgotten it. Yup, I was panicking.

"All right, I'm going to go, but I'll meet you tomorrow at the doctor's at ten o'clock sharp, yes?" I asked.

"Yes," she said. She grabbed my hand and gave it a quick squeeze. "And thank you, Sam. I really appreciate it."

"Appreciate what?" a deep male voice asked from behind me. I felt it rumble inside me from my scalp down my spine all the way to my feet. I closed my eyes. Ben.

Em looked nervous as if she'd been caught planning a bank heist. She licked her lips and said, "Her h-help with th-the teen programming."

Never mind caught planning a heist. Em sounded as if she'd been caught in the bank vault with the money in her hands. I jumped in.

"It's going to be an amazing evening of walking tacos, cake in a mug, you name it."

"You had me at tacos."

Ben slid into the seat beside me, setting a stack of books on the table. I glanced at the titles. One was in a horrible pixel font that made everything look squared off and, to me, completely illegible. The rest were easier to decode but still too much work for me.

"Are you a fan of hers?" he asked me as he held up one of the books.

"I haven't read her," I said. I tried to sound uninterested.

He looked shocked. "Really? But Lauren Beukes is a horror author. Even your icon Stephen King raved about her book **The Shining Girls**."

"Meh." I shrugged.

Em frowned as she glanced between us. I knew she could tell I was in over my head and she was trying to figure out how to help me.

"Have you read this one?" he asked. It was a different book by an author I didn't recognize.

Honestly, book people can be such badgers.

"No," I said. At least that was true.

"Why don't you borrow it?" he asked. "You can give it a shot. I guarantee it's not 'meh.'"

I glanced at him. He was so eager to share his books. It was ridiculously adorable, and I didn't want to let him down, but I also didn't want to torture myself with trying to read the book. I could feel a headache start even thinking about it.

"Thanks, but I'll just catch the movie," I said.

"You can't. There isn't a movie version," he said.

Damn it! Thankfully, I didn't say this out loud. Instead, I picked up the book and looked at the print on the back. It jumped. It did backflips. It was like trying to read a computer monitor while it was spewing code. Bleh.

"Sure, I can give it a try," I said. I have no idea why these words came out of my mouth.

Em looked at me with her eyebrows raised up above her glasses as if to say this would be a good time to mention that I have dyslexia, but I shook her off. Why did I have to mention it? It wasn't as if this thing with Ben and me was going to last more than a few weeks. Heck, it might even fizzle after a few dates. Just because a guy was hot did not mean he was a good date, although, after that kiss, I found it hard to imagine that Ben was a bad date.

"Mr. Reynolds, I've been looking for you all over the building." A middle-aged woman wearing a navy blue and pink floral dress strode toward us. Her mousy brown hair was highlighted, curled, and sprayed into a cloud on her head. Her style reminded me so much of pictures of my parents from the eighties. It was as if she were frozen in time.

"And you've found me, Mrs. Bascomb," Ben said. He sounded friendly, but she didn't even crack a smile in return. She merely stared at him over her reading glasses. Her gaze took in Em and me, and it was clear she did not approve of Ben chatting with us while on the clock.

"This is the contract for the cooking program with the teens," she said.

"Excellent," Ben said. "This is Samantha Gale, who will be doing the program. The contract is for her."

Mrs. Bascomb studied me, taking in my tie-dye dress with a look of disapproval that was hard to ignore.

"This is very irregular and last minute," Mrs. Bascomb said. "These papers are supposed to be signed and turned in before the start of the summer reading program." Her disapproval slid over to Em, who studied the notebook in front of her as if she hadn't heard the censure in Mrs. Bascomb's voice.

"You'll need to sign these right away," Mrs. Bascomb slapped the papers onto the table in front of me. She clicked a pen and handed that to me, too.

"Oh . . . um." Em met my gaze. She must have seen the panic in them. "Sam should probably look it over before signing just to make sure it all checks out."

"We don't have time for that," Mrs. Bascomb said. "These need to get to human resources right away."

"Mrs. Bascomb, I'm sure Ms. Gale can take a few minutes to look over the contract without the world coming to an end," Ben said. His voice was calm but also very firm. Mrs. Bascomb let out a huff and crossed her arms over her chest.

I stared at the papers in front of me. I could feel them all watching me. "Talk among yourselves," I joked. "I'll just be a minute."

Em got the message and immediately asked Ben about his latest motorcycle trip. He told her he'd taken it up to Nova Scotia recently and was hoping to do it again soon. While they spoke, I studied the papers in front of me. I couldn't read a thing. Panic was making it even worse. I could feel my heart beat in my throat, and I clicked the pen nervously with my thumb. Mrs. Bascomb shifted from foot to foot, letting out an audible sigh as she loomed over me.

Hoping I wasn't signing away a kidney, I scribbled my signature in the first blank space I could find. I handed it to Mrs. Bascomb with a smile and said, "Here you go. Thank you."

She glanced from me to the paper. Her face squinched up in a frown and she asked, "What's this? Is this a joke?"

I felt all of the blood drain from my face. Em and Ben stopped talking, and they turned to see what had Mrs. Bascomb in a tizzy.

She dropped the paper down in front of me and

tapped it with a pink-painted nail. "You signed where the human resources person is supposed to sign. You're supposed to fill out all of the pertinent information up here, print your name, sign your name, and date it."

"Oh, sorry," I said. My face felt hot. I stared down at the top of the table. The old familiar sick feeling of shame welled up inside of me, choking me, making me want to run, to cry, to hide, to be anywhere but here.

"Mrs. Bascomb," Ben began, but my tormentor talked right over him.

"Sorry?" she mimicked me. "You realize I now have to go all the way downstairs and print another one? What were you thinking?"

"Hey!" Em protested. I glanced up at her and saw her eyes flash. She was coming in hot. Mrs. Bascomb didn't care. She was on a roll.

"I mean, it's so basic, can't you read simple instructions?" she asked me.

And there it was. The truth was out. I thought I might throw up. I swallowed, forcing the lump in my throat to ease. I rose from my seat, keeping my gaze on the ground.

"No, actually, I can't. I have dyslexia ," I said. "Excuse me, I have to go."

I stumbled away from the table and bolted for the door. I couldn't look at Ben. I didn't want to know what he thought of me—the disgust or disappointment or, even worse, pity—I couldn't bear it. Not from him.

"Samantha!" I heard him call after me, but I kept running.

At home, I wandered around the house. Stephanie had decorated the upstairs hallway with large framed photographs of me and Tyler, growing up. Several of me were from before I'd even met her.

There was one taken when I was four. I was in a yellow bathing suit with bright pink flowers on it, a sun hat askew on my head and a pail and shovel in my hands. The lumpy start of a sandcastle was in front of me, and I was concentrating on carrying the bucket of water to the moat. It was before I started school, before I became the kid who couldn't read, before I felt defective, less than, dumb.

I felt my throat get tight, and tears burned in the corners of my eyes. I remembered that horrible day during sophomore year in high school. We were studying plays, and each of us had been assigned a part from **Blithe Spirit** by Noël Coward. On the day that we were to perform, one of the girls in my group had a minor nervous breakdown and threw up all over herself. The teacher told me I was to read her part, Elvira, instead of Ruth, the one I had spent weeks memorizing even though we were allowed to read from the scripts.

It was the only time in my life I ever thought of doing myself an injury to get out of something. If I could have unobtrusively punched myself in the face, I would have.

Instead, I marched to the front of the class and botched most of my lines. Stammering and stuttering, I tried to string together the sight words in my head before I spoke. The laughter started quietly at first.

Kids were pressing their heads together and whispering behind their hands. I heard more than one person say, "She can't read. Is she stupid?"

I began to panic. My heart was racing, my hands were sweating, and Mrs. Ward was staring at me in disgust. Looking back, it might have been horror, but she was a mean woman who enjoyed her power and gave out detentions like they were lollipops, so I suspect she was truly disgusted. After all, it was the end of the first semester and I was passing her class, barely, but I was passing, so I had fooled her for at least four months.

Finally, at the end of the scene, with poor Danny Rubens trying to carry the whole thing while looking at me as if I'd started speaking ancient Greek, I pronounced the word **ghost** with an **f** sound because I panicked and **gh** is pronounced like an **f** at the end of tough, so in my freaked-out brain I latched on to what I remembered, and butchered the word. After that, the kids nicknamed me Simple Sam, I was considered to be an idiot, and my high school career was dusted and done.

As if the bullying wasn't enough, my parents had separated the year before, Dad had started dating Stephanie, and she was pregnant with Tyler. Not surprisingly, my parents weren't speaking to each other, leaving my guidance counselor in charge of my academics. I was tested and found to be severely dyslexic but with a very high IQ. Naturally, because no one knew what to do with that information, I was placed in all remedial classes. It was not awesome.

I sank onto the top step of the stairs and let the remembered humiliation wash over me. The tears came hard and fast, and I was surprised by how much the memory still hurt. Clearly, Mrs. Bascomb outing me in front of Ben had opened up a door that I thought I had sealed shut and blockaded with razor wire and guard dogs.

It took the better part of the morning to pull myself together. So what if Ben thought I was an idiot? I'd dealt with worse. At least, now he knew the truth so I could stop trying to hide it. I'd spent my entire childhood coming up with coping mechanisms to disguise the fact that reading was problematic. It was exhausting and I refused to spend my adulthood like that.

I took out my phone and sent Tyler a text, using the voice-to-text option, telling him I'd meet him at the far end of the library parking lot for pickup. I didn't explain why.

I glanced back at the picture of me on the beach,

and suddenly I wanted to be her, free from all of the judgment that life was going to throw at her, just enjoying the day. I stood up and hurried to my room to put on my bathing suit. I knew exactly where I wanted to spend the time I had to burn until I picked up Tyler—Inkwell, my happy place.

Chapter Ten

The sand was scorching hot, so I didn't take off my sandals. Better to have it annoy me as it sifted through my shoes than to burn the bottoms of my feet. I staked out a spot next to a small dune sporting a tuft of seagrass and unfolded my beach chair. It was quieter here along the perimeter.

Families crowded the water line, and sunbathers took up the middle of the beach. There were more umbrellas than there used to be, as people had smartened up about the sun. I had on a wide-brimmed straw hat of Stephanie's, and I'd also slathered on the sunscreen. Even though I tanned easily and never burned, I was very aware of how the sun could damage the skin. No thank you.

I unpacked my water, as well as my phone and my earbuds, planning to listen to some music while I chillaxed and thought about my happy hour recipes, planning the logistics, while I watched the waves roll in. Nothing could touch me here, or so I told myself.

I was five songs in when a shadow fell across my legs. Great. Like the beach wasn't big enough, some doofus decided to crowd me. I lifted the brim of my hat and peeked out from beneath it.

Standing there in his khaki slacks and dress shirt, with his library ID on a lanyard around his neck, was Ben. I blinked, wondering if I was hallucinating in the midday sun. He grinned and lowered his sunglasses, looking at me over the top of them. Nope, not hallucinating unless I was full on dreaming. I pinched myself right in the curve of my elbow. Ouch. No, not dreaming.

"You're a little overdressed for the beach," I said.

"I'm not here for the beach." He dropped the tote bag he was carrying on the ground and snapped open the folding chair he had slung over his arm. He set it beside mine and sat down. He didn't look repulsed by me. I supposed that was something.

"I had an idea," he said.

"What idea?" I asked. Then I frowned. Was Ben one of those guys who were always trying to fix everyone's problems? That would absolutely not work for me. I decided it was best for both of us if I shot his "idea" right out of the sky. "If this is about me and reading, let me spare you the effort. I've tried everything, but there is no fixing the way my brain is wired. Reading is hard and difficult, and even when the font is dyslexic friendly and the words have better spacing, it still takes me a really long time to read and, frankly, it's exhausting."

"Samantha," he said. It occurred to me then that he always said my full name, as if he savored every syllable, and not the short version of Sam that everyone else used. Truth? I liked the way he said it. It made me feel a tug somewhere deep inside, but I wasn't ready to examine that too closely at the moment.

"I would never assume there's some quick fix for a neurodivergent brain," he said. "My idea was just that I could join you for my lunch break."

"Hmm." I was dubious. "How did you know I was here?"

"Tyler mentioned that you like to come to Inkwell Beach on your bike since it's the closest to your house. He said something about being forced to paddleboard with you this weekend, so when you weren't at home, I figured . . ."

"I'd be here?"

"Yeah."

I didn't know what to say. I glanced out at the ocean. The vast blue-gray waves really were a spot-on match for his eyes. I appreciated that he was here to check on me. He was a nice guy, and he probably wanted to make sure my feelings weren't hurt by Mrs. Bascomb's incredible rudeness.

"I'm okay," I said. I pushed some sand with my feet. "Really."

"I had a conversation with Mrs. Bascomb." He carefully removed his brown leather shoe from his foot and poured the sand out. Then he peeled off his sock, shook it out, and stuffed it in his shoe. He did the same with the other foot. There was a ridiculous amount of sand in his shoes. I tried not to laugh.

He rolled up the bottom of his pant legs and settled back in his chair. I wanted to reach over and loosen his tie or roll up his sleeves, but I didn't.

"A conversation, huh?" I asked. I tried to picture that—couldn't—and turned to study his face. The wind tousled his thick, wavy shoulder-length hair. I couldn't see his eyes because of his sunglasses, but the set to his jaw was tight, and a muscle clenched in his cheek. "Why do I sense that might be an understatement?"

"The word 'conversation' does imply there was give-and-take," he admitted. "There wasn't. She's been put on notice to check her behavior or I'll put a note in her file about her aggressively hostile demeanor. And just so you know, you aren't the first person with whom she's been rude and difficult. This has been brewing for a while. I'm sorry you were the tipping point."

"She does have a blunt force trauma way about her," I said.

He laughed. His full lips parted, and his head fell

back. It felt good to make him chuckle like that. As if he felt me watching him, he turned and lowered his sunglasses, allowing his gaze to meet mine. His expression grew abruptly serious.

"I am very sorry that she hurt you, Samantha," he said. "Part of me wants to go ahead and put that note in her file without giving her a chance to improve."

My hurt feelings were all for that, but it seemed unfair. Everyone should have a chance to try again. That being said, I'd met Mrs. Bascomb's type before, so I doubted it would do any good. I'd had years of her sort of well-meaning advice, which were variations of "just focus" or "try harder." Bleh. Still, I did own a part of this mess.

"In all fairness, I should have told you about my dyslexia when we met, but it's a surprisingly awkward factoid to work into conversation with a hot reader guy."

One of his eyebrows lifted as he continued to peer at me over the top of his shades. Mercy, that look turned his hotness up to scorching. I wondered if it was going to leave burn marks on my lips, my throat, the line of skin just above my bikini top. I reached for my water.

"Did you just call me hot?" he asked.

"Maybe." I shrugged. I took a long sip, trying to maintain my cool.

"Are you flirting with me, Samantha?" he asked. His voice was a low, deep growl that made a cloud of steam rise in my core.

"Nope, just stating the obvious." I cleared my throat and kept my face blank.

"Well, that disappoints . . . sort of." His grin was positively wicked and impossible not to respond to. I let my lips turn up just a little in the corners.

"Real talk," he said. "If horror isn't your genre, what is?"

And just like that. Total buzzkill.

"I'm not a reader, remember?" My voice was tight and now I just wanted him to go away. I didn't want to talk reading or books or any of that stuff that made me feel shitty about myself.

"Apologies," he said. "I meant in film. What is your favorite genre of film?"

"Why?"

"Humor me."

"You're going to judge me," I said.

"Librarians never judge," he countered.

I stared at him.

"Okay, the good ones don't judge."

We held each other's gaze. I sensed he wasn't going to leave me in peace anytime soon.

"Fine, but this is not public information." He lifted his hand to his mouth and gestured like he was zipping his lips shut. I nodded my head once. "All right, I like rom-coms. Happy?"

"I feel like I should have guessed that about you,"

he said. "You give off such positive energy, it makes sense."

Was that a compliment? It felt like a compliment, and my toes curled into the sand in pleasure.

"So, what are you planning to do with this top secret information?" I asked.

"You'll see," he said. He turned away and dug through the canvas bag he'd brought. He pulled out a large paperback book. It had a bright-pink-and-aqua-colored cover with illustrations of a man and woman and an airplane. Whatever.

"What part of 'I have dyslexia' do you not understand?" I sighed. Frustration was making me defensive and curt. Did he really think he could just hand me a rom-com, and I was going to be healed or something? Like all I needed was the right genre? Did he have any clue as to how much this pissed me off?

"Hush." He looked me over again, as if memorizing the sight of me, from the tips of my Vixen red toenails to the brim of my floppy sun hat—**oh my!** His gaze was bold, taking in me, as if he was committing the sight of me wearing a bathing suit in my beach chair to memory. "This is how I flirt."

Flirt? That shut me up. I tried to ignore the thrill that thrummed through me. He reached into his bag and handed me a sandwich wrapped in paper. "Tyler also said your favorite sandwich is a double-cream Brie and fig jam on lightly toasted sunflower honey loaf."

He'd brought me a sandwich? Wait. Tyler knew what my favorite sandwich was? I wasn't sure which of these things shocked and pleased me more.

If I hadn't been absolutely starving, I'd have dropped the Brie and fig and kissed him full on the lips. Luckily hunger won out, keeping me from embarrassing myself. I ripped off the paper and took a bite. Delicious.

Ben reclined in his chair and put his water in the cup holder built into the armrest. He leaned back and said, "Just listen."

"Fine, but only because you brought me a sandwich." I didn't want to look like a complete pushover. I took another bite and leaned back in my folding chair like a reluctant teenager.

"Chapter One," he said. I glanced over at him. I opened my mouth to say I have no idea what because he raised his hand in a "stop" gesture and continued reading. "'I'm getting married.'"

I hunkered lower in my seat, enjoying my perfectly toasted sandwich. I supposed I could listen for a page or two.

A seagull paced at the edge of a nearby blanket, obviously hoping I would share. I paid him no mind. A family of four played Frisbee in the surf nearby. I hardly noticed them. The sun inched across the sky, but as Ben read, I had no sense of time passing.

His voice enthralled me, weaving the story around me in such a way that I was there on the page, looking at the world through the character's eyes, seeing what she saw and feeling what she felt. He didn't change voices when he read, there was no falsetto for the females, but he shifted his tone a little bit, just enough to indicate another person was talking. I laughed. I sighed. A workaholic woman was on her way to Europe to find the three men she'd once loved to see if she could remember how to be happy and in love again. I was completely invested in her journey.

A chime sounded right in the middle of his sentence. He shut off the alarm on his phone and closed the book.

"Wait!" I cried. "You can't leave me hanging! She's in Ireland and about to find ex-boyfriend number one."

"Hey, at least I didn't toss the book into the ocean," he said.

"That was an accident," I protested. Then I gasped. "Is this revenge?"

He laughed and then put his hand over his heart. "No, I would never."

I watched in dismay as he put the book back in his bag.

"What are you trying to accomplish then?" I asked. I couldn't believe how irked I was that story time was over and in the middle of a chapter! So rude!

"Nothing. I always read on my lunch hour, and I thought maybe you'd enjoy it, too."

"So, you **are** trying to fix me," I accused.

"That makes it sound as if I think you're broken," he said. His gaze was as true as the tide. "But I don't think that. Not at all."

The sincerity in his voice forced me to correct him. I didn't want him to think more highly of me than I deserved.

"Oh, I'm pretty broken," I said. He didn't argue, just tipped his head to the side in that way he did when he was listening. "I didn't find out that I had dyslexia until I was in high school, and by then, I'd developed so many coping mechanisms to deal with it that I actually thought I was doing fine."

"Strong survival instinct," he said.

I smiled. "I suppose. What's weird is, looking back, I knew something was wrong, but by the time I knew enough to tell my parents I was struggling, their marriage was unraveling and I didn't want to cause them any more stress, so I just figured out how to decode the world enough to survive."

"I bet you're wicked smart," he said. "Like genius-level intelligent."

I glanced at him in surprise and drew in a shaky breath. It was the first time someone had discovered I had dyslexia and assumed I was smart instead of dumb. It shocked me. It made my eyes fill with tears, and a hard knot formed in my throat. Yes, it meant that much to me. After years of being dismissed as stupid because of my learning differences, Ben had spun it around on me. I didn't know what to say, and it was taking everything I had not to cry.

I took a beat to pull it together. He was being kind. I appreciated it more than I could ever say, but as much as I would have liked to, I couldn't pretend that what he said was true.

"The critical voices in my head don't see it that way, but thank you." I was trying to keep it light. He wasn't having it.

"Tell those voices to shut the fuck up," he said. He pushed his sunglasses up onto the top of his head and leaned toward me, clearly wanting to emphasize his point. "I mean you have to be off-the-charts brilliant. There's no way a child could keep up academically like you did unless you were thinking three moves ahead of everyone else. That's freakishly intelligent."

I stared at him. His gaze held mine, and his eyes didn't have a shadow of a doubt in them. He genuinely believed I was brilliant. I had no idea what to do with this information. I wanted to laugh. I wanted to cry. I wanted to hug the stuffing out of him. I did none of those things.

"I've never thought of it that way," I said. "Huh."

"How did you get outed?" he asked.

I thought about Mrs. Ward and the play. I didn't want to risk a break in the dam of tears I was pushing back, so I kept it short. "At the last minute, a teacher reassigned parts for a play we were reading in class. I was assigned a new part and couldn't memorize my lines ahead of time." I glanced at him with a rueful look. "It was bad, as in 'crash and burn with no survivors' bad."

"I'm sorry." His eyes were kind and full of empathy.

I felt the tears well up again, but I blinked them away and asked, "So if you don't think I'm broken and you're not trying to fix me, why the story?"

"Cooking is your thing, right?" he asked.

"Hundred percent."

"True confession time," he said. "I hate cooking. No, 'hate' is too weak a word. I loathe, despise, and abhor it."

"Don't hold back," I said, repeating his words to me on the ferry when we first met. "Say what you feel."

"Oh, believe me, I am," he said. "If I had it my way, I would eat out for every meal, I'd never ever cook. In fact, my house wouldn't even have a kitchen."

I put my hand to my throat. "Blasphemy!"

"I know," he said. He raised his hands in the air. "I'm a knuckle-dragging boor, a philistine to the culinary arts. But the truth is I loathe everything about cooking. It bores me to tears. So here's my question to you, why do you love it?"

Stunned by his revelation—I mean, who hates cooking when you have to eat to live?—I turned from him and stared out at the water. The waves were rolling up higher and higher on the beach as the tide made its way in. How could I answer his question in a way that would make sense to him? Cooking beside my vovó had been a part of my life as soon as I could stand on a stepstool beside her. It calmed me. It allowed me to be creative. Under her gentle guidance, it was the one place where I felt exceptional.

"It just makes sense to me," I said. "Taking ingredients and making something new out of them, something that didn't exist before, that tastes amazing and sustains the body, it feels like a special sort of magic."

"Magic. That's how I feel when I read a book," he said. "It's like opening a portal into another world, allowing me to escape the one I'm trapped in."

"I can see that," I said. "While I was listening to you, I felt as if I were in a pub in Ireland, looking for an ex-boyfriend and wondering what I would say if I found him."

"Exactly. Just like when I tasted the food you created at that delicious happy hour, I was in awe of what you were able to conjure. Since you shared your love of cooking with me, it seemed reasonable, when I learned why you're not a reader, to share what I love with you, which is stories."

"You really aren't trying to 'fix' me?" I asked.

"No," he said. "As long as you don't ask me to cook, I won't ask you to read."

I laughed. Now his scheme was coming into focus.

"But you'll eat what I cook and I'll listen to your stories, so we're really just sharing what we love with each other."

"Yeah," he said. His gaze was tender, and I felt my throat get tight when he asked, "Do you think that's possible?"

I had no idea. No one had read to me since I was a kid, which I had loved. I could still remember leaning over my mother's arm to see the illustrations in the picture books. My favorite was **Where the Wild Things Are** by Maurice Sendak, and I'd had her read it over and over and over again until I had the entire book memorized and could say it with her. Naturally, this became one of my earliest coping skills.

And for many reasons, not just sentimental ones, **Stargirl** by Jerry Spinelli, the last book my dad read to me when I was eleven, before my parents decided I was old enough to read to myself—ha!—was also a favorite. How could I not love a book about a girl who was not like anyone else and who was totally okay with it? The memories were as thick as the fog that frequently engulfed the island. It was a revelation to realize how much I had loved those stories, and how much I had missed listening to someone read to me.

I studied Ben's face. Did I see pity or mockery there? I didn't think so. Still, I was cautious. "Does this mean you're going to keep reading to me?"

"That depends," he said.

"On?"

"What are you doing for dinner tomorrow night?"

I laughed. Oh, I liked this man. I liked him a lot.

"Tomorrow night?" I asked.

"Yeah, I have to go to Chilmark to see my mom tonight, but I'm free tomorrow if you want to go out to dinner with me. Just so we're clear, you don't have to cook for stories. I'm interested in you for more than your cooking."

Be still my heart.

"Then we can do some reading," he continued. How did he make reading sound so sexy? I felt a bead of sweat run down between my breasts. "And find out what happens when our heroine gets to Paris."

"I might be interested in that," I said. I was absolutely interested in that.

"Great," he said. "Then it's a date."

He gave me a pointed look to see if I protested his word choice. I did not. I saw the intent in his gaze and I didn't wave him away. Instead, I waited, perfectly still, while he leaned in and kissed me as if sealing the deal. His mouth was gentle, and he lingered for a moment as if he just couldn't help himself.

When he leaned back, I had to force myself not to follow him like a moth to the porch light because he'd certainly given me a case of the flutters. He had to get back to the library, so we folded up our chairs and left the beach together. We agreed that he'd pick me up tomorrow when he got off work. I reminded him to bring the book, which made him smile.

I rode my bicycle home, pedaling through the quaint Oak Bluffs neighborhood, wondering what this shift between Ben and me meant. Were we dating? Well, we were going on a date, so—yes? Or were we just getting to know each other? Did that make us friends? Friends with potential? All of the above? I had no idea, but I was eager to find out.

Chapter Eleven

Tyler was outside waiting for me when I arrived at the library. I glanced at the clock on the dashboard. I was five minutes early. I pulled up alongside the curb, wondering if something had gone wrong.

Tyler climbed into the passenger seat and fastened his seat belt.

"Everything all right?" I asked. I tried to sound like I wasn't expecting an answer, because I'd noticed over the past few days that the more invested I was in Tyler's life, the more he shut down and shut me out. Honestly, it was like having a prickly little hedgehog for a sibling.

"Yup," he said.

Monosyllabic answers. My favorite. But I knew better than to keep asking questions. If I kept asking, he'd just go full vow of silence on me.

I navigated the neighborhood, keeping an eye out for tourists while moving at a crawl. It was the perfect summer evening, when the heat of the sun was waning and a cool breeze was picking up. I could smell

someone grilling something yummy, and I wondered
how difficult Tyler would be if I wanted to make
something adventurous for dinner like spicy beef
flatbread with yogurt and cucumbers. Hmm.

"Why did Ben want to know what your favorite
sandwich is?" he asked apropos of nothing.

I was just pulling into our driveway and pretended
to be concentrating on not hitting the curb to buy
myself some time, as I wasn't sure how to answer.
Would Tyler be appalled if he knew Ben and I were
interested in each other? Would he think I was infringing
on his library turf?

"He brought me a sandwich on his lunch hour," I said.

"Why?"

"Because he's nice," I said. This was all true.

"Yeah, he is," Tyler said. "But bringing you a
sandwich seems like above and beyond, so what gives,
and why is your friend Emily sitting on our porch?"

I snapped my head in the direction of the house.
Sure enough, Em was perched on the edge of one of
the chairs. Her shoulders were hunched, and she looked
as if she was bracing herself for bad news.

I shut off the engine and said, "I'll explain more
later. Right now, I need to talk to Em."

Tyler glanced from me to her and back. "Okay."

He hopped out of the car and strode up the steps.
He waved to Em as he passed, unlocking the door and
disappearing into the house.

I climbed up the steps. "Hey."

Em shot to her feet. "Sam, I'm so sorry. I should have tackled Mrs. Bascomb to the ground and stuffed that stupid form into her mouth before she could say any of that mean stuff. I hate bullies. I'm a terrible friend and I'm just so fucking sorry."

I blinked. Em was not a swearer. Having worked in high-pressure kitchens with lots of rough-and-tumble culinary types who needed the occasional profanity laced instructions, cursing was really more my forte. I gave her a small smile, trying to let her know it was okay, even though in regard to Mrs. Bascomb, my feelings were still a bit raw.

I gestured for her to sit back down, and then I did the same. "It's not your fault. You're certainly not responsible for the thoughtlessness of that old shrew."

Em put her hand on her forehead and leaned back. "Maybe not, but I should have been quicker to shut her up and shut her down. I just feel awful. Ben was furious."

My ears perked up. "Furious?"

"Oh yeah," she said. "The former director, Louis Drexel, was more of a figurehead. Between you and me, Mrs. Bascomb really ran the library for the last five years of his time with us. She set the schedules, did the payroll, went to the meetings, basically all of the administrative stuff, while he played **FreeCell** on his computer."

"Oh." I didn't want to feel sympathy for the mean lady, but I felt a twinge of something. It wasn't right that she'd been doing the heavy lifting without compensation.

"Do **not** feel sorry for her," Em said. "She is not the type of person who should have any authority at all ever. She's vicious, and even a little power, like having you sign a contract, goes right to her head. I'm positive she was looking for a reason to pitch a fit because Ben okayed your program after the deadline and, you know, rules."

"Will this cause a problem for you?" I asked. I was feeling alarmed that my cooking program was going to be an issue.

"No, that sort of thing happens all the time. Mrs. Bascomb's just mad because when Ben arrived, he stepped up and took charge of the library like a real director and she lost all of her authority and she's . . . well . . . pissed."

"Oh," I said. "I don't want to get you guys in trouble."

"You won't," Em said. "Ben made it clear to her that he was going to go after you and make sure you didn't file a complaint about her insensitivity with human resources."

"I wouldn't do that," I said. I leaned back in my seat feeling as if everything had gotten so messed up all because of me. Ugh.

"You know that, and I know that, and Ben probably knows that, too, but Mrs. Bascomb doesn't and honestly, she needs to do a little self-reflection on the way she deals with people," Em said. "Believe me, you did us a favor, although I'm still sorry she was such a bitch."

"I hope you're right," I said.

We sat silently for a while. I glanced at the neighbor's yard. Their white picket fence propped up a tumble of bright pink summer roses and blue hydrangeas. There was a buzz in the air as if the bees were working overtime to gather all the pollen.

"Ben took a looooong lunch," Em said. She smoothed the skirt of her dress, which was already wrinkle-free.

"Did he?" I asked.

"Aw, come on," she said. "I'm your best friend and I have no life and I need to live vicariously through you. Give me details. I saw Ben talking to Tyler, so I know he was asking him where to find you."

I flashed on the beach, sitting with Ben, enjoying my sandwich while he read to me. It had been a perfect afternoon. I wasn't ready to share it yet, however. I wanted to savor the details and keep them to myself for a bit.

"He found me," I said. "He brought me a sandwich and we talked."

"Talked?" she asked. She was grinning, and she pushed her glasses up on her nose.

"Yes, talked," I said. "We were on a public beach, you know, with families and stuff. Not really private enough for anything else."

"That disappoints," she said. "I was really hoping for some 'how did sand get there?' deets." She made an alarmed expression and I laughed. She tipped her head to the side and added, "I'm glad you're okay."

I waved a dismissive hand. "I'm fine. I've dealt with much, much worse." Like being passed over for a job I deserved, I thought, but I didn't say it.

"Are you still up for tomorrow?" she asked. "You don't have to come with me."

"I'll be there."

"Okay then." She rose from her seat and leaned over me, giving me a big hug. "But if you change your mind . . ."

"I won't change my mind."

She smiled, and I could see the relief in her eyes. She waved and headed down the steps. I waved back and yelled, "It's going to be all right."

She lifted her arm and sent me a thumbs-up. As I watched her walk away, I hoped with all my heart I wasn't lying.

"So, you and Ben, huh?" Tyler stepped out onto the porch, carrying two glasses of iced tea. He sat in the chair Em had vacated.

"Are you going to yell at me?" I asked.

He leaned forward and handed me the iced tea. The

glass was dripping with condensation, so I suspected he'd poured the tea and waited, probably listening, until the right moment to join me.

"Nope." He leaned back in his seat and took a long sip.

I watched him, wondering what was going through his teenage brain. I took a sip, too. It was cold and refreshing, and I noted he'd even taken the time to slice a lemon wedge and drop it in the glass. There might be some culinary hope for him yet.

"In answer to your question, I don't know about me and Ben," I said. "Right now, we're just friends who kind of dig each other, but we're very different."

"Because he's a librarian and you're dyslexic?"

"It's not the most obvious of pairings."

"Was Emily mad because you made a play for her man?" he asked.

"What? No!" I cried. "I didn't make a play. I met him on the ferry before I even knew he was her boss, and besides, she's not interested in him."

"Then why was she here, looking so freaked out?" he asked.

"There was a thing at the library earlier," I said. I didn't want to talk about it. "It was dumb, but Em felt responsible, which was ridiculous. We're good now."

He raised his eyebrows and just stared at me, waiting. He looked so much like our dad that I found myself blurting out what happened in short form. The pretending to Ben that I could read and Mrs. Bascomb outing me as dyslexic and the crippling shame I felt at the revelation. I did not include the date I had planned with Ben or Em's doctor's appointment. I did have some boundaries.

"Wow, that totally sucks," he said.

"It happens." I said.

"Often?"

I shrugged. "More than I'd like but not as much as it used to."

He nodded. He looked like he was processing this. When he met my gaze again, he asked, "Did you resent me?"

My heart sank. Was I really supposed to answer that honestly? I was fourteen when he came along, ending any **Parent Trap** fantasy I'd had about my parents getting back together. Of course I resented him.

"In what way do you mean?" I asked. Maybe, like when he was a toddler and fixated on a specific toy, I could divert him.

"Because school is easy for me, because I'm not dyslexic," he said. He looked sheepish.

"No!" I said. I was so relieved he was asking about school and not his actual existence that I sagged against the back of my chair. "Never. I'm relieved you won't have to struggle like I did."

"I just wondered because . . ." He put a hand on the back of his neck, and his face became slightly pink, as if he was embarrassed.

"Because?" I prodded.

"You didn't come around as much after you graduated high school," he said. The words exploded out of him in a volley of hurt and confusion. He glanced away quickly, but he had just shown me a wound that I couldn't ignore because I had done that to him. Was this why he'd been so chilly when I arrived this summer?

"Oh, Tyler, I'm sorry. That had nothing to do with you," I said. "Dad and I had a very different idea about my continuing education, and I was so furious with him that I didn't want to visit him. You and Stephanie were collateral damage."

He turned back to face me. "You know I was four when you left for college."

"I remember," I said. "You used to carry around this really disgusting stuffed dog named Skip. If it were real, I would have thought it had mange."

"You remember Skip." Tyler grinned. "I still have him."

"I hope his condition has cleared up," I said.

He laughed, then grew serious. "I suppose it was because I was just a kid and didn't understand, but I always thought you stopped coming around because you didn't like me."

I felt my heart squeeze hard in my chest. This was

the same thing I'd thought when my parents separated—that somehow it was because of me, which was why I'd worked so hard to hide my academic struggles. I thought I could fix things if I just did better in school.

"You figured out that it wasn't you, though, right?" I asked. I felt like the worst big sister in the whole wide world. The truth was I'd had so much going on as a teenager that Tyler hadn't really been on my radar as much more than a member of Dad's new family.

The look he gave me was one of chagrin. "Not really, no, but I think I'm figuring it out now. Things change when you're a teenager."

"Yeah, they do," I agreed. "I am sorry. I wish I'd been a bigger-hearted person as a teenager. When my dyslexia was discovered, my entire life imploded. All of the covert coping mechanisms I'd developed and depended upon for years were exposed, making them useless. I felt like I woke up one day and I was blind. Still, that's no excuse. I should have been more aware of you and your feelings."

"You're here now," he said.

I smiled. "Don't let me off the hook so easily. You should definitely leverage this."

"See? That's the sort of big-sister advice that's been missing in my life," he said. "So, since you mentioned it, I've been wanting to learn how to drive—"

"Whoa, whoa, whoa, my dude," I said. I held up my

hands in a "stop" gesture. "I was thinking you could get me to make you a sandwich."

"We can start there," he said. He wagged his eyebrows and I laughed, but I feared there was a battle of wills up ahead, and I wasn't sure I could win.

I parked outside the doctor's office in Edgartown. The lot was small, and the gray shingled building with white trim was standard Edgartown housing. I noticed Em's car, an old Honda hatchback, was already in the lot. I jogged up to the front door. It slid open when I stepped on the mat, and I strode into the small waiting room as if I was on urgent business. I was. Em was my ride or die in the friendship department, and whatever was ailing her, we were going to figure it out, because I simply couldn't imagine my life without her in it.

Em was sitting in the corner with a clipboard. She glanced up at the sound of the door and waved me over when she saw me. She looked scared.

I took the chair beside her. "Hi."

"Hi," she said. "Can you believe the amount of paperwork? And it's always on paper. I thought we were in the digital age."

"They probably just want to keep you busy so you don't worry."

"I'm not worried," she said.

I lifted one eyebrow.

"I'm not. Okay, maybe I am a little." She hung her head. Her auburn hair curtained her face. I put my arm around her shoulders and gave her a quick squeeze.

"Let's save the worry until we have something to worry about," I said.

"Okay." She sniffed. "But what about my hair?"

"Huh?"

She lowered her voice. "What if it's cancer and I have to have chemo and I lose my hair?"

I was not prepared for this discussion this early in the morning. "We could tattoo your head."

She made a face. "Seems painful."

"Okay, then we could get some really cool hats. You'd look adorable in a beanie."

"Without eyebrows?"

"We can draw them on, angry ones if you want. If not hats, you can get some supercool wigs," I suggested. She looked distraught. "Now just hear me out. Dolly Parton has like three hundred and sixty-five wigs, one for every day of the year."

"I am not Dolly Parton," she said. She waved a hand in front of her diminutive chest.

"Well, no, but she's a big promoter of literacy, so you have that in common," I said.

Em laughed. "Yeah, me and Dolly Parton, I can see where people would get us confused."

I smiled at her, relieved that her panic seemed to have ebbed.

"Emily Allen?" a woman in scrubs called from the door.

We both glanced up, and then Em scrambled to pick up her things.

"Do you want me to come back there with you?" I asked.

"Would you mind?" she asked.

"Not at all," I said. I felt like this was very altruistic of me, because the truth was I hated doctor's offices. In my world, they were to be avoided at all cost. I was most definitely of the "rub some dirt on it and get back in the game" school of medicine.

The woman in scrubs took the clipboard. I held Em's handbag and book while she was weighed and had her blood pressure taken. We were shown into a tiny exam room, where we waited for what happened next.

Em sat on the paper-covered patient table while I took one of the two plastic chairs. I tried to think of things to say that might calm her down, but I was drawing a blank.

"Read any good books lately?" I asked.

Em turned her head away from the human anatomy poster she was studying, and looked at me. A small laugh bubbled out of her. Maybe it was nerves, but her laugh got bigger and bigger until I was laughing at her laughter, and not because I'd said anything particularly funny.

"I'm so glad you're here," she gasped as her laughter wound down.

"Me, too," I said.

A knock sounded on the door, and we straightened up. A petite woman entered the room. She was middle-aged, judging by the silver just starting to appear in her black hair. She wore glasses and carried herself with an air of no nonsense.

"Good morning, Emily," she said.

"Hi, Dr. Ernst," Em said.

Dr. Ernst looked at me with one eyebrow raised in question.

"Hi, I'm Samantha Gale, a friend of Emily's," I said.

"I appreciate you being here." She smiled at me, and it was a warm and gentle smile. Then she said, "You're not squeamish, are you?"

"Nah, I'm a chef," I said. "I once butchered an entire cow."

She blinked at me. "Well, okay then." She turned back to Emily. "Now, you know how I feel about this procedure. A biopsy is serious, and there is always a risk for complications."

"I understand," Em said.

"When we get the results, we are going to have to have a real conversation about your situation," Dr. Ernst said.

"Yes, ma'am," Em said.

Biopsy?! Situation?! This couldn't be good. I felt my insides grow cold with the dread that my friend might be really sick.

I tried to picture Martha's Vineyard without Em. I couldn't do it. She was as much a part of my memories here as the rugosa roses that bloomed in summer, the warning blast of the ferry's horn when it was about to depart, and the sound of the surf as it pounded the shore. I simply could not lose her.

Chapter Twelve

Mercifully, the biopsy didn't take that long. Em had a big old bandage on her neck that looked like she was trying to hide the world's biggest hickey or a vampire bite.

"Are you sure you can drive home?" I asked. "I should have driven you here. Why didn't we do that?"

"Because you needed to take Tyler to robotics."

"He could have walked." I waved my hand at her. "How about I follow you home? Just so I know you arrive okay."

"I don't think that's necessary," she said. "I mean, I'm still numb, but if it will make you feel better—"

"It will," I interrupted.

"Okay."

I followed her in her ancient vehicle across the island from Edgartown back to Oak Bluffs. It was only a twenty-minute drive along the Beach Road and, as always, when I drove over the Jaws Bridge, made iconic by the film, I slowed to watch a few tourists taking the plunge off the bridge. I remembered doing that on a dare as a teenager, and I wondered if Tyler had ever done it. It was a rite of passage back in my day, but I doubted that his crowd felt the same way. Suddenly, I felt practically middle-aged. Ugh.

Em parked in front of her house, which was much like ours, with a big front porch and hydrangea bushes in full bloom. I parked behind her and got out in case she needed help getting settled with pain meds or anything.

I also needed to talk to her about this biopsy. While it was most definitely not my business, I was still going to grill her. Oh yes, I was. Patient privacy did not extend to best friends.

"You don't have to walk me to the door," she said. "It's not like it's our first date."

Her smile was wan, and I could tell she was tired.

"Oh, I'm walking you in," I said. "Then I'm making you a cup of tea."

"Fine," she said.

"Where is your mom?" I asked. Em had moved home after college, and even though she frequently talked about getting her own place, she never had. I wondered about that, and realized this was one of the many conversations we should have been having over the years. I promised myself I would do better.

"She's shopping the outlets in Maine with my aunt," she said. "They won't be back for another week."

"Ah, so that's why you did the biopsy today," I said. "So, she wouldn't worry."

"Yeah." She unlocked the door and pushed it open. I glanced around. The Allen house was exactly as I remembered it. Same granny square afghan across the back of the couch, likewise the potbellied woodstove in the corner. It even smelled the same, like lemon furniture polish and lavender potpourri. In many ways it felt more like coming home than my own house did.

Em collapsed onto the couch while I went right into the kitchen and put the kettle on. I fished around in the pantry until I found the herbal teas. I chose a mellowing chamomile.

While the kettle heated up, I went back to check on Em. "Need anything?"

She shook her head. "I was so nervous, I didn't sleep at all last night, which was why I took the day off. I'm just going to lie here and listen to some audiobooks."

I remembered having Ben read to me, and I felt my face get warm at the memory of his low voice painting pictures in my mind and luring me deeper into the story with every page.

"You all right?" she asked. "You look flushed."

"Yeah, I'm fine," I said. It was moment-of-truth time. "I need to tell you something."

"Okay," she said. She sounded groggy and I hesitated.

The kettle hit optimum whistle just then, and I'd be a liar if I said I wasn't relieved. I was nervous about telling her I was going on a date with Ben. Not that Em would mind, but that talking about it made it a thing. And if it was a thing, it had the potential for disaster. I wasn't sure, given the rough few months I'd just had, that I was up for more of that.

I fussed with the tea, making two mugs with honey and a splash of milk, and then carried them back to the living room. I put Em's down on a coaster on the coffee table, which was a challenge, as it was piled high in books, and took a seat in the armchair across from her.

I sipped my tea. Hot and honey-sweet. Perfection.

"Spill it," Em said. She was lying down with her head on the armrest, and her eyes were shut.

"Spill what, my tea?" I asked.

"Yes, but not the tea in your mug," she said. "The 'T,' as the kids say, meaning the gossip, the skinny, the dirt."

"I wouldn't call it gossip exactly," I hedged. Stalling maneuver number 305.

"Right. Sam, I know you. You have no sense of personal boundaries, and if you want to say something, you usually just throw it out there."

"That makes me sound so rude."

Em opened one eye and swiveled her head in my direction. "I was there with you on the T when you asked the woman with the pet python about her relationship with the snake."

I snorted. "In my defense, they were entwined quite passionately. It's not my fault she viewed him as more of a child than a lover."

"And the time we were walking around Boston Common and you asked the man in the superhero costume what his origin story was."

"He had a pretty good one," I said. "Compelling narrative, being birthed out of a giant squid and forced to live with mortals."

Em laughed, then winced and put her hand on her neck. "Ouch."

"Sorry." I took another sip of my tea. "All right. I have two things on my mind. I'll start with the one that is less important. To revisit our conversation yesterday, when Ben brought me the sandwich, he also asked me out."

Her eyes popped open. "He brought you food, then asked you out? Oh, he's definitely into you."

I wanted to jump to my feet and do a fist pump. I didn't. **Slow your roll there, Gale**. Technically, Ben and I were going on our first date tonight. It could turn out to be the stuff of nightmares, so it was best to check my expectations.

Em sat up and sipped her tea. She put it back on its coaster and sank into the sofa. "I think I'm going to fall asleep, so you'd better get on with asking me questions."

"Okay, I need you to promise me that you really have no interest in him. I know you said no before, but just so we're clear, I would absolutely cancel with him if you felt even a little something for him in that way, because I figure you have dibs, plus you're my best friend, and sisters before misters and all that."

"Dibs?" Em asked. "Like he's the last ice cream sandwich in the freezer or something?"

"Did you just compare a man to an ice cream sandwich?" I asked.

"Yeah, you're right," she said. "That's unfair to the ice cream sandwich."

"Harsh." I laughed.

She shrugged. "For the record, to be perfectly transparent so that you have no worries about my feelings toward my boss—oh, horror!—no, I am not now nor have I ever been interested in or attracted to Ben."

"But he's so hot," I said.

"Meh," she countered.

"How many pain pills did you take?" I asked. "After that assessment of Ben's hotness, I'm actually concerned."

She laughed and waved a hand at me. "I'm just teasing. He's cute enough, I just . . . I don't know . . . I want something **more**."

I thought about the guy who had brought me a

sandwich and read to me, whose blue-gray eyes reflected the sea, and whose kisses made me dizzy in the best possible way. If that guy was any **more**, I'd melt into a useless puddle of goo.

She smiled at me. "Go out with him, Sam. It's pretty clear you're warm for his form."

"I am no—" I cut off my own protest. "I am, totally, all of that."

"And when's the hot date?"

"Tonight."

"Tonight?" She sat up. "What are you doing here? You have to get ready! Where are you going? What are you wearing?" She looked me up and down. "You're not wearing that, are you?"

"No, of course not." I glanced down at my frayed jeans shorts and Guns N' Roses T-shirt. "I'm going to add my leather jacket and combat boots. Duh."

She looked appalled, and I laughed.

"I'm just joking," I said. "Although, I didn't think I was going to have a hot date while I was here, and I'm not sure I packed anything other than some casual sundresses that are definitely more stroll on the beach than fancy dinner out. Having worked chef's hours forever, most of my dates have been breakfast dates, so I am out of touch with what's trending."

"Let's go." She pushed herself off the couch and headed for the stairs.

"Wait. Aren't you supposed to be resting?"

"This is an emergency," she said. "I can rest when we have you properly outfitted."

I picked up her tea and mine and followed her upstairs. Her bedroom was at the top and to the right, but other than location, I wouldn't have recognized it. Gone were the piles of clothing on the floor, the candy wrappers on her nightstand, and the boy band posters that had adorned the walls back in the day.

Now it was painted a matte sage green with cream trim, and everything was neat and tidy, except for her favorite white cardigan, which was draped across the arm of a chair. The seat cushion was dented, and judging by the stuffed bookcase beside it, I imagined this was where Em spent most of her time.

It made me pause. Why wasn't she going for Ben? They were both readers. It just made sense, like attracts like, right?

"No, no, no," she muttered as she slid clothes across the rod in her closet. "Too simple, too slutty, desperate, not desperate enough."

"Oh, I don't know," I said. "I'm pretty desperate."

"No, you're not," she said. She didn't even look at me. "You just haven't had a chance to get out there."

"Em, I haven't had a boyfriend since I took the chef job at the Comstock. We're talking **years** here, and it's not because I was too busy."

She turned to face me and took the tea I held out to her. She pushed up her glasses and said, "You are one of the friendliest people I know. You're also smart, funny, and a total knockout, oh, and you're an amazing chef. If you're single, it's because you don't really want a boyfriend."

"Oh, Em, I wish everyone saw me the way you do," I said. "But the fact is, once a guy finds out I have dyslexia, he usually ghosts me."

"But why?" she cried. "Look at you, with that thick mane of black hair, that heart-shaped face, and those long legs!" She tugged me in front of a full length mirror. "And that's just the packaging. You have so much to offer. How could any man walk away?"

"Well, if I remember what my last boyfriend, Bruce, said when he dumped me after a few months and the truth came out, it went something like this." I paused to clear my throat and lower my voice. "'I'm sorry, Sam, but I can't see you anymore. I'm not getting any younger and the fact is I'm looking for wife and mother material. I can't risk your unfortunate disability being passed down to my kids. It's all about the genetics, nothing personal.'"

"He. Did. Not." Em's fingers tightened on her mug until they turned white.

"Oh, he did," I said. "Spoiler alert, it was pretty effing personal to me."

"What was his last name?" she asked. "Boron or something."

"Brenowicz," I said.

"That's right," she said through gritted teeth. "Does he still work in the Pru?"

"Why?" I asked.

"Because the next time I'm in Boston, I'm going to find him and punch him in the face," she said.

All of a sudden my throat got tight. I took a sip of tea, and said, "I love you."

"I love you, too," she said. Then she snapped her fingers and pointed at me. "Red."

"Red rover? Red roses? Red sky at night? Sorry, you lost me."

"Red dress," she said. She spun back to the closet, dug deep until she disappeared up to her armpit. "I bought this last year with the idea that red would make me bolder."

"Did it?"

"No, more like jaundiced." She pulled something wrapped in plastic out of the depths and draped it across the bed. "But with your coloring, you will look amazing."

I put my tea down and pushed the plastic aside. The dress was cherry red, and it look like it was designed to hug every curve. I looked from it to her.

"This is some dress, Em," I said. "And you're wrong. You could totally wear this dress, and you would blind men you'd be so hot."

She flushed with pleasure and laughed. "Thank you, but I don't think it fits my personality. Try it on."

"If you're sure," I said. I noticed the tags were still on it. "You could always sell it."

"No." She shook her head. "I don't want to. I think this dress was just waiting for you."

"All right," I said. I slipped off my clothes while Em took the dress off its hanger and lowered the zipper. She handed it to me and I pulled it over my head, letting it fall into place. Em gently zipped up the back.

"Oh, Sam," she said.

I could tell without even looking that the dress fit me to perfection. I stepped in front of the full-length mirror and glanced at my reflection. The soft red fabric hugged my curves without appearing to be sausage casing fighting a losing battle. Sleeveless with a scoop neckline, the dress was simple but flared out at mid-thigh, making it flirty instead of severe. Given my usual boxy chef attire, I felt like an onion that'd been peeled to its core.

"Wow," I said. "I'd forgotten I even have breasts."

Em laughed. "And then some."

I turned to face her. "Are you sure?"

"Positive." She sighed. "This reminds me of all those summer nights when we'd get dressed up in our skinny jeans and halter tops and hang out at the arcade. Remember what Twihards we were?"

"But only for the movie," I said. Then I flashed a peace sign. "Team Edward."

"Forever." She put her hand over her heart.

I glanced at her where she stood sipping her tea and smiling at me, and her bright white neck bandage caught my attention.

"Hey, Em," I said. "My other question was, What did Dr. Ernst mean about the biopsy and your situation?"

She put her hand on her neck, self-consciously covering the bandage.

"Sorry, I know it's none of my business, but that is the second question I wanted to ask you. Well, it's really the first, but I was trying to ease you into a sharing place," I said. "What's going on? How likely is it that you have cancer? How worried should I be?"

"Don't be worried," she said. "I appreciate the concern, I do, but there was just a weird lump in my neck, the size of a lima bean, and I asked Dr. Ernst to biopsy it just to be sure it isn't anything to be worried about. I'm sure it's nothing, and in a few days, that will be confirmed."

She didn't look sure of anything of the kind. Rather, she looked terrified.

"Oh, Em, how can I be so selfish talking about a stupid date when you have big, bad life stuff happening?" I asked.

"Are you kidding?" she asked. "This is great. You got me out of my own head for a while, and I really needed that."

I stepped close and hugged her.

"You'll tell me if it's something serious?" I asked. I

rested my chin on her shoulder, the one on the unbiopsied side. "Promise me?"

"I promise," she said.

We stood together for a moment, silently appreciating the lifelong friendship we shared.

"All right," Em said. She broke the hug by stepping back. "That's enough. Now we need to talk about your hair."

"My hair?" I asked. "What's wrong with my hair?"

"Nothing a comb and some product won't fix," she said.

She was trying to divert us from our fears over her biopsy. I knew it. She knew it. And I knew I would have done the exact same thing.

"So, no single ponytail out of the side of my head then?"

"Ha! Watch yourself or I'll dig out my mom's old banana clips."

"Hello, 1980s," I said.

"Yeah, no, we'll let them rest in peace," she said. She crossed herself and I laughed.

My throat was tight, however, and I was worried. Worried about what she wasn't telling me and full of regret that I hadn't been here more for her over the past few years. I was going to fix that. I was. I just didn't know how yet.

Chapter Thirteen

"Are you sure you'll be all right by yourself?" I asked Tyler for the fifteenth time. "I could cancel and stay."

"No!" he shouted. He shot a glance at me from the television screen, where he was playing a video game. "Sorry, that was for the idiot I'm playing with. Stop!"

I frowned but then realized he was again yelling at a person on his headset. Suddenly, being out for the evening seemed like more of an escape plan than a date.

A knock sounded on the door, and I started. I was nervous, actually nervous.

Tyler must have registered this, because he dropped his controller on the coffee table and pulled off his headset. He glanced at me and stood up. Then, with a mischievous grin, he said, "I'll get it."

Oh no!

"Tyler, don't you dare embarrass me," I hissed as I followed him to the door. "I'm warning y—"

"Ben, come on in," Tyler said.

Ben's broad shoulders filled the doorway as he entered. He was wearing a pale gray dress shirt, open at the throat, that molded to his muscular frame, and black pants. He was clean-shaven, making him even more handsome, as if that was possible, and I found myself wondering what it would feel like to kiss him without the scruff of a beard. With his square jaw revealed, the man looked positively edible, and I would have bet my favorite whisk that it hadn't taken him two hours to get ready.

Ben's eyes went wide at the sight of me, and his gaze swept over me like a lick of fire. I shivered, in a good way, feeling as exposed as a pedestrian in the middle of the crosswalk when the light changed.

I was wearing spiky black sandals and the red dress, and had let Em tease my hair until it was a Texas-sized mass of curls and was only lacking a beauty queen's tiara. In other words, I looked nothing like my actual self, which was probably a good thing. Or not?

"Okay, kids, there are a couple of ground rules," Tyler said. He rubbed his hands together, clearly enjoying himself. "Sam needs to be home by ten, and you are to go nowhere except the restaurant and back. Am I clear?"

"Sure." Ben's gaze lingered on my body, appreciating my newly painted toes, my shaved legs, the curves of my hips and breasts, before he met and held my gaze with a look of desire that made my body hum. I felt a thrum, like the vibration of a low note, deep in my belly resonating out to my skin.

"Great, you two have a good time and I'll see you at ten," Tyler said. He bounded over to his video game and put his headset back on.

"Sure. Wait. What?" Ben asked. He frowned at Tyler as if he was just registering his words.

I laughed. I walked to the couch and hugged Tyler around the shoulders from behind and whispered in his ear, "Nice try. I'll be home when I get home but I **will** be home. No shenanigans, and call me if you need me."

He hugged my arm to his chest and grinned. Then he whispered, "You look amazing, Sis. Try not to break his heart."

"Uh . . . thanks," I said. I was so startled by his use of the nickname Sis and the compliment that I didn't know what else to say. "See you later."

"Later." He gave us a thumbs-up and went back to his game.

"Curfew at ten, huh?" Ben asked as he held the door open for me.

"Tyler enjoys embarrassing me," I said.

"As any good little brother should," he said. He paused on the porch and said, "You are devastatingly beautiful, although those words feel really inadequate right now. Honestly, I think I might have lost consciousness for a second when I saw you."

I grinned. He looked so befuddled by his reaction to me that I couldn't help it. There was nothing more charming than a man who was rendered speechless at the sight of the woman he was interested in.

"Would it make you feel better if I told you that my first thought upon seeing you was that you looked edible?"

"Edible?" he laughed.

"Chef." I pointed to myself. "It's the highest compliment I can give."

"In that case, I'm delighted to be your main course." He wagged his eyebrows suggestively, and I laughed again.

He took my hand in his and walked me to a sports car parked in front of the house.

"No motorcycle?" I asked.

"That's for third dates," he said.

"Ah," I said.

The night air was warm, but a cool breeze was blowing in from the water, perfuming the air with its briny tang. As we drove along Beach Road, I glanced at the ocean and noted that the moon was reflected on its dark depths all the way to the horizon.

When I was a girl, I had been absolutely obsessed with **The Little Mermaid**, and I always wondered what it would be like to live under the sea. Probably, there were no Jamaican lobster and little boy flounder sidekicks, but still, the daydream held fast. I glanced at Ben. I wondered what he had dreamed about as a boy. Had he been an athlete? A nerd? Popular?

"Were you as much of a gamer as a teen as Tyler is?" I asked.

Ben glanced from the road to me. "Oh, yeah. Why are you worried about him?"

"I feel like he spends all of his time inside, either at robotics camp or on his video games," I said. "I've tried to get him to the beach, but it's like he's allergic to the sun. You haven't seen him shying away from garlic and drinking blood on the sly, have you?"

Ben laughed. "No, but I suspect he's at the age where the beach is way too risky. Too many people to see you in your bathing suit, especially as a teen where you're skinny, acne loaded, and can't exactly control your reaction to the sight of women in bikinis."

"Ah, the horror!" I agreed.

"Maybe he just needs something else to do in the great outdoors," he said. "Does he sail?"

"No."

"Tennis?"

"No."

"Golf?"

"No," I said. "I do not know of any hobbies he has outside of being an electronics nerd."

"Hmm." Ben mulled this over. "I might have an idea. Let me talk to Ryan and see about the logistics, but I think the robotics camp would benefit from a field trip with sunshine, hiking, and bugs. It'll be great."

His enthusiasm made me smile. "Just don't tell him

I had anything to do with it. He'd never forgive me for exposing him to fresh air."

Ben nodded. "Understood."

He drove through the narrow streets of Edgartown. I didn't ask where we were going since I suspected that him taking me, a chef, out to dinner would be as stressful as me trying to buy a book for him. How would I know what he hadn't read already or what he enjoyed? Nightmare.

"How did you decide what restaurant to take me to?" I asked.

"I did my research to make certain our first date isn't a bust over the appetizers. Very modern librarian of me, I know."

"Indeed," I said. "You picked Bailey's, didn't you?"

"Bailey's? Is that what you're thinking? Oh, this is embarrassing," he said. "I was just planning to have us go down to the dock and fish for our supper."

"And me without my tackle box," I said.

"Tragic," he said. "I suppose we'll just have to hope they have room for us at the restaurant."

He parked and strolled around the back of the car to open my door for me. Normally, I would open my door myself and meet him halfway, but it was hard to navigate the dress and the heels and my handbag. I was woefully out of practice at being a girlie girl.

Ben offered his hand and I took it, letting him pull me to my feet. His fingers were strong and warm and he didn't let go of me, but instead held my hand as we walked to the restaurant.

Bailey's had a small sign hanging outside on the corner. The gray shingled building with the white trim looked like every other Martha's Vineyard edifice, but it boasted a long porch with white rocking chairs, and inside the tables had white linens and comfy chairs, inviting diners to linger.

I hadn't eaten there since the former owners sold the place several years ago. My dad had delivered this news with the solemnity of a man reporting a death in the family. Once the new owner took over, however, my dad and Stephanie gave it a test run and declared it would remain the family place of celebration. Wouldn't Dad be pleased that I was going on a first date here? I wondered if I should tell him when he checked in from Europe. Nah, it could keep until he got home. Still, I knew he'd approve and somehow that made this date feel even more meaningful.

The hostess sat us at a lovely table for two by a window and handed us menus. I glanced at mine. The font was not dyslexic friendly and there were no pictures. Thankfully, I already knew the menu by heart.

The waitress came by and took our drink order. Knowing I was going to get seafood, I went with the house white wine. Ben ordered the same. I felt him watching me over his menu. I sensed he wanted to say something but wasn't sure how. I decided to put him out of his misery.

"I should warn you, when I eat out, I hit every course, appetizers, entrée, and dessert," I said. "But I'm also a very good sharer."

He nodded and I saw his shoulders drop ever so slightly. "That sounds great."

"Do you want to share the seared scallops?" I asked.

"Excellent choice." He kept watching me.

"And for an entrée, I am torn between the swordfish or the roasted cod."

"Those look great," he said. "If we each order one, we can share."

"Perfect," I said. I put my menu down. Dessert could be ordered later. He was still studying me. "And now you're wondering how I could read the menu so easily?"

"No." He shook his head and then nodded. "Okay, a little bit."

I smiled. I liked his honesty, so it was time for my own.

"Truthfully, Em told me you had asked about my favorite restaurants. So I went online and studied all of the menus so I was prepared. Sorry. Do you think I'm a big fraud?"

He shook his head. "You're not a fraud. You're

amazing. I can't even imagine how you manage to run a kitchen and think so many steps ahead. It must be like being in a foreign country where you can speak the language but can't read it."

"That's a very a good analogy, but I'm not amazing," I said. "Dyslexia is more than just a reading disability. It causes my brain to be busy all the time. I swear, some days it's like a hive of bees up there, and my organization isn't great because I get distracted easily. Honestly, running a restaurant kitchen was hard, and I only pulled it off because I had a great crew."

"Still impressed," he said. "Are you headed back to Boston when you're finished chaperoning Tyler?"

"I don't know," I said. "I left my position at my former restaurant, so I'm going to be looking for a new one, but I don't know if it will be in Boston or if I'll go someplace else. How about you? You're the interim director, are you going back to academia at the end of the summer?"

"Like you, I don't know." His gaze held mine. "I suppose it'll depend upon how this summer plays out."

I felt my body temperature rise under his warm regard. Did he mean between him and me? Was I ready for that? I wasn't. At best, all I had to offer was a summer fling. I was about to say as much when our waitress arrived with our wine.

I ordered our meals and she departed. As I watched her leave, I noticed Ben was studying a fiftysomething man in the corner, seated with his wife. My heart sank. This again.

I took a bracing sip of my wine, and he turned back to me.

"Sorry," he said. "I was just—"

"Checking out a middle-aged man at another table?" I asked.

"When you say it like that, it sounds so pervy," he said. But he was smiling.

"You were going to explain this . . . interest . . . of yours to me before," I said.

"But we were interrupted," he said. "Repeatedly."

"Right." I took another sip. I really hoped this wasn't where he told me he had some kink that I was unprepared to deal with. It had happened before.

"The truth is I'm looking for someone," he said.

"Someone?" I encouraged him.

He hesitated. He took a sip of wine. He let out a sigh and glanced out the window. I suspected this was an intensely personal matter for him.

"Not to push you," I said. "But you know my deep dark secret. I promise you can trust me with yours."

Ben met my gaze. His mouth curved up in one corner in a rueful half smile. It was an acknowledgment of the unevenness of our relationship.

"You're right," he said. He took a deep breath. "Have you ever heard of Moira Reynolds?"

"The artist?" I asked. "Who hasn't? I mean, she's

probably the most famous contemporary artist in New England right now."

"She's my mother," he said.

I felt my mouth form a small O and my eyebrows reached my hairline.

He looked chagrined. "Yeah, that's the usual reaction from anyone who knows her, which is anyone in New England."

"I . . . she's . . . really?"

He laughed. It was a full-on belly laugh. "Crazy, right?"

"She's just, well, she's a legend," I said. "Being so talented and eccentric and all. No offense."

"None taken," he said. "You seem familiar enough to imagine what my childhood was like."

I shook my head. "Nope, I really can't. I mean, she chained herself to a lighthouse once." I paused to lower my voice into a whisper. "And she was naked."

"Yeah, going to school the day after that happened was brutal," he said. "Being raised by her was like being hazed for a frat. I never knew what to expect, and it was usually unpleasant. Actually, I think I would have preferred a frat."

"Ooh, and I thought I had 'stuff' from my childhood," I said.

"Fair to say we both do," he said. "But I did have my grandparents, my mother's parents, who were supportive and loving and, thankfully during my teen years, exceedingly normal."

"Your mother is known for her sculptures, isn't she?" I asked.

He nodded.

"And if I remember right some were very . . ."

"Pornographic?" he suggested.

"I was going to say 'sensual'," I said.

"'Pornographic' would be more accurate. Yeah, that was a fun phase of her artist's journey to go through," he said. "Don't get me wrong, I am proud of her, but she wasn't like other mothers. There were no cookies after school, no chaperoning field trips, and no sitting in the stands when I pitched a no-hitter. In fact, from the time I could walk and form full sentences, she gave me complete autonomy. I can't tell you how many times I had candy for dinner."

"Really?" I asked. "Because as a candy freak, I have to say that's pretty cool."

"I thought so, too, until I started to catch on that other parents were a bit more invested in their kids' health and well-being than my mom was," he said. "It's not that she didn't love me, I knew she did and does in her own way.

"But it was as if she was tuned in to some other frequency, some wavelength that only Moira could hear. My grandparents took custody of me when I was ten because the truant officer reached out. I hadn't been to school in a month. I stayed with them on the Cape until I graduated high school."

"Did you see your mother during those years?" I asked. This seemed so sad, even sadder than my parents' divorce.

"She came to stay with us a few times a year, a week here or there, holidays and my birthdays," he said. "I loved seeing her, but like my grandparents, I was always okay when she left. She just sucked all of the oxygen out of the room, you know?"

"I know the type," I said. I had met some chefs during my career who didn't leave enough air in the kitchen for a flambé. "You said you were going to see her last night. How did that go?"

"Not well," he said.

The waitress delivered our appetizer, and we leaned back to give her access to the table. When she left, we picked up our forks and each speared one of the perfectly browned scallops.

"What happened?" I asked. I felt as if Ben's relationship with his mother might be the key to knowing him, and I didn't want to get sidetracked, not even by food, right now.

"I asked her for the millionth time who my father is, and she, also for the millionth time, refused to tell me," he said.

Chapter Fourteen

"You don't know who your father is?" I asked. My fork was halfway to my mouth, frozen in place. I couldn't even imagine.

"Nope, not even a name." He sounded resigned, and I desperately wanted to get up and hug him. I didn't.

"Why won't she tell you?" I was mystified. It wasn't like he was a boy who might suffer psychological damage if he discovered his dad was a murderer or a convict or something. He was a grown-ass man who wanted to know who had spawned him. I was irate on his behalf.

"She's very cagey," he said. "She doesn't say no outright, because then I could kick up a fuss or argue. Instead, she just changes the subject."

"How?" I asked. Granted, my dyslexia made me a bit of a badger when it came to asking questions so I could understand things, but how did this woman manage to shut down a conversation of this sort by changing the subject?

"It's hard to explain." He took a bite of his scallop, and his eyes closed as he savored it.

It was quite the sensual look, and I wondered if he looked like that when he—I shook my head. **Focus, Gale!** Still, just the sight of him with his eyes shut and a look of enjoyment on his face made my whole body get hot as if I had a fever. I bit my own scallop, barely tasting the divine buttery garlic and perfectly seared edges, which was tragic.

"Okay, you be me," he said. "And I'll be her and you'll get a better sense of what I'm dealing with."

"Okay." I swallowed my scallop. "Hey, Mom—"

"No." He shook his head. "I've never called her Mom. She felt it diminished her individuality as a person to be defined by the role of mother. I call her Moira."

I stared at him.

"Wow, that's a lot to take in," I said.

"Tell me about it."

"All right. Hey, Moira," I said. I glanced at him to see if this was okay. He nodded. "I was filling out some forms the other day, and in the place where it said 'father,' I drew a blank. Any ideas on what I should be writing there?"

"Why would you fill out forms about your parentage? Are you a slave to the patriarchy?" he asked. His voice was higher but definitely strident.

"Oh."

"Hmm."

We both stabbed another scallop and contemplated the situation.

"Moira, I've got this hereditary condition in my man parts that requires a matching donor," I said. He glanced at me across the table, and his eyes glinted with amusement, and his lips twitched. "Any idea where I might find a match?"

"Ask James," Ben said. Then he added as an aside, "That's what she calls her father, my grandfather, who is an awesome guy, by the way."

"It's supposed to be a paternal match from the father's side," I said. I lowered my voice and tried to sound stern.

"Parthenogenesis," he said.

"I . . . what?" I gave him a confused look as I tried to wrap my head around the science-loaded word.

"Did you know that there are species of animals that procreate with no male participation?" he asked.

"Is that even possible, outside of a cell splitting?" I asked.

"Oh yeah, reptiles, fish, all sorts of animals have these 'virgin births,'" he said.

"Moira," I tried to sound forbidding. "You did not have a virgin birth, and I'd like an answer to my question."

He looked at me or, more accurately, looked past me. "Have I shown you my latest piece? It focuses on the moment of ejaculation from a female perspective."

I choked on melted butter.

"I . . . I've got nothing," I said. There was no place to go in this conversation.

"And end scene," he said.

We ate the last two scallops in silence.

I took a sip of wine. Our waitress arrived with our entrées and whisked our appetizer plate away. I pushed my plate into the center of the table and Ben did, too, so we could share more easily.

The swordfish was amazing, and so was the cod. I was trying to decide which I preferred, but my brain kept chugging back to his mom and his quest to find his father.

"I'm assuming there's nothing on your birth certificate," I said.

"Correct," he said. "I ordered it from the state when I was in college and thought, 'Aha, I've got her.' But no, she'd left it blank."

"And your grandparents have no idea who your father is?"

"No, they asked her, too," he said. "As my grandmother tells it, Moira showed up very pregnant in the winter of nineteen ninety. When they asked who the father was, she refused to say, and since their relationship was already strained, they didn't want to push it. So that was that. She's never spoken of him to anyone as far as I know."

"I don't want to cast aspersions on your mom," I

said. I made a pained face because it truly hurt me to have to say it, but it had to be done. "Have you considered that she doesn't know who your father is?"

"I would welcome a list of names," he said. "Even if it's as long as my arm. At least then I would have a starting place."

We ate in silence, contemplating the dilemma that confronted him. I had no great ideas, unfortunately.

"So, when you told Em and me that you were looking for someone that day at the library," I said. "You were talking about your dad."

He nodded. There was a soul-deep sadness in his eyes that pulled at me.

"All right, I'm in," I said.

"In what?" He gave me a side-eye.

"I'm in the hunt. Let's do this. Let's figure out who your father is," I said.

"While I love your enthusiasm, I haven't had much luck," he said. "I don't have much to go on, and I don't want you to waste your time or be disappointed."

"I'll only be disappointed if we don't try," I said. I reached across the table and put my hand on his arm and gave it a gentle squeeze. "You deserve to know."

He looked up at me. His eyes glistened, just a little, as if he was feeling too much and the emotions were trying to escape through any available route. It endeared him to me. Seeing his pain made me want to ease it the way his presence helped my busy brain calm down.

His voice was gruff when he said, "It's killing me not to pull you into my arms and kiss you right now."

Guh. I was rendered mute by the intensity of his stare.

"Oh my," the waitress said. She had arrived at our table and stood entranced as if she was caught in the sexual tension force field that seemed to be swirling around us. "Shall I bring your check?"

"Yes, please, and a slice of cheesecake to go," I said.

Ben burst out laughing, which eased the fever a bit. I let go of his arm with great reluctance and finished my wine in one swallow.

The check and cheesecake arrived in minutes. Ben paid the tab and hustled us out of the restaurant and into the summer evening. Around the side of the building, he stopped and turned to face me. I had a paper bag of cheesecake dangling from my fingers. He didn't care.

He cupped my face in his hands, and his gaze latched on to mine, full of lascivious intent. It was a deliciously wicked look on his handsome face. I couldn't move, I couldn't breathe, the anticipation as sharp as the first bite of an amazing-looking dessert. Would it taste as sweet, or was I doomed to disappointment?

My insides tightened as if bracing for impact, and then his mouth was on mine, and it was such sweet relief. I gasped. He deepened the kiss, and my buzzing brain went into hyperfocus on him. The lush press of his mouth against mine. His tongue sweeping across my lower lip, wooing me under the tender assault. The scent of him, not an aftershave or cologne, but a scent that was particularly him, warm and musky like the woods after a fresh rain.

Instinctively, I leaned in closer until my front was pressed up against his. I dropped the cheesecake so I could twine my arms about his neck and pull him in even closer. He hummed in approval and slid one hand into my hair while the other moved to my lower back, holding me in place while he broke the kiss and moved his lips along my jaw to settle just below my ear.

I arched my back and tipped my head, giving him full access. I forgot we were in public, on the street, and I might have started to undress him had he not pulled me into a fierce hug and held me while his breath rasped in my ear and his hands slid up and down my back as if trying to tamp down the fire that raged between us.

"Well, that escalated quickly," he said. He took a small step back, allowing the air to move between us. I wanted to close the gap again. Instead I laughed.

"You made me drop my cheesecake," I said. "This might set a new bar for future kisses."

He scooped the paper bag up and peered inside. "It appears to have survived the fall. Does this mean when I kiss you, it'll only be successful if you drop things?"

"Hmm," I considered. "To be truly successful, you'll

have to kiss me when the only thing I can drop is my clothes."

"Mercy." He blew out a breath and looked adorably wide-eyed. He took my hand and we walked to his car. He put the cheesecake inside and said, "Want to take a walk? I think I need to cool off a bit."

"Same," I said.

We strolled down narrow streets busy with summer tourists. There was laughter and conversation, and we swerved around a family, a couple of senior citizens, and a pack of teens. The night air was cool, but it pulsed with that intoxicating feeling of summer that to me always meant freedom from school, books, lessons, and the constant anxiety of trying to hide my learning issues. Summer on the Vineyard had always been a magical respite for me. It hit me again how much I'd missed it.

We wandered down Cooke Street until we reached a small inlet. Ben gave me a sideways glance and asked, "Beach?"

"Always." I kicked off my sandals while he did the same with his shoes, and we left them in a happy tangle of straps and laces for when we returned.

Small boats were tied up, scattered across the water, but it was quiet as everyone was off foraging for their dinners. The beach was deserted. The breeze made me shiver, and Ben put his arm around my shoulders and pulled me close. My side locked into his with my head resting on his shoulder.

"I wonder if my parents walked along this beach," he said.

I slid my arm around his back, settling my hand just above his waist. He was all muscle. I tried not to get distracted.

"I suppose it's possible," I said. "What was your mom doing on the island that summer?"

"She worked as a waitress at one of the restaurants," he said. "She was a student at the Rhode Island School of Design at the time, so being here was her summer getaway. My grandparents would have preferred that she live on the Cape with them, but she isn't one to do what's expected of her."

She sounded like a woman after my own heart minus the naked and chained to a lighthouse thing, oh, and the not telling her son who his father was.

"You're sure it was during her summer here that she got pregnant?" I asked.

"It checks out on the timeline," he said. "I was born in March of 1990, which puts her in the middle of summer on the Vineyard when she got pregnant."

"Do you know what restaurant she worked at?" I asked.

"I know it was on the island," he said. "But not the name. She says she doesn't remember, which I find hard to believe. Honestly, it feels hopeless."

We walked toward the water. The waves were small in this tucked-in little cove. Our toes were licked by the surf, just a tease and tickle, before it slid back down the sand into the bay.

"Well, it's a good thing you looped me in," I said, trying to lighten the mood. "I happen to be an Agatha Christie superfan."

Ben looked at me in surprise.

"**Masterpiece Mysteries**, featuring Miss Marple and starring Julia McKenzie, specifically," I clarified.

He grinned. "What about Hercule Poirot?"

"Those are fine, but Miss Marple has so many more layers than Inspector Poirot," I said. "Her cases are much more satisfying."

"How do you figure that?"

"Because Marple is an unassuming older lady who observes the world around her and deduces what happened, while Poirot is an actual detective," I said. "To have her sleuthing makes her character much more multidimensional while it's expected with him, because it's literally what he does."

"Huh. I never thought of it that way. We're going to have to have a movie marathon so I can compare the two."

"You're not just going to give me the win on this?" I asked.

"Librarian." He pointed to himself. "Research is required."

I laughed, delighted to have movie nights with him

to look forward to. "We're going to have to canvass the island like detectives."

"I've already searched the library archives, the old gazettes, but no luck so far," he said. "She wasn't an artist then, so there's no mention of her."

"I can talk to Stuart, the owner of the Tangled Vine Inn, where I'm catering on Fridays," I said. "He was friends with my parents and probably remembers Vineyard hot spots from back in the day. I can also check with my family. I have cousins and an aunt who used to own places out here. They might remember something. I'd ask my dad, but he won't be back for a couple of weeks. There's always the Portuguese club, too. They've been here for generations."

Ben hugged me close. "Careful. You're giving me hope, Samantha."

I tried to ignore the flush of pleasure I felt when he called me by my full name. No one called me that. It made it uniquely his. I was grateful it was dark out so Ben couldn't see me blush. It had been a long time since a guy had shown more than passing interest in me, and I was soaking it up like a wilted flower in a gentle rain.

We walked back to the spot where we'd left our shoes. We brushed off our feet as best we could before slipping our shoes back on. There was still some sand between my toes but I didn't care. I was too consumed with our quest.

I wondered what would happen if we managed to find his dad. What if he was here on the island already? The thought made me try to picture them meeting for the first time. I had a very **Field of Dreams** father-son reunion playing in my head, but then was that what Ben wanted?

He took my hand and we walked back through the narrow streets to his car.

"What will you say to your father when you see him?" I asked. I kept my voice light, or tried to.

"When I was a little kid, I just wanted him in my life," he said. "I used to daydream about him arriving at the door and sweeping me into his arms and holding me tight. I thought he'd be the one person in the whole wide world who understood me and loved me just for me."

My throat got tight, picturing him as a little boy, yearning for that unconditional love.

"Then, when I was a teenager, I pictured tracking him down and punching him right in the mouth," he said. "I was so angry."

"I understand that," I said. Having been an angry teen myself, this made perfect sense to me.

"I mean, I love my grandparents, and they provided a very loving and happy home for me, but when everyone else has parents and your mother can't be bothered to be a mother and you don't even know your father's name . . . yeah, I was pissed."

We turned onto Water Street. I let go of his hand to allow a couple of teenagers to pass between us. I was charmed when he immediately reached for my hand again, folding his fingers around mine in a warm grip.

"And now?" I asked. "How do you feel now?"

"Not angry," he said. "And I don't have any illusions that he'll want me in his life. I'm fairly certain Moira never told him about me, otherwise I assume he'd have shown up in my life at some point."

I waited while he thought it over.

"I guess what I want to know is, Do I look like him?" he asked. "I know I have some of my mother's features, but where did the rest of it come from? Do I have his eyebrows? His ears? Does my love of pickle, bacon, and peanut butter sandwiches come from him?"

"I think that just means you're weird," I said. I was trying to keep it light because, honestly, he was breaking my heart.

Ben laughed and my shoulders dropped in relief. I had never had to face these questions. Despite my parents' divorce, I had never doubted their love for me, never, not once. Sure, my dyslexia had been a challenge for all of us, but my parents had supported me to the best of their abilities. They hired specialists, tutors, reading coaches, even a counselor when the emotional toll became too much. And I knew where I came from, that I looked mostly like my dad but with my mom's slim nose, her long-fingered hands, and her tenacious personality. My mom and I chatted every Sunday on the phone, and when I'd lived in Boston, we did brunch every other week. I had the sudden urge to call her just to thank her for being such a loving mom.

We arrived at the car, and Ben opened the door for me. I slid into the passenger seat, moving the cheesecake to the floor. He shut the door after me and strolled around to the driver's side.

When he took his seat, he glanced at me, and his look was rueful.

"I hope this wasn't a downer of a first date," he said. "I don't usually overshare like that."

Well, didn't that make me feel special? I didn't know what to say, so I leaned across the console and put my mouth on his, saying with a kiss what I couldn't say with words.

He didn't move, letting me take control just like I had let him before. It was intoxicating. I pressed my mouth against his. I heard him swallow. I put my hand on his shoulder, to pull him closer and to steady myself as I deepened the kiss. I liked the shape of his lips and the way they fit mine.

When I parted my lips, encouraging him to do the same, I heard him grunt. The muscles of his shoulder bunched under my fingers, as if he was really trying to rein himself in. That simply wouldn't do. I slid my tongue into his mouth, seeking the taste of him.

Ben's control snapped. Ha! He reached for me with both hands and hauled me up against him as much as our seats would permit. His large hand pressed against my back while his other hand cradled my head, tilting it just enough to open the kiss wide. Heat and desire began to sizzle inside me, and I shifted restlessly, trying to get even closer.

The piercing honk of a horn sounded, and we both jumped. Ben didn't let me go but glanced out the window. I turned my head and followed his gaze. A car alarm was blaring and its lights flashing. It was three cars away, and a man was standing beside it, desperately pressing on his key fob while his wife looked exasperated beside him.

"Excellent timing there," I said. I pressed my forehead into his shoulder, trying to calm my racing heart.

"Yeah," he agreed. He leaned close and kissed me quick. Then he let me go and turned to start the car. I slumped against my seat, and he glanced at me and winked.

It was a wicked wink that made me blush, but it also reassured me that what I was feeling, this crazy, giddy, attraction, wasn't one-sided. He was feeling it, too.

We arrived at the house twenty minutes later. It was just getting dark, and the porch light was on. I could see the light on up in Tyler's room. I wondered if I needed to tell him we were home or if he was too deep into his video games and wouldn't notice either way. Dilemma.

I climbed out of the car before Ben could reach my door. He took my free hand, as I had the bag with the cheesecake in the other. We walked up the walkway, and I could feel first-date awkwardness hitching a ride with us.

Did I invite him in? What if he thought he was spending the night? That was a no-go. I was not having a man over with my little brother in the house. Too weird, and I was pretty sure Dad and Stephanie would be unhappy.

Still, I wasn't ready for the night to end, and we had cheesecake. If Ben left, I would probably eat the whole slice myself as a delicious substitute for sex. Which was a terrible choice because the cake would do my already bottom-heavy ass no favors, and the satisfaction would be temporary, ending when the cheesecake was gone, unlike a good orgasm, which could leave me sated until—oh, who was I kidding? If the man made love as well as he kissed, I'd never get enough of him.

"Can I make you some coffee?" I asked. "It would go well with dessert."

"Sounds great," he said. "After all, we need to fortify."

He held up his other hand. It was the book from the beach. Even on the inside my grin felt huge. I'd been hoping he'd remember, but I didn't want to be pushy. Truly, the man could have read the phone book to me and I would have been ecstatic, but picking up where we left off was so much better.

I let go of his hand and unlocked the front door. I

stepped inside and he followed. I closed the door behind us. The blast of music and the thumping sounds of someone stomping on the floor came from above. Tyler was practicing his dance moves. Not exactly the romantic vibe I'd been hoping for.

"We could read on the porch," Ben suggested.

I nodded. "I'll make the coffee and bring it out."

"I'll help."

He didn't help. Instead, he distracted me. He was a solidly built man who took up quite a lot of real estate in our small kitchen, which made maneuvering around him a challenge.

It did not help that his hands seemed to be everywhere when he brushed the hair off my shoulder as he reached around me to grab the coffee out of the cupboard that I indicated, or when he cupped my hip to slide me to the side so he could open the silverware drawer for forks for the cheesecake and spoons for the coffee. When he stood directly behind me to reach over me to the shelf where Stephanie kept the large wooden tray, I inadvertently—I swear—leaned back so that I was pressed against him from thigh to chest.

He dropped the tray and it clattered to the floor. Oops.

Chapter Fifteen

Neither of us moved to pick up the tray. The music and stomping upstairs did not skip a beat. I could feel the heat of Ben at my back, and I pressed the curve of my derriere right where I knew it would get his attention. Honestly, I felt a little crazy, like a cat in heat.

Ben let out a hiss and his big hands landed on my hips. For one delicious second, he pulled me in tight and then pushed my hair to the side, and his lips landed on the curve of my neck. It was my turn to hiss. He let out a low chuckle that rumbled in his chest against my back.

The beep of the coffee maker broke the spell. Ben let me go, and I reluctantly moved away to pour the coffee.

"Do you think there's something about us that we keep setting off alarms?" he asked.

I laughed and turned to face him. The look in his blue-gray eyes smoldered, and the laughter dried up in my throat.

"I'm pretty sure it's you," I said. This time I did fan myself.

"And here I was going to say it's you," he said. He

mimicked my hand fanning and I laughed again. I couldn't remember the last time being with a man had felt so easy.

Even with my closest friends, like Em, I felt self-conscious about my dyslexia and the weird ways it cropped up in my life, but with Ben I simply felt okay. His acceptance was so completely without judgment or reservation. I wondered if his mother had taught him that outlook, or maybe it was self-taught from growing up with an artist. Either way, I appreciated it so much.

He plated the cheesecake while I prepared our coffee. He handed me the book and picked up the tray. I led the way to the front porch. We chose to sit beside each other on the love seat. There was a reading lamp on his side, which I was certain was there for Stephanie to read in the evening on the porch. The sound of Tyler's music was mercifully muted.

We sipped coffee and shared the cheesecake. Ben pushed the last bite to me and I let him. Very gracious of me, I know.

We settled back into the soft cushions, and Ben reached for the book. He opened it and held it with one hand, lifting his other arm up, inviting me in. I curled up into his side, and we both put our feet on the coffee table, relaxing into the space as if it had been made just for us. I didn't think I'd ever felt as content as I did in that moment.

"Ready?" he asked.

I nodded, eager to listen.

His voice was deep and resonant, painting pictures with the words that invited me through the portal he spoke of, and I was happy to follow wherever his words led me.

The banter between the hero and heroine made me laugh, and the angst of the heroine's inner struggle spoke to me. I knew how she felt, an outsider, trying to find her way in a world that could be cold and cruel. But the hero understood her, he was there for her, despite his own pain. My heart broke for him as he tried to leave his past behind and find something new with her.

The sky darkened. Streetlights popped on. Pedestrians passed by on their way home from dinner or visits with friends. Ben read on, pausing only now and then to glance at me after a funny line or a particularly poignant scene.

I nestled into his warmth as the summer night cooled. His hand moved up and down my arm in a soothing motion that didn't actually soothe as much as it made me aware of him. The rough rub of his calloused fingers on my skin, the masculine scent of him, the slow rise and fall of his chest as he breathed. I felt as if this was exactly where I was supposed to be.

The heroine of the story was in Paris, and as Ben read, I could see the lights of the city, feel the cool air, and revel in the moment she and her companion decided to celebrate what had been a disastrous night for her by going to the top of the Eiffel Tower. I had never been to Paris, but the author's words put me there.

When the couple slow danced on the top of the tower, listening to Édith Piaf sing, I pressed closer to Ben as if I was in the story with them. His voice dropped as he described the heroine, taking the initiative to kiss the man she was with even though he wasn't the man she had come to Paris to find.

My own heart hammered in my ears, and I felt the heroine's desire bubble up inside of me as if it were my own, wooed by Ben's voice as he lingered on certain words, drawing out the feelings of the characters and igniting my own longing for this man sitting beside me.

When the scene ended, Ben paused. He glanced at me, and I saw the same heat in his gaze that I knew must have been in mine.

"Oh hell," he said.

He tossed the book onto the seat of the chair beside us and pulled me up onto his lap. I didn't even have a chance to get settled before his mouth was on mine and he was kissing me as if I was everything he had ever wanted in life.

I knew exactly how he felt. My hands dug into his wavy dark hair and I marveled at its softness beneath my fingers. His clean-shaven face was already sprouting stubble, and the rough rub against my skin kicked my pulse into high gear. His lips moved from my mouth to that sweet spot behind my ear and then slid down the side of my throat to nestle in the curve of my shoulder.

A moan escaped from my lips, and I heard him hum in response as his mouth moved lower to the exposed skin above the neckline of my dress. I arched my back, wanting more.

"Ahem."

I didn't register the new sound. Nothing could penetrate the haze of lust that had engulfed me.

"Ahem."

I would have ignored it, but Ben didn't. Instead, his mouth left my skin. I felt feverish in the cool night air as he raised his head. He looked past me toward the front door, and seeing the chagrin on his face, I turned.

Standing with his arms over his chest, looking like a dad who was busting his kid for breaking curfew, stood Tyler.

"Now that I've got your attention," he said. There was a laugh tucked into his voice. "I need to ask what your intentions are toward my sister, Ben."

Ack!

I rolled off Ben's lap with all the grace of a turtle stuck on its back.

"Tyler!" I squawked. "What are you doing out here?" I tried to sound indignant, as if I hadn't been the one caught making out on the front porch.

"Protecting my sister's virtue," Tyler said.

That surprised a laugh out of me. My virtue had been gone for a while.

"We were just reading," I said. This was, quite possibly, the most ridiculous thing I had ever said for a variety of reasons.

"I could see that," Tyler said. His tone was as dry as toast, and Ben snorted.

"Face it, Samantha, we're busted," Ben said. He put his hand on my back in a reassuring gesture.

I glanced at him to see if he was mad at the interruption. Instead, he was smiling. **Smiling!** He turned back to Tyler, looking duly chastened.

"My intentions toward your sister are honorable," he said. He raised his free hand in the air as if making a pledge. "I promise."

"This . . . Tyler . . . you can't just . . ." I sputtered. Truly, I had no words.

"I'll leave you to say your good nights then," Tyler said. He looked at me. "You have ten minutes, Sis. Don't make me come back out here."

Sis. It was still jarring to hear him call me that, and he took advantage of my surprise and stepped back inside, closing the door behind him.

I stared open-mouthed at the house. When I turned to Ben, I blinked as if I could not believe what had just happened.

"Did my little brother just chaperone me?" I asked.

"Yup," he said.

He stood up. "Good thing, too." He tucked my hair behind my ear. "It would be awfully easy to get carried away with you."

And just like that the heat was back. It shimmered in between us like something magical, and I wondered if Tyler was really going to time me. How carried away could we get in ten minutes?

"Better not risk it," Ben said as if he could read my mind. He pulled me in and enveloped me in a hug that did not assuage the rampaging lust in my heart. "I'll see you tomorrow?"

"Yes," I whispered in his ear. "And bring the book."

He grinned. "That's my girl."

The idea of being his girl made my insides flutter. I leaned up and kissed him, trying not to linger and failing.

"Ahem." This time the clearing of the throat came from the open window overlooking the porch.

I broke the kiss and pressed my forehead to Ben's collarbone. Tyler was killing me. Had I been single and living alone, I would definitely invite Ben to stay the night, but I wasn't. As I walked him to his car, I tried to tell myself this was better. We were taking it slow. If it all blew apart early on, I would have fewer regrets.

Yeah, right. I also might murder my little brother.

The thought caught me off guard. I had a brother. I mean, I'd always known I had a brother, but I'd always sidelined him as a pesky younger half brother and had never let him in my life as an active participant. To my surprise, I discovered I kind of appreciated his ham-fisted attempt to look out for me.

"Good night, Samantha." Ben kissed me once more and then climbed in his car and drove away. I missed him before he reached the end of the street.

I turned and walked back to the house. I locked the door and switched off the porch light. I found Tyler sitting at the kitchen table eating the largest bowl of ice cream I'd ever seen, and it was covered in whipped cream and rainbow sprinkles.

"How does that fit into your narrow margin of acceptable foods?" I asked.

"Ice cream is a food group all its own," he said. He pushed the bowl toward me in an unspoken gesture of sharing.

I took a spoon out of the drawer and sat down next to him. I dug into the mound of gooey deliciousness and popped it into my mouth. We ate silently until the bowl was empty. Tyler took our spoons and the empty bowl and rinsed them out in the sink.

"Are you in love with him?" he asked. His voice cracked in the middle, and he shifted awkwardly on his feet as if he didn't like asking but felt he had to.

I had no idea what to say.

Chapter Sixteen

"It's a bit early to know," I said. I thought about how Ben made me feel when I was with him, and I added, "But I like him an awful lot."

He nodded. He stared at his shoes. "Are you mad that I interrupted you guys?"

I felt my face get warm. I had no idea how far things might have gone if Tyler hadn't appeared.

"Um, no," I said. "I mean I guess I appreciate that you were looking out for me."

"Yeah?" he asked.

"Yeah," I said. I was surprised by how much I meant it. "I've never had anyone do that before."

"Well, it was your first date," he said. He sounded as prim and disapproving as a spinster. "No need to rush things."

I thought about the pull I felt for Ben every time he was near. It didn't feel rushed so much as it felt right, but I couldn't explain that to a fourteen-year-old. He'd discover it for himself soon enough. Hopefully not on my watch.

"You're very wise, Tyler Gale," I said.

"Are you mocking me?" he asked.

It was there in his eyes, the ones exactly like my own. How guarded he was. How much he didn't want to be hurt by me.

"No," I said.

I got up from my seat and crossed the kitchen to stand beside him. Then I hugged him. It was disconcerting to have my head barely reach his shoulder. He stood frozen for a second and then hugged me back.

"You're a really good brother," I said.

I felt his chest swell beneath my cheek.

"You're an okay sister," he said.

I stepped back and gaped at him. And here I thought we'd been bonding. "Just okay?"

"Well, you'd be awesome if you'd teach me to drive," he countered.

"You're fourteen," I protested.

"Almost fifteen," he argued. "And how old were you when you stole that car?"

I gasped. "You know about that?"

"Are you kidding?" He turned and led the way out of the kitchen. I shut off the lights as we went through the house to the stairs. "Everyone knows about that. It was the talk of Oak Bluffs for years."

"For the record, I was fifteen," I said.

"So, still underage," he said.

"I am not teaching you how to drive," I said. I tried to sound as if this was my final word on the subject.

"I'll do the dishes for the rest of the month," he bargained.

"No."

"I'll take out the trash."

"You do that anyway."

"Fine, I'll do all the laundry."

I paused in front of my bedroom door. Now I had him.

"Oh, even my delicate unmentionables that have to be hand washed?"

He made a pained face as if I'd asked him to pull a tick off my butt. He was clearly wrestling with this one, and I was sure I was going to win.

"Okay," he said. "I can use salad tongs or something."

I barked out a laugh. "You are not using salad tongs on my undies."

He stood in the doorway of his room, which was next to mine, and clasped his hands in a pleading gesture. "Please, Sam? I'll be your best friend."

"I already have a best friend."

"Aw, come on, why not?" he asked.

"Because of a thousand reasons," I said.

"Like what?"

"We can start with it's dangerous, we might wreck the car, I have no idea how to teach someone to drive,

Dad and Stephanie definitely did not have this on the approved list of activities for us to share, and because if something happened to you, I'd never forgive myself," I said.

"That's only five reasons," he protested.

I blew out a breath. Were all teenagers this tenacious?

"Five **big** reasons," I said.

"Just take me out for a practice run in a parking lot," he negotiated. "If it doesn't go well, I'll never ask you again."

"Why don't you have Dad teach you? Or your mom?" I asked.

"Dad says you broke him," he said. "Something about blowing through a red light and having his life flash before his eyes. And Mom is too nervous. She tried to take me once and she started to hyperventilate. You're my only hope, Obi-Wan."

"I'll think about it," I said.

He jumped up and down.

"Thinking about it is not a yes," I said.

"But it's also not a no. G'night, Sam." He jumped into his room and slammed the door before I could say another word.

"Good night," I called through the closed door.

I went into my room and kicked off my shoes and hung up the dress. I glanced at the clock on my nightstand and noticed it was almost midnight. Huh. Ben and I must have been reading for hours. I felt a thrill zip through me.

Oh, I knew I had only been listening to him read and not actually reading myself, but it made me wonder if maybe I'd enjoy listening to other books being read aloud. My mother had tried to get me to listen to audiobooks before but my busy brain seemed to resist and my attention usually wandered, forcing me to backtrack and try to figure out where I'd tuned out. It was too much work to constantly catch myself, and I'd lost interest. But maybe it was worth another try.

I got ready for bed and was just slipping under the covers when my phone chimed with an incoming call. I grabbed my phone, wondering who would call this late and worried that it might be an emergency. Maybe Dad and Stephanie forgot about the time change. Ben's name flashed on the screen and I answered.

"Hey," I said.

"Hey," he replied. "I just wanted to make sure you weren't in too much trouble with your chaperone."

"Well, he didn't ground me, if that's what you mean."

"Good," he said. "Actually, it was just an excuse so I could call you."

Warmth bloomed inside of me.

"Oh?"

"I can't sleep," he said.

"Me neither," I said. It wasn't a lie given that I hadn't actually tried yet.

"I always read myself to sleep, but I didn't want to read ahead without you," he said.

"That would be an unforgivable offense."

"I thought so, too," he said. I could hear the rustle of pages in the background. "Where were we?"

"Kissing on top of the Eiffel Tower," I said.

"Ah, yes." I could hear the smile in his voice. "Ready?"

I settled back against my pillows and put the phone on speaker. "Yes."

Ben resumed the story right where we'd left off. And just like that I was in Paris again and it was beautiful.

Tyler and I arrived at the library bright and early. This was no small feat given that I had stayed up until the wee hours of the morning listening to Ben read. When we both started yawning, we called it a night but it was with much reluctance.

As Tyler trotted off to robotics, I looked for Em. She was standing in front of a book display, arranging the books in what I assumed was an attempt to grab the attention of readers. I glanced at the sign above the shelf. It read **Travel Books**. The font was surprisingly easy to read, and the banner included pictures of famous places from all over the world. Perfect for summer.

"Nice display," I said. I saw a book with a picture of the Eiffel Tower on it, and my mind flitted back to the novel Ben was reading to me. After some relationship turmoil, our heroine had left Paris and was en route to Italy. I couldn't wait to hear more.

"Thanks," Em said. "Is the sign okay?" She pointed to it and I nodded. She gave me a shy glance and said, "I've been reading up on how to make things easier for people with dyslexia to read. It said to use sans serif fonts and inter-letter and character spacing of thirty-five percent."

I didn't say anything. I couldn't. Suddenly, my throat had closed up and my eyes burned.

"Are you all right?" Em asked. "I didn't offend you, did I?"

"No," I said. My voice came out wobbly. I glanced at the ceiling. "I just have something in my eye."

She caught on then that I was having a moment. She walked to the reference desk and came back and handed me a tissue.

"Thanks," I said. I dabbed my eyes and blew my nose. "And thanks for that, too." I gestured to the display. "It means a lot."

She looked pleased. Her hair was in a messy bun and she was wearing her favorite cardigan over a pale yellow dress. The bandage on her neck had been replaced by a smaller adhesive bandage.

"Have you heard anything?" I asked.

Her smile slipped away and she put her hand over the bandage. "Not yet."

"I'm sure it's going to be all right," I said.

She nodded quickly, too quickly, and I knew she was

worried. She shook her head and then glanced around
the room to see who was about. The reference area was
empty—not that I was looking for Ben, but I absolutely
was.

"Enough about that," she said. "How was the date?
Did he pick you up on his motorcycle?"

I laughed. That would have been something in the
red dress. I'd have had to ride sideways.

"No," I said. "He had a car."

"Where did you go? What did you do? Come on, tell
me everything," she said. "I have to live through you
since I haven't had a date in forever."

"We need to fix that," I said. "You're too awesome
to sit on the shelf."

"Can you stay on island after the summer?" she
asked. "You're very good for my self-esteem."

"Likewise," I said. I then gave her the highlight reel
about the date, not sharing the personal information
that Ben had told me since I didn't feel it was my
place. She did get a solid belly laugh out of Tyler
busting us for making out on the porch.

"I like that kid," she said.

"Me, too," I agreed. I was a little surprised by how
much I meant it. "So, listen." I paused. Clearly, Em was
my friend, and after seeing her display, I knew she
wouldn't judge me, but I did so hate feeling vulnerable.
"I, um, I was wondering, how do I go about checking
out audiobooks?"

She tipped her head to the side, considering me. With her overly large glasses she looked like a friendly, inquisitive little bird, and yet I still felt stupid for asking.

"I mean, I know, it's not like really reading," I said. "But I've recently discovered that listening to books is kind of cool."

"What do you mean it's not like reading?" she asked. Her pale green eyes flashed with something that looked like indignation.

"Well, because I'm not actively reading, you know, single-mindedly with my eyes on the words and shutting everything else out."

"So what?" she asked. She looked fierce. "Sixty-five percent of the population learns visually, while thirty-five percent are auditory learners. You just happen to be one of those."

I had not known this statistic and it immediately made me feel better.

"I'll tell you something else," she said. "People who learn words by reading them are shit at pronunciation."

I burst out laughing, which I was certain was what she intended.

"It's true," she said. "I can't tell you how many times I've embarrassed myself by pronouncing a word wrong because I learned it by reading. Audiobooks prevent that and you still learn the theme and all that other junk."

"Junk, huh?"

She shrugged. "You know what I mean. How you connect to a story is your choice, whether it's from reading or listening or watching."

"All right," I said. "I'm sold. Show me what you've got."

Em took me to the computer catalog. She sat down and walked me through the Cape Libraries Automated Materials Sharing or, as locals called it, the CLAMS online catalog system, searching my preference for audiobooks. She then used my library card to download a volume by the same author Ben was reading to me.

As she pointed out other books I might enjoy, I surreptitiously glanced around the library looking for Ben. No sign of him. Huh.

"Ben is in a meeting with the Friends of the Library," she said.

"Oh." I felt my face get warm and she smiled. "Did you want me to tell him you were looking for him?"

"No, not necessary," I said. "I have to go to the store and prep for Friday's happy hour at the inn."

"Do you need me to help that night?" she asked. She rose from her seat.

"No, but thank you. Stuart said he'd have some of his regular staff available." She looked disappointed so I quickly added, "But I'd love it if you'd come and hang out. It's always nice to see a friendly face, plus Finn Malone is working as a bartender and I know he'd love to catch up."

She cheered up immediately. "All right, I'll be there."

I noticed that while we'd been talking, she hadn't touched the bandage on her neck again. It was as if she'd forgotten about it. It occurred to me that she needed something else to think about. I thought the mystery of who Ben's father was might be of interest. I'd ask him first, of course, but I was hoping he'd allow me to include Em. It could be what she needed to take her mind off her worries.

"Excellent," I said. "See you later?"

"I'll be here." She sounded resigned, as if her life was a set routine with no deviation. Or maybe she was worried about the results of the biopsy and she was thinking she was here but not for much longer. Either way, I was concerned about her.

I gave her a quick hug. "Thanks for your help."

"You bet." She turned back to her display and I headed for the stairs.

I had just exited the building and was halfway down the walkway when I heard someone shout my name. I thought it might be Tyler. It wasn't.

Ben came striding toward me. He had a rolled-up piece of paper in one hand and he looked full of purpose. Oh my.

"What are you doing tonight?" he asked.

My eyebrows rose. So eager! Wasn't that flattering?

"Listening to my brother torture the neighborhood with his music while he practices his sick dance moves," I said. "Why? Do you have a better offer?"

"Yes," he said. He held up the papers. "I came in early this morning and went through the digital archives. I made a list of restaurants that were open on the island in 1989. I then checked to see which ones were still open, and it's a much shorter list, but still, I'm going to stop at each one and ask if they have any record of my mother being a waitress there. Come with me?"

"Yes!" I cried. My inner sleuth was loving this. "However, I am going to require compensation for my time."

It was his turn for the eyebrow lift. "Okay." He dragged out the word. He studied my face as if trying to figure out what I was thinking. "How much?"

"Two chapters," I said. "And no quitting in the middle of them."

"Two?" he scoffed. Then he grinned, and it made my head spin. "You could have gotten three."

"Ack!" I cried in mock dismay. "I knew I should have asked for more."

A couple of patrons came up the walkway, and Ben took me by the arm and said, "I'll walk you to your car. Please tell me you parked out of sight of the building."

"I am in the far corner," I said. "Why?"

"Because I'm planning to kiss you, and I need to know if I have to drag you behind the book drop or not," he said.

His voice was that gruff growl that made my heart bang around in my chest as if looking for an escape hatch to get to him. I laughed but the intensity in his gaze clued me in that he meant business.

"Well then." I glanced at the Gale family SUV. "I think if you walk me to my car, we'll be all right."

He fell into step beside me and put his hand on the small of my back as if he just had to touch me. I wasn't used to that, to being the object of someone's desire so blatantly. It was intoxicating stuff but also terrifying.

I was afraid I was falling too fast for a guy with whom I likely had no future. I had no idea where I was going when summer ended. I might have to pull up stakes and move to another city for a restaurant job, and I definitely did not want to have to drag a broken heart along with me. I had thought I could keep this just a summer fling, but I could tell my feelings were beginning to get engaged. This was not good.

"What are you thinking?" he asked as we stopped beside my car. "I can practically hear the cogs in your brain churning."

"Honestly?" I asked. I leaned against the car and gazed up at him.

"Preferably," he said.

"I want to be clear that this"—I paused to gesture between us—"is only for the summer." I bit my lip. I felt stupid saying it out loud, but I needed to be clear that these weeks were all I had to offer. I was trying to protect myself, obviously, but him, too.

He nodded. "Is there any particular reason this came up right now?"

"Maybe."

He leaned down until his face was level with mine and he met my gaze. "Care to share?"

"No," I said. I tipped my head back and stared at the big beautiful blue sky. Why had I decided this was the moment to have this chat?

"Is this because the balance in our relationship, excuse me, our summer situation is off?"

"What do you mean?" I asked.

"You're my friend and you're helping me find my dad," he said. "But I'm not really helping you with anything, so the scale is unbalanced."

Friend? Really? I tried not to dwell.

"I didn't really think of this as a transactional relationship," I said.

"No, just a short one." He grinned at me to let me know he was teasing. He leaned beside me and said, "What's something you want?"

You. The answer in my mind was swift and sure. Thankfully, I did not say it out loud. Instead, I said, "A job."

"Hmm." He scratched the scruff on his chin. "Not owning a restaurant, I can't help with that. What other dreams do you have?"

"I want to write a cookbook," I said. I clapped my

hand over my mouth. "Forget I said that. I never said it. It's a dumb idea."

"What? No!" he cried. "That's brilliant."

"Um, shockingly, writing isn't my strong suit," I said. "And I'd have to jot down the recipes from scratch by myself, because my vovó did everything from memory. She never wrote anything down. I want the cookbook to be all of the recipes she taught me while growing up, but like I said she kept them all in her head and she left them all in mine." I tapped my temple with my finger. "Although I appreciate your enthusiasm."

"Samantha," he said. His voice was a low sexy drawl, and it curled around my insides just like his hands reached out and pulled me up against him. "I can be your scribe and write down your recipes while you cook." He leaned down and kissed me, catching me with my mouth open, which he took full advantage of. When I was thoroughly dazed and bemused, he leaned back from me and deployed one of his highly suggestive, wicked winks. "I'll be your secretary and your sous-chef, if need be."

Oh wow.

Chapter Seventeen

After a day spent day dreaming about my cookbook, I
was back in the library parking lot at five to pick up Tyler
from camp. He climbed into the passenger seat, flinging
his backpack into the foot well and looking like he wanted
to rip someone's head off. I was sensing a post-robotics
pattern here. But maybe he was just hangry.

"You all right?" I asked.

"Yeah."

It was the most loaded **yeah** I'd ever heard. I
wondered what my dad would have said if he were me.
When I thought back to my teen years and my sullen
moods, I remembered that my dad had pretty much
said nothing. I tried to do the same even though it's
not my nature to ignore a person who is clearly in the
throes of something.

I drove out of the lot and down School Street,
meandering through the narrow roads until I reached
our house. When I parked the car, Tyler grabbed his
bag and stomped into the house. There was no thank
you, no how was your day, no nothing.

As the door slammed behind him, I was pretty sure teenagers had been created as a warning for anyone contemplating parenthood. These were not the fun years. I had only to look at my own adolescence to know this was true.

In an effort to get the kid to chill out, I made plain pasta and garlic toast. Then, because I'm me, I grilled some linguica and made a side salad. He didn't have to eat it, but it was there if he dared step out of his food comfort zone.

"Tyler! Dinner!" I yelled.

"I'm right here," he said. He was standing behind me.

"Oh." I started.

He slouched into the kitchen and threw himself into one of the dining chairs. He looked at the food on the table and grunted.

"You made plain pasta?"

I shrugged. "You seemed to need comfort food."

"Thanks." I wasn't sure if he meant it or if good manners had just been nagged into him by Stephanie.

"You're welcome," I said. We dished our food and I noticed he took some of the sausage and a little bit of the salad. Not enough to keep a hamster alive, but I still figured it was a win. Then he drowned it in ranch dressing. I held back my sigh. Barely.

"Want to tell me what's wrong?" I asked.

He stabbed one of the rigatoni as if it was an

enemy's eyeball. Then he dropped his fork and looked at me. "It's you."

"Me?" I choked on a cherry tomato. I coughed it down and asked, "What did I do? Is this because I won't teach you to drive?"

"No," he said. "I just heard from Ryan that you're teaching a teen cooking class at the library."

"So?" I asked.

"So, a bunch of the robotics kids have signed up," he said. His voice was very dramatic.

I chewed carefully, considering why this might be a problem, and came up with nothing. "I'm not getting why you care."

"Because you're my sister," he said.

"And this is a problem because . . . wait, it'll come to me," I said. I frowned in concentration. "I know— you've told everyone that you don't have parents, that you were spawned by a pine cone and you don't want me to show up and ruin the narrative?"

"Hi-la-ri-ous." He shoved a forkful of pasta into his mouth. I waited but he didn't say anything more.

"My dude, Em asked me to teach a class on how to make your own fast food, to celebrate the middle of the summer reading program," I said. "I didn't think it was a big deal. Do you want me to cancel?"

"No. Yes. Maybe."

"You're going to have to pick one," I said.

"It's just . . ." He dropped his fork and ran his hands through his hair.

My stomach clenched and I realized there was only one reason my brainiac brother wouldn't want me anywhere near his friends. He was ashamed of me. My dyslexia. My neurodivergent brain probably made me a freak in his overachiever eyes. I couldn't really blame him. He definitely moved in an elevated circle of smarty pants and I would tarnish the rep he had established.

"You don't have to say it," I said. "I get it. I know I'm not like you and your crowd."

"Duh," he said.

Ouch!

I glanced down at my plate. I was not going to cry. He was a teen. What his peers thought meant everything to him. I wasn't going to be the one to embarrass him. I'd save that task for my dad with his goatee and skinny jeans.

"I mean, I'm barely hanging onto my popularity as it is after that fiasco with Amber," he said.

"Right." I nodded. I took a sip of my water, hoping it would dislodge the hard lump in my throat.

"Having the cool Gale sibling razzle-dazzle everyone with her culinary genius will leave me with zero street cred," he said. "I'll look like the lame nerd that I am."

"Sure, I get . . . Hold on. What did you say?"

"Yeah, you're like a legend on the island," he said.

"Do you have any idea what it's like following in your footsteps?"

"But I was always in trouble," I said. My role in the family had always been that of the black sheep, the problem child, the disappointment, and even though I was a grown-up and had put years between teenage and adult me, I still cringed at a few of my more brainless exploits.

"Which makes you supercool," he said. He shook his head as if mystified by this. That made two of us.

I sat back in my chair, absorbing the fact that the taint of shame I'd assumed my brother felt about my dyslexia and troubled youth didn't exist. He wasn't ashamed of me. Huh.

"That's messed up," I said.

"Tell me about it," he agreed.

"So, that's why you don't want me to teach the class?" I asked.

"I know it's stupid," he said. "But Sophie already talks about you all the time, and I just can't compete."

I glanced down at my plate, trying to hide my smile. My little brother thought I was cool. Mind blown. This was so not what I'd been expecting.

"Well, I'm pretty sure she doesn't want to date me. Tell you what," I said. "I would feel really terrible canceling on Em right now. She has a lot going on and I don't want to add to that."

He sighed. "I know. I shouldn't have asked."

"But I'm going to need a sous-chef," I said.

He held up his fork, which was loaded with pasta. "I literally can't even make microwave popcorn without burning it."

"Good," I said. "That stuff is nasty."

"You're missing my point."

"No, I'm not," I said. "You just haven't had me to teach you before. It's time you started learning Vovó's recipes. We'll practice cooking together and then when I do the program, you can cook with me. You can be the rock star."

He stared at me across the table. "You'd do that?"

"Absolutely."

"Do I get to wear a chef coat?"

"I might be able to find one that will fit you."

He grinned, and a piece of dark green lettuce showed in his teeth. I grinned back. This sibling thing was so unexpectedly awesome.

In a crazy moment of unchecked magnanimity, I said, "And I'll teach you to drive."

"What?" he gasped. "Seriously?"

"Yes, but there will be rules. And you have to do everything I say," I said.

"I will. I promise."

He was so eager I wondered if I'd just been snookered. But then he smiled at me and I simply didn't care. I was going to teach my baby brother to drive. What an epic bonding experience this would be. And wasn't that exactly what Dad had hoped for? Besides, it was just driving. What could possibly go wrong?

"See you, Sam!" Tyler dashed through the living room on his way out the door.

"Hold it! Stop right there!" I pulled an earbud out, pausing the story. I was sitting on the couch, listening to the rom-com Em had downloaded for me while I waited for Ben. "Where are you going?"

"Out with some friends from robotics," he said. He paused by the door. "That's okay, right? Um . . . I mean . . . I could stay home if you want."

"No," I said. It was the first time I'd seen him go hang out with kids outside of camp. I sensed this was a very big deal.

"Who all is going?"

"Are you going parental on me now?" he asked.

"My dude, I've been cooking for you and chauffeuring you around, so I've already been doing the parental thing, thanks for noticing," I said. "I just need to know who you're with in case you go missing so I can choke the life out of them for letting something happen to my baby brother."

He held up a finger. "Not a baby."

"Little brother."

He shook his head. "Not little either."

"Fine. My younger brother," I said.

"It's Cameron, Sophie, Blake, and Hector." He was shifting on his feet, clearly ready to run. So, of course, I needed to torture him with more questions.

"Is Cameron a boy or a girl?" I asked.

"What does that matter?"

I rolled my hand, gesturing for him to answer.

"Girl," he growled.

"Okay," I said. "I just wanted to make sure Sophie wasn't outnumbered."

"Can I go now?"

"Be home by ten," I said. I gave him the same raised eyebrow look he'd given me when I went out with Ben.

"Of course." He bounced out the door, letting it slam shut behind him.

He'd been home every night since I arrived, and I'd been worried that his only friends lived inside his game system. It was weird to have him out and about even though I was going out myself.

On the one hand, I was ecstatic that he'd made in-person friends, but on the other hand, what if something happened to him? This was another new emotion for me in regard to my brother. Worry. I cared about him—a lot—and the weight of responsibility for him felt heavy.

I settled back in my chair and rewound the book. The readers were a man and a woman alternating as the book switched points of view. They were both good, really good, but they weren't Ben. I closed my eyes, listening, letting the story wash over me. I was a million miles away, figuratively speaking, in Phoenix, Arizona, where the book was set, when I felt a hand on my knee.

Naturally, I screamed. And not a little yelp but an ear-piercing, "kick out at the person standing over me, screeching like I was being assaulted" sort of scream. The person jumped back with his hands in the air.

Chapter Eighteen

I raised my fists in a fighter stance while my phone dropped from my lap to the floor.

"Sam, it's me," Ben said. His hands were still raised. "Just me."

"Oh, geez," I gasped, and pulled out my earbuds. "You scared the shit out of me."

I pressed my hand to my chest to try and calm my racing heart. I doubled over and my hair fell around my face. I'd been so lost in the story I hadn't heard him enter the house.

"I'm really sorry," he said. "Normally, I wouldn't have just walked in, but I could see you through the window, and you weren't answering my knock and I got worried. Those are some crazy self-defense moves you've got."

"Are you mocking me?" I asked through my curtain of hair.

"No," he said. He shook his head, but his eyes were glinting with suppressed laughter.

"Don't you dare laugh at me," I said. "I can still

kick you and I'm sneaky enough to do it when you won't see it coming."

"I have absolutely no doubt that you could kick my ass if you put your mind to it," he said. He sounded like he was trying to mollify a savage. Given how I'd leapt off the couch in attack mode, he wasn't totally wrong.

I rolled up to a standing position, tossing my hair back. Ben bent down and scooped up my phone. He glanced at the display. "You're listening to her other book."

"Yeah," I said. I put my earbuds in their case, feeling embarrassed, which was ridiculous.

Ben of all people would not judge me for listening to an audiobook. I just didn't want him to think I was doing it to impress him or anything.

"How is it?" he asked.

"I like listening to you read more," I said. Which was the truth. "You know, if you ever want to give up the glamorous library world, you could absolutely read books for a living."

"You mean like a voice actor?" he asked.

"Yes," I said.

He laughed, amused by the idea.

"You'd be brilliant," I insisted.

"I'll definitely keep that in my back pocket," he said. "Have you recovered from your scare?"

I nodded.

"Good." He held up the piece of paper with his list on it. He was wearing jeans, biker boots, and a charcoal gray T-shirt that highlighted his perfectly defined muscles. Truly, the man was not like any librarian I had ever seen before. "I figured we could start here in Oak Bluffs. Depending upon how far we get, we can tackle the other towns."

"Sounds good," I said. "I'm guessing Giordano's and the Ritz Cafe on Circuit Avenue are our starting places?"

He looked at me in surprise.

"What?" I asked. "Everyone knows they've been open since the thirties and forties, they're iconic. My dad was in a band in the eighties and they played the Ritz all the time. It's one of his claims to fame."

"Your dad is a musician?" he asked.

"Drummer. In his wild youth, before he became an insurance salesman," I said.

It hit me then when I said the words out loud that my dad's midlife crisis could be because he'd envisioned a different life for himself, and now that his kids were almost grown, he felt it was his last chance to be the musician he'd once dreamed of being. Huh.

We set out immediately. Walking through the quieter section of Oak Bluffs, I appreciated the scent of the summer roses on the evening air, the sound of the crickets, the murmur of conversations as we passed front porches. Despite the ever-revolving summer tourists who came and went, Oak Bluffs maintained its small-town feel, where the year-round people and the annual summer residents knew one another and looked out for one another. There was comfort in that. I knew if either Tyler or I were ever in trouble, there was a small army of people we could count on for help.

"What are you thinking?" Ben asked.

"That I've been away from here for too long," I said.

He seemed to understand the regret in my voice, and he held out his arm. I scooted up against his side and wrapped his arm around my shoulders. We walked through town like that until we reached our first destination.

Giordano's was packed with a wait line going out the door. Ben asked to talk to the manager, and the hostess's eyes went wide as if she feared a complaint.

"I just have a question about a former employee," he said.

She nodded, looking relieved, and disappeared. We cooled our heels in the front of the restaurant until a woman arrived. She carried herself with authority and greeted us with a smile.

"Hi, I'm Naomi, how can I help you?" she asked.

"This is a long shot, I know," Ben said. "But I was wondering if there's anyone who might remember a waitress who worked here in the summer of '89?"

He reached into his pocket and took out a photograph. He handed it to Naomi, who'd probably been a baby back then or, like me, not yet born.

She glanced at the photo and back at Ben. "I can

check and see if our personnel files go back that far. Do you have a name?"

"Moira Reynolds," he said.

Her eyes went wide. "The artist?"

He nodded.

She shook her head. "If she had worked here, I would know. That would be serious bragging rights, as in her portrait on the wall with flashing lights around it, you know what I'm saying?"

Ben nodded. "Oh, I know. She wouldn't have been famous back then, so maybe no one realized."

"It's possible," Naomi said. "Give me your number and I'll check the records and ask around."

"Thanks, I really appreciate it," he said. He took a business card out of his pocket and handed it to her.

"Can I ask why you want to know?" she asked.

Ben hesitated. I suspected he didn't want to share the details of his personal life and was conflicted about what to say. I didn't have these issues.

"We're librarians and we're doing research on people of consequence on the Vineyard before they were famous," I said. "For the library archives and all."

"Oh." Naomi gave Ben the once-over, and I knew she was thinking the same thing I'd been thinking earlier. The man didn't look like a librarian to her either. "That's awesome." She gave him a little wink. "I'll be in touch."

"Great, I appreciate it," he said. He took my arm and ushered me outside. "Quick thinking."

"Thanks," I said. "I feel that the quest for your father should be on a need-to-know basis, don't you think?"

"Definitely," he said. "The Vineyard is small and I don't need it getting back to Moira that I'm actually doing boots-on-the-ground recon until it becomes unavoidable."

"She doesn't know you're looking for your dad?" I asked.

"Not in an overt way," he said. "I think she's counting on me containing my search to old library archives and stuff, which have been a bust, since I have nothing to go on."

We walked down Circuit Avenue, around clusters of tourists and residents, toward the Ritz Cafe. We'd be lucky if we were able to get in given that this was the hot spot to catch live music in Oak Bluffs—or the whole island, for that matter.

Unsurprisingly, the Ritz was hopping. A rock band was playing, and it was standing room only. Ben and I squeezed in, muscling our way to the bar, where a harried bartender took our order.

"I don't know how anyone will hear us when we ask about your mom," I said.

"What?" Ben shouted over the music.

"Exactly," I replied.

We were crowded up against a wall. Ben put his arm around my front and stood at my back, letting me lean against him while we sipped our beers and enjoyed the show. The singer was a female. She had short, curly hair and full red lips. She was wearing a glittering dress and high heels, and she stalked in front of the band, her voice a bluesy combination of rock and spoken-word poetry. It was impossible not to bob my head to her groove.

We finished our beers, and when the band took a break, Ben leaned over the bar and asked to speak to the manager. The bartender shook his head.

"He's not here tonight," he said. "If you want, I can have him call you."

Ben handed him a business card. We left our empties on the bar and headed out the door. The night air was refreshingly cool after being in the crowd.

"I can't say that this feels very successful," he said.

"We might have better luck in the daytime when they're not so busy," I said. "Do you have any weekdays off?"

"I can probably manage one," he said.

"Excellent, we can hit the older restaurants in Edgartown like the Square Rigger and l'etoile," I said. "Of course, there's always Coop de Ville and Net Result in Vineyard Haven, too. We have a lot of places to check out. Don't give up yet."

We walked toward the large town green that was the first point of entrance to Oak Bluffs from the ferry. The tall gazebo was empty but kids were running across the grass, and several people were enjoying ice cream cones.

Again, Ben put his arm around my shoulders and pulled me close, then kissed the top of my head and said, "Thanks."

"For what?"

"The pep talk," he said. "I needed that."

He looked so forlorn. I just wanted to help him in any way I could. The thought of not knowing my dad, I couldn't conceive of it. Despite the divorce and his current midlife conundrum, my dad was one of my closest friends. I'd be lost without him.

"'I can't carry it for you, but I can carry you,'" I said. I waited to see if he'd recognize the quote.

"Samwise from **The Return of the King**." Ben looked impressed.

"Another movie that was better than the book," I said.

He gasped and staggered, leaning heavily on me. "Heresy! Although I have to say the **Lord of the Rings** movies were very, very good." He straightened up.

"And in all fairness, I never read the books," I said. "Or listened to them either."

"It appears you have a lot of listening to do, Samwise," he said.

The nickname made me smile but the reference to listening instead of reading made me feel dumb, less than, stupid. I felt my gut clench. How long before Ben, too, thought of me as Simple Sam?

In every relationship I'd ever been in, at some point

the boyfriend of the moment would find the burden of my dyslexia to be too much. It usually happened when the guy was embarrassed that I struggled to read a menu, or a meme he wanted to share, or in one case a grocery list—in my defense, that particular guy had terrible handwriting—and then the ghosting began.

I glanced at Ben out of the corner of my eye. Should I say something or let it pass? I didn't want our evening to be ruined by my insecurity, and I definitely didn't want to bring attention to my deficiencies, but I didn't want to pretend that nothing was wrong. I felt it was important that he understand how much my dyslexia had shaped me.

"I like that nickname," I said. I swallowed the lump in my throat. "It's much better than the one I got in high school when everyone found out I struggled to read."

He stopped walking and went very still. I could see he was bracing himself as if he expected a big wave to hit.

His voice was very soft when he asked, "What nickname was that?"

"Simple Sam," I said. I tipped my head back and stared up at the sky. "Kids can be very on point in their cruelty."

"Maybe some can," he snorted. "But not those kids."

I looked at him in surprise.

"You are one of the most complex people I've ever met," he said. "And I mean that in a good way. You have a memory that is like a vault, you can problem solve in ways that my tiny brain can't even come up with, you're wickedly funny and so damn resilient that I am in awe of you. Truly, whoever gave you that nickname was a moron, and if you happen to have a name and address, I'd be happy to go crack some skulls on your behalf."

I blinked. My throat was tight. Was that how he saw me? Really?

No. He's just being nice to you because he feels sorry for you. My inner critic was right there to slap away any positivity.

"You're very kind," I said.

"No, I'm not. You should see yourself the way I see you," he said. He turned so we were facing each other. "You are a culinary wizard precisely because your brain is wired completely differently. You intuit things that the rest of us can't even imagine because you are extraordinary."

I had no words. What he said meant so much to me that I simply couldn't speak. I rolled up on my toes, wrapped my arms around his neck, and hugged him tight. He was warmth and strength and kindness, and I just wanted to be absorbed into him. His arms slid around me, pulling me into him as if it was my special place.

I rested my head on his shoulder and said, "Thank you."

"Just stating the facts," he said. He propped his chin on my head.

A tear slipped out, melting into the fabric of his shirt. It was an amazing thing, the way this man made me see myself through his eyes. It humbled me. It made me want to return the favor, but the only way I could would be to help him find his dad. I didn't say this, however. Instead I leaned back to meet to his gaze.

"I like you," I said.

His smile was adorable. "I like you, too."

"No, I **really** like you," I said. It was as close as I could get to confessing the feelings that were simmering inside of me.

"Listen, I really like you, too," he said.

A thrill coursed through me that I immediately checked. This was a summer situation, nothing more. I was only here for another month and he was an interim director, not permanent. He'd be headed back to his academic job soon, too.

"Speaking of listening, you didn't happen to bring our book with you, did you?" I asked.

"Of course I did," he said. "I never go anywhere without something to read. It's in the top box on my bike."

"Yes!" This was some couple time I could get behind.

"Ready to go home?" he asked.

I glanced at the time on my phone. It was nine thirty. "Tyler is supposed to be home by ten. I should be there first."

"Understood." He turned up one of the paths that cut across the grass by the gazebo.

As we walked, I said, "Maybe if you told your mother you were actively looking for your father, she'd be more inclined to help you."

He looked unconvinced. "My mother can be . . ."

He didn't finish and I bit my tongue to keep from guessing, but adjectives like **difficult**, **stubborn**, and **mean** swirled around my brain.

Which was why I was surprised when he said, "Guarded."

I waited for him to explain.

"She's not on any social media, she doesn't grant interviews, she's reclusive, and she's fiercely protective of her privacy. Even when she's performing public art, like the lighthouse episode, she doesn't talk to the press."

Interesting. In a world where everyone seemed to want to have their voice heard twenty-four seven—even when they had nothing significant to say and were very angry if they didn't get their allotted fifteen minutes of fame—this was unexpected.

"Then I suspect she's going to freak out when she finds out that you're actually asking people about her and whom she might have been dating in 1989," I said.

"Understatement," he agreed. "But it's a risk I'm willing to take."

Chapter Nineteen

Three voice messages and two texts were on my phone when I pulled it out of my shoulder bag after my trip to the grocery store the next day. They were all from Em. I called her back immediately, my fingers trembling as I held my phone and asked Siri to call her.

"The results are back," she said. "From the biopsy."

"And?" I unloaded my canvas bags onto the counter.

"Dr. Ernst wants me to come in," she said. "She wants to talk to me in person. I got the message in the patient portal instead of the test results. What do I do, Sam?"

My heart dropped to my feet. This had to be bad. Really bad. As in, months-to-live bad.

"I'm sure it's fine," I bluffed. "She probably wants to talk to you in person so there's no miscommunication."

"Hmm. She could say, 'You're fine,' on a voicemail. Why does she want to do it in person?" Em persisted.

"It's probably just protocol," I said. "Biopsy results are complicated, you know, all that sciency stuff. She's being thorough." I wondered if I sounded like I knew what I was talking about, because I was slinging more bullshit than a politician.

"You're right," she said. She sighed in relief. "It's likely just standard operating procedure."

We were both silent, praying that this was true.

"Will you come with me?" Em asked at the same time I said, "What time is your appointment?"

"Ten tomorrow morning," she said as I said, "Of course I'll go with you."

We hung up a few minutes later. I waited a bit and then sent her a funny GIF of a hot male nurse taking temperatures. You do what you can.

When I picked up Tyler after robotics, I was standing by the car when he got out of class. The parking lot was mostly empty, so I figured this was as good a time as any to start teaching him to drive.

He looked at me quizzically, and I said, "Catch."

I tossed him the keys. His eyes went wide but he grasped them in his hand.

"Now?" he asked.

"Why not?"

The pure joy that lit his smile made me laugh. "Easy there, Speed Racer. We're going to take it slow."

He nodded and jumped into the driver seat. Was he even going to wait for me? I ran around the front of the car and climbed in the passenger's side.

"All right, what do you do first?"

"Crank the tunes!" He made a rock and roll sign with his hand and bobbed his head.

I made my face blank and lifted one eyebrow. "No."

"Just kidding," he said. "You adjust the seat and mirrors and buckle up."

I let out a breath. The kid was in robotics and he played video games. Surely his hand-eye coordination and basic grasp of machinery would make this easy peasy.

He started the car. And he started it again. The car let him know it was displeased.

"The engine's already running," I said.

"It's so quiet." He looked surprised. "I never noticed that before."

"Hmm." I pressed my lips together to keep from saying anything.

I wondered if I should send Dad and Stephanie a pic of this. Nah, they'd just worry, and that seemed cruel to do to them when they were on an epic trip.

We'd just gotten a message this morning with a picture of them in front of the ruins of the Acropolis. They looked happy and Dad, mercifully, had been wearing shorts and not those embarrassing jeans. He still had the chin hair, though. I wondered if Stephanie had managed to ditch the awful pants off a plane, boat, or train somewhere. I would have.

"All right, I parked facing out so all you have to do

is put it in drive and ease your way out of the parking spot," I said.

Tyler checked both ways four times. The lot was clear with only staff cars in the far corner, as tonight was one of the library's closed evenings. He stepped on the gas and we shot out of the spot. He slammed on the brakes and I felt the bite of my seat belt across my chest—that was going to leave a mark—as it kept me from slamming into the dash. I dropped back against my seat and blinked. Okay, maybe **Mario Kart** was not the best driving instructor.

He looked at me in horror. "Are you all right?"

"I'm fine," I said. "You?"

"Yeah, I'm okay," he said. But he was wide-eyed, pasty, and sweating.

"It's okay. Try it again," I said. "We're just going to go around the parking lot. We won't head out onto the open road because you're not old enough for your permit and the Martha's Vineyard police and I have a history, so we'll be keeping respectful boundaries."

"Good idea," he said. "We should work up to main roads."

No argument here.

This time he stepped on the gas and we eased into the lot. He overturned the wheel and then had to correct, which he also overdid. We made one very painful loop. And then another. Then I had him make the same loop but going in the opposite direction. By the time he stopped and put the car in park, we were both ready for me to take over.

"That was an excellent start," I said. "We'll just keep at it until you get comfortable."

He shut the engine off and turned to face me. "Thanks, Sam. That was like a million times better than when Mom attempted to teach me the basics."

"You're welcome," I said. I climbed out of the car and saw Ben across the parking lot. He was getting onto his motorcycle. He didn't see us and I suddenly felt ridiculously shy. Did I shout his name and wave? Pretend I didn't see him? Ugh.

This was stupid. I was here picking up my brother. Ben knew I did this every day. It wasn't as if I was stalking him or that he would even think of me stalking him. Still, I felt weird.

Our conversation from yesterday lingered in my mind. Ben was determined to help me write my cookbook. But what if it went badly and I disappointed him? Would finding his father make up for that?

Whoa, whoa, whoa. I had to slow my roll. Why did I care if I disappointed him? When I'd told him this was just for the short term, Ben had called this a summer situation, and just because that term lacked definition and made the hive of bees in my head busy, busy, busy didn't mean I needed to sweat us not making it for the long term. We were just for the here and now. No need to make things complicated.

As if he could feel my gaze on him, Ben glanced over his shoulder in the direction of our car. His mouth curved up immediately at the sight of me, and my shoulders dropped in relief. I soaked in the image of him as he strode across the parking lot wearing a lightweight black leather jacket over jeans and a T-shirt. Mercy.

"I was hoping I'd see you today," he said.

"Yeah?" My voice came out embarrassingly high and squeaky. I immediately feigned a cough. **Chill, Gale**.

"I was wondering if you're free on Saturday to do some more amateur sleuthing."

"I should be available, but I'll know better tomorrow," I said. I thought about my appointment with Em and hoped I'd be available to go with Ben. If Em got bad news, I didn't plan to let her out of my sight. At least, not until she had a plan of action. Thankfully, I had my happy hour for tomorrow evening all prepped and ready to go. I was getting a solid rhythm with this new chef gig.

"Great." He glanced at the car. Tyler was watching something on his phone, so Ben kissed me quick and then came back for more.

The mutual attraction flared to life, and the next thing I knew he backed me up against the car, cupped my face, and was kissing me with a single-minded intensity that made my entire world narrow to one focus point. Him.

I forgot where we were. I forgot my name. All I knew was that I could have spent the rest of my life kissing this man and it would never be enough.

The sound of a horn broke through, and Ben and I separated. I glanced at the car, and Tyler was leaning out of the passenger window and grinning at us.

"Now that I have your attention . . . ahem." He cleared his throat. "Will you be joining us for dinner, Ben?"

Ben looked at me. His hair was disheveled—**did I do that?**—and his lips were swollen. He looked as dazed and confused as I felt. I smoothed my Blind Melon T-shirt, one of my dad's favorite bands from back in the day, and tried to pull it together.

"I'm making one of Vovó's dishes, shrimp Mozambique," I said. "I use a pepper sauce, you might not like it."

"He'll like it," Tyler said. "Even I like it and I hate everything." It was a fair point.

"Just to be clear." Ben raised both of his hands like a scale. "My choices are a frozen pizza at my house or authentic Portuguese cuisine at yours?" The hand for his house rose while he dropped the other.

"Apparently." I nodded.

"I will race you to your house."

I laughed and pointed at Tyler. "Beginning driver."

"I will follow you at a respectful distance to your house." Ben grinned at me, and I was charmed all the way down to my socks.

"All right," I said. "Meet you there."

The drive home was quick. I spent most of it watching Ben on his motorcycle behind us and trying not to get into an accident.

"You're crushing hard, aren't you?" Tyler asked.

I whipped my head in his direction. "No . . . maybe . . . totally. I mean look at him. He's hot and funny and smart and nice."

"Yeah, he's the whole package." Tyler sighed. "It makes it impossible to dislike him, which I should because all of the girls in robotics talk about him all the time. It's annoying."

"On the upside, you are relieved of your sous-chef dinner duties tonight," I said. "Ben can take your place."

"See? How could I possibly dislike the guy who gets me out of hard labor?"

I parked in the driveway, and Tyler banged out of the car and up the steps. I caught up to him while he was unlocking the door. He glanced over his shoulder and said, "Don't forget to call me for dinner."

"I would never," I protested.

The sound of a motorcycle drew my attention to the street. Ben cut the engine, climbed off the bike, and removed his helmet, shaking out his dark hair.

"Hello, Sis, you in there?" Tyler waved his hand in front of my face, breaking the spell. I shook my head and turned to find him laughing at me.

"Stifle yourself," I said. He laughed harder and dashed upstairs to his room.

I waited in the doorway for Ben, taking a moment to appreciate how very different this summer had turned out from my expectations and in such a good way. When did that ever happen?

Ben was carrying a brown leather backpack, and I hoped it meant that he was bringing our book.

"Come on in," I said.

He followed me to the kitchen and placed his backpack on the counter while I grabbed my apron from the hook on the wall and pulled it over my head. I turned around to find Ben holding up his phone and taking my picture.

I held up my hands to ward him off. "Ack, no! I'm a hot mess."

"Never," he argued. "Besides, this is the first official picture for your cookbook."

"You want to work on that now?" I asked. I wasn't mentally prepared for that.

"Why not?" He pulled out a laptop and looked at me expectantly. "You cook and I'll write it down. We can go from there."

"But I . . . so much of it is guesswork . . . I don't . . ." My voice trailed off. This was what I wanted, and yet I was gripped with a paralyzing fear of failure at the thought of attempting to write a cookbook.

As if he understood, Ben put down his phone and grabbed my hands, giving them a quick, reassuring squeeze. "Don't think about the cookbook right now. Just focus on dinner and we'll see where it takes us."

"Just dinner." I nodded.

"Yeah." He grabbed Tyler's blue apron from the other hook and slipped it over his head. "Tell me what you're doing while you cook, and I'll do the rest."

I met his gaze and allowed myself to think—what if, what if I could actually do this?

"All right." I said. "Let's get this party started."

"That's the spirit." He moved to stand beside me.

I had been a professional chef for almost a third of my life. I was confident in my culinary abilities. But I had never had a distraction like Ben in the kitchen with me. Wanting to jump on your sous-chef and have your way with him was not a challenge most chefs had to deal with.

I shook my head to clear it. **Focus, Gale.** I used a two-quart pan to start the rice. Then I put a large pot on the stove and turned the heat to medium. Ben opened up his laptop and started typing.

"What are you typing?" I asked.

"Large pot and medium heat," he said.

"Oh." Feeling like a dope, I went to the refrigerator and started pulling out my ingredients. Mercifully, to save time, I had done the prep work before I picked up Tyler. I grabbed my items and placed them on the counter by the stove.

I unwrapped a stick of butter and dropped it in the pan. Ben was watching me and I met his gaze and said, "One stick of butter."

He grinned and started typing. Okay, maybe this wouldn't be so hard. I gathered more ingredients while the butter melted completely and started to sizzle.

"Half an onion, diced, sauté for five minutes."

Ben continued typing. "That smells amazing." He lifted up his phone and took another photo of me beside the stove. I glowered. "What? You look adorable."

I rolled my eyes even though I was flattered, no question. "Six garlic cloves, minced, sauté also for five minutes."

I tended the rice, adding the grains to the boiling water. Then I reached for the key ingredient in a small mason jar.

"What's that?" Ben asked.

"The pepper sauce," I said. "Or as Vovó called it, pimenta moída."

"Is it homemade?" he asked.

"Yes. You can buy a variation of it at most Portuguese markets but Vovó taught me to make it, so I always prepare my own." I opened the jar and spooned out the savory crushed peppers.

He looked at me expectantly and I said, "One heaping tablespoon of pimenta moída."

"We'll have to include a recipe for that in the book, too," he said.

I stared at him. His confidence in me and this project confounded me.

"What?" he asked.

"You." I waved my hands at him, indicating his entire person. "You make it all seem . . . possible." I felt a fluttering in my chest that I assumed was excitement about actually starting the cookbook, but I didn't know how to embrace the feeling, so it came out of my eyes in big fat tears.

"Samwise, are you crying?" Ben asked. He left his laptop and came around the counter to hug me from behind.

"No, it's the onions," I lied.

"Ah." He kissed the top of my head. "Do we need to stir this?"

"Yes," I answered but I didn't pick up the wooden spoon I'd placed on the counter. I didn't want to leave his arms. Ben reached around me with one hand to grab the spoon. He held it over the pot until I put my hand on his. Together we stirred in the pimenta moída into the garlic and onions.

"It needs a pinch of salt." I sniffed.

Ben's cheek was resting against my temple and I

felt him smile. He put the spoon down and reached for the salt, pouring a tiny amount into his palm. I used my free hand to pinch it and toss it into the simmering ingredients.

"Tell me about your vovó," he said.

This was not a simple request. Vovó had been such a positive force in my life that there wasn't a corner of my existence that she didn't inhabit in one way or another. I pictured her in my mind and recalled the scent of the perfume she always wore, a soft floral fragrance that reminded me of a rainy day in spring.

"She was short, stout, and bespectacled. She kept her red agate rosary tucked safely in the pocket of her crisp gingham apron. She went to the salon every Saturday and had her white hair set in big fat curls so she'd look her best for Sunday mass."

I leaned back against Ben and his arms tightened about me.

"Vovó was bighearted and easy to make laugh. She never had a cross word or a criticism to say about her family. Her children and her grandchildren were her reason for being. As teens, we couldn't get a hug from her that didn't include a twenty-dollar bill tucked into our hand."

I paused. My throat was tight and I had to swallow before I could continue.

"She baked bread every single day." My voice

dropped to a whisper as I added, "And I think she knew."

Ben became very still. "Knew what?"

"That I couldn't read," I said. "She grew up in a house with parents who only spoke Portuguese, so English was her second language and she spoke it very well, but I think she learned as a child to be an observer. She watched people to fill the language gap. We had that in common, and I think she knew that I struggled to read. That's why out of all of her grandchildren, she taught me the family recipes. I think she recognized I was going to need an occupation that I could manage, and cooking was what she knew, so she gave it to me."

More tears spilled and Ben's arms tightened around me. I relaxed against him while I tried to pull it together. After a beat, I turned in his arms and said, "I've never told anyone that before."

"She meant a lot to you," he said.

"She meant everything to me," I corrected him. "That's why writing this book of her recipes is such a huge responsibility. I can't get it wrong."

"You won't," he promised. "You're brilliant and determined and you'll do her justice."

I met his gaze, and a feeling of certainty came over me. It occurred to me then that I trusted Bennett Reynolds implicitly. It was equal parts thrilling and comforting and terrifying.

"What is taking so long? I'm starving." Tyler burst into the kitchen. He stared at us and then said, "Seriously? This is a food preparation area." He waved at us with his hands. "You, over there." He pointed for Ben to get back to his laptop. "And you, tell me what goes in next."

Ben released me but not before planting a kiss on my lips, and whispering, "You've got this."

I met his gaze and nodded. I might have this but he had me. Oh, he had me, all right. The guy had no idea how much he truly had me. In fact, he might never be rid of me.

My morning consisted of dropping Tyler at camp, doubling back home to change, and then rushing out the door to pick up Em for her doctor's appointment. I'd insisted on taking her, fearing that if it was bad news, she'd be in no state to drive.

As I motored through the neighborhood, I marveled at how full my days were. When I'd originally agreed to come to the Vineyard to chaperone Tyler, I'd assumed my summer would be filled with rigorous days of paddleboarding, beach volleyball, and maybe some tennis with my dad because it made him happy. I'd done none of that.

Em was waiting outside her house when I arrived. Her eyes were big behind her glasses and she looked pale. I'd bet she hadn't slept at all last night and she probably hadn't eaten either. I pulled up to the curb and she hopped in.

"Have everything you need?" I asked.

She opened her shoulder bag and peered inside. I could see the edge of not just one but two books.

"You sure you don't want to go grab another book?" I teased.

She smiled. "It's okay, I have an e-reader app on my phone."

I considered telling her I was being sarcastic, but thought better of it. I was now rocking several books in my own audiobook library, so I was no longer in a position to mock. The realization that I had a toe in the book nerd club made me smile. I'd sure never seen that coming.

We arrived at the doctor's office ten minutes ahead of time. Em signed in and we took two seats in the corner of the waiting room. A wall-mounted television was playing the local morning show out of Boston and there were two other patients in the room in addition to us. No one was watching the program, as everyone was looking at their phones.

Em grabbed her book and I relaxed back in my seat to watch the TV since they were running a segment on making your own guacamole. The local chef wasn't a person I recognized, but even from across the waiting room I could tell he was using too much cilantro.

We sat quietly waiting for her to be called. I glanced at Em as I mentally critiqued the chef. She seemed completely absorbed in her book. Her gaze was focused on the page, her posture relaxed. Reading was an immersive experience. I felt a small pang of envy but then shrugged it off. Just because I could listen to a book while I did the dishes didn't make it not immersive. It just freed up my hands.

The chef on the television was overmixing the avocado. It wasn't supposed to be a puree. Chunks should be able to be dug out of the guacamole with a chip. How did this guy not know this? I was completely annoyed, when I felt Em's hand on my arm, drawing my attention to her.

"Are you all right?" I asked.

"Yes, but Dr. Ernst is ready for me." Em gestured to where a woman in scrubs stood by a partially open swinging door.

"Do you want me to come with you?" I asked.

"If you don't mind," she said.

"Not at all," I said. "I'm here for whatever you need."

"Thanks, Sam," she said. "You're a good friend."

We gathered our things and followed the woman in scrubs down the hallway to a patient room. Em sat on the exam table. The long paper strip that covered it crinkled as she shifted. I took one of the two hard plastic chairs. I felt like the mother of a child at the pediatrician's office. Probably because Em looked so vulnerable sitting there waiting to hear.

What if it was bad news? What if it was the worst news? What could I possibly say?

The door opened and Dr. Ernst walked in. She was carrying a folder, which I suspected was Em's chart.

"Hi, Emily, how are you?"

"Good," Em said, then added, "unless you're here to tell me otherwise."

"Hi," Dr. Ernst greeted me as she put the chart on the counter. "I assume you want to have your friend here while we discuss the results of your biopsy?"

"Yes," Em said. "Please."

I gave her an encouraging smile.

"All right." Dr. Ernst leaned back and considered Em. I thought my heart might burst out of my chest from anxiety. This was not the face of a person bringing good news. "First, let me tell you that the results were negative. The lump was benign. You do not have cancer."

"Woo-hoo!" I yelled and jumped to my feet. They both turned to look at me. Dr. Ernst in amusement, and Em as if she couldn't comprehend such good news.

"Um, sorry." I sank back onto my seat and tried to read the room. Darned if I could figure why we weren't all jumping around in giddy circles.

"How accurate is the biopsy?" Em asked. "I read that core needle biopsies have false negatives."

"That depends upon whether an adequate sample was taken," Dr. Ernst said. "In your case, there was."

"But how do you know?" Em persisted.

I glanced at her in surprise. She was looking very determined but why? She'd gotten great results—the best results—why was she questioning the outcome?

"Emily, do you remember the conversation we had when you first discovered the lump, the appointment before the biopsy?" Dr. Ernst asked.

"Yes." Em's gaze slid away from the doctor with a look that I could only identify as embarrassment.

"And do you remember what I said to you?"

Em glanced at me as if she didn't want to say it in front of me. I tried to look encouraging. No matter what I was in her corner.

"You said there was no indication of cancer, that you didn't think a biopsy was necessary, and that you were only doing it so that I would stop obsessing about tumors and dying," Em said.

I felt my eyebrows lift in surprise. I tried to hide it but doubted I was successful. This sounded an awful lot like Em was a hypochondriac. I didn't know what to say or where to look. I wondered if Em regretted having me in the room. Probably.

"The biopsy has proven my initial diagnosis to be accurate," Dr. Ernst said.

"But—"

"No, there are no buts about this. You do not have cancer. You are not dying."

Em's mouth formed a tight line as if she was forcing herself not to say anything.

"I do have a referral for you but it's for a therapist to help you get to the root of what's really bothering you," Dr. Ernst said.

"You think I'm crazy," Em said. She sounded angry.

"No." Dr. Ernst shook her head. "I think something is troubling you and it's manifesting in phantom health concerns." She handed Em a business card. "Dr. Davis can help and you can always call me if you need me."

"Thanks," Em said. She didn't sound grateful. She sounded depressed.

Dr. Ernst rose and left the room. When the door shut behind her, I had no idea what to say. This was not at all what I had expected. After a very awkward pause, I turned to Em and asked, "Ready to go?"

"Yes, please."

Neither of us spoke until we were halfway to Em's house. It might have been the quietest ride we'd ever shared. I racked my brain thinking of the right phrase, a comforting sentiment, something, anything that would make her feel better. I pondered what I would want someone to say to me if I genuinely believed I was ill but the test results said otherwise. Support. I would want one hundred percent, have-my-back, no-doubt-allowed support. Okay, I could do that.

"You can get a second opinion," I said.

Em was staring out the window, looking at the ocean as we blew down Beach Road. The view was clear, and a fine line appeared at the horizon where the dark blue of the water met the pale blue of the sky. A clash of blues. It hit me again how much I'd missed it.

"Thank you, but no. I don't think I'll be asking anyone else," she said. "That was humiliating enough."

"No, it wasn't," I said. I'm sure it felt like it was, but embarrassment and I were old friends. You get over it. I would have told her this, but she didn't need to have her feelings filtered through my experience. I could see she was feeling bad about herself, and I couldn't let that stand, just like she couldn't let me think listening to a book was less valid than reading. "It is never ever wrong to follow up on a health concern."

"I wasn't, though, was I?" Em asked. "I essentially forced them to take tissue out of a fatty lump in my neck because I thought I was dying. Who does that? Crazy people."

"Harsh!" I said. "And you're not crazy, don't say that. Dr. Ernst very specifically said something is troubling you. That's exactly like having something physically wrong with you, and that's why she referred you to another doctor. See? Still a medical condition."

"Hmm." She hummed. But she straightened her back, looking less defeated.

"Any idea what it could be?" I asked.

"No," she said. "My life is . . . fine. But the truth is I **have** become a bit of a hypochondriac. If someone sneezes near me, I'm convinced they've given me the flu. If I have a headache, it's brain cancer. Stomachache, and I'm sure my appendix has ruptured. I spend all of my free time on medical websites. Between you and me, I think they're trying to kill me. Every medical condition ends up in death."

I huffed out a laugh and quickly squelched it. "When did all of this start? Because you were never like this before."

"I didn't have time before," she said. "When we were growing up, we were always busy, but ever since I moved back after college, my life just got really, really small. Now I don't go anywhere or do anything except work and home, day in and day out, rinse and repeat."

Her words snapped on the light bulb in my brain. This made sense. I knew exactly what was wrong. I turned to her and said, "That's it!"

"What's it?" Em looked confused.

"Why you're convinced you have cancer or a tumor and that you're dying. You just said it."

"Really?" she asked. "What did I say?"

"Quite simply, you're bored, or as the expression goes, you're bored to death."

Em stared at me. She blinked and her jaw dropped. She looked like I'd just slapped her.

"No, I'm not," she said. "I love my job and . . . and . . ."

Her voice trailed off as I stopped at a stop sign. I turned to look at her and raised one eyebrow.

"You forget I've known you since we were kids. I'm sure you love your career, but this isn't the life you always dreamed of. Do you remember? You never planned on living on the island permanently, you were always going to go off and see the world," I said. "You wanted to work as an archivist, or with special collections, preferably in a foreign country if I remember right."

"People change." Em shrugged.

"Not that much they don't," I countered. The car behind me honked, and I waved in acknowledgment and started driving. "Don't get me wrong, I love having you here on island with me, but **why** are you here?"

"You know why," she said.

"Spell it out for me."

"My dad left us for **that** woman and my mom couldn't be alone," she said. "You know that."

"Couldn't be alone or didn't want to be?" I asked. "There's a big difference."

Em didn't answer. She didn't have to. I knew Mrs. Allen well enough to know that she was hanging on to Em with a tenacious grip. Mr. Allen had left Mrs. Allen right when Em graduated from college. Em moved back to help her mother acclimate to life on her own, but then she never left. I had thought she'd made peace with it and discovered she liked living on island in her childhood bedroom, but if she was rolling into full-on hypochondria, then clearly she was unhappy.

"I don't know," Em said. "It's just so much easier doing what she wants. No drama or guilt that way."

"But what about what you want?" I asked.

Em glanced out the window. I wondered how long it had been since anyone had asked her what she wanted.

"I'm twenty-eight," she said. "And other than the four years I was away at college, I've never lived off island. You know, I thought I would have seen some shit by now."

A laugh busted out of me and she smiled. I parked in front of her house and she hopped out.

"Do you want to go walk on the beach or something?" I asked. "We can keep spitballing ideas about what's bothering you, because despite my advanced psychological degree, I'm sure there's more to consider."

Em laughed. "You've given me a lot to think about, Dr. Gale, reminding me of what I used to want."

I grinned. She was laughing at my jokes. I took it as a good sign.

"I think I need to do some solo thinking, and I'm going to see if I can get an appointment with Dr.

Davis," Em said. "Before my mom comes back from her trip."

"I think that's an excellent idea. Call me if you want to talk," I said.

"I will. Thanks, Sam, for . . . everything."

"That's what besties are for," I said.

She closed the car door and walked up the walkway.

I rolled down my window when she was halfway up the steps, and called out, "And stay off the medical sites on the Internet."

She nodded and sent me a double thumbs-up before she disappeared into the house.

Chapter Twenty

Ben texted me shortly after I arrived home. Actually, **texted** implies that it was one message. It was not. It was a very lengthy message followed by several shorter messages including links to websites and books and articles. A quick scan indicated that they were all instructions about writing a cookbook. There were so many. I immediately felt too overwhelmed to try and read through them all.

Straight talk. I hate receiving texts unless they are very short or in GIF form. I'd much rather call a person and speak directly instead of texting back because, quite frankly, my spelling is atrocious. People laugh at it, heck, I laugh at it, but I wasn't ready for the hot librarian guy, whom I really wanted to see naked, to laugh at it.

Because I knew he was at work and likely couldn't take a call, I did what I usually did when I was feeling overwhelmed: I did nothing. His string of texts sat on my phone, ignored. Normally, I'd have opened the app that can read my texts to me and replied with a voice to text, but he'd left so many I was undone.

Last night, when I'd opened my heart and shared with him about my vovó and why she was so special, that I believed she knew about my neurodivergent brain and had done what she could to help, I'd felt as if he and I had a soul connection like the one I'd shared with her. I'd thought he understood me on an elemental level, but now his string of texts mocked me like a reminder of how incompatible we were.

Sure, I could have waded through the texts and articles and my phone could read aloud his messages in its horrible robotic voice, but that wasn't the point. The point was that I'd fooled myself into believing that he saw me, really saw me, when this string of messages proved that he didn't. Not at all.

I decided to spend the rest of the morning working on my happy hour menu for that evening. Preparation was always critical for me when taking on a big job. I needed to time things out and memorize the flow. I had changed up this week's menu, trying to be more efficient. While the guests had loved the peixinhos da horta, it had required me to keep running back to the kitchen to use the fryer. This week, I was going with shredded pork in a vinha-d'alhos, and by making it beforehand, I could keep it warm in a heated chafing dish during the happy hour.

I tried to focus on the task at hand. Still, the entire

time I prepped, my eyes strayed to the phone and the messages sitting there. I had to pick up Tyler later today. Maybe I would see Ben and I could explain. Explain what? That I was embarrassed? That his text string made me feel deficient? That clearly a big-brained booklover like him could never be content with a word-repellent girl like me even for the short term? I didn't want to. These were the salad days in our summer situation, and I hated to have him think of me as incapable of even texting him.

I felt a tear well up in one eye and I swiped it away with the back of my hand. I wished it was the pepper I was chopping but it wasn't. It was the same old mean voice in my head that called me stupid and useless. I reminded myself that this thing with Ben was just a fling. So why did I care? Because I was on the precipice of falling hard for Ben, so maybe this was the moment I should call the time of death on the relationship, end it, and spare myself the impending heartbreak.

I shook my head. No. I liked Ben, more than liked him, and I wanted to be with him for as long as I could. When the day came that we went our separate ways at the end of the summer, as he returned to his university library and I, hopefully, found gainful employment again, that would be the natural end.

For now, I would enjoy Ben while we were together and hope that at the end of it we could remain friends, because I couldn't see a future for a guy whose happy place was wordy academia and a girl who struggled to read, no matter how much I loved listening to him. The cookbook project and shared reading would eventually get old for him, and I wanted us to part before he looked at me as a burden, because eventually guys always did.

It was noon when Ben called.

I picked up right away. Newly resolved to enjoy him for as long as our time together lasted, I was eager to hear his voice.

"Hey, you," I said.

"Hey." He sounded tense.

"What's wrong?" I asked.

"Is everything okay?" He cleared his throat. "I mean, you haven't texted me back, so I was just wondering."

I felt my panic press against the inside of my skin as if it could leak out my pores in a flop sweat. What was I supposed to say? The truth? Ack! No, no, no. I desperately didn't want Ben to know I'd been wrestling my inner self-esteem demon all morning. Why hadn't I just sent the man a thumbs-up emoji? Honestly, I had to acknowledge that, like Em with her bout of hypochondria, I sometimes made my life way more difficult than it needed to be.

"I . . . um . . . I . . ." I stammered. Honestly, it was almost like I was **trying** to come across as slow-witted.

"You know, if you don't want to get together tomorrow night, that's okay," he said. His tone was gentle.

"No, it's not that," I said. "I just . . ."

"Talk to me, Samwise," he said.

I laughed. I felt anything but wise, and the irony of the nickname struck me as funny in a sad sort of way. I opened my mouth to remind him of my reading issues but I couldn't do it. I just couldn't trot it out there again. It already colored so much of our time together.

"I'm actually elbow deep in minced peppers," I said. "Any chance we could talk later when I pick up Tyler from camp?"

"Sure. I'll be here," he said. He sounded wary.

"Okay, I'll see you later then." I totally sounded like I was blowing him off. This was so bad. I knew it was my pride and I just needed to remind him about my dyslexia, but I simply couldn't make myself do it.

"Okay." He sounded bewildered in one of those "what the hell just happened?" voices that guys use when women confound them.

I ended the call and went back to work, chopping the red peppers, my plastic-glove-covered palms sweating as I lifted the cutting board and scraped them into the large pot on the stove. I was adding ingredients, stirring until the marinade was bubbling in a low boil, when the doorbell rang.

"Just a second!" I yelled. I wondered if it was Em.

Maybe she'd sorted her feelings and wanted to talk. That would be a nice distraction from my own relationship angst. I stripped off my gloves and threw them in the trash, then I put the lid on the pot and set the timer.

The kitchen looked like a small typhoon had hit but I forced myself to ignore it for the moment and hurried to open the door.

"Sorry, I was—" My words caught in my throat. Standing in the doorway in a dress shirt and khakis was Ben, clutching a big bouquet of bright yellow coreopsis and daisies, some of which still had their roots attached. I wondered whose yard he'd pilfered them from, and the idea of him doing this for me made me want to laugh and cry in equal measure, so naturally, I just stood there blinking at him.

"I am a fucking idiot," he said. "Forgive me?"

I looked from the flowers to him and back. "Huh?"

"Like an insensitive a-hole, I sent you a text—**a text!**—and not even one text. There were like ten with messages with links and whatnot. The string was practically long enough to be from the **Epic Cycle**." He shook his head. "Forgive me, Samwise?"

This man. Would he ever stop surprising me? I'd been wrong about him. Maybe he'd forgotten for a beat, but right now in this moment he made me feel seen and understood for the first time in my life, and it was everything.

I couldn't help myself. I took the flowers in one hand and then I jumped on him. "Yes, I forgive you."

He staggered back a step at the surprise attack but rallied as I twined my arms around his neck and my legs around his waist. I planted my mouth on his as he cupped my bottom with one hand and wrapped an arm around my back, holding me against him while I kissed him with all of the desperate longing that I felt.

His mouth yielded beneath mine, his lips parting to allow me entry. I deepened the kiss, trying to show him how much I had come to care for him without having to say the words. I ran my lips down the side of his throat and bit him gently on the curve of his shoulder.

I heard him kick the door shut behind him before he strode farther into the room.

"I missed you," he said. His voice was a fierce, low growl and I felt it echo in my bones.

"I missed you, too," I said.

He moved across the living room, and when he sank onto the couch, my legs fell to each side so that I was straddling him, which was thrilling. I leaned back and dropped the flowers into my water glass, which I'd left on the coffee table. It would have to do for now.

When I turned back to him, he was making a face as if he was in pain. I sat up on my knees, lifting my weight off him.

"Sorry, am I crushing you?" I asked.

"Uh . . . no," he said. He reached behind himself and pulled something out of his back pocket.

"Ha!" I laughed. "You brought our book."

"I figured if you were really sore at me, I'd start reading and get you to forgive me by withholding the good stuff," he said.

"Ah!" I gasped. "That's devious."

"A man does what he has to do," he said. He opened the book. "In fact, where were we?"

I went to slide off him, eager to listen.

"No, don't move," he said. He glanced at me from beneath his thick dark lashes. So hot. "I like you right where you are."

I felt a slow-boiling heat roil up inside of me. He splayed one hand across my abdomen, holding me in place, and then he began to read.

It was the love scene, the big moment where our hero and heroine finally give in to the lust that has been buzzing between them for most of the book. I would have thought I'd be mortified to listen to a guy read about a man going down on a woman, licking her, sucking her tits, sliding his cock into her. But nope. It was insanely hot.

Possibly, it was because I was distracted by his thumb, which he slid beneath the waistband of my shorts, seeking the aching center between my legs. He stroked in relentless circles, making my breath catch and my hips tilt as I pressed against the friction, wanting more. He did not give me more, however.

Instead, Ben kept reading in his dead-sexy voice. He drew out every word, savoring the description of the woman's shattering orgasm as the male object of her desire thrust into her repeatedly. His voice was making my brain buzz, and my entire body was beginning to throb. I was overheated and knew I was going to require a bucket of ice and fan just to keep from combusting on the spot if he kept it up. He kept it up.

He flicked opened the buttons on my shorts, giving himself full access while he continued to read. The heroine was staking her claim this time. As she made love to her man, Ben deviously slid one finger into me while still rubbing that deliciously sensitive pressure point with his thumb. I was practically incoherent with blind lust, and then he slid a second finger inside me and I about blacked out. His voice was low and gritty, and he leaned forward to whisper the words of the story in my ear.

My orgasm came up so hard and fast, I grabbed the book out of his hands and tossed it aside while I arched against his wicked fingers and the magic they were unraveling inside of me. His eyes glinted with satisfaction, which was ridiculous because I hadn't done anything for him at all.

When the spasms finally stopped, and I could

breathe like a normal person and not someone who had just run a 10K, I collapsed against him. He held me close, his hands running up and down my back, trying to soothe me, but it didn't work. I wanted more.

"How long are you here for?" I asked as I kissed his chin and behind his ear, and ran my lips down the side of his neck.

"The rest of my lunch hour," he said on a hiss. He glanced at his watch. "About fifteen minutes."

"Perfect," I said. "That's when my marinade will be ready."

"Is that a euphemism?" he asked.

I laughed. "It can be our code word for sex. I'll just look at you and say, 'You want some marinade?'"

"So hot." He laughed. Then his face grew serious. "Actually, it smells amazing."

"I'm sorry, are you getting distracted from sex with me by food?" I asked.

His gaze when he looked at me was tender. "Samantha, I am not going to rush the first time we're together by trying to beat the timer on your oven."

"Oh." My disappointment made it sound like a three-syllable word.

He kissed me. It was slow and deep and thorough, and I was certain I'd convinced him to change his mind, when he broke the kiss. His chest was heaving a little bit and I flattered myself that at least I was making it difficult for him. He leaned back and refastened my shorts.

"I'll pick you up tomorrow night," he said. He lifted me up and set me on my feet. My head was still fuzzy, when he added, "I was thinking about our conversation in the parking lot the other day."

"Conversation?" My short-term memory was on the fritz at the moment. I blamed him.

"When you declared this was just for now because we'll both be leaving at the end of the season, and I called this a 'summer situation,'" he reminded me.

"Oh, right. What about it?"

"You know I was just kidding, right?" he asked. He reached out and cupped the back of my head with his very large square man hand and pulled me up against him. "I feel like I need to clarify that this isn't temporary for me."

"It isn't?" I asked. I hadn't realized he was joking, when at the time I'd been very serious about labeling it a fling.

"Nope." He slid his hand down to my lower back, holding me close. It was lovely.

"Well, that begs the question, What am I to you?" I asked. My heart was racing, my breathing was shallow, and I felt this ridiculous fluttering feeling in my chest. I think it was hope.

"More than a friend," he said. "But the term 'girlfriend' isn't right either. It's so high school. There is nothing high school about how I feel about you."

The glint in his eye was pure porn. Oh my.

I cleared my throat and tried to get my synapses firing amid the lust fog.

"How about your special lady friend?" I asked.

"Hmm, no."

"Your plus-one?"

"Meh."

I rolled my eyes. "Well, it's too soon to be your significant other or your partner."

"Is it?" he asked. "Is there a time requirement on these things?"

I swallowed. I felt as if the conversation was getting away from me.

"But you're the interim director here," I said. "You'll be leaving the Vineyard soon."

"Maybe," he said. "I'm not making any plans until I know who my father is and I find him."

"Oh," I said. "I just assumed . . ."

He waited. When I didn't say more, he raised one eyebrow and asked, "Assumed?"

"That we'd go our separate ways in a few weeks because of work and life and . . ." My voice trailed off.

"If you're asking me if I want this to end with the summer," he said, "the answer is no. I just found you, Samwise, and I feel like you're my . . . person."

And just like that everything I had believed to be true—that this was a fling, that it was temporary, that we'd go our separate ways in a matter of weeks—was obliterated.

Ben leaned down and kissed me. I didn't know what I thought about us lasting longer than a few months. Most of my relationships barely made it through one season. I had no frame of reference for anything longer. But when his mouth claimed mine, I discovered I didn't care. I was in as long as he was in.

Beep. Beep. Beep.

We broke apart and glanced around the room. Was it a phone, a fire alarm, what? Then the smell infiltrated my brain.

"My marinade!" I cried. I let him go and dashed for the kitchen. Grabbing my pot holder, I lifted the lid off the pot. A plume of savory steam rose into the air. I grabbed a big spoon and began to stir. It hadn't gotten scorched. Phew!

Ben was standing in the doorway, watching me as if I was endlessly fascinating to him. Not gonna lie, it felt good to give the critical voice in my head something to stew about.

Flattered to be the object of his attention, I removed the pot from the heat and crossed the room. I pressed myself up against him. He got the hint and lowered his head so I could kiss him with all of the wicked intent in my heart. I was just about to climb him like my own personal beanstalk when the kitchen timer went off again, making me jump.

"Argh!" I grumbled. "I was sure I shut that thing off."

Ben was laughing.

"What?" I asked. I hit the button on the oven and turned back to him.

"There we go, setting off more alarms," he said. He shrugged as if unsurprised that our chemistry was potent enough to cause havoc all around us. Charmer.

"I have to get back. See you tomorrow, Samwise." He kissed me quick and then left.

"Bye!" I called after him.

My brain went into hyperdrive as soon as the door shut behind him. **He sees you as his person. He thinks this will last longer than just the summer. You're going to disappoint him. He'll get sick of your disability. He'll dump you. It'll be worse the longer you're together.**

"Oh, for fuck's sake, shut up," I said to the voice in my head. Then I dunked some freshly made bolo lêvedo into my marinade and scarfed it down, because good food makes everything better.

Chapter Twenty-One

No one had a record of Moira Reynolds working for
them during the summer of 1989. Ben and I spent two
weeks hitting every restaurant on the island that had
been open at the time, and no luck. We'd looped Em
into the quest but even with her mad research skills, we
hit a dead end. There was simply no trace of Moira
Reynolds on the island that summer. It was as if she'd
managed to disappear her past. How did a person do
that?

At my third happy hour at the inn, I made a point
of asking Stuart Mayhew, the owner, about Moira, but
he said he hadn't arrived on the island until 1991 and
had never met her. Despite this setback, I crushed it at
that happy hour and Stuart was very pleased. Both Ben
and Em were there to cheer me on, which I
appreciated.

I knew that Ben was taking the lack of a lead hard
and trying not to show it. We watched old British
mysteries together, trying to up our detective game,
and we worked on my cookbook. He sat on a stool in

the kitchen, writing the recipes on his laptop as I cooked. When I went to throw in a pinch of this or a dash of that, he made me stop and measure the ingredients. Tyler frequently joined us, and I knew that Vovó would be so happy to know that the boy she didn't get a chance to watch grow up was learning the family recipes.

Robotics camp was going well, and I noticed that Tyler's conversations seemed to begin and end with Sophie. Three and a half weeks had passed since Dad and Stephanie departed. I sincerely hoped that they returned before things got serious—as in, we needed to have a talk—between the two teens.

When not searching for his dad, Ben threw himself into his job as library director, and he and Ryan took the robotics campers on a field trip where they used drones to map the island. It was all Tyler talked about for the next two days.

At the four-week mark for summer reading, Em and I, with Tyler's assist, held our teen cooking program, Teen Chef, which was a massive success, if I do say so myself. Tyler and I wore matching chef coats and he was very close to being a perfect sous-chef, anticipating what I needed before I knew I needed it. He also charmed the socks off the girls in the crowd with his quick wit and dazzling smile. I couldn't have been more proud.

At the end of the night, when the kids were making

their own food under our supervision, we cranked the tunes until I saw Ben arrive in the doorway of the conference room, looking very much like the library director that he was. In his white dress shirt and gray slacks with his tie loosened, he had a hot professor look about him that was hard to resist.

I left Tyler to oversee the group and met Ben at the door. "Are we being too loud?"

"Nah, we're about to close," he said. "Maybe the noise will encourage those who would normally linger right up until the very last second to leave in a timelier fashion."

"Happy to help," I said.

"Looks like your influence has extended to more than food," he said. He tipped his chin at the crowd behind me, and I turned to see Tyler leading a dance party.

He had Sophie and Cameron on each side of him, and he was showing them how to shuffle dance just like I had shown him—flamingo, pyramid, flamingo, pyramid. Then he went fast and his running man was so smooth. I clasped my hands in front of me. I was as impressed as the girls.

"Sam!" Tyler saw me watching and waved me in.

"Be right back," I said to Ben.

"Of course," he said. He leaned against the doorway, making himself comfortable while he watched.

"Can you show them the T-step?" Tyler asked. "I'm still working on that one."

"Sure," I said.

I demonstrated slowly. Tyler joined me. Then we went fast, and I could hear the kids talking behind us. They sounded like they approved. We changed it up, trying to trip each other up with different dance steps. When the song ended, we were gassed.

Tyler held out a fist and I knuckle bumped him. He then slapped my open palm with his and then the back. He hooked his thumb with mine and lifted both our hands in the air. He laughed at my look of confusion.

"We have to have a Gale sibling handshake," he said.

"And that's what you came up with?" I asked. "We'll be working on that."

"Tyler, that was amazing." Sophie Porter, the girl who'd been at my first happy hour with her parents and who was clearly the object of Tyler's affection, bounced up to him.

He looked down at her with a twinkle in his eye that reminded me of our dad. "Was it amazing enough for you to go on a date with me?"

I sucked in a breath. He just asked out a girl! In front of me! In front of everyone! Ack! What if she said no? The kid was throwing himself out of the plane without a parachute. I was equal parts awed and aghast.

Sophie blushed a pretty shade of pink and said, "Yeah, I'd like that."

I expelled a huge breath that I hadn't known I was holding. Sophie spun away from Tyler and went to tell her friends the news while he moved to stand next to me with some righteous swagger.

"Pretty ballsy move asking her out in front of everyone," I said to him out of the corner of my mouth.

"I'm a Gale," he said. He shrugged as if it was nothing. Then he grinned at me and added, "I think it was my sick dance moves that sealed the deal. Thanks, Sis."

My heart about exploded out of my chest. Until my dying day, I would never get tired of hearing him call me Sis.

"Anytime, Bro," I said.

He turned to look at me and it was there in his eyes. He felt the same way I did. That a piece that had been missing in our lives had finally been found. I hugged him tight and after a slight hesitation, he hugged me back. In front of his friends and everything.

I released him and pointed to a trash can. "Okay, sous-chef, start cleaning up. This place is a mess."

"So bossy!" he complained, but it was negated by his smile.

I watched as he joined his friends. They all started cleaning, and then I slipped outside into the cool night air. I just needed a minute to process.

Ben joined me a few moments later. "You all right, Samwise?"

"Yeah," I said but my voice wobbled. "I just . . . I didn't know . . . for the first time ever I really feel a sibling bond between me and Tyler and it's so freaking cool. Why didn't I come out here sooner? Why did I waste so many years?"

Ben put his arm around my shoulders and pulled me into his side. "You're here now."

"But so much time has been lost," I said. A tear spilled down my cheek, stopping in the corner of my mouth. It tasted like regret. "And I can't ever get that back."

"No, you can't." His voice was low, heavy with his own heartache.

"Oh, I'm sorry," I said. I turned in his arms and cupped his face in my hands. The scruff of his beard gently scratched my skin. "Here I am whining about reconnecting with my brother when at least I have him here to reconnect with."

"It's okay," he said. He turned his head just slightly and placed a gentle kiss in my palm. My skin tingled where his lips lingered. He raised his head and pulled me into a hug. "You and Tyler give me hope that when I find my dad, we'll have that sort of special connection, too."

I slipped my arms around his back and hugged him hard. I wanted so desperately for him to find his father, to have an answer to all of his questions, yes, even about why he liked peanut butter, bacon, and pickle sandwiches. So gross.

The truth of the matter was I cared about this man so much that I would have done anything to help him in his search. Sadly, I was left with hollow platitudes that were as unappetizing as jarred tomato sauce.

"We'll find him," I said. "We'll find your father. Don't give up yet."

The look in his eyes was full of doubt, but he didn't say anything. I could see the stars behind his head, and I thought that was the perfect framing for this beautiful man.

He leaned down and kissed me and everything melted away. Regrets, sadness, anxiety, there was no room for those emotions when Ben's lips were on mine. I pressed up close to him and threaded my fingers through his hair. I parted my lips and the kiss deepened. A thrum of desire purred inside of me, and I thought if I didn't get to be with this man soon, really be with him, I might actually die from an acute case of lust.

"Ben—oh, sorry!"

We broke apart, exchanging a look of mutual frustration before turning to walk back to the building.

Em stood in the doorway. She was actively staring at the ground as if in deep conversation with her shoes. "Sorry," she said again. "But one of the library board members is here, asking for you. I would have told her you were gone for the night, but she saw your motorcycle out front."

"It's okay," Ben said. He ran a hand through his hair and straightened his tie. "Thanks for having my back." He turned back to me and in a low voice asked, "What do you think about hanging out at my place tonight?"

"Sure," I said. "We can strategize our next move in our search for your dad and maybe do some reading or work on the cookbook."

"Not exactly what I had in mind when I suggested my place," he said. His look was pointed, and I felt a thrill rocket though me.

"Oh . . . okay." I nodded. "Tyler is going out with his friends after the program. I'm a free agent for a few hours."

"Excellent. Wear the chef coat," he said. He wagged his eyebrows and with a wink, he left to go meet with the board member.

I heaved a massive sigh as I joined Em in the doorway.

"You've got it bad," she said. "You didn't even sigh like that over Timmy Montowese back in the day."

"I didn't?" I asked. "That's shocking because Timmy has been the gold standard by which I have judged all other men."

Em laughed, which was my intention. She looked

younger when she laughed. Less weighed down by life, I supposed.

I waited a beat and then asked, "How are you doing?"

She turned to look at me. She pushed her glasses up on her nose, her eyes wide behind the lenses. "I'm better."

"As in all better?" I asked. That seemed fast.

"No," she said. "But Dr. Davis was able to fit me into her schedule, and at our first session, I got a very good vibe off her. I think she can help me figure things out."

"That's great, Em," I said. I glanced at her neck where the bandage had been and now there was just a little pink pucker of new skin.

"I applied for a job in Ireland, and if I get it, I'm going to leave the island," she said. Then she turned to me as if shocked that she'd said such a thing. "Please don't tell anyone I said that."

"Of course not," I replied.

"I have to figure out how to tell my mom," Em said. "I expect it will be difficult."

"I'm here," I said. "For whatever you need. To practice what you want to say to her or to arrive at your bedroom window in the middle of the night in a flying car to whisk you away to wherever you want to go."

Em laughed. "Just like in **Harry Potter and the Chamber of Secrets**."

"Movie was better than the book," I said. Just to rile her.

She gave me an arch look that said quite clearly she was not going to take the bait. I grinned. These librarians were so easy.

"When will you leave?" I asked.

"I have to get the job first," she said. "That's why I'm waiting. Well, that and Dr. Davis said I need to do some work on myself before I make any hasty leaps into the unknown."

"That seems reasonable," I said. "Do you want me to promise to kick you in the behind if you lose your momentum?"

"You don't have to sound so eager," she said. Then she nodded. "Yes, please."

"I'll be gentle," I said.

She laughed, and we headed back inside.

I gave Tyler some money so he could go into town with his friends, because apparently they hadn't eaten enough walking tacos, chicken and waffle sandwiches, cheese fries, and milkshakes and were off to forage for more food. When they left, I saw him offer his hand to Sophie, and when she took it, I felt my heart melt a little bit. Then I had a flash of fear. What if Sophie broke Tyler's heart? How would I deal with that? I had no idea. I sent a silent plea out to the universe that if my brother got hurt, it was not on my watch.

When I finished packing up my car, I drove over to Ben's place. I kept my chef coat on, per his request, and only felt a little ridiculous when I knocked on his door.

Ben's place was an adorable two-bedroom cottage, tucked away on a cul-de-sac near the library. It was set back from the road in a copse of leafy oak trees. A climbing rosebush with pink blossoms the size of my fist went up one side of the porch and down the other, creating a magical archway over the house.

I had been over before but usually we just ducked in and then left, because we were on our quest to find his dad and I didn't like to leave Tyler home alone. But tonight, for at least a little while, I was off duty and we were not sleuthing.

Ben opened the door, and before I could even say hello, he was pulling me into the house and into his arms as if he hadn't seen me in a week instead of a half hour.

"You wore the coat," he said.

"Sure, I can roll with that kink," I said.

He laughed. "Truthfully, I just didn't want you to take too long to get here by changing first."

"And here I thought it was the outfit that had you so hot and bothered," I said.

"Not that it isn't sexy," he insisted.

"Please, I look like the Pillsbury Doughboy," I said. "Which is not a bad thing in a professional kitchen where it's best to be gender neutral but not exactly how I want to present for a hot date."

"Hot, huh?"

"Scorching." I unfastened the top button on my chef's coat. Ben's eyes locked on my fingers as I slowly undid one button after another.

I had a little **boom chicka wow wow** music playing in my head, and I strutted past him and into the living room. I unbuttoned enough of my coat to drop it halfway down my back and reveal one shoulder. I tossed my hair, pouted my lips, and looked at him from under my lashes in what I hoped was a come-hither look.

Ben's only response was a low growl from deep in his throat as he leaned back against the closed door and watched me. I had never stripped for a guy before, and I would have thought I'd be clumsy or inhibited but no, because it was Ben. Ben who accepted me as I was, who didn't care about my reading issues or attention deficiencies. He'd called me his person and I realized, as I bared all in front of him, he was my person, too.

I dropped the coat off my other shoulder. I was wearing a white racerback tank top and the standard black chef pants I always wore. I twirled the chef coat over my head and tossed it in the air to land in a heap on the brown leather couch.

I toed off my sneakers and stepped out of them. I faced Ben, holding his gaze while I unfastened my pants. I was about to lower the zipper when he pushed off the door and strode across the room toward me.

The look in his eyes was fierce. It made my heart race. He caught my hands with his and pulled me close.

"Easy," he said. "We have time, plenty of time."

He cupped my face and lowered his mouth to mine. I didn't know if it was the weeks of built-up desire or whether he was just that good, but when his lips met mine and he licked across my lower lip, I felt a hot flame of desire ignite my core. I wrapped my arms around his shoulders, and he slid his hands down my sides and grabbed me about the waist. He picked me up without breaking our kiss and I wrapped my legs around him.

He turned and carried me to the stairs. My love of food does not make me a light girl but he carried me effortlessly up to his bedroom. He kicked the door shut behind him, and I dropped my legs from around his waist and slid down the front of him until I was standing. I tugged off my tank top in one smooth motion.

Ben looked like I'd just struck his personal match, and I could feel the heat in his gaze on my skin. I reached for his shirt, and he put up no resistance.

The only thing better than professional-looking Ben was shirtless Ben. Hefting all those books had given the guy some serious definition, and I traced my fingers over his pecs and down his abs. He shuddered. It was glorious.

He caught my hand with his and tugged me close until we were skin to skin. He plundered my mouth with his tongue, and I felt a wanting surge inside of me that was all-consuming. I wanted him. All of him. And not just for tonight but for—I pushed the thought away.

I didn't want to get caught up in thoughts about the future. I just wanted to be here now, fully present, and savoring every second with him.

I unzipped my pants, shoving them down my legs and leaving them in a puddle on the floor. Usually, I preferred to slyly slide my clothes off when I was already in bed and under the covers, but with Ben, I simply didn't care.

He stood, flexing his fingers as if itching to touch me. His head was lowered slightly as he stared at me from under his thick black lashes. I had never felt sexier or more desired in my life.

When I reached for him, he put his hands on my bare waist and lowered his mouth to mine in a slow-moving, sensory-drugging kiss that made my ears ring. I reached for his pants and he helped, kicking off his shoes and leaving his pants on the floor next to mine.

I would have continued but he tugged the tie holding the braid in my hair. Using both hands, he sifted his fingers through the waves until they fell about my shoulders.

"I have wanted to do that every day since we met," he growled.

He lowered his head and slid his mouth across mine, licking at my lower lip, before he kissed his way to my ear and then down my throat.

I arched my neck, giving him full access, and he worked his way down to the tops of my breasts where they were framed by my bra. A flick of his fingers at my back, and my bra was gone. With a murmur of approval, he lowered his mouth, gently sucking one nipple and then the other between his lips.

My blood ran thick and hot, and I could hear my heartbeat in my ears. My fingers found their way back to his boxers and I managed to push them down, shoving them over his hips. He returned the favor and we were now bared in front of each other, flaws and all, but neither of us seemed to care. To me, he looked perfect, and judging by the way he was looking at me, an intoxicating mix of worship and tenderness, I knew he felt the same.

How incredibly freeing it was to be with someone who was so open. I didn't hide anything from him. I wanted him. I wanted to experience his hands on my skin. His weight on top of me, and him inside of me.

"Are you sure?" he asked. Even now with his

impressive erection in full participation mode, he was putting me and my feelings first. My god, I loved him.

I could have told him that, right then and there, but I didn't want to freak him out by saying it, so instead, I simply said, "One hundred percent."

I took his hand and pulled him to the bed. It was neat and tidy right up until I ripped the gray-and-white quilt back and climbed onto the mattress, pulling him along with me. It felt deliciously wicked to be in the bed where he slept. I pictured him here, reading to me over the phone at night, and I wondered whether he wore pajamas to bed or read to me when he was in the raw. Why did the mere idea of that make my eyes cross?

I kneeled on the bed and he joined me. I couldn't resist running my hands over his warm skin, the corded muscles in his neck and shoulders. He closed his eyes as if my calloused and scarred chef's hands were a balm.

I leaned forward put my mouth in the dip of his collarbone. He sifted his fingers through my hair, gazing down at me with such affection, I felt it bloom in my heart.

"When you read to me on the phone at night," I said, pausing to slide my lips up his throat and over his chin to his mouth. "Are you naked?"

That surprised a laugh out of him. I felt the puff of breath against my mouth. He leaned close and kissed me and said, "Is there a fantasy involved here, because

I don't want to ruin it by admitting that I sleep in footie pajamas."

It was my turn to laugh. I could just see him in a giant pink bunny suit, and the fact that even that seemed sexy to me informed me that I was a goner.

"Just curious," I said.

"Ah, I think you'll just have to spend the night on one of our dates and find out," he said.

His hands slid from my knees, detouring up the inside of my thighs and around my hips to my backside. He lifted me up, lowering me onto my back, and then he was above me. I tried to catch him and pull him down on top of me. It felt as if I'd been waiting forever to have him right where I wanted him, but he outmaneuvered me.

He scooted down the bed, kissing one knee and then the other. His mouth slid, hot and wet, up the inside of my leg, skipping over my throbbing center, to slide down my other leg and kiss my knee.

I let out an aggrieved groan, and a smile curved his lips as he glanced at me from beneath his thick dark lashes. That look. Until I drew my last breath, I was quite certain I was going to remember that look and how it made me feel. Desired. Cherished. Loved.

He settled in between my legs, and when his mouth settled on the sensitive bundle of nerves that was aching for his touch, I thought I might fly apart. Ben didn't let me. He was relentless in pushing me right to the edge and then pulling me back. It was the sweetest torture I had ever known, and I wasn't sure if I wanted to curse him or sing his praises. Perhaps both.

Finally, when my back was bowed, my heels were digging into the mattress, my fingers were twined in his hair, and I was tingling from my head to my feet, he relented. Using his tongue and his fingers, he pushed me right over the precipice into a swirling light storm that rippled down every nerve ending in my body.

I couldn't move. Every breath I took sent aftershocks through my body. I'd had a lot of orgasms but never one like that.

Ben kissed his way up my belly, lavishing attention on my breasts, and sliding up the side of my throat to nestle into the curve of my shoulder. Summoning my muscle memory, I forced my arms to move and I slid my hands up his arms and onto his shoulders. His blue-gray eyes met mine and I could tell he was quite pleased with himself, as he should be. But of course I couldn't let that stand.

I leaned up and forced him onto his back. He let me. I wanted to do to him what he'd done to me. I wanted to taste every inch of him, and I trailed my lips over his skin, working my way to his erection. I made him suffer for it. By the time I took him in my mouth, he was covered in sweat and his hands were trembling.

"Samantha." He said my name on a gasp and I knew he was right there. But he wasn't letting me have my way. He gently lifted me off him and reached over to the nightstand to grab a condom. I helped him slide it down his length, and then he moved in between my legs. His gaze held mine as he slid into me, and it was everything.

He put his hand under my hips and lifted me up. I braced myself against the mattress, meeting his every thrust by clenching tightly around him. He grunted and I moaned. It felt that good. My release hovered right there, mine for the taking, but I waited until I felt him. His entire body tightened and he swelled in my core, and then I let go. My orgasm unfurled inside of me in a glorious burst of shimmering colors. I had never felt anything like this before and I knew, way down deep inside, it was because I was in love with him.

The words were right there. When he gathered me in his arms and kissed me, I thought they might slip out on a whisper. But they didn't. Instead, I kissed him back, wondering if my lips were giving me away. If I kissed him differently now that I knew how completely he owned my heart.

He slipped from the bed and disposed of the condom. I thought I should go. It might be for the best, so I didn't rush things between us by making a premature declaration of **feelings**. I didn't get the chance to flee. He was back in the bed before I could gather my wits, which were scattered like rose petals all over the bedding. Before I could say a word, he gathered me in his arms and pulled the sheet up over us. Then, to my delight, he pulled out our book and began to read to me.

I rested my head on his chest, feeling his heart beat beneath my cheek while I listened, and I knew I had never felt as purely connected to anyone as I did to this man.

Chapter Twenty-Two

Despite my own state of blissful coupledom, I couldn't help but notice that Tyler and Sophie quickly became inseparable. I thought being in robotics all day would have been enough for them, but no. Every evening was spent with Sophie at our house or Tyler at her house. I was not prepared for this teenage lovefest.

Ben and I were sitting on the porch one evening, watching **The Alphabet Murders** on my laptop and discussing the case, when Tyler came home from a date with Sophie. He practically floated up the front steps and his lips were seriously swollen, so either he'd been attacked by bees or he'd been kissing the girl.

"Hi, Tyler," I said. "Did you have fun?"

He didn't answer but drifted across the floor with a dreamy look in his eyes. At the door, he turned to look at me as if it just registered that I had spoken.

"Yeah, ice cream sounds great." The door shut behind him.

Ben paused the movie and said, "Whoa."

"I know. He's been like that all week," I said. I

fretted my lip as a horrible realization dawned on me. I turned and stared at Ben with wide eyes.

He looked at me in concern. "What's wrong?"

"Oh god, I think I'm going to have to have the S-E-X talk with him," I said. "Just so I'm clear, I'd prefer to jump off the Jaws Bridge with a great white circling me in the water, thank you very much."

"Yeah, I'd definitely choose the shark," he said.

"Not helping," I retorted. "I wonder if I could do it with emojis or food or anything other than actual words?"

He laughed. "Either way you'll put him off eggplant forever."

I clapped a hand over my face. "I can't deal with this. I mean, I remember when he was five and obsessed with Spider-Man. If you sat in a chair for too long, he'd tie your shoelaces to the legs and pretend he'd shot you with webs. He even did it to the family priest, Father Roberts, who did a face-plant when he got up. That was a fine Gale family moment. What happened to that kid? I miss that kid."

"Maybe you don't have to say anything," Ben said. "I mean, he's only fourteen."

"Almost fifteen," I said. I was snuggled up against him while we watched the movie, but now I leaned back so I could see his face when I asked, "How old were you?"

"The first time?" he asked.

I nodded.

"Seventeen," he said. "And before you ask, let me just say, it was awful. I had no idea what I was doing and despite the glorious two minutes of actual sex that happened before I came, at the end of it I felt cheap and gross."

"Why did you feel that way?"

"I didn't love her," he said. He pointed at the house with his thumb. "Not like that."

"Reaffirming my need to talk to him," I said. "Damn."

"What about you?" he asked.

"I was eighteen," I said. "I had a mad crush on him, and it was lovely as first times go. But then he left for college, and when he came back a few weeks later, he'd found a 'smart' girl to be with and he dumped me." I tried to keep my voice light but a sliver of hurt revealed the unhealed wound.

"Proving that having a college education does not mean you're not a moron or an asshole," Ben said. It was his library director voice of authority. Dead sexy and it made me feel surprisingly better.

I kissed him, but before it could get hot and heavy as it tended to with us, I pulled back and said, "I'd better go talk to him."

He nodded. "Call me if you need backup."

It was weird, having this person that I could lean on. I had been a solo unit for so long that I wasn't used to it. I walked him to his motorcycle, which was parked in front of the house. He pulled me close and when he kissed me, it was all I could do not to demand he take me with him.

He climbed onto his bike, straddling the seat. Was there anything sexier than a man on a motorcycle? No, I was certain there wasn't.

I stepped back, giving him space. He picked up his helmet and slipped it on. He fired up the bike, and over the purr of the engine, he said, "Just so we're clear. Unlike my first time, my feelings for you make it impossible for me to feel anything but **wow** after a night with you."

He winked at me and then revved his engine as he took off down the street. Did he mean what I thought he meant? My heart was thumping hard in my chest, and I felt a smile curve my mouth. Ben Reynolds had **feelings** for me. When I turned back to the house and jogged up the steps, I was quite certain I had the same dazed look that Tyler had worn.

My not-so-little brother was seated at the kitchen table with a monster bowl of ice cream in front of him. I grabbed a spoon and joined him.

"So . . ." I said.

Tyler pushed the bowl so it sat between us. Chocolate ice cream with whipped cream and sprinkles. Perfect.

He looked at me, waiting for me to say more. I took

a spoonful to fortify myself, and only after I swallowed
did I elaborate.

"You and Sophie."

Tyler flushed and said, "What about us?"

"As your temporary guardian, I think I need to ask
how serious it is."

"No. Nope. Nuh-uh."

"What?"

"We're not having this conversation." He gestured
between us with his dripping spoon, leaving splats of
chocolate on the table. I grabbed a napkin from the
holder and wiped them up.

"What conversation?"

"The sex conversation," he said.

I gaped at him, my face a mask of innocence.
"What makes you think I want to talk about that?"

"Just because you and Ben—"

"Stop right there," I said. I felt my own face get
warm.

"Ha!" he said. "Not so much fun now, is it?"

"It was never going to be fun," I said. I scooped up
more ice cream, not caring if I got brain freeze. "I just
need to know that you're being careful." I paused,
feeling a pain in my head that had nothing to do with
the ice cream. "Like do you need me to buy you
condoms or anything?"

"Ah!" He let out a horrified yell. "I've barely even
kissed her!"

"Oh, well that's good," I said. "You've just been together so much I was worried that things might be moving too fast."

"Really feeling uncomfortable right now," he said. He shoveled some more ice cream into his mouth as if he could end this conversation if he cleaned out the bowl.

"All right," I said. "There's just one thing that we need to talk about and then I'll stop torturing you, I promise."

He closed his eyes, no doubt hoping he'd be abducted by aliens before I continued.

"I know they cover the basics of sex"—he made a strangled noise that I chose to ignore—"in health class, but do they talk about consent?"

He looked physically pained and made a moaning noise. His face was now as red as a beacon, and if he perched on East Chop, he could stand in for the lighthouse out there, no problem.

"When you're . . . you know . . . you have to listen to her," I said. "Simply put, no means no, and it doesn't matter when she says it or if she said yes and then changes her mind. No means no. I don't care if you have to slam it in a door to get a grip. Understood?"

"Got it! Can I go now?" he asked. "I'm feeling a sudden need to climb into a blanket fort with all of my stuffed animals."

"Go," I said. He practically ran from the room, and I yelled after him, "But no snuggling them if they say no!"

"Ah!" he yelled all the way up the stairs.

So that went well.

To make up for embarrassing the heck out of him, I took Tyler to our favorite breakfast spot on the Vineyard. It was a hole-in-the-wall coffee shop called the Grape. They were known for their coffee and their pastries, my favorite being the cinnamon-raisin roll. Buttery, flaky pastry loaded with raisins and veins of cinnamon. I could eat four in a sitting and have no regrets.

As I stood in line to place our order, Tyler stared at the wall of photos in the small dining room. The Grape had been here forever and hosted live music, poetry slams, and assorted fundraisers for everything from saving the rain forest to helping refugees. Family owned and operated by the Camara family, they only hired Camaras. It was one of the reasons Ben and I had scratched it off the list of places where his mother might have worked.

I paid for our bag of pastries and joined Tyler by the wall. He was staring at one picture in particular and frowning.

"Hey, Sam, have you seen this before?"

He pointed to the photo. It was old and slightly faded. There was a red neon date in the lower right-hand corner but I couldn't read the numbers, as they were all squared off and impossible for me to decipher. I looked at the people in the photo instead.

Standing to the right was a man with dark hair, styled in a mullet—never a good look—and he was holding a pair of drumsticks and grinning. **Dad!** On the left, in profile, was another musician, holding a guitar. He was tall and lanky, wearing a T-shirt with a Ramones logo on it, and his golden brown hair was long and wavy, reaching just past his shoulders. In between the two men stood a woman. She and the guitarist were gazing at each other with such raw longing, I felt as if I was intruding on their moment.

She was not my mother, and I didn't recognize her as a person I'd known on the island as a child. I looked more closely and noticed she had familiar blue-gray eyes, a straight nose, and full lips. I gasped. It had to be Moira Reynolds.

"Well?" Tyler asked. "It's Dad, isn't it?"

"I think it might be," I hedged. I had no idea what the picture meant. I tapped the corner. "What's the date?"

"Nineteen eighty-nine," Tyler said. "Man, that's an old photo. I can't believe Dad is rocking a mullet. How did I not know this? I mean, I knew he was a drummer in a band back in the day, but this is just mortifying."

I forced a laugh and looked at my watch. "We'd better go or you're going to be late or, to normal people, on time for camp."

"Okay," he said. "But I have to take a picture of this. In case it is Dad. Mom will die when she sees that hair."

He took out his phone and snapped a picture. I was too stunned to do anything. My dad knew Moira Reynolds? I scanned my memory trying to recall if Dad had ever mentioned her to me. I didn't think so. **What did this mean?**

"Can you do me a solid, Bro?"

"Sure," he said without hesitation. This sibling thing really was the bomb.

"Message me that picture, please, but don't show it to anyone else," I said. Tyler looked at me in question. "I can't explain why right now, just promise me, no one at the library, okay? It's important."

"Okay," he agreed. No balking, no fussing, just a simple yes. Man, I loved this kid.

I dropped off Tyler and hurried into the building, looking for Em. She'd talk me down from my panic. I did not see Ben, thank goodness, because I didn't know if I could keep myself from blabbing about what we'd found.

Not finding Em in her usual spot on the desk, I scanned the library. There were several librarians at work throughout the building but I didn't know any of them, except Ms. Bascomb, and I was not up for talking to her. I popped into the teen area and waved down

Ryan Fielding, the robotics camp counselor. He was young, fresh out of college, with a thick head of dark hair, black-framed glasses, a pointy chin, and a wardrobe that consisted of a colorful carousel of T-shirts from cartoon shows. Today it was SpongeBob.

"Ryan, have you seen Em?"

He glanced past me at the desk where Em usually sat in the morning. "I think she works this evening, so she's probably off this morning. Do you want me to check her schedule?"

"No need, thanks," I said. I waved to Tyler and dashed from the building. I sent a message to Em using voice to text. My words must have conveyed my upset, because she was standing on her front porch when I arrived.

I parked and hurried up the front steps. She handed me a mug of coffee like a true best friend. She waved for me to sit in one of the wicker rocking chairs, and she took the other.

"What happened?" she asked after I'd taken a sip. "Your text has me completely freaked out. What do you mean your dad had a mullet and you might have found Ben's father? How? Where?"

"You're freaked out?" I cried. "My dad knew Ben's mom. How could I not know this?" I rocked back and forth, trying to self-soothe. It didn't work.

"When you say he 'knew' Ben's mom, in what sense

are you referring?" she asked. She reached across the space between us and put her hand on my chair arm, slowing me down.

"I don't know," I said. I stopped the chair and turned to face her. "They're in a picture together with another guy." I handed her my phone. "Look."

Em glanced down at the screen, where I had the picture open. She studied it quietly for a moment. Then she blew out a breath as if she couldn't believe what she was about to say.

"You don't think your dad and Moira . . ." Her voice trailed off.

"Ah!" I clapped my hands over my ears. "Don't say it. Don't even think it."

Em started to laugh. "You're tripping out."

"Little bit," I agreed.

"Breathe, Sam," she said. "I was just messing with you. Sorry." She turned the picture back to me. "You can practically feel the sizzle between Moira and the guitar player. Your dad looks a few years younger than them. I seriously doubt he's Ben's father."

"Ah, you said it!" I cried. "What do I do, Em?"

She glanced at me, and her face grew serious. "You have to tell Ben."

Chapter Twenty-Three

"Oh no," I said. I shook my head. "That's crossing a line."

"What line?" Em asked. "You told him you'd help him find his father and this is the best clue you've found all summer."

"Except my father is in the picture, too," I said. "Um . . . awkward."

She shook her head. "Why are you making a big deal out of that? Remember when he asked for your help? He said it was because your family had been here for generations and knew everyone on the island. It makes perfect sense that your father is in the picture and potentially knew his father."

I sipped my coffee. It was hot and bitter and tasted like dread, or maybe that was just me.

"What's wrong, Sam?" she asked. "I feel as if you're not telling me something."

"Ben was just supposed to be a summer fling," I said. I set my chair to rocking, but slowly, more meditatively this time.

"And?"

"My feelings changed," I said. "I thought we didn't have enough in common, that we could never last for the long haul, but we both love mystery shows, I've been teaching him to paddleboard, we read together—okay, he reads and I listen—and now he's helping me with the cookbook—"

"Right," she interrupted me. "All those activities you do together is what has shifted your feelings for him, but not the way he looks at you as if you're everything he ever wanted in a woman." The sarcasm was thick enough to spread with a knife.

My face got hot and I felt like I had to protest even though my heart was crying, **Yes! Yes! Yes!** I cleared my throat. "I'm sure he does not look at me that way."

"Oh, but he does," Em assured me. "It's revolting and matched only by the way you look at him." Her voice softened as if she was delivering bad news. "Sam, you're in love with him."

"No, no, no, no." I vigorously shook my head as if rattling my brain loose would add weight to my denial. "I'm not ready for that."

"Too late," she said. "Think of it this way, you'll have plenty of time to recalibrate on the drive to Chilmark."

I frowned. "Chilmark?"

"Isn't that where Ben is going today?" She calmly

sipped her coffee, looking like she hadn't just devised the most outrageous course of action.

"Yes, he's visiting his mom this afternoon. What are you suggesting?" She stared at me. "No! I can't present this to him now." I cried. "I need time."

"Sam, I hate to point out the obvious but summer is more than half over. If Ben is going to find out who his father is, he can't waste a second," Em said. "You need to go to his house and show him."

"I could also just text it to him," I said.

"You're going to explain that your dad is in a photo with his mom and some other random guy in a text?"

"Too complicated?" I asked.

"A bit," she said.

I put my coffee on the small table between us and scrubbed my scalp with my fingers. I felt as if I was going mad. What would I want Ben to do if the situation was reversed? Oh, that was easy. I'd want him to bring the picture to me. I nodded.

"All right," I said. "I'm going."

"'The most difficult path is usually the right one to take,'" Em said. "The protagonist of my favorite author, Siobhan Riordan, always said that in her series."

"She's the young adult fantasy author you loved when we were in middle school, isn't she?"

Em nodded.

"Wise woman." I picked up my mug and swallowed

most of the coffee. It was hot, scalding even, but it got my head in the game. I rose to my feet. "I'm doing the right thing, yes?"

"Absolutely," she said. "Call me when you get done."

"Definitely." I rose to my feet, and Em put her coffee down and stood, too. She hugged me quick and said, "You've got this."

With a forced smile, I jogged down the steps back to my car. I started the engine and pulled out onto the road. I debated calling Ben but I didn't want to explain about the picture over the phone, which would be only slightly less confusing than a text. I arrived at his cottage in minutes and was half relieved to see his motorcycle there and half full of dread.

I had no idea what I was going to say. I shut off the car and pulled out my phone. I glanced at the photo. Maybe this wasn't his mom. The thought filled me with relief, and I promptly felt terrible, because if it was his mom, then this was the first real clue we'd had to a possible father for him, and I wanted him to find his dad, I really did.

I stepped out of the car and approached the house. The pink roses were still blooming, attracting bees, and their somnolent buzz was the background noise to my heart, which had decided now was a great time to start pounding. I was nervous about showing Ben the picture for a variety of reasons. I was halfway up the short steps to the porch when the door opened and he grinned at me, which improbably made my heart beat even faster.

"Good morning, Samwise," he said. "This is an unexpectedly awesome start to my day. Come on in."

I stood on the steps, staring up at him. He truly was a fine specimen of a man with his wavy dark hair, broad shoulders, and thick-lashed blue-gray eyes. I didn't want to get his hopes up and I didn't want to crush him, but Em was right, I had to show him the picture. My conflicting emotions must have shown on my face, because he frowned and reached for me, pulling me in for a hug.

"What's wrong? Are you okay? Is it Tyler? What can I do?"

I leaned into him, taking a long breath of the scent that was uniquely his. I swear it was a concoction of old books, coffee, and laundry detergent. Then I stepped back and handed him my phone, displaying the photo. My voice was soft when I said, "I think I found something."

He took my phone in his large square hand and glanced at the display. His eyes went wide and he glanced back up at me and asked, "Where did you get a picture of my mom?"

Well, that answered that.

Chilmark was the exact opposite corner of the island from Oak Bluffs. It was a twenty-five-minute drive, assuming we didn't run into any tourist traffic. We got lucky as we cut right through the island on Barnes Road, passing the airport. Yes, the place JFK Jr. was supposed to land his plane. I was a little kid when that tragedy happened, but even so I remembered that July and how the entire island had felt the shock waves of another Kennedy tragedy. Frankly, my mother still wasn't over it.

My grandmother's childhood on Martha's Vineyard had been vastly different from mine. The island had not been the retreat for the wealthy that it now was. It had been a poor community up until after World War II, when people in New England discovered it, Nantucket, and Cape Cod as summer vacation destinations. It didn't get global attention, however, until Chappaquiddick. According to my grandmother, that's when everything changed.

I had grown up only knowing the Vineyard as a popular destination for presidents, actors, and other famous types. Part of its allure was that the locals never fussed over the famous. We still don't, as far as I know, treating everyone as just another summer guest. I could see the appeal but to me it's where my father's family carved out their slice of America. The Gale roots were deep on the island, and I was again regretful that I had been so neglectful of this place I loved.

We turned right onto Edgartown–West Tisbury Road.

Traffic slowed in West Tisbury, and I had second thoughts about this venture.

"Maybe you should talk to your mom on your own," I said to Ben. He was sitting in the passenger seat, looking a bit shell-shocked. When he'd seen the date in the corner of the picture, he was certain that the guitarist was his father.

"Tell me again how you found this," he said. "My brain went a little fuzzy when I saw it."

I told him how Tyler had spotted it on the wall of the Grape and recognized our father, and then I saw his mom and noted the similarity to him. Ben nodded.

"This has been our best lead all summer," he said. "I can't believe it was just on a wall in a bakery."

"Date stamped, no less," I said.

We continued on to Chilmark. On the southwest corner of the island, near Aquinnah, this was one of the smaller towns on Martha's Vineyard with a population of 1,200 people, give or take. Ben directed me onto a narrow road, where I turned in to the driveway of a series of gray shingled cottages. The buildings were perched on a bluff and overlooked the Chilmark Pond and the Atlantic beyond. I wished I had my paddleboard with me.

A minivan was in front of the second building and I parked beside it. We climbed out of the car. The small houses were quiet and I wondered if anyone was home.

I had a moment of hope before I remembered that
Moira must be here since she was expecting her son.

Ben reached out and took my hand in his, and we
strode toward the two-story wood-shingled house with
the white trim and wraparound deck. There was a
mermaid weather vane on a cupola on the top of the
house. To me, it looked like the bare-breasted sea
nymph was pointing for me to go back the way I'd
come and not return.

"You didn't tell me you were bringing a guest," a
voice called to us from one of the smaller cottages.

We stopped and pivoted in the direction of the
voice. Standing in the open door of what appeared to
be a studio was Moira Reynolds.

Her hair, brown with streaks of silver, was in a
messy bun on top of her head. She wore a white T-shirt
beneath a pair of battered blue jean overalls, and on
her feet were black lace-up work boots just like the
ones Ben wore to ride his motorcycle.

She didn't smile. There was no welcoming softness
to her features, which were makeup-free. Her
countenance was stern, made even more so by the faint
lines that creased her eyes and mouth. One eyebrow
was raised in question or challenge, I wasn't sure which
but I definitely suspected that either way I was not
welcome.

"Hi, Moira," Ben greeted his mother. They didn't hug

or even smile at the sight of each other. "I hope an extra for lunch isn't a problem."

"Of course not, a little notice is always appreciated, however." She tipped her chin up as she studied me. Her blue-gray eyes were just like Ben's but without his warmth. When her gaze swept over me, it left me cold. Her mouth tightened.

"And how are you, Samantha Gale?"

Hearing her say my name made me pause. Had Ben told her about me? My ridiculous heart fluttered around my chest with something that resembled hope. I tried to mentally slap it down. So what if he had? It didn't mean anything. I gave him a side glance. Judging by the surprise on his face, he hadn't told her about me. Well, okay then. "I'm sorry, have we met before?"

"No, but you look just like Tony," she said. "That Gale DNA is unmistakable."

I nodded. This was true. "So, you know my father?" I asked, thinking this would give us an opening to mentioning the picture.

She didn't answer, instead she studied me and frowned. I sensed she was having an internal debate. "I just made tea. Would you two care for some?"

She waved her hand, indicating that we should follow her.

Moira disappeared into her studio and we followed. The work space had an open floor plan. It was one enormous room, packed with shelves full of sheets of metal of varying sizes, industrial-looking machinery, and tools for which I didn't even have names.

A large art piece stood in the center of the space, and I studied it. The metal had been shaped into what looked like a spiral of copper fire, and on the inside the voluptuous silhouette of a woman had been formed, also in copper but with a rich teal patina. Given what Ben had told me before about her evocative art, I wondered if this was Moira's representation of the female orgasm. I didn't think so. Despite the curves of the woman, it didn't give off a sexual vibe.

A large wooden worktable was littered with other bits and pieces, and at any other time I would have been curious about her work. As I took in the muscular biceps Moira was rocking, I decided those questions could wait.

She led us through the building to a stone patio outside. The view was breathtaking. A lush rolling hill descended into a line of trees that surrounded the pond. Just beyond which I could see a narrow line of sand, separating the pond from the sea.

It was exactly the sort of spot where you'd expect to find the studio of a renowned artist. She gestured for us to sit in the padded chairs that surrounded a rectangular glass table. There was a glass ashtray sitting in the center with what looked to be the nub of a joint in it.

"Make yourselves comfortable. I'll go get the tea," she said.

She disappeared back into the studio. I sat down and Ben took the seat beside mine. My leg jogged up and down. I could hear the birds singing, feel the warm sun on my face, but it didn't help my nerves. I had the feeling a confrontation was coming and I really didn't like those. I did everything I could to avoid them, in fact.

The briny smell of the ocean was carried ashore on the breeze, and I took a deep breath and held it, releasing it slowly. I wasn't calm but it took the edge off. The urge to run was still there just under the surface, and I wondered for a second if I could make it to my car. Before I could act on this impulse, Ben put his hand on my knee.

"Samwise, relax, it'll be fine." he said. His low voice plucked that chord right in my belly, making me shiver in a good way. "Hey."

I turned to look at him and he leaned over and kissed me. I expected something swift and sweet. It wasn't. He cupped my face with both hands and kissed me with a thoroughness that left me breathing heavy and forgetting my name.

The door banged open, breaking the spell. Ben leaned back from me as Moira stepped out of the studio with a tray, bearing a teapot and three china cups. Ben rose from his seat and reached out to take it from her and she let him, casting a speculative glance between us. Okay then.

"Fortunately, I brewed a large pot before you arrived. You're saving me from overcaffeinating myself, so your timing is excellent," she said. Her smile was forced and it didn't reach her eyes.

I suspected this was the pep talk she'd given herself in her studio and not how she really felt about a stranger turning up in her driveway. She was a formidable presence, and I was grateful for the tea that Ben handed me, as my throat was coated in anxiety and very dry.

Once we were all seated with our tea, Moria turned those oh-so-familiar blue-gray eyes on me. She didn't say anything. Just stared like an owl. It was unnerving.

I waited for Ben to say something, to mention the picture, but he didn't. My extroverted self, the part of me that charmed everyone to distract them from my neurodivergence, took the wheel.

"You have a lovely place here."

Moira said nothing. Just sipped her tea. Ben had set his cup on the table and wasn't drinking. The tension between them was like a fourth guest, and I almost offered to pour it some tea.

"I imagine it must inspire your incredible work," I said.

This was a statement of fact not a suck-up move, I swear. Still she said nothing but stared past me out at the ocean. Ben had called her guarded. Spectacular understatement, that. My need for Ben to say something was suddenly at war with my desire to get the hell out of there. I decided to give him a conversational nudge.

"You're probably wondering how Ben and I became friends and why he brought me here to—" I began, but she interrupted me.

"I'd say you're more than friends with my son," Moira said. Her face was impassive. I had no idea how she felt about that.

"Moira." Ben's tone was a warning. My face grew warm. So he had told her about me? What had he said? How should I respond? Moira gave me nothing to work with, but Ben stepped into the arena like a gladiator.

"Martha's Vineyard is small," he said. "I imagine you heard that Sam and I have been spending time together from someone on the front porch of the Chilmark General Store?"

Moira's eyebrows lifted. She didn't say anything, and I took that to mean that Ben's guess had been accurate. I almost sagged with relief. I disliked the thought of him talking about me to his mother because, frankly, she was terrifying.

He'd told me his childhood was unconventional, but I hadn't appreciated how not full of rainbows and puppy dogs it had been until I met her. I glanced at Ben. The sun shone on his dark shoulder-length hair. His close-trimmed beard framed his full lips and accented his cheekbones, but it was his eyes that drew me, rolling me in like a seashell on an incoming tide.

He looked tired, not from lack of sleep, but rather from a soul-deep weariness. This battle with his mother over the identity of his father was taking a toll on him. It hurt my heart to see it and it made me mad.

"So, you two are dating?" Moira asked.

I didn't wait for Ben to answer this time. "Ben and I haven't decided what we are, which is between us." This was true. We'd never really nailed down what we wanted to call each other, other than our person. I glanced at Ben and saw raw admiration in his eyes. I imagined very few people held their own with his mother. I sat up straighter. "I consider Ben an important part in my life, which is why I've been trying to help him find his father."

I turned back to Moira. Her lips flattened into a tight line and her blue-gray eyes were matte. They didn't sparkle like sunshine on the waves like Ben's did.

"Why would you do that?" she asked. She didn't sound angry, merely perplexed.

"Because I asked her to," Ben said. It went unspoken that it was because Moira refused to tell him.

"What's important to Ben is important to me," I said. I glanced at Ben and nodded. He held out his hand and I put my phone in his palm.

He held it up so his mother could see. "The man in this photo, the guitarist, is he my father?"

The world went perfectly still. The birds stopped singing, the breeze halted, even the waves on the beach ceased while we waited for her answer.

She took the phone out of his hand and studied the picture. Her face softened and a small smile turned up the corners of her lips. It felt as if her inner thermostat rose a couple of degrees, not approaching any sort of genuine warmth, just removing the frost.

"I remember this," she said. Moira glanced at me. "Your father was a wonderful drummer. He had more enthusiasm than talent but sometimes that's more important."

She handed the phone to me and I waited for her to tell me about the guitar player, but she didn't. I handed the phone back to Ben, sensing he wanted to keep possession of the picture.

"My brother, Tyler, found the picture on the wall of fame at the Grape, the bakery in town," I said to Moira. "It's from 1989."

"Really?" She sipped her tea.

Ben looked up at his mother and then back at the screen. He rubbed the knuckles of his free hand against his chest as if trying soothe himself.

"Who is the guitarist?" Ben pressed Moira.

"Everyone loved your father," she said to me, ignoring Ben.

I studied her face. There was a faraway look in her eyes as if she was reliving a precious moment in time.

"Tony Gale was everyone's little brother," she continued.

"And the other man?" Ben asked. His voice was fierce. "Who is the guitar player?"

Moira stared at him and then she stood up, pushing her chair back. She turned to me. "Did you see the piece I'm working on?" It was clear that I was to follow her. "Come, I'll show you."

I glanced at Ben. His eyes narrowed and his jaw was clenched, and I remembered the conversation we had where he had pretended to be his mother. His impression had been more spot-on than I realized. She simply ignored our questions. Maddening!

Perhaps, if we double-teamed her, we could wear her down. I fell in behind Moira as she strode into the studio. She gestured to the piece that looked like a large metal flame with the woman inside. She stood in front of it, studying it.

"It's not there yet. It needs something," she said. She turned to me. "What do you think of it?"

Oh, shit. Was this a test? Was this how she'd determined whether she would answer our questions or not? I had no idea what to say. I'd never really had a great passion for art. I liked some things and didn't like others. Modern art bewildered me, and mall art made me queasy.

"It's impressive," I said. Bullshitting 101, try to appease the other person's ego.

"Why?" Moira asked.

"Because it's massive," I said. I stared up at the piece. I wasn't wrong, but I sensed this was not what she was looking for. We were so screwed.

"Here's my artist's statement." Moira plucked a piece of paper off a nearby table and handed it to me. "Read it out loud."

"Uh . . ." I glanced at the paper. Of course it wasn't in a dyslexic-friendly font.

"I'll read it," Ben said.

"No," Moira said. She stared at me. "Her."

My nerves were pulled so taut I thought they'd snap. I thought about bluffing. I could pretend I didn't have my glasses or that there was something in my eye, but I didn't. Instead, I handed the paper back to her.

"I can't," I said. "Not without time to study it properly."

She blinked at me. I suspected her fame had created a bubble of assuredness for Moira Reynolds where she seldom if ever heard the word no. She hadn't a clue what to do with my refusal.

"Why?" she asked.

"Reading isn't my thing," I said.

She gaped at me. "You can't read?"

I shrugged. I didn't have to explain my dyslexia to a woman who refused to answer basic questions from her own son. My life was not hers to judge.

She started to laugh. "Oh, that's rich," she said. She turned to Ben. "You've had your nose in a book since you were a toddler and you're with her, a woman who can't read?"

"Moira, stop," Ben ordered. His voice was sharp, a siren not to take another step forward.

She ignored him and laughed even harder. I felt my old friend shame sling its arm around my shoulders and squeeze me in a half hug that left me feeling cheap, dirty, and less than. I couldn't even look at Ben.

"Tell me," Moira said. "How do you amuse yourself—reality television? Or are you a celebrity stalker?"

I knew I should clarify that not reading wasn't a personal preference, but in that moment I disliked her so intensely I couldn't even speak.

"Moira, enough!" Ben snapped. He stepped between her and me as if his physical presence could protect me from her words. I glanced past him at Moira. She was glaring at him, with her fists clenched and jaw tight.

"It's all right, Ben," I said.

"No, it isn't," he said. "You don't know anything about Samantha. How dare you mock her? She happens to have dyslexia."

"Ignorant by circumstance or by choice," Moira scoffed. "What's the difference?"

Ouch! That stung.

I saw Ben's shoulders stiffen. Fury was radiating off him in hot waves and I reached for his hand. Not that I thought he would do anything, but I wanted to give him an anchor if he needed it.

"There's a big difference," he said. "Much like the difference between being a kind, generous, and loving person and being a mean, stingy, and hateful one."

Moira's head snapped back as if he'd slapped her. Through gritted teeth, she hissed, "Get out!"

"Let's go, Ben," I said. "We're wasting our time here." I turned to leave, pulling one hundred and ninety pounds of furious male with me.

At the door, I paused. I remembered Ben had told me that my neurodiversity allowed me to see things others couldn't, so I took a last look at her piece and said, "I don't need to read your artist's statement to grasp the concept of your piece. I'll tell you exactly what it is represents."

"Oh?" Moira's eyebrows went up in disdain.

"It's an overpriced collection of junkyard scraps cobbled together in a provocative shape by a woman who can't form an emotional attachment to another human being." I swept my arm at the sculpture. "This represents a woman so closed off to the world she can't even acknowledge the personal pain she's in, and she's being consumed by it."

Moira's face was impassive.

"How'd I do?" I asked. I didn't wait to hear her answer.

Chapter Twenty-Four

The door slammed shut behind us and I half expected Moira to make an appearance, but she didn't. Ben looked numb. I wondered if I had offended him by insulting his mother. I knew their relationship was strained, but she was still his mother and there were boundaries. I mean, I could make fun of my dad's midlife crisis, but I'd put a hurt on anyone outside of the family who did the same.

"I'm sorry," I said. We crossed the driveway and stopped beside my car. "I shouldn't have criticized her sculpture."

"Are you kidding me?" Ben asked. "That was amazing. No one has stood up to Moira Reynolds in forever. You were spectacular."

Well, okay then. We climbed into the car and I drove Ben back to his place. He was quiet for most of the ride. I glanced over a few times and watched him zoom in and out of the picture, studying the guitarist until the guy was mere pixels. I wondered what he was thinking and what he'd do now, but I didn't ask. I suspected he needed a moment to think.

I parked in his driveway and we both got out of the car. He pulled my phone out of his pocket and handed it to me. "I sent the picture to my phone."

"Good," I said. "I know your mom isn't being helpful, but I'll send the picture to my dad. Maybe he remembers who the guitarist is."

Ben's eyes lit up with hope. "I look like him." His voice was tentative, as if he was testing out the words.

"I think so, too," I said.

Ben's gaze met mine and his eyes danced with excitement. "I'm going to find him, Samwise."

"It looks very promising," I said. I gave in to my feelings, wrapped my arms around his neck, and hugged him tight. "I'm so happy for you, Ben."

He lifted me up so my feet were dangling, and then he kissed me. It was deep and thorough and I was breathing heavy at the end of it.

"I would never have gotten this far without you," he said. "I can't ever thank you enough."

"No need. We're a good team, Bennett Reynolds."

"Yes." He kissed me. "We." He kissed me again. "Are." He kissed me a third time but this time he lingered. When we broke apart, I wasn't even sure of my own name.

"I'm going to catch the ferry and drive up the Cape and pop in on my grandparents. I want to know if they recognize this guy. It's a long shot, but I have to try."

"Great idea," I said. "And if I hear from my dad, I'll let you know."

Ben grinned and it was like getting hit in the chest with a rainbow. I had never seen him so happy, and I have to say, happy Ben was hot.

"I'll call you," he said. He kissed me again, pinning me up against the side of my car and plundering my mouth as his hands locked on my hips and held me still until I was a throbbing hot puddle of need. When he broke the kiss, his gaze met mine. "You amazing woman. What did I do to deserve you in my life?"

My throat closed up. No one had ever considered me a blessing. I wanted to cry. Instead I cracked a joke. "Sinned, no doubt, lots of overdue library books or something."

He laughed, a deep belly laugh, and kissed me again. When he released me to gather my wits, I watched as he threw his leg over the motorcycle and pulled on his helmet. With a roar of the mighty engine, he shot down the driveway back to the main road. I watched until he faded from sight, feeling all of the love in my poor heart follow him on his journey.

I had a few hours before I needed to pick up Tyler, so I headed home. I would text the photo of my dad from there. I drove through Oak Bluffs painfully slowly to avoid the tourists. When I arrived at my house, it was to find a minivan parked in front. I turned in to our short driveway and parked.

I climbed up the steps to find a person seated on our porch. I jumped and put my hand over my heart. Moira rose to her feet. She was watching me with an inscrutable look on her face.

She shook her head at me. "You have no idea what you've done."

I also had no idea what she meant, but a shiver of foreboding wiggled down my spine all the same. I hoped it was just Moira's flair for the dramatic. I eased past her to the door. Given her inability to help her own son locate his father, I had no interest in hearing anything she had to say.

I almost made it. Almost. I'd unlocked it and had my hand on the doorknob when Moira called after me. "I was sorry to hear about your parents' divorce."

Why would she bring that up? I whipped around to face her. There was a look of triumph in her eyes.

"Your dad came to stay with me on the Cape while they were separated," she explained. "Did you know?"

What?! I wanted to protest, to argue with her, but I was so shocked. I just stared.

"He spoke of you often," she continued. "It was a lovely time when he stayed with me, two adults finding each other again after so many years apart. Ah, well. Have a nice day, Samantha."

Before I could say a word, she turned, strode down

the steps, and climbed into her minivan. I stepped forward, ready to go after her, but then stopped. That's what she wanted me to do. She was trying to instigate something. I was not falling for it.

I watched her minivan drive away, and then I locked my front door and drove straight to the library to find Em. I needed her insight and wisdom. Her humor and tact. I needed her to sit on me to keep me from driving back to Moira's and forcing her to talk using a headlock and thumbscrews if I had to.

I found Em in the staff workroom. I sat in the chair next to her desk and told her everything, almost collapsing from a lack of oxygen at the end of my tale of woe.

"Good call in coming here," she said. "Getting into a brawl with your boyfriend's mother is not a great plan."

"But she—"

"I know."

"And she—"

"You can't win this way, Sam. She's holding all the information and is keeping it close." Em patted my arm.

"What do I do?" I asked her. "She just stood there and insinuated that she had some sort of relationship with my father. Shouldn't I have challenged that?"

"You need to talk to your dad first," Em said. She typed on her keyboard, checked something on her computer monitor, and then shelved the book in her hand onto the book truck beside her. She picked up the next book.

"I tried on the ride over here," I said. "But he and Stephanie are on the cruise portion of their trip and their cell service is terrible. I left a voicemail but who knows when he'll get it."

"Maybe you'll get lucky and he'll get it today or whatever day it is where they are. In the meantime, you need to stay away from that toxic narcissist." I glanced at her in surprise and she explained, "I have not lived with my mother for all these years to not understand what one looks like."

I sat back in my seat. I didn't know what to say. Em continued working on the book records. My brain was buzzing with all of the possibilities, sifting through all the outcomes I could envision.

"I have to tell Ben," I said.

"Do you?" Em asked.

"If what Moira said is true, that my dad stayed with her when my parents were separated, which would have been after Ben went to live with his grandparents, he might not know about it. But what if he does and he just doesn't remember? What if he and my dad meet and Ben's all, 'Hey, I remember you. You came out of my mom's room wearing her robe'?"

Em burst out laughing. "I'm sorry." She snorted. "Really sorry, but the picture of your dad wearing a lady's robe. Too much." Clearly, she hadn't seen him in his skinny jeans.

I dropped my face into my hands. "Em, what am I

going to do? There is no way I can keep this from Ben. He's going to find out."

"And what if he does?" she asked. "What's the worst that can happen?"

"It's confirmed that our parents are exes," I said. I made a face like I'd just bitten a raw cranberry. "That would be the worst. I mean, how could Ben hang out with my dad knowing that my dad and his mom . . . **Ack!**"

"It was a long time ago," Em said. "You have to give Ben some credit."

"Maybe, but what about me? I'm not prepared to have Dad and Ben meet knowing what I know," I said. "It would be so weird."

"Admittedly, it is odd," she said. "But it's not end-of-the-world stuff. I mean, it's not like your dad is his da—"

"Don't say it," I cried. I clapped my hands over my ears. She laughed and shook her head.

"My dinner break is in an hour," she said. "Want to join me so we can discuss in greater detail?"

"I wish I could," I said. "But I have to pick up Tyler and feed him." I stood up and leaned down to hug Em. She gave me a tight squeeze back.

"It's going to be all right," she said. "Your dad will be back soon, and you can ask him if what she said is true. It could be that she was just messing with you. She clearly has her issues."

"You're right," I said. "I just don't know how to face Ben. I mean, what am I supposed to say? 'Hey, I think our parents might have hooked up and how about those Red Sox?' This is a total nightmare."

"Sam!" Em said my name in that sharp way people do when they want your full attention. I met her gaze and she continued, "You're panicking, and I say that as your friend and a person who has an intimate relationship with panic."

"You're right," I said. "Moira was clearly unimpressed with me and this is likely her petty revenge."

"Exactly," Em agreed. "You have nothing to worry about. You just need to figure out how to share this new information with Ben. It'll be fine. You'll see."

Despite Em's confidence in me, my version of figuring it out was to avoid Ben for the next few days. In my defense, I had taken on several catering jobs for Stuart at the inn, one of which was a very high-profile wedding rehearsal dinner, so my free time was booked solid.

Thankfully, I barely had a moment to think about anything—except for the occasional internal debate about my father and his friendship with Moira. I really couldn't imagine anything happening between them, but her words nagged me like a bug bite I shouldn't scratch and yet I did, making it itch like fire. I thought about calling my mom, but I didn't want to drag her into the past, especially if she didn't know. Besides Em was right, why would I believe anything Moira had to say when her entire modus operandi was to mess with people? Argh.

I tried calling my dad again, but this time instead of voicemail there was no answer. The call just dropped. Curse you, spotty cellular service!

While I waited to reach my dad, I barricaded myself in my safe space, the kitchen. Stuart was impressed with my work ethic—ha!—and made some comments about the potential for me to be hired on permanently. My bank account certainly felt healthier for the work, and I felt better about myself.

I had felt like such a loser for getting passed over at the Comstock. The critical voice in my head was quieting down about that since I was working, but it ratcheted up in regard to my personal life. Only now, it was the voice of Ben's mother in my head. **You've had your nose pressed in a book since you were a toddler and you're with her, a woman who can't read?**

It played on a continuous loop, fanning the flames of my insecurity. I knew the best way to handle it was to talk to Ben, but, quite frankly, I was nervous. Ridiculous, I know.

Two days passed with no contact with Ben other than voicemails. His grandparents hadn't known who the guitar player was. He'd asked around the island but no one recognized the mystery man in the photo. I didn't answer my phone but let every call go to my messages.

I knew his schedule well enough to call him back when he couldn't answer.

Finally, the evening of the wedding rehearsal dinner on the patio of the Tangled Vine arrived. It was an amazing event. Every dish I served met my very high expectations, and the guests were incredibly generous with their compliments and praise. It was a small gathering with just the two families and their attendants. I watched from the kitchen as the groom gazed at his bride with a look of such love and affection, I felt my heart pinch. Could this be Ben and me someday?

Not if you don't tell him what's going on, the voice in my head chastised me. I hate it when it's right. I needed to reach out to Ben and soon. I decided I'd call him when I got home and tell him everything I knew. What was it Em's favorite author wrote? The most difficult path is usually the right one to take. So be it.

At the end of the night, I finished packing my gear in my car and hit the button on the fob to close the back hatch. When I heard it latch, I came around the side to the driver's door.

"Hey, Samwise." And there was Ben, as if I'd conjured him with all the longing in my poor heart.

Chapter Twenty-Five

"Hi, Ben." My voice came out high and tight. He must have heard something in my stressed tone because his small smile flattened, his brow furrowed, and he looked confused.

He pushed off the car and stepped toward me. I stiffened. Not because I didn't want him to touch me, quite the opposite. I was afraid if he did, I'd latch on to him and never let go.

He stopped, accurately reading my body language, and leaned back a little on his heels. His gaze moved over me as if taking in any changes a couple of days might have wrought.

"Have I done something?" he asked.

"No," I said immediately. I might have been too firm in my denial, because his eyebrows went up and he didn't look like he believed me.

"You've been avoiding me," he said.

I didn't deny it because I didn't want to lie. Instead, I stared at the ground, trying to gather my thoughts.

He'd caught me off guard and I wasn't prepared to see him or tell him what I'd learned.

He misinterpreted my look, because why wouldn't he, and he said, "Listen, if you don't want to see me anymore, you can tell me. I know you wanted to keep this short term, and I'm not that fucking fragile."

The way he said it, fierce and defensive, made it clear that he actually was. It hit me then that as much as I was afraid of being rejected, so was he. Small wonder given that iceberg of a mother he had. That was mean, I didn't care. I knew I had been incredibly selfish by not being direct with him.

"It's not that," I said. "Listen, I need to talk to you, but I want to get my thoughts together before I do." Also, I really wanted to hear from my dad, but I didn't want to go into that.

He stepped close, not touching me, but near enough that I could smell the scent that was particularly him, old books and leather and a hint of coffee. I wanted to wrap it around me like a blanket. Heck, I wanted to wrap him around me like that. I didn't.

I gazed up at him, hoping that he could see in my expression what I felt, mostly longing but also **feelings**. We were just outside the area lit by the inn's spotlight, but whatever he saw made him relax just the tiniest bit.

"When?" he asked.

"Tomorrow evening, after work, come to the house

for dinner," I said. "I'll make something amazing. We can talk then."

He nodded. "All right."

He took a step back and I felt as if my heart was shrinking in my chest, collapsing in on itself, with every inch of space he put between us.

"Samwise, maybe now isn't the time, but I feel as if I should tell you—" he began, but I interrupted.

"Let's save that for tomorrow," I said. I didn't want any declarations of feelings until we ironed out his mom and my dad and how we felt about that and about each other around that.

He looked hurt. I felt terrible but I knew it was for the best in the end. When I told him I loved him, and I would, I didn't want to have any weirdness overshadowing it.

"Okay," he said. He reached into his pocket and took out a small digital recorder. He held it out to me.

"What's this?" I asked. I took it reluctantly as if I didn't know what to do with it, which was not completely inaccurate.

"I didn't know what to expect tonight," he said. "I was prepared for the worst. So I recorded myself reading the rest of our book for you, because I know you'll want to know how it ends. It's all queued up. Just press play."

"Oh, Ben." My voice was wobbly and tears filled my

eyes. The thoughtfulness of his gesture wrecked me, completely wrecked me.

"Good night, Samwise," he said. He turned and strode over to his motorcycle, which was parked just beyond my car. In one fluid motion, he climbed on the bike and put on his helmet. With a flick of his wrist, the engine fired to life and he was gone.

"Tyler, will you set the table?" I asked. I was in the kitchen putting the finishing touches on dinner. I had chosen to go with the Azorean comfort food my vovó had taught me to make. So it was tuna steaks and asparagus with red bean cake for dessert.

"But I'm meeting Sophie," he protested.

"Not before dinner," I said.

"What? Why?" he asked. He stood in the kitchen doorway, looking disgruntled.

I glanced up at him. I was about to heat the oil for the tuna steaks and didn't have time to debate.

"Because I'm your sister and I need you," I said.

His eyes went wide. Small wonder. I had never played the sister card before.

"What's going on?" he asked. "I thought Ben was coming over for dinner."

"He is," I said.

"Are you guys fighting?"

"No, but I have to tell him something, and I could use you as a buffer," I said. "I don't want to put you in a weird spot, but if you're here, maybe he'll relax a little bit before I have to lower the boom."

"Oh my god, are you pregnant?" He gaped.

"No!" I cried. "Why would you even think that?"

He shrugged. "Maybe it's because of that stellar sex ed talk you gave me."

I glared. He grinned.

"But seriously, I would make a fabulous uncle, just sayin'," he teased.

"Hush your mouth," I said. "It's about his search for his father."

Tyler knew the bare minimum about Ben's quest, just enough to make his face turn serious.

"Oh," he said. "Okay, Sis, I'll text Sophie that I can't meet up until later."

"Thanks," I said. "I really appreciate it."

I watched as he texted his girl with one hand, wearing a ridiculously adorable grin, and set the table with the other. It occurred to me that if everything did go sideways with Ben, at least I still had Tyler. The thought was oddly comforting.

Everything was ready. I would quickly sear the steaks after he arrived, and so long as Ben was on time, it would taste amazing. I was just pouring water into the glasses when I heard steps on the front porch, and then the screen door banged opened. I took it as a good sign that Ben felt comfortable enough to just come in.

"Hello? Kids?"

Tyler and I both froze. That was Dad's voice. As one, we crossed into the living room to find Dad and Stephanie, standing there.

"Mom! Dad!" Tyler cried and then he darted across the room and swooped them both into a hug. When he let them go, I took his place.

"Hi!" I cried. "You look amazing." They both had a post-vacation glow that was impossible to deny.

"Thank you," Stephanie said. She kissed both of my cheeks just like Dad had. "Although the jet lag is making me feel like I'm an exhumed mummy."

"We saw those!" Dad chimed in.

"Did you bring me one?" Tyler asked.

Dad laughed and hugged him again. He ruffled Tyler's hair and said, "Did you grow while we were gone?"

"It's the vegetables Sam's been making me eat."

"You got him to eat vegetables?" Stephanie asked. "I think I'm in shock."

I laughed. It hit me then how much I'd missed them.

"Big sisters who bribe little brothers with driving lessons can achieve amazing things," I said.

"Driving?" Dad choked.

"Only in vacant parking lots," I assured him.

"Let's table that until I've slept for at least six hours straight," Stephanie said.

Tyler stepped out onto the porch to retrieve their bags in an overt display of helpfulness. I suspected it was a teenage diversionary tactic to distract them from the thought of him behind the wheel.

"We didn't expect you for a few more days," I said. "Nothing happened to cut short the trip, did it?"

"No, we just missed you guys," Dad said. "Europe was . . ."

"Incredible," Stephanie breathed. "But we missed home, so we left Athens a couple of days early."

They exchanged a sheepish glance, and I hugged them both again. It was good to have them here, even though I had really enjoyed getting to know Tyler and spending time with him one-on-one.

"Dad, I left you a couple of voicemails and some texts, but you never responded," I said. "Did you get them?"

My father shook his head. "I managed to run over my phone with a scooter in Rome. Was it important? Everything okay here? I assumed you'd reach out to Steph if there was a problem."

"Of course," I said. I resisted the urge to do a facepalm. Why hadn't I texted Stephanie, too? Argh. "Everything's fine here. I was just touching base."

"Hey, look who I found outside," Tyler said. He pushed the door open and Ben came in behind him.

"Ben, hi," I said. In the hullabaloo of my parents' arrival, I'd forgotten all about dinner. "Come in."

I saw Dad and Stephanie exchange another glance. Their kids were giving them lots to chat about later. I hurried across the room and took Ben's hand in mine. He sent me a questioning glance as we wound our way through the luggage Tyler had stacked at the bottom of the steps. I smiled.

"My parents got back early from their trip," I said. "My dad broke his phone, which is why I haven't heard from him."

His eyebrows went up. "So, I'm meeting your dad?"

"Is that all right?"

"More than all right," he said. "Maybe he can identify the guitar player."

"Exactly what I was thinking," I said. I did not mention what his mother had said about my dad coming to live with her. I'd deal with that later when it was just me and Dad.

I realized that everything could still blow up in my face, and I had no idea how to change course. There was no way out of it except through it.

"Stephanie, Dad, this is my . . ." I paused to glance at Ben. I was not sharing with them that he was my person, not yet. That was entirely too much information. I cleared my throat and said, "My friend Ben Reynolds."

Ben's gaze darted to my face, but I kept my focus on my dad. He glanced from me to Ben, then held out his hand, and with a welcoming smile, said, "Nice to meet you, Ben. Call me Tony."

"All right." Ben smiled as they shook.

"A pleasure, Ben," Stephanie said.

"Likewise," he said.

I watched my dad's expression. Did he recognize Ben? Had he put the names together? Was I going to have to spell it out for him? My dad was asking Ben what brought him to the Vineyard, and Ben was talking about his interim run at being the director of the public library. Stephanie perked up at this because she was an avid reader and librarians were her favorite people.

There was no recognition on my dad's face or on Ben's either, for that matter. Finally, I couldn't take it anymore. "Dad, Ben is Moira Reynolds's son."

Dad blinked twice. He turned from me to Ben. "You don't say." He clapped Ben on the shoulder and added, "I see it now. You look just like her."

"I get that a lot," Ben said. He looked nervous and he glanced at me. I knew he was checking to see if I thought now was a good time to show my dad the picture. I nodded and pulled out my phone.

"Dad, Tyler and I found this photo at the Grape. This is you and Moira Reynolds, isn't it?" I asked.

I opened up the photo on my phone and showed it to him. He stared at it for a moment and then he laughed.

"Oh, honey, don't look at this," he said to Stephanie.

I felt a beat of panic. Why didn't he want her to see Moira?

"I have a mullet," he said. "I'm going to have to make sure all copies of this photo are burned."

I relaxed. So no big deal about Moira then. Cool.

Stephanie glanced over his shoulder at the picture. "Oh, Tony, that's . . ." She burst out laughing.

"Precisely," he said.

"So, you knew Ben's mom?" I asked. My voice came out tight and I took a deep breath, trying to loosen the knot in my throat. It didn't work. Tyler was frowning at me over our dad's shoulder and I grimaced. I knew I was being a complete freak about all this.

"I sure did." He turned the phone so Ben could see. "Your mom back in the day."

"Yeah, I've seen the picture," Ben said. His voice was tight. "Nineteen eighty-nine, right?"

Dad glanced at the photo again. "Indeed. Peak year for the mullet."

"You don't happen to remember who the guitar player in the photo is, do you?" I asked.

"Of course, I do," he said. "Steve Lennon—lead guitar in our band, the Procrastinators."

"Were he and my mom . . . ?" Ben's voice trailed off. He looked intensely uncomfortable. Given that I was going to be asking my dad the same thing about Moira and him, I got it.

"He and your mom what?" Dad asked. "A couple?"

"That, yeah." Ben nodded.

"I'll say they were," Dad said. "I mean, your mom was so cool, every guy in the band had a crush on her, but Moira only had eyes for Steve."

"It's him." Ben turned to me. "I know it is. Now that I have his name, I have to go confront her with this."

"Confront?" Dad asked. His eyebrows rose and he pulled on his chin whiskers. I wondered if this was a new habit. Despite the goatee, he was wearing the usual dad clothes of baggy shorts and a polo shirt. No sign of the skinny jeans anywhere. Maybe the trip had tamed his midlife crisis.

"Go," I said to Ben. "We'll catch up later."

"All right." I walked Ben to the door. He leaned in and kissed me quick. His eyes sparkled with excitement, and he cupped my face with one hand. "We still need to talk about us, Samwise. There are things I need to say." His voice was soft, for my ears only.

I pressed his hand to my cheek and responded quietly. "Me, too," I said. "See you later?"

He nodded. He turned to Dad and Stephanie and said, "It was nice to meet you, but I have to run."

"Nice meeting you, too, Ben. Come by anytime," Stephanie said.

Dad was glancing between us with a curious look, but he smiled and said, "We'll see you soon."

I accompanied Ben out to the porch. He was practically vibrating with excitement.

"Don't speed," I said. Then I made a face. "Ugh, I've been chaperoning Tyler too long. I sound like a parent."

"No," Ben said. "You sound like a woman who cares about her man."

"My man?" I asked. My heart started thumping triple time.

"Who would be me," he said. "In case that wasn't clear."

I laughed. He hugged me one more time, and I tried to shake off the ominous vibe that it was goodbye, but my gut was twisted up with anxiety as I watched him get on his motorcycle. I had a bad feeling about his conversation with his mother. I tried to tell myself it was because she was mean, to be frank, but it was more than that.

What if Ben learned that his father was in Australia or something? Would he just leave? I wouldn't blame him if he did. But where did I, where did we, fit into that scenario? I tried to put the doom aside. I'd worry about that when it happened. Maybe the guy was just living in Falmouth and would be ecstatic to hear from Ben. Yeah, that could happen. Why fear the worst and not hope for the best?

Because the worst is what always happens to

you. Not true! I argued with the voice in my head. My proof was that Ben had happened to me and he was the best thing ever.

I watched as his taillight disappeared, and hoped that for once Moira would be honest with her son and tell him the truth. I returned to the living room to find Tyler running the luggage upstairs.

"Well, this was all unexpected and I'm eager for details, but I am desperate for a long, hot soak in the tub," Stephanie said as she climbed the stairs. She paused to send my dad a pointed look. "Get the details and fill me in?"

"Roger that," Dad said. He turned to me. "Looks like we have some talking to do."

He had no idea.

Chapter Twenty-Six

"Would I be a complete jerk if I begged you to finish cooking dinner?" Tyler asked from the entrance to the kitchen. "I'll even eat the green stuff."

"Green stuff?" Dad asked. "As in vegetables? You hate vegetables."

"They're not so bad," Tyler said.

Dad raised one eyebrow and looked at me. "What sorcery is this?"

I smiled and then glanced at Tyler and said, "Can you make the salad? Dad and I will be right there."

"Sure." Tyler vanished.

Dad's jaw dropped. "I have so many questions."

"So do I," I said.

He tipped his head to the side. "What's up?"

"Dad, I had a rather awkward conversation with Moira. She told me that when you and Mom separated, you went to live with her on the Cape," I said. "Is that true?"

My dad took a second to process the question and then he nodded. "Yes, I did," he said. "Things weren't good with your mom and me, and Moira was an old friend. I needed a place to go, so when she invited me to the Cape, I went."

I sucked in a breath. I felt like I'd been shot. How could my dad have had a relationship with Moira Reynolds and I didn't know about it?

"Dad, were you involved with her?" I cried. I felt like I was having a flashback to my teen years when it felt as if all Dad and I did was yell at each other. Still, I pressed on. "Did you have an . . . er . . . intimate relationship with Ben's mom?"

"Whoa," Tyler said. "Didn't see that coming."

As one, Dad and I snapped our heads in the direction of the kitchen. Tyler stood there, holding a cucumber and a peeler.

"I was just wondering if you wanted it peeled completely or striped," he said. "But this is way more interesting."

"I can explain," Dad said.

"Peel it completely, Tyler." I gestured for him to go back into the kitchen.

"Oh, no." He shook his head. "If Dad is spilling T about the fam, I want to hear it."

Dad looked at me. "What is he talking about?"

"'T' is slang for gossip and 'fam' is family," I said.

Dad blinked then shook his head. "It's fine. He can hear what I have to say."

"Cool, can Sam cook while we talk?" Tyler asked. "It

is not hyperbole that I will die if I don't eat soon. I'll even eat the asparagus."

I turned around and took in his gangly teenage body. The boy needed to eat, and I could do that. "I'm going to hold you to that. Let's go."

The half-prepped dinner was easy to finish off, and in a matter of moments, Tyler, Dad, and I were enjoying tuna steaks and asparagus, while I kept a plate warm for Stephanie. I had a feeling we were going to need the omega-3s from the fish to power through the family convo that was about to take place.

"About Moira," I said to Dad. "Start explaining."

"Were you having a midlife crisis then, too?" Tyler interrupted. I sent him a quelling look and he shrugged while loading his plate.

"Midlife crisis?" Dad asked. "I'm not having—"

"Aren't you though?" Tyler asked. "The beat-up sports car, the goatee, and your drum set at home, which has taken over the garage."

"Don't forget the skinny jeans," I added.

"No, please forget the skinny jeans," Tyler said. "We're begging you."

I snorted a laugh and Dad glanced between us.

"I like my jeans," Dad protested.

"We'll discuss them later, back to Moira," I prodded him.

"It was a random happenstance," he said. "Your mother and I were in the process of separating and I took off to the Cape for the weekend to clear my head. I ran into Moira at a coffee shop and crashed with her for the weekend, instead of spending money on a hotel. I slept on her couch for three days and then came home, packed up, and moved in with Vovó until I found an apartment."

"So, you didn't hook up?" I asked.

"By 'hook up' do you mean . . . ?"

"Yes, that's what I mean."

"No." Dad shook his head. "We weren't . . . She's not . . . To be clear, we were and are just friends. Why is this so important to you?"

"Because I'm dating Ben, and having my dad be involved with his mom in the past would just be too weird."

"It's not that weird," he said.

"Oh yes, it is," Tyler said. He slugged back half of his milk, leaving a white mustache on his upper lip. "I think what Sam really wants to know is if your weekend with Moira is what ended your marriage to Sam's mom?"

"Yeah, that," I said. "Just to be clear."

"No," Dad said. "Our marriage had been over for a while by the time I left. While I loved your mother, Sam, and still do as a friend, I just couldn't live with her."

"I know," I said. My mom, Lisa, was a type A personality, and Dad was absolutely a B. Honestly, I have no idea how they ever got together from the start.

"That's good to hear," Tyler said. "You know, I've often worried that Mom and I were your backup family."

Both Dad and I went very still. Tyler, oblivious to the stunned reaction his words elicited, shoved more asparagus in his mouth. My pride at getting him to eat vegetables was stunted by the sick feeling in my stomach caused by the worry that I had somehow contributed to his feelings of being second best. Had teenage me, in all of my rebellious anger, caused Tyler to feel this way?

Dad glanced at my face and correctly interpreted the stricken expression I could feel pinching my features. Dad's big strong hand landed on my forearm and he gave me a fatherly pat. "No, don't think like that. Any blame for your brother feeling like second string is mine and mine alone."

He turned to Tyler. "Buddy, I don't know what to say. You and your mom and Samantha are everything to me. I suppose I didn't manage the guilt I felt about the end of my first marriage very well and for that I am deeply sorry. I love you all so much. It breaks me to think you believe you're a backup anything."

He stared down at his plate. I could see there were tears in his eyes. This time I reached over and put my hand on his forearm at the same time that Tyler did. We both gave our dad a gentle squeeze.

"Don't worry about it," Tyler said. "I have recently come to appreciate that it's never too late to establish a strong family bond. Right, Sis?"

"One hundred percent, Bro," I agreed. He held out his hand and we exchanged the complicated handshake we'd been working on. I messed it up and started laughing. Then I leaned over in my seat and hugged him. Tyler didn't know it but he had staked a claim on acres of real estate in my heart. I figured it was time I told him, so I said, "I love you."

"I love you, too," he replied.

A weird noise came from across the table and I let go of Tyler and looked at Dad. He was sobbing. Not old school clear-your-throat-and-move-on boo-hoos, oh no, this was big, emotional, drowning-in-his-feelings bawling.

Tyler and I both hopped up from our chairs and hugged him.

"Are you all right, Dad?" I asked.

"Is this jet lag?" Tyler asked. "Because other than when Vovó passed away, I don't think I've ever seen you cry."

"I'm fine and no, it's not jet lag," Dad said. He picked up his napkin, dabbed his eyes, and blew his nose. "It's you two, you're friends now," he said. His voice broke on the words.

Tyler and I grinned at each other.

"We're more than that," I said. "We're siblings."

"Yeah," Tyler nodded. "And just wait until you see us dance."

"What?" Dad asked.

"Long story," I said. "Dad, I don't want to pry into

your personal life—okay, that's a lie. The truth is I need to know more about you and the summer of 1989."

Tyler and I sat back down and Dad said, "Does this have to do with that picture?"

"Yes."

He studied my face. "Does this have to do with your friend Ben?"

I nodded.

"Okay. Nineteen eighty-nine. Best summer ever. The Procrastinators were rockin' the island, we had gigs every night either here or on the Cape." He turned to Tyler. "Pro tip: If you ever go into music, always pick the guitar. Women love the guitar, plus it's a lot easier to break down than a drum kit."

"Noted," Tyler said. He laughed. Then he pointed his fork at Dad's remaining tuna. "You gonna eat that?"

"Fish, you're voluntarily eating fish?" Dad asked. Tyler nodded. "Take it."

As my brother forked the tuna steak onto his own plate, Dad looked at me and said, "A miracle, you've worked a miracle here."

I smiled. I appreciated the flattery, but I was on a quest. I pulled out my phone and opened the picture again. I turned it so my dad could see it, and I tapped the screen.

"Dad, this guy Steve Lennon, what's his story?"

"For starters," Dad said. "He was the most incredible musician I've ever played with. He could channel Stevie Ray Vaughan like nobody's business. And he had the best hair. He was a cool guy, too. Quiet, but wickedly funny when he dropped a one-liner on you."

I frowned. "What do you mean 'was'? Did he move away? Quit music?"

"No," Dad said. His face grew somber and there was a deep sadness in his eyes. "He died. Ten years ago. Steve was killed in a motorcycle accident."

Chapter Twenty-Seven

All of the blood rushed from my head to feet. I felt woozy and rested my forehead in my hand. No, no, no. This was bad, so bad.

"Are you okay, Sam?" Dad asked.

"Dad, this is really important," I said. "Ben was born in the spring of 1990."

"So he's a few years older than you," he said. He looked like he was processing the age gap.

"Not the important part, Dad," I said. "Ben doesn't know who his father is. Moira won't tell him and there's no name listed on his birth certificate."

"Oh." Dad's face became serious. "I see."

"Moira got pregnant with Ben in the summer of 1989. You were there," I said. "Do you think Steve Lennon is Ben's father? Did Moira date someone else? Anyone else?"

Dad ran a hand over his eyes while he thought about it. "As I remember it, Moira and Steve were inseparable that summer. If she was pregnant, I'd bet the house on Steve being the father."

Oh no, poor Ben. Even though the heartbreak wasn't mine, I felt the pain and despair that was coming for Ben. He was never going to get the chance to meet his father, to hug him, to ask him if he liked peanut butter, bacon, and pickle sandwiches.

I wasn't aware that tears were coursing down my cheeks until Dad took my hand in his. "Hey, are you all right?"

I shook my head. Then I hugged him hard around the neck. "In case I haven't told you often enough, I love you, Dad."

"Thanks, kid," he said. He hugged me back and patted my back. "What's going on? Why are you so upset?"

"She's in love with Ben," Tyler said. "He reads smutty books to her when they sit on the porch together."

"Tyler!" I let go of my dad and threw my napkin at him. "How do you even know that?"

"Sophie and I may or may not listen to you from inside the house." He wagged his eyebrows.

"Sophie?" Dad asked. He turned his head slowly toward Tyler and raised one eyebrow in inquiry.

"Tyler has a girlfriend," I said. I looked at my brother, who was pink with embarrassment and I added, "Payback's a bitch."

Tyler stuck his tongue out at me and I laughed.

"Dad, can I borrow the car? I need to go see Ben," I explained.

"Take it," he said. "I'm about to go to bed. I don't even know what time my body thinks it is."

"Thanks." I hopped up from my seat and kissed his cheek. "And thanks for doing the dishes, Tyler!"

"What?" he cried. "But I have a date!"

"About that date," Dad said. "I think we need to have a talk."

"Oh god, not again," Tyler muttered.

I left them to it and grabbed the keys and banged out the door. I considered driving all the way to Moira's but thought better of it. Who knew how long they would talk, if they even talked at all.

Instead, I drove over to Ben's house. Judging by the lack of a motorcycle, he wasn't home. I wondered how it was going with his mother, and I felt my anxiety spike. Did she know about Steve's passing, and would she tell him?

I climbed out of the car and stepped up onto the small porch on the front of the house. There was one cushioned love seat under the window and I sat down. I could smell the heady fragrance of the pink roses thick on the night air as they arched over his porch. I debated calling him, but no. Not now. This was between him and Moira.

Instead, I reached into my shoulder bag and pulled out the digital recorder he had given me and hit play. His deep voice started our book right where we'd left off and I let it comfort me as he drew me into the story. I missed having him beside me, his warmth and strength. I drew my knees up to my chest and wedged myself into the corner of the seat. I closed my eyes, entering the story fully.

I'd listened to two chapters before the sound of a motorcycle's engine broke through his narration. I stopped the recorder just as he drove up the driveway, parking beside my car. I stuffed the recorder back into my bag.

His body language told me nothing. I watched as he cut the engine and put down the kickstand. His movements were the smooth, practiced motions of a person who has done something so many times it's accomplished without thought. He swung his leg over the seat and took off his helmet, setting it on the back of the bike.

He stood for a moment, contemplating his motorcycle. His shoulders were slumped and his head hung down. And that's when I knew that she'd told him. He knew.

"Ben." His name came out of my mouth on a breath. He turned to face me and then he was striding toward the porch to me. The look on his face, the grief in his eyes, was an expression of such pure devastation, I felt it all the way down in the bottom of my soul.

I rose from my seat and crossed the porch, meeting him at the top of the steps. I wrapped my arms around his neck, trying to ease his pain.

Ben stiffened. His hands grabbed my waist and he tried to pull me off him, but I clung like barnacle.

"Samantha, I can't . . . I don't . . ."

"Shh," I said. "Just let me hold you, just for a moment."

He dropped his hands, giving in, and I hugged him hard, running my hands through his hair and across his shoulders. While we'd been searching, I had listened to him talk about meeting his father a hundred times. He had to be gutted.

When he started to tremble, I knew he was coming undone and it was my job to hold him together. He clutched me close and buried his face in the curve of my neck. I ran my hands down his back, trying to soothe the raw pain. I felt my eyes burn when I heard a muted sob and felt his hot tears against my skin.

"In all the years I dreamed of finding him, I never even considered that he could be . . . gone." His voice cracked with emotion.

I kissed his hair and tightened my hold. "I'm sorry. I'm so sorry."

He set me back on my feet and cupped my face. "I need you," he said.

"I'm here," I said. "For you, for whatever, I'm here."

He nodded. He held my hand, lacing our fingers together. He unlocked the door and I grabbed my bag with my free hand. We went inside but didn't speak.

There was nothing I could say to take away his suffering.

Instead, I kissed him again and again. He pulled my tank top over my head and I did the same with his T-shirt. The rest of our clothes followed swiftly after that. We were pressed together, skin to skin, but it wasn't enough.

I took his hand and led him up to the bedroom. I shoved back the covers and pulled him onto the mattress. He hesitated, but I didn't. I could feel a chasm form between us, as if he felt his burden was too heavy and he was releasing me. I rejected that. I wanted the distance between us gone. I wanted my Ben back, the kind, loving man who made me feel good about myself because he accepted me exactly as I was.

Parting my legs, I pulled him on top of me. Barely taking the time to use protection, I guided him into me. I needed to look into his eyes and know that he was mine. When I felt him thrust deep, I thought I could bring him back and wipe away the grief struck expression from his face. But Ben didn't meet my gaze.

He made love to me as if he was trying to outrun his feelings, but I wouldn't let him leave me behind. I cupped his face in my hands when I knew I was getting close, and I stared into his eyes. I wanted to tell him how I felt, that I loved him, that I wouldn't leave him, that he was welcome to take whatever solace he could in me, but the words were stuck, lodged somewhere in my chest by a heart that was afraid to be broken.

Instead, I kissed him. I told him it would be all right, and when I felt him climax, I followed, hoping that I could keep him with me somehow. We were sweaty and panting for breath. My heart was thumping hard in my chest in the aftermath.

Instead of the usual postcoital snuggle, he stared at the ceiling. He looked as if he were lost. It broke my heart. I nudged him off the bed and into the shower and I washed us both. He stood with his head bowed, letting the water sluice the soap off his skin. When the hot water started to run cool, I shut off the tap and led him out. I dried him with a towel and then quickly patted my own damp skin.

"Thank you," he said. He kissed me and pressed his forehead to mine. "I'm sorry I'm such a mess."

"Don't apologize. Come on," I said. "Let's get some rest."

We climbed back into bed and I wrapped myself around him, hoping I could be a lifeline for him as the grief of realizing he would never know his father pulled him into an abyss of regret and sorrow that swallowed him whole.

"She knew he'd died," he said. "She's known for years."

It was early morning. Sleep had been elusive and

we finally gave up. We'd made a large pot of coffee, poured it into two travel mugs, and headed to the beach. It was cold at this time of day, the darker side of dawn, and the fog was thick. We didn't care.

The only other people out here were some surfers and a few people walking their dogs. The rising sun was trying to blast through the thick haze but wasn't having any luck.

Ben sat on the blanket, and I curled up into his side mostly for warmth but also because it felt important to maintain physical contact with him. I was his tether.

The day had a gloomy, sorrowful vibe to it, which I supposed was appropriate. Even though his father had passed ten years ago, Ben had just learned of it and he wasn't just grieving for the man, he was also mourning the relationship he was never going to have with him.

I felt his body get tense beneath my cheek, and I knew he was processing the hurt. I lifted my head to look at him and over the sound of the waves, I asked, "Why do you think she didn't tell you?"

He shrugged. "Hard to say. Moira doesn't think much past her own needs and wants."

"But she knew you were looking for him," I said. This was what I couldn't understand or forgive. She had let Ben search for his father, fully knowing that Steve had passed away and that her son would be devastated at the end of it, yet she'd said nothing.

"She said he was the only man she'd ever loved,"

he said. "She also said that she never told him about me because she didn't want to keep him from pursuing his dream of being a rock star. He died never knowing he had a son."

We silently watched the waves. Their steady rhythm was hypnotic given my lack of sleep.

"Did he have any other family?" I asked.

"Moira says no," he said. "He was an only child and his parents passed away shortly after his death. So there's no one. No one to tell me what he was like, no one to share photos with me, no one who can tell me . . ." He paused, his voice gruff. "No one who can tell me whether he would have liked me."

Raw hurt made his voice rough. I had no words of comfort, so I looped my arm around his waist, letting him know I was here and I wasn't leaving. For the rest of the day and the following night, I kept a hand on him at all times. It was a weird sort of grief bubble we were in, mourning a person we didn't know and a father-son relationship that would never be.

When we collapsed into bed on the second night, I waited until Ben fell asleep before I crept out of the bedroom and called my dad. He had stopped by earlier in the day and collected his car, but we'd been hiking the beach.

I gently closed the front door of the house behind me before I hit my dad's name in the contacts.

"Sam, how are you doing?" he asked. "How's Ben?

Stephanie wants to know if she can bring you guys some food."

Inexplicably, hearing my dad's voice, with all of his fatherly concern gushing out of the phone, made my nose sting and my eyes water. It hit me how lucky I was to have him, screwy midlife crisis and all.

"Aw, she's the best, but she can stand down, although the offer is much appreciated," I said. "Ben's not really eating. He's in shock, I think."

"Tyler told us Ben spent his summer searching for his father. I can only imagine how crushed he must be," Dad said. "Is there anything I can do?"

"Actually, I'm glad you asked," I said. "Do you have anything—photos, notes, videotapes, anything at all—of your old band, the Procrastinators?"

"You want me to look for anything I have with Steve in it?" he asked.

"Exactly."

"I'm on it," he said. "I'll do a deep dive in the attic."

"Thanks, Dad," I said. "Sorry to have called so late."

"You're my daughter. It's never too late to call me," he said.

My throat was tight when I said, "Thanks. I love you, Dad."

"Love you, too."

I ended the call and slipped back into bed beside Ben. He was snoring softly. Given that we'd only gotten a couple of hours of sleep the night before, I knew he had to be exhausted. I curled up around him, wishing I could ease his sadness. The warmth from his body relaxed me and I fell asleep within minutes.

I awoke the next morning and found myself alone. With my eyes still closed, I reached across the sheets, seeking Ben. His side of the bed was cold. I sat up immediately, shoving the covers aside. I glanced in the open door of the bathroom. The light was off and the room was empty.

There was no noise coming from anywhere in the small house. I grabbed one of Ben's flannel shirts and slipped it on over my tank top and underwear and headed for the kitchen. The coffeepot was on and the carafe was half-full.

I glanced outside at the porch but Ben wasn't there. It was then that I noticed his motorcycle was gone. I hurried to get my phone out of my bag.

There was one voicemail waiting in the queue. I knew before I opened it that it was Ben. My fingers shook when I pressed play.

"Hi, Samwise. Sorry to tell you this over the phone but I didn't want to wake you. I have to go away for a while. I have to figure some stuff out. Stay as long as you want in the house. I'll . . . I guess . . . I'll be in touch. Take care."

The message ended. I played it again and then again. Away? For a while? What did that even mean?

I hit the callback button but it rang once and switched right over to voicemail. Damn it!

Why was he pushing me away? Didn't he know that I was here for him? That I'd be here for him? That I loved him?

How would he know that when you were too chicken to tell him? the voice in my head chided me. I sighed and tossed my phone back into my bag.

I shuffled to the kitchen and poured myself some coffee. The heat and bitterness were the punch to the face I needed. I took a shower, tidied up the place, and walked home. It was only a few miles away and it gave me time to think.

Where would Ben have gone? Back to Moira's? To his grandparents'? To work?

I took my phone out and called Em. She answered on the second ring.

"Sam, is everything okay?" she asked. "Ben's on a sudden personal leave for a few days, and everyone is wondering what happened. Is he all right?"

"No, he's not," I said. I told her about what we'd learned about his dad, and Em blew out a breath.

"Moira is making my mother look like a saint," she said. "And that's saying something."

"Agreed," I said. "Hey, Ben left while I was sleeping this morning, so I didn't get a chance to talk to him." I hated admitting this because it made me feel as if I'd been dumped, which I very well might have been, but I had to ask. "If you hear from him, will you call me?"

"Of course," she said. "But I'm sure you'll be the person he reaches out to first."

And that is why Em was my best friend forever. She always said just the right thing when I doubted myself.

"Thanks," I said. "Talk later?"

"Definitely."

I walked through the neighborhood toward home. The sun was out and the temperature was climbing. I passed through the Campground, which is essentially a town green in the center of the famous gingerbread cottages, and the massive open-air iron tabernacle with its stained glass windows holding court in the center.

I paused at the entrance. I wasn't a praying sort, which I figured meant that if I offered one up, maybe it would get moved to the head of the line. I thought about Ben. I pictured his grief and I simply asked for strength for him to get him through these dark days. If any place could be a conduit to the divine, it was the tabernacle.

I continued walking to the cottage. When I arrived, Stephanie was sitting on the front porch, reading. She glanced up, worry in her eyes, which she quickly masked with a welcoming smile.

"Sam, are you all right?" she asked. She put aside her book. It had a drawing of an ancient Greek or

Roman man on the cover, so I assumed she was studying up for the coming school year. "Can I get you anything? How's Ben?"

"I'm fine," I said. I sat in the seat beside her. "I don't know how Ben is. He left this morning before I woke up."

"Left?" she asked. "Do you know where?"

I shook my head. "He didn't tell me in his message."

"Men," she said. She shook her head as if she found the entire gender confounding. I was right there with her.

"Are you referring to Dad's midlife crisis?" I lowered my voice and whispered, "Are you guys okay?"

"We're fine or we will be," she said. She stared past me at the driveway where Dad's project car was. "As soon as he gives up the skinny jeans. I can handle the car, and the goatee is kind of sexy but the skinny jeans have to go."

I laughed. "You have my full support on that mission."

She smiled, a genuine heart-melter of a smile, and asked, "Do you love him?"

Chapter Twenty-Eight

The question caught me off guard, which was ridiculous, because this was Stephanie. She never missed so much as an eye twitch. Of course she noticed how I felt. I nodded and a tear spilled down my cheek. "Yeah, I do."

"Oh, honey." She leaned over the arm of her chair and wrapped her arms around me. I sank into her softness, which carried the maternal scents of lemons and laundry detergent.

Stephanie had never gotten much of a chance to mother me. I had spent our first years hissing and spitting at her so much that she'd always treated me like a stray cat that she fed from time to time but wasn't sure was feral or not. I couldn't blame her. By the time I had matured a bit and was decent to her, I was a grown adult and out on my own.

This was the first time I could ever remember needing her, really needing her, and I was so grateful she was here.

She brushed my hair back from my face and kissed my head. "It's going to be all right, Sam. He'd be an idiot to let you go, and he did not strike me as an idiot."

"You only met him for a minute," I said.

"Still, a man with his formidable intelligence—Tyler has told us all about him—is not going to let a catch like you get away. Not if he's worth having, he isn't," she said.

"Thanks," I said. "Have I told you that you're the best bonus mom ever?"

She laughed. "Yes, repeatedly."

"Well, I'm right."

"Thank you." She let me go and I sat up straight already missing her warmth.

"Where's Dad?"

"He's been up in the attic all morning," she said. "You sent him on quite a quest."

"That's right," I said. "I'd better go see if I can help. If this causes him to start wearing parachute pants and a Members Only jacket, I apologize in advance."

"No need," she said. "Even those would be an improvement on the skinny jeans."

I laughed and pushed to my feet. I headed into the house, hoping my dad had found something, anything, that might help Ben get an idea of who his dad was.

The screen door swung shut behind me, and I saw my dad sitting at the kitchen table with a large cardboard box in front of him. He was holding an old-fashioned cassette player and wearing an ancient pair of headphones. His eyes were closed and he was listening to something, the tinny sounds of which I could just make out.

"Hi, Dad," I said. Obviously, he didn't hear me so I stepped close and tapped him on the arm.

"Ah!" He jumped. When he registered that it was me, he pulled his headphones off while fumbling with the cassette player. "Sam, you'll never believe what I found. Session tapes."

I gave him side-eye. "I have no idea what that means."

"When we formed the Procrastinators that summer, we were dreaming big of getting signed, being rock stars, touring the world—as you do."

"As **you** do," I corrected him. "And?"

"And I have hours and hours of tapes of conversations, song recordings, stupid jokes, and a couple of fistfights."

"Rock and roll." I made the universal hand gesture. Dad grinned.

"So, what happened? Why didn't you guys make it to the big time?" I asked.

"I had to go back to college, Mikey the bass player had enlisted in the military and was shipping out, and Doug our lead singer had a bit of a drinking problem and by the end of the summer his family staged an intervention and he was sent to rehab. Steve was the only one who remained a musician."

"Really?" I asked. I sat down in the chair beside his.

"Yeah, I did some digging and found out that he became a studio musician in Nashville and taught guitar lessons as well," he said. "He never made it to the big time, but he was working in the industry and he was well respected."

"I think Ben will be happy to hear that," I said.

"Want to listen?" Dad asked.

"Yeah." I wondered if I'd be able to pick out Steve's voice. I wondered if he sounded like Ben.

Dad handed me the headphones. I slipped them on and he pressed play. He set the cassette player down and I watched the little wheels turn in the see-through window. There was a drum riff and then someone said, "Dude, that was excellent."

A guitar solo busted out and there was some more chatter. A debate about who might see them if they got booked at the Ritz Cafe, some trash talk about who was the best musician in the band, someone belched, and then there was an earnest discussion about becoming a national touring act.

They all sounded so young and full of dreams. Someone demanded they play what was going to be their hit single, "Lazy Susan." Then the click of drumsticks could be heard as the drummer—**my dad!**—counted them in. I listened to the song and it wasn't terrible. In fact, despite the distortion and garage band vibe, it was catchy as hell.

I reached out and shut the cassette player off. "You guys were great."

My dad's face got a little pink with embarrassment. "We were idiots but we sure had a lot of fun. There are a bunch more of these cassettes. Steve is on all of them, not just playing but in conversation, too."

He reached into the box and took out several packets of old pictures. "I have these as well. Steve's all over these and there are several with him and Moira. You can see how much they loved each other."

"Dad, this is great," I said. "I can get copies made."

"Nah, I'll do it," he said. "I haven't looked at this stuff in years. Ben can keep the originals. I hope it brings him some comfort."

"Will you help him figure out which voice is his dad's?"

"Of course, we can listen to the tapes together if he wants and I can fill in the gaps."

"I think he'd appreciate that," I said.

My dad reached across the table and put his hand on mine. "Is everything all right with you? You seem sad."

"Just tired," I said. "It's been a pretty intense couple of days."

"I'll say," he said.

"Have you and Stephanie recovered from your trip?" I asked.

"Mostly," he said. "Although she has asked me to rein in my midlife crisis a bit."

"Just the jeans," I said. "Get rid of the jeans."

"Really? But I thought I looked—"

"No." I shook my head.

"Done," he sighed.

I didn't hear from Ben for several days. Every morning, I awoke and checked my phone, but there were no messages. I wondered where he was and how he was doing. I thought about calling but I wanted to give him the space he needed. It was not easy when all of my instincts were telling me that I should be with him.

Em called at midmorning while I was sitting on the porch, watching cooking videos. I had to plan for my next happy hour, which thankfully gave me something else to think about.

"Hey, Em."

"He's here."

I paused the streaming video on my tablet.

"Ben's at the library? Right now?"

"Yes," she said. "But Sam . . ."

"But what?" I asked.

"He's delegating all of his projects and packing up his desk," she said.

"What?" I cried. "Did he quit?"

"I don't know," she said. "We haven't been told anything official but it sure looks that way."

"I'll be right there," I said. I ended the call and

dashed inside the house to grab the box of band memorabilia. Dad had finished sorting and copied whatever he wanted. He'd said I was welcome to give the rest to Ben. I grabbed the car keys from the counter and headed out the door.

Tyler was at camp and Dad and Stephanie were off on a bike ride. There was no one to tell where I was going, so I sent a voice text to my dad, letting him know I had the car.

The drive to the library was short and I'd done it so many times this summer, I thought I could probably do it blindfolded. I parked in the lot and immediately regretted that I hadn't taken the time to do my hair or put on makeup, but I didn't know how long Ben would be here, and it felt imperative that he have these mementos of his dad.

I hefted the box in my arms and strode up the walkway. Em was waiting by the door.

"His office is in a nonpublic area," she said. "I'll escort you back there."

"Thanks," I said. My voice was tight. I hadn't seen him since we'd fallen asleep together a few nights ago. I had no idea how he'd react to seeing me.

Em paused by a partially closed office door, and she rapped on the frame three times.

"Come in," Ben called.

"Good luck," Em said. She gave my arm a squeeze and I sucked in a steadying breath.

I pushed the door open with the box, feeling the nervous flutters in my belly gain in size and strength until I thought I might achieve lift off. Sadly, I didn't.

"Hey," I said. "Doing some cleaning?"

The first thing I noticed was how exhausted he looked. His eyes were sunken and his chin sported thicker stubble than usual. His clothes were wrinkled and his hair was disheveled, as if he'd run his fingers through it repeatedly.

"Samantha," he said. His eyes went wide. He looked surprised to see me. So it was not a "drop everything and embrace me" moment. Instead, he stayed behind his desk, keeping his distance. "I was going to call you."

"Were you?" I asked. The piercing pain in my chest was a surprise and I realized it was because I didn't believe him.

He hung his head. "I'm sorry. I'm just not in a good place right now. I figured it was better if I just . . ."

I waited. He didn't finish his sentence. I dropped the box of tapes and photos onto his desk. I could feel my temper heating up.

"Just what? Left?" I asked. "Were you even planning to say goodbye? Where are you even going?"

My voice was rising with each word, and I turned around and kicked the door shut so that no one would hear us.

"I don't know, Samwise," he said. His voice was

soft, and the nickname that always made me smile now felt like a gut punch, because I didn't feel wise. I felt like an idiot.

"Don't call me that," I snapped.

"Listen," he said. His voice was tight. "I can't do this right now." He gestured between us. "I've got too much stuff to figure out."

He was pushing me away, cutting me out. It shouldn't have hurt so much. We hadn't been together that long, but I'd thought the two days we spent together processing his father's death had meant something. Clearly, I was wrong.

"This is for you," I said. I pushed the box across the desk. He opened his mouth to protest. Seriously?

"Before you say something stupid," I began, but then paused to take a calming breath. His eyes went wide at the harshness of my tone. Whatever. "These are things my father found in the attic that are from his days in the band the Procrastinators with your dad. He said you could keep them and if you want help identifying your dad's voice on the tapes, he's happy to assist. I know it's not like finding your father, but at least you'll be able to hear his voice and his laugh and get to know him a little bit."

Ben stared at the box and then he looked up at me with gratitude in his eyes. "Samantha, I don't know how—"

"Don't thank me," I said. "Thank my dad." Because it actually fucking hurt to even look at him, I turned and headed for the door. Over my shoulder, I said, "I find it pretty ironic that you're shutting me out the same way your mother has always shut you out. I thought you wanted more than that." I shook my head. "I hope you find whatever it is you're looking for, Ben."

I closed the door behind me with a soft click. Then I bolted for the exit before the tears filling my eyes cut loose. Ben was leaving. I'd probably never see him again. I told myself I didn't care. If he left me this easily, he wasn't the man I thought he was, and everything that had happened between us was exactly what I'd said it was from the beginning. Just a summer fling. No big deal. Right.

A week passed and there was no word from Ben. Em had been appointed interim director in his absence and she was not happy. Her mother had come home from her trip and they'd had a terrible fight when Em said she was moving out. So now she was doing a job she wasn't getting paid for, and her mother made her life a living hell with crying jags and guilt trips whenever she was home.

Over enormous margaritas, served to us by our friend Finn, we earnestly debated the pros and cons of hopping on a plane to Australia and seeing if we actually could run away from our problems. Too bad we were both broke.

My last happy hour at the inn was a huge success. My family came to try out my latest creations, and Tyler and I wowed our parents with some of our slick dance moves.

At the end of the evening, my dad had the DJ play Keith Urban's "Only You Can Love Me This Way," and he led Stephanie out onto the dance floor just like he had on their wedding day. Tyler and I exchanged a glance, and he mouthed the words **Look, no skinny jeans!** I burst out laughing and we joined them on the floor.

I was just contemplating cleanup, when Stuart, the owner, arrived. He glanced around the packed terrace and said, "You have made this **the** Friday happy hour spot on the island, Sam. Well done."

"Thank you. It's been fun," I said.

"I'd like to hire you permanently as my events chef, Sam."

"What?" I gaped.

"Happy hours, weddings, all of that, what do you say?" he asked.

"Meaning I'd live on the island permanently," I said. This was a major life change for me.

"Here or I have another inn in Savannah, Georgia, if you'd prefer," he said. "You're too talented for me not to try and keep you."

"Can I think about it?" I asked. "I'm still hoping to finish the cookbook I started."

"Of course, and just to sweeten the pot, you can arrange your cooking schedule around working on the book," he said. "I want to be clear that even if you say no, if you ever change your mind, you have a job with me."

After all of the economic uncertainty I'd struggled with and the self-blame I'd endured for getting passed over, this was a balm to my soul. I wanted to cry I was so relieved. Instead, I smiled and said, "Thank you, Stuart. That means a lot."

"You're an incredibly talented chef, Samantha Gale," he said. "Don't let anyone tell you differently."

"I won't," I said. I waited for the voice in my head to refute his words, but all I heard was blissful silence.

I realized that my critical inner voice had become quieter and quieter over the summer, and I realized why. Ben. He had helped me see myself through a different lens and the voice that usually chopped me down to size had been replaced by his voice in my head. His voice telling me that I was something special. In that moment, I missed him with an intensity that almost dropped me to my knees.

Stuart walked over to my father and Stephanie to say hello. The men had gotten reacquainted and Stephanie was determined to find a nice woman for Stuart to date. I wished her luck with that. I didn't think Stuart had left enough space in his heart for anyone besides his late wife, and I sure understood that, but Stephanie was nothing if not persistent.

Two weeks later, Tyler's robotics camp ended and there was still no word from Ben. The campers had presented their designs at a conference in Boston, and Tyler and his team had achieved their dream to be accepted into the elite STEM high school funded by Severin Robotics. Tyler was thrilled. I'm sure it helped that Sophie was going, too.

While waiting to hear from Ben, I had stalled on deciding my future as long as I could, but time was up. When Stuart asked me again if I'd made a decision about working for him, I said yes and I chose the Savannah job. I couldn't imagine being on the Vineyard without Ben. We had scoured the island so thoroughly looking for any trace of his father that I couldn't go anywhere on the island without missing him.

I packed my sad little bag, and my family took me to the ferry to head back to Woods Hole, where I'd catch a bus to Boston and stay with my mom for a week before I headed to Savannah. Em had put in for vacation and was planning to follow me in a few weeks. We were both looking forward to it.

I hugged Stephanie. She held on a little longer than usual and said, "Thank you for being here this summer. Is it too soon to ask you to come back next summer?"

"Nope," I said. "I'll be here at least for vacation. I have to check and see how Tyler's driving progresses."

My dad sighed. "I suppose that means I have to continue teaching him in your place."

"Don't worry, Dad," I said. "I taught him everything I know."

"That's what I'm afraid of." He opened his arms and I stepped into his hug. We stayed like that for a few seconds, committing the moment to memory. Dad kissed both of my cheeks. "I'm going to miss you, Sam."

"Savannah's not that far away," I said. "I'll be back to visit, definitely around the holidays."

He nodded.

I turned to Tyler. We exchanged our complicated handshake and then I said, "Like Dorothy said to the Scarecrow, 'I think I'll miss you most of all.'"

Tyler's eyes watered and he nodded. Then he cleared his throat and said, "I'm coming to Savannah on fall break, so find a cool place to live that has a foldout couch."

"Deal," I said. Then I hugged him. Despite my heartbreak over Ben, I had gained an awesome brother this summer and for that I was so very grateful.

People were streaming around us to get to the ferry. I had to go. As I looked at my people with the village of Oak Bluffs behind them, I felt my heart squeeze tight. I loved them all so very much. It hurt quite a lot to leave them, but I couldn't stay.

I swiped at the tears on my face and said, "I'd better go." I forced a smile. "I'll text you when I get to Mom's."

Dad hugged me one more time. The three of them stood waving as I walked up the gangway to board the boat. I showed my ticket and stepped onto the ship. My heart was heavy but I knew I'd made the best decision for me. Georgia would be a fresh start, and after this crazy summer I surely needed one.

I moved to the railing on the lower deck, where I could see my family. I waved and they all waved back. I took out my phone and snapped a quick picture of them. I wanted to remember them just like that.

The ferry let out a sharp blast to let us know we were heading out. For a few seconds, I actually debated getting off the ship so I could stay on island and wallow in memories of Ben. Stupid, I know. Since our dustup in his office, it had been radio silence from him, telling me more clearly than words that he was over whatever it was that we had.

No, he isn't. He loves you as much as you love him.

I waited for the voice in my head to call me stupid, but it didn't. For the first time I could ever remember, the voice actually sounded kind. I tried to ignore it.

And you deserve to be loved like that because you are worthy.

Okay, now my inner critic was going too far. Tears filled my eyes and I blinked them away. I knew the voice was just repeating the things Ben had said to me when we were together. I missed the sound of his voice so much. I took out the digital recorder he'd given me and put my earbuds in. I glanced at Oak Bluffs. I wanted to have his voice talk me out, as I left the place that was going to hold my heart for a very long time.

"Samantha!" a voice shouted. A man's voice. Ben's voice! I looked at the recorder. I hadn't hit play yet.

I glanced around the deck and then at the upper one. I didn't see him.

"Samwise!" he shouted again. I spun around to see him running up the gangway.

OMG! The engines were on, the water was churning, the cars had all been loaded. We were departing! Was he out of his mind?

"Ben, don't!" I cried.

I dodged around the other people on the deck and ducked inside where the exit to the gangway was. An employee was standing there, clearly waving Ben off. Ben did not care.

He saw me and, with a determined look in his blue-gray eyes, he jumped!

Chapter Twenty-Nine

"Ah!" I shrieked. I clapped my hands over my mouth.

The ferry employee, a well-muscled middle-aged man, grabbed Ben's arm when he would have slipped backward, and yanked him inside, slamming the door after him.

"Are you crazy?" he shouted at Ben. "What the hell, man?"

Ben wasn't paying any attention to him. His gaze was fixed on me.

He was wheezing, but he said, "I love you."

"Aw, shit," the guy said. He glanced between us. "I see how it is."

He wandered away to stand with some of the passengers, who were clearly enjoying the drama unfolding in front of them.

"I love you," Ben said again. His gaze never left my face.

"Ben, I . . ." I cried. Was it too late? Had that ship sailed, as it were? I wanted to laugh and cry at the same time. I didn't know what to say.

"And you love me, too," he said. "I know you do."

I opened my mouth to speak but the words wouldn't come. I was petrified. Ben was my one in a million. I knew that. And as such, his capacity to hurt me was unparalleled. How did I know he wouldn't just flake on me again?

"I don't think I can do this." I gestured between us.

I felt the small crowd that was watching deflate. They were hoping for some over-the-top happily ever after, but it was my heart on the line and I wasn't going to sacrifice it, not for anyone, including Ben.

"Listen, I know I fucked up," he said. "I shut you out when I should have pulled you in, but I didn't know. I didn't know that a relationship could be like that."

"Like what?" I asked. I stared at him. He was saying what I desperately wanted to hear, but I was too afraid to believe.

"Those two days where you didn't let me out of your sight after I found out about my father . . . I've never experienced anything like that," he said. He pressed his lips together. I could see he was struggling to keep from breaking down. His voice was raspy when he continued, "I've never had anyone jump in the foxhole with me before."

My throat was tight. I knew his life hadn't given him the sort of support that mine had, and I was glad to have shown him another way, but could I endure it if he pushed me away again? I didn't think so.

"I'm sorry, Ben," I said. "I can't."

"Can't?" he asked. "Or won't?"

"Does it matter?" I asked. "We had an amazing summer fling, but it's over now. I've taken a job in Savannah. I'm leaving."

I heard a sigh from behind me and glanced over my shoulder to see the cluster of people watching us. One woman was clutching her hands in front of her chest. She looked like she wanted to knock me down and take my place. I had to get out of there.

"I'm sorry," I said to Ben. I turned and went back out to the deck where I'd been before he'd made his dramatic entrance. The wind whipped at my hair. I didn't care.

"Samantha," Ben said. He appeared at the railing by my side. He reached out and took an earbud out of my ear and put it in his own. He took the small recorder out of my hand and hit play.

The sound of him reading our book filled one ear. He smiled at me as if this proved something.

"I just wanted to know how the story ends," I fibbed.

He took his earbud out and switched off the recorder. He pulled the other earbud out of my ear and said, "I can tell you how the story ends."

"You'd better make it the abridged version," I said. "The ferry will be docking in Woods Hole in forty-five minutes."

Ben glanced out at the deep blue water. The sun shone on his dark hair, highlighting the copper strands. I felt the familiar thrum in my chest that happened every time I looked at him.

"All right," he said. "The story ends like this."

He leaned on the rail and I did, too. If he was going to tell me how our heroine finds her happily ever after, then I was all ears.

"Our heroine has fallen deeply in love, but she's afraid of how vulnerable she feels," he said.

I nodded. I knew there was a reason I liked her.

"Our hero has cocked it all up," he said.

I raised my eyebrow in question.

"Not in a good way," he said. "But after the hero realizes that he's made a mess of things, he declares his feelings for our heroine in the middle of a vineyard in Tuscany."

"He does?" I asked. This was the part I had just been getting to in the book.

"No, wait," Ben said. "He didn't do that."

"He didn't?" I asked. I had been so sure.

"No," Ben said. He met my gaze and held it. "He declared his feelings for her after he jumped aboard the ferry from Martha's Vineyard because he realized, when he heard that she was leaving the island, that he'd been a self-centered asshole and that he couldn't bear the thought of his life without her in it every single day."

"Our book does not take place in Martha's Vineyard," I said.

He reached out and took my hands. "Doesn't it, though?"

I swallowed the lump in my throat.

"You showed me what a real relationship is," he said. "I want that, Samwise. I want it with you. Despite my recent freak-out, the town has offered me a permanent position as director of the library. I'm thinking of accepting, but only if you'll be here, too. Stay with me on the Vineyard, Sam. Let's build a life together here."

I stared at him. A flurry of images of us flashed through my brain—getting pastries at the Grape, paddleboarding in the ocean, catching bands at the Ritz Cafe, celebrating Grand Illumination, curling up together on the porch in the evening watching our mystery shows or while he read to me—it was everything I'd ever wanted.

It hit me then that over the past few weeks, we'd already built the foundation of that life. We'd had to prove ourselves to each other, we'd had to slog through some misunderstandings and some very real trauma, and sure, we'd both made mistakes but we were here, standing together, reaching for each other. That meant something.

It was in that moment that I felt it. My fear that Ben would eventually get bored or embarrassed by my neurodivergent brain and leave me just melted away. Like the book of Ben's that I'd accidentally tossed into the ocean on the day we met, all of my anxiety about us was gone as if it had been pitched into the sea. I was free. I felt a tear spill down my cheek.

"I love you," I said. His face lit up, his eyes sparkled, and a smile curved his lips. "But I can't commit to us—not yet."

His face fell. I reached into my bag and took out my phone. Ben turned away from me and stared at the ocean. He looked defeated.

I pressed the name I was looking for in my contacts. He answered on the first ring.

"Hi, Sam."

"Hi, Stuart," I said. "Listen, can I change my mind?"

Ben straightened beside me. One eyebrow went up and he was watching me so intently, it messed with my brain waves. I glanced away.

"You're not taking the job?" Stuart asked.

"It's more that something has come up, and I was just wondering if I could take the job on the Vineyard instead?" I asked. I glanced back at Ben, who was looking at me with an extremely exasperated expression as if he didn't know whether to kiss me or dunk me in the ocean, which was pretty hilarious.

"Absolutely," Stuart said. "I haven't filled the spot here yet, and I know your dad will be as thrilled to have you stay as I am."

"Cool, thanks," I said. "I'll stop by and see you tomorrow."

"Looking forward to it," he said.

I ended the call. I had just lowered my phone when Ben cupped my face and kissed me. I heard a cheer go up from inside the ferry. Our audience had gotten their happily ever after, after all.

"Say it again," Ben demanded. He pulled me into a hug and my lips were right by his ear.

"I love you," I said. He sighed and a shudder rippled through his powerful frame.

"I love you, too." He kissed me, a long, lingering "oh, how I've missed you" sort of kiss. When he leaned back, he looked at me and asked, "If Stuart hadn't said you could stay on at the inn, would you really have ended us for your career?"

"I think the more important question is: If I had gone to Savannah, would you have waited for me?" I asked.

"No," he said. No hesitation. No thinking it over. My heart dropped. Had I just made the biggest mistake of my life in choosing a man who wouldn't even wait for me?

"I would have followed you," he said. He kissed me and then stared into my eyes with a depth of love and affection I'd never received from a man before. "I'd follow you anywhere, Samwise. You are my heart."

"And you're mine," I said.

RECIPES

═══

Liquid Sunshine Cocktail

2 ounces lemonade
1½ ounces vanilla vodka
1 ounce limoncello
2 ounces club soda
crushed ice
1 curled lemon peel or lemon slice, for garnish

Put several ice cubes in a rocks glass. Pour in lemonade, add vodka and limoncello. Finish with the club soda and garnish of choice.

(For a mocktail version, leave out the vodka and limoncello, and use one pump of vanilla-flavored simple syrup.)

=====

Pimenta Moída
(Portuguese Pepper Sauce)

1 pound Fresno chilies
2 tablespoons sea salt
¼ cup distilled white vinegar
½ cup water

Cut the peppers in half and remove the stems and most of the seeds. Grind the peppers in a food processor until coarsely chopped. Add the salt. Transfer to a saucepan and cook over medium heat for 5 minutes until the peppers soften. Remove from heat and add the vinegar and water. Let the pepper sauce cool to room temperature. Transfer to a glass jar with a tight seal and store in the refrigerator. Pepper sauce will keep for 3 to 4 months.

Bolos Lêvedos
(Sweet Muffin Cakes)

¼ cup warm water
1 package active dry yeast
pinch of sugar
4 eggs, room temperature
1 cup sugar
½ teaspoon salt
2 cups warm milk
7½ cups flour
¼ cup butter, melted

Pour the warm water into a small bowl and add the yeast with the pinch of sugar. Set aside.

In a standing mixer, blend eggs, the cup of sugar, the salt, and warm milk. Add the flour, rehydrated yeast, and butter until fully incorporated. It is a wet dough and will be sticky. Knead the dough for five minutes. Let it proof (rise) until it has doubled in size. This will take 1½ to 2 hours.

Preheat the oven to 325 degrees. Dust the countertop with flour and knead the dough for another 3 minutes. After kneading, shape the dough into discs about 3 inches in diameter. Place them on a parchment-paper-covered baking sheet. Cover them with a cloth and let them rise for 1½ to 2½ hours. Using a large frying pan, cook the bolos over medium-low heat for a few minutes until lightly browned on both sides. Transfer back to the baking sheet and bake in the oven for 10 to 12 minutes.

Torresmos (Azores Marinated Pork)

4 pounds pork spareribs

4 tablespoons pimenta moída

5 garlic cloves, crushed

1 cup red wine

1½ tablespoons sweet paprika

pinch of salt

1 cup vegetable oil

½ teaspoon ground white pepper

½ teaspoon ground black pepper

Cut the ribs into large pieces and set aside. In a large plastic bag, mix the pimenta moída with the garlic, wine, paprika, and salt. Add the meat, seal the bag, and mix well. Put the bag in the refrigerator for 3 hours (minimum) or overnight (even better). To begin cooking, place the meat and the marinade in a large thick-bottomed pan on the stove, add the oil, and cook on high for 10 minutes. Cover, reduce the heat to very low, and cook for 2 hours and 45 minutes. The meat should become very tender and fall off the bone. Stir occasionally. Adjust the pinch of salt to your taste and sprinkle the meat with the white and black pepper. Cover, and cook for another 5 minutes. Remove the pan from the heat and let it rest for 10 minutes. Drain the fat from the meat and serve.

Acknowledgments

This book simply would not exist without the generosity of others. So many shared their creativity, wisdom, and personal stories with me that I am going to endeavor to thank them all and, hopefully, not miss anyone.

Christina Hogrebe, my agent, said, "I have a great title for you" and indeed she did. Thank you for gifting "Summer Reading" to me and letting me run with it as my starting blocks.

Kate Seaver, my editor, has the rare talent of being able to read my first drafts and know exactly where I need to expand and contract my work. There are so many scenes that came out of Kate asking for more and the story is infinitely better for her input. I feel incredibly fortunate to have such an insightful editor helping me reach my fullest potential.

Special thanks to the design team at Berkley, specifically Kristin del Rosario and Katy Riegel for embracing the idea to print **Summer Reading** in a dyslexic-friendly font and to design the interior with that accessibility in mind as well. Your enthusiasm and talent is much appreciated.

Much gratitude to the crew at Berkley—Amanda Maurer, Jessica Mangicaro, Chelsea Pascoe, Kim-Salina I, and Stacy Edwards. I could not ask for a more supportive group of people. Truly, you're the best!

For my beta readers, Kat Carter and Chris Speros, thank you so much for your support and for sharing your neurodivergent stories with me. Your life experiences and personal knowledge of dyslexia informed Sam's character so much. She became fully realized only with your input, and I'm ever grateful.

Eternal gratitude to my Portuguese family—Maria Fontes, Natalia Fontes, Laura Monteiro, and Melissa McIntyre. Thank you for sharing with me your heritage and your culinary skills. I will always cherish our time spent in the kitchen together—"Mais sal!" I feel very blessed to call you mi familia.

Many thanks to my boots-on-the-ground research team—Susan McKinlay and Austin McKinlay. How many miles did we walk on the Vineyard? Thank you both for one of my favorite days, and I think we need to go back!

As always, much love and thanks to my men—Chris Hansen Orf, Wyatt Orf, and Beckett Orf. I love you to the moon and back. Thanks for listening to me when I go on and on and on and on about my work in progress. Your patience and fortitude are unparalleled.

Lastly, I want to thank the writers and readers who virtually keep me company on the long days spent in my office by myself—my assistant, Christie Conlee, or, as I think of her, my magical unicorn; my plot group buddies, Kate Carlisle and Paige Shelton, who let me dominate the conversation and never tell me to shut up—truly, your patience baffles me—my blog pals, the Jungle Red Writers, all so talented and wise and generous with both; and my readers. You always show up, you buy the books, you encourage me, and you make me laugh. I've said it before, but it's the plain truth—I have the best readers ever, and I adore you.